the summer we met

THE DESTIN DIARIES

HOPE HOLLOWAY
AND
CECELIA SCOTT

Hope Holloway & Cecelia Scott

The Destin Diaries Book 1

The Summer We Met

The Destin Diaries

Chapter One

Vivien

"Excuse me?" Vivien Knight scowled at the dashboard as if she couldn't believe the words that came through the phone speaker. "You want me to change my *name*?"

Ryan grunted, a sign of his true frustration whenever Vivien didn't give in and let her husband—okay, soon-to-be *ex*-husband—have his way.

Which was, if truth be told, never. She *always* gave in. He *always* got his way.

But change back to her maiden name? That was just...too much.

"Come on, Viv," he said, sliding into his sales voice, the one that won add-ons and upgrades and big fat closing profits for Ryan Knight Homes, his successful custom home-building business. "It'll be way less complicated if you use Vivien Lawson."

Way less complicated for *who*? As if she couldn't guess.

She'd been Vivien Knight since they got married twenty-six years ago. She'd built a solid reputation as an interior designer with that name. Yes, she'd worked exclusively for Ryan Knight Homes. Why wouldn't she? Ryan was her husband.

For six more weeks, anyway.

"But I have a website and business cards," she said, hating that she could hear the first notes of concession in her voice. She sat up and squeezed the steering wheel, determined to feel her backbone. Even if that spine did sometimes seem more like a wet noodle than the titanium rod she dreamed of having. "Vivien Knight Designs is...a thing."

She heard his caustic laugh, rich with derision. "Viv, you opened the business, what? Six months ago? You've had a few measly jobs re-doing living rooms. No one cares if you switch back to Lawson."

Measly? How dare he—

"The old name really makes sense now that you've left the company."

Left? She almost wailed. She hadn't *left*. Ryan had a midlife crisis, filed for divorce, and threw away their marriage—and his top designer—in the process.

"So, will you start using it right away?" he asked, plowing through his close. "You don't have to have it legally rubberstamped, just change your website or start answering your phone with your old name."

The phone that wasn't exactly ringing off the hook? She swallowed hard, tasting defeat.

"I have to think about it," she said, eyeing the Atlanta traffic ahead of her.

"There's nothing to think about," he said, which translated to *I have asked, therefore, you will do.*

As it had been since the day she'd met him, two weeks out of college when she got a job answering phones at Ryan Knight Homes. The handsome builder/owner, seven years her senior, had taken a liking to her. She'd liked him right back. However, he was her boss, so he called the shots, and that set the tone from courtship through marriage and even, evidently, through the dissolution of that union.

Vivien had always made the concessions, probably because she'd been trained for that by a controlling and demanding mother.

At the thought of Maggie Lawson, she glanced at her GPS. She'd better end *this* uncomfortable conversation to mentally prepare for the *next* one. She still didn't know why her mother had summoned her three grown children for a Sunday afternoon meeting, but her gut said it couldn't be good.

"What's to think about?" Ryan pressed when she didn't respond.

"I have other things going on today," she said, knowing the excuse sounded lame.

"Like what?" he asked. "Where are you going?"

"To Crista's," she replied, referring to her younger sister. "To see my mother."

That's all he needed to know about her life and schedule—he wasn't part of her family anymore.

"Good," he said. "Then you can ask Maggie about changing your name back. She'll jump on the chance for you to be a Lawson again."

True. And he knew Vivien couldn't say no to her mother, either.

Which was the crux of her problem. She never stood up to powerful people. Middle child, peacemaker, conflict-hater—that was Vivien Knight...er, *Lawson*, if Ryan got his way.

She shook her head and took a deep breath, ready to say no. Just...*no*.

"I'll call you tomorrow and let you know," she said instead.

Okay. Not exactly *no*, but at least it wasn't a full-blown *roll over and surrender*.

"Just change it, Viv," he said, unimpressed with her attempt to call this one and only shot. "Why fight it? You know it's the right thing to do."

Was it? She'd never considered going back to her maiden name during this season of personal upheaval. Heck, she'd just taken off her wedding ring a month ago and only because it had gotten loose from a lost appetite.

Maybe she *would* go back to Lawson, maybe she *should*. But she wanted the decision to be hers, not his.

"I have to go," she said, finally eyeing the exit that would take her to her sister's house. "I'll text you when I make a decision."

Without waiting for his response, she stabbed the button on her steering wheel, disconnecting the call. The move gave her a jolt of satisfaction that she longed to feel more in her life.

"Vivien Lawson," she whispered, imagining saying it to a new client.

It sounded...familiar.

As she drifted into the exit lane, she inched up in her seat to steal a glance at her reflection in the rearview mirror. Her golden-brown eyes looked shellshocked and uncertain, the light gone. Her caramel-blond hair had grown darker, too, draping around hollow cheeks during this long winter of discontent.

Maybe she should change her name *and* her hair color. And everything else about her life. Would that put the spark back in her eyes? The bounce back in her step? The joy back in her heart?

Doubtful. This divorce had wrecked her.

Driving past the lush lawns and tall oaks of Crista and Anthony's suburban neighborhood, her mind slipped back to that moment when it all started, nine months ago.

That morning, she'd awakened to the sound of her husband sobbing in the bed next to her. She'd opened her eyes and found Ryan sitting up in bed, literally ugly crying into his hands.

In a teary confession, he told her he was no longer in love with her and hadn't been for a long time.

No, he hadn't cheated, hadn't even considered it. He just wanted "more." He wanted romance and excitement and the thrill of a new life. He wanted meaning and purpose and significance. He wanted...a divorce.

She'd never seen it coming and, no surprise, she hadn't really fought him. How could she? He wouldn't consider counseling, a temporary separation, or a second chance. It was *over*.

Before she knew what hit her, attorneys were

involved and papers were drawn up and assets were divided. Pretty soon, her own well-loved home in a pretty development like this was on the market and, shortly after, under new ownership.

In a fog, she'd rented a townhouse, emotionally supported by her twenty-four-year-old daughter. Lacey had leaped at the chance to leave her own tiny apartment and move in together.

Although he helped her financially, Ryan thought it best if she quit the company so they'd have a clean break, promising he'd use her as a freelance designer.

But that had yet to happen.

So, yes, maybe it was best if she changed her name back. She could be a Lawson woman again, and who was stronger than a Lawson woman? Namely, the steel Magnolia—no pun on her mother's name—she was about to see for some mysterious reason.

Didn't matter why—when Maggie Lawson said jump, her three middle-aged children leaped, pirouetted mid-air, and stuck the landing.

Their mother expected nothing less.

With exactly one minute to spare, she turned into her sister's two-story brick Colonial, where Maggie now lived in a mother-in-law suite on the first floor. Vivien's brother was sitting in his BMW looking at his phone when she pulled up next to him.

Eli instantly smiled and was out in a flash.

He came around the front of her SUV, greeting Vivien as she opened her door, looking more Sunday casual than she was used to seeing her buttoned-up big bro. Instead of business dress, he wore a T-shirt and sweats, and his salt-and-pepper hair was soft and windblown.

Even at fifty-three, he was a handsome man, mostly because of all the goodness on the inside of him.

"Hey, Viv. How's my favorite sister?"

She shot a warning look as she climbed out. "Hush. You know Crista probably has Ring cameras and mics everywhere."

He laughed, his blue eyes glinting with a bone-deep happiness few people truly possessed. And that was remarkable, considering all this widowed father had been through.

He'd not only survived the shocking death of his beloved wife in a private plane crash almost fifteen years ago, he'd gone on to build a thriving architectural firm and raise two amazing kids. Well, one amazing, and one who *would* be amazing if he'd settle down and do something with his life.

"You look...not thrilled," Eli remarked as she opened the back door to get her bag.

"I'm fine."

"Really?" He regarded her closely, his eyes narrowing as though he could read all her thoughts—which he often did.

"Just getting bulldozed by my husb—er, ex," she told him.

"Now what does he want?" Eli asked, no love lost for the brother-in-law he'd never quite connected with, but not for lack of trying.

"He wants me to go back to Vivien Lawson."

Eli's face lit up. "I love that! It's who you are."

"Really?" She made a face. "It's who I *was*. Maggie's daughter. Then Ryan's wife."

He leaned in. "Now you can be Vivien, an independent woman with no one else calling the shots."

She sighed, grateful he got her like almost no one else, but annoyed that she was such a cliché. "I guess. I'm not exactly a woman of, uh, independent means."

"You could be."

Waving off the platitude—which actually sounded possible when he said it—she squinted at Crista's house, bathed in early March sunshine.

"Do you have any idea why the Queen has called us to court?"

She expected him to give a wry snort, but he inhaled slowly, running a hand over his jaw, shadowed by weekend beard growth.

"It's...business."

Business? Maggie had no business. She was a seventy-eight-year-old widow living with her youngest child. Other than being a loving live-in grandmother to Crista's seven-year-old daughter, Maggie's *business* was tending roses and...grudges. She was an expert at both.

"What kind of business?"

Eli just gave her a look of amusement and mystery. "You'll see."

"Hey." She jabbed his arm with the same force she would have used when they were twelve and fifteen, pestering each other constantly. "Tell me."

"I can't."

"Why not?"

"Have you met our mother? Everything is on a need-to-know basis."

She rolled her eyes. "The CIA should have such an operative," she joked. "Just give me a hint. I need to know what I'm walking into. Does this have to do with the trip she's taking next month? The garden tour thing in the Netherlands?"

"No."

"Eli! Give me one word, please."

He smiled. "Okay. It's about...our inheritance."

She sucked in a breath. "Is she all right?" Vivien pressed her hand to her chest. Her mother might be an irritating, judgmental, and controlling woman who ran the family with the proverbial iron fist, but Vivien could not bear a world without her.

Just then, the front door opened. "You know I can see you standing out here gossiping like a couple of old ladies," Crista called. "Mom's waiting."

They shared a quick look.

"FOMO," Vivien muttered. "Still the baby sister who cannot stand to be left out of anything."

Eli snorted. "Come on. Let's go."

"Wait." She snagged his arm. "Is she sick? Why would she want to talk about our inheritance?"

"She's fine. Just trust me on this, Viv. It's going to be great."

This time, it really didn't sound like a platitude, but a promise. She sure hoped so.

EVERY TIME VIVIEN entered Crista and Anthony's home, she felt a sense of family. Not just because Eli's architecture firm had designed it, Ryan Knight Homes had built it, and Vivien had decorated every room.

But because Crista Merritt, a forty-three-year-old dark-haired beauty, had made it a family oasis for her husband and daughter, plus the addition of their mother. Maggie had moved in when she'd turned seventy-five a few years ago, and the arrangement worked perfectly—for them.

Vivien could never live with their mother, but Crista seemed to thrive under Maggie's watchful eye. Well, she was a perfectionist, so meeting their mother's exacting standards suited Crista's personality well.

"She's on the back patio," she said simply, giving them both air kisses and leaving no doubt who "she" was. "And before you ask, I have no idea. She told Anthony to take Nolie out for the day so we have complete privacy, *sans* explanation."

Of course she did. *Privacy* was Maggie Lawson's stock in trade.

Vivien looked from one sibling to the other, a pit forming in her stomach as the seriousness of this hit her.

"I'm worried," Vivien admitted.

"Don't be," Eli assured her. "Just brace for... blessings."

Vivien shot him a look, long used to her brother's uber-positive outlook drawn from his deep faith. But this wasn't just Eli being a believer—he obviously had more information than Vivien or Crista.

"You know what it's about, don't you?" Crista asked him.

He shrugged. "Oldest has privileges," he teased. Sort of. He did have some privileges, being the man of the family since their father had passed away nearly thirty years ago.

But if any of them had special "Maggie privileges," it was Crista, who was by far the closest with their mother. So why didn't *she* know?

As they followed Crista through the tastefully appointed home, Vivien's mind whirled with possibilities.

If Eli knew and he wasn't unhappy, then this meeting wasn't because Maggie was dying. But why else would she want to discuss their *inheritance*?

Which couldn't amount to *that* much. After all, everything their father had ever accumulated had been seized by the government when he'd gone to prison for fraud and embezzlement, leaving them penniless.

Maggie loved to use that word—*penniless*. Whenever Roger's dark past came up, Maggie would remind them that she'd been left *penniless* with Crista only twelve, Vivien a teenager, and Eli still in college. She blamed the government, of course, not her darling white-collar criminal of a husband.

With true grit, unrelenting focus, and, yes, a backbone of ice-cold steel, Magnolia Lawson had managed to usher her kids into adulthood and navigate the world alone. Now, *that* woman was a fighter.

And no one—least of all Vivien—fought back, but only because they'd lose.

Crista opened a French door, taking them to her expansive deck—an add-on that cost a fortune but was worth every dime. Maggie stood at the far corner, leaning on the railing with the spring green trees and rolling hills as her backdrop.

Her short silver hair, sleeked back from her high cheekbones, fluttered slightly in the March breeze. She wore crisp khakis and a pale blue cardigan that matched her eyes. Her ever-present Yorkie, Aunt Pittypat, was tucked in her arms, showing off a pink ribbon on her furry head.

Despite the dog named after a character from *Gone With the Wind*—or possibly because of that—Magnolia Fredericks Lawson was the picture of a confident Southern woman who could bless your heart and shut your mouth with the same smooth smile.

Most of all, she looked as vibrant as Vivien could remember, taking away some of her worry.

"Come and sit," Maggie said after both Vivien and Eli had given her light hugs, gesturing to a group of four chairs surrounding a stone firepit.

Crista sat closest to their mother. "Everything is okay, right, Mama?"

Maggie smiled, settling Pittypat on her lap. Her expression was always softened for her youngest child, the only one who still called her Mama. To her face, Vivien and Eli used Mom but mostly, it was just Maggie, a name synonymous with...power.

"Yeah, you have us a little concerned," Vivien said.

"Just dive in and tell them," Eli suggested to Maggie.

Vivien frowned. "Tell us what?"

Her mother took a slow, deep inhale, and let out the breath with a sigh that sounded almost pained. Vivien's heart shifted. She knew that sigh. She knew that pain. There was really only one thing that made this woman sad.

"Is this about Dad?" Vivien asked.

"Yes and no," she replied. "Because with his help from wherever he rests in peace, I am about to change all of your lives."

They all sat in silence as Maggie lowered Pittypat to the deck and looked from one to the other, as though the moment was too dramatic for her eight-pound baby to endure.

"Who remembers Destin?" she finally asked.

Destin? Vivien had to bite her lip to keep from gasping.

Whatever this was about, it had to be major for her mother to even utter the *word* Destin.

Maggie gave them a minute to process her question, enough time for Vivien to mentally open a box of memories that began and ended on the blissful white sands of a beach town in Florida's Panhandle.

To her, Destin meant freedom and sunshine and laughter, bonfire nights and delicious days. Mostly, it meant three months of non-stop fun with summertime besties Kate and Tessa Wylie.

Destin epitomized Vivien's teenage years, since she'd spent the seven most formative summers of her life there.

But it wasn't a place, a topic, or a memory Maggie *ever* voluntarily mentioned. In fact, Destin in general, and the Wylie family in particular, were considered off-limit subjects that were never discussed in Maggie's presence.

So Vivien tried to play it cool. "Our summers in Destin are some of my best memories," she said.

Starting in 1989 for seven consecutive years, the Lawsons spent the whole summer there, sharing a beachfront vacation cottage with the Wylie family. The Wylies —friends of her parents from college—came from Upstate New York and had twin daughters Vivien's age.

Vivien, Kate, and Tessa had been twelve when the Destin summers started and had just graduated high school when they ended.

And, boy, had they ended.

"Some of the best memories for *you*," Crista countered. "Because you had friends. I was the tag-along baby that no one wanted."

Eli smiled at her. "You managed to worm your way into things, though. You were always—"

Maggie held up her hand. "This is about the house," she said, as if to gently remind them not to even whisper the name *Wylie*.

"The beach house we rented?" Vivien asked. "I thought it got blown away right after we left for the last time. Wasn't there a big hurricane that year? Opal?"

Maggie and Eli shared a quick and indecipherable

look. After a second, he nodded, encouraging their mother to continue.

"There was, but that house didn't get completely destroyed," Maggie said. "Badly damaged, yes, but it was repaired."

"Okay," Vivien said, drawing out the word as she wondered how Maggie knew that, and why it mattered.

Her mother lifted one perfectly drawn brow, as if to underscore the importance of what she was about to say. "In point of fact, we didn't *rent* it, not that last summer anyway."

Crista frowned, as confused as Vivien. "What do you mean?"

"Your father purchased the property that last summer, as a gift for me."

He had? That was news.

Her mother wet her lips, obviously taking her time before she continued. "But, as you recall..." she said softly, "that fall, things changed."

That was one way of putting it.

Dad had been carted off in handcuffs and, months later, he was found guilty on a mountain of charges for using his architectural business as a front for white-collar crimes. The U.S. government took everything they had to repay his clients' losses and cover unpaid taxes. That must have included this beach house Vivien didn't even know they'd owned.

"So, does the government still hold that primo property?" Vivien asked.

"Actually, *I* do," Maggie said softly, earning a blink of surprise from both Crista and Vivien.

Eli just looked like he knew all of this already.

"Roger purchased the house in cash, and I was able to, uh, protect that one lone asset," Maggie told them, speaking in a hushed tone, as if an IRS agent might be hiding under the deck. "The sale went through that August, Roger was arrested in September, and the hurricane hit in early October. Because of the chaos, the insurance mess, and all the confusion about the status of the damaged house, I was able to...do that."

To *do that*? Did she mean *break the law*? And had they been called here to find out they somehow had to pay back this debt to the government? Vivien's heart dropped at the possibility of yet another emotional and financial blow.

"How did you keep the place?" Crista asked, obviously as in the dark as Vivien.

"I knew a local Destin attorney who helped me legally place the home in a secure trust since my name was also on the deed, shielding the asset, and then he handled the repairs," Maggie told them. "Over the years, he managed the property and supervised rentals, which have been brisk and profitable. In fact, the house has been generating income for thirty years."

Vivien dropped back against the chair, her jaw nearly hitting her chest as she thought about how the government helped itself to everything that could be associated with Roger Lawson.

"Don't tell me," she guessed. "We owe all that back to the government now. With interest."

Maggie gave a quick laugh. "Gracious, no! We've passed the statute of limitations on the government seizures. They cannot have the house, thanks to a loophole the size of a pin that my attorney's son found. It's ours, free and clear."

"That's astounding," Crista said.

"It sure is," Vivien agreed, relieved they didn't owe millions for her father's bad, bad decisions. "That's prime beach property in a top tourist destination."

"You have no idea," Eli said with a smile. "Gulf Shore Drive is a true jewel in Destin's crown. Back in the early nineties, it was a fairly desolate beach with a smattering of little cottages like the one we stayed in every summer. Now, it's a prized strip of mini-mansions that sits directly on the sand, flanked by condos at either end. There are fewer than twenty home sites on that stretch, one more stunning than the next, with mind-boggling value."

"And that little house is still there?" Crista asked, sounding as shocked by this news as Vivien felt.

"Not exactly," Maggie said. "Once I learned we were past all possible legal hurdles, I made the decision to bring Eli into it. I needed a talented architect, and I needed someone I could trust."

Eli was certainly both of those.

"Believe me, I was as shocked as you are," he said to his sisters. "But the plan was solid, and I promised I'd keep it to myself until the time was right."

"What plan?" Vivien asked, still trying to make sense of all this.

"Mom used a small portion of the rental income to keep the house in shape all these years, banking the rest," Eli said. "Then, almost a year ago, she turned over a size-able sum to my company and we razed the original house, drew up plans for a three-story, six-bedroom beauty—with a separate apartment over the garage. I'm happy to announce that building is just about complete."

Vivien drew back with a gasp, feeling like *she* was the one hit by a hurricane. Six bedrooms and a separate apartment directly on the beach?

"That must be worth millions!" she exclaimed.

"It is," Maggie said, the first smile pulling at her lips. "We can't legally sell it for profit until thirty years after your father's death, which, you all know, will be later this year, in November. But when we do, we will divide the profits among the three of you."

Wait a second. Did she say—

"No!" Crista exclaimed. "You can't give it to us! That money is yours, Mama!"

"Actually, according to the law, I have to give it to you," she explained. "That's the loophole. Since your parent passed away by natural causes in prison, it can be passed to you three—but only you three. When he died, it ended the legal ability to seize even his assets, but by that time, they had everything and left me..."

Not exactly penniless, Vivien thought. Of course, no one knew because...Maggie.

"You can sell it for an excellent price," Maggie

continued. "And that will set you all up quite nicely for the future."

For a moment, Vivien couldn't breathe, but Crista shot out of her chair, draping her arms around their mother with a wail.

"This is too much. Too much! You can have whatever you need, forever and ever. I can't..." She shook her head, blinking back tears. "I can't believe this."

Vivien wasn't the crier that her little sister was, but she had to admit her throat felt thick with emotion. "This is unbelievable, Mom. Thank you."

But no sooner were the words out than she had to wonder, *What's the catch?* Because there had to be one. After all, this was Maggie.

"Don't thank me," Maggie said. "Thank that brilliant lawyer down in Florida and this man right here." She smiled at Eli. "His architectural vision was inspired and got us everything at cost, much of it with his own sweat equity." She added a sharp look to Vivien. "I would have had Ryan Knight Homes build it, but..."

But Ryan currently sat in the top spot in her mother's rather long blacklist.

"I will say this," Eli interjected quickly. "It's definitely one of the most beautiful residential properties I've ever done. I didn't like keeping quiet about it, but..." His eyes, the same cornflower blue as Maggie's, lit with that inner joy he always had. "I think this surprise was worth the secrecy."

"So that's where you've been going on so many business trips," Vivien said, only realizing now that her brother, usually so close and candid, had been weirdly distant lately. She'd blamed her divorce, but this made more sense.

He nodded. "I gave Mom my word."

And his word was pure gold.

"You won't believe how much Destin's changed in thirty years," he added. "But Gulf Shore Drive is still one of the most beautiful places imaginable, and this house?" He gave a chef's kiss on his fingertips.

"Have you been there, too?" Vivien asked Maggie.

"No." Her mother's smile disappeared. "I will never step foot on that property."

Oh, boy. They just hit the Wylie landmine.

"Then I won't go there either," Crista announced, always standing in solidarity with their mother, whether she knew the whole story of the estrangement or not.

And Vivien doubted anyone knew *this* whole story. She was certain it had gone to the grave with Dad...or to New York with the long-lost Wylies.

Whatever had caused the families to part was a deep, dark secret that Maggie refused to discuss. Eli and Vivien had speculated now and again, but to be honest, they didn't remember the details. Who could blame them?

Their whole world turned inside out after that last summer—Vivien had started college, Dad had been arrested, and the family had slipped from comfortably middle-class to barely making ends meet.

All but Crista had to get jobs in order to survive, and life had shifted to something new and not always good. A year later, their father had a fatal heart attack in his prison cell.

In the grand scheme of things, before email and social media, the loss of her girlhood friends from summers in Destin had faded into the background, eventually forgotten.

"Well, I'd like to go there," Vivien said, already longing for the feel of that soft sand under her feet and a nice long walk down memory lane.

"That's good to hear," Eli said, stealing one more look at their mother. This time, Maggie nodded as if to give him the go-ahead to drop more news. "Because Mom and I would like you to stage it for sale, Vivien. It's empty now, and houses at that price point have to be decorated perfectly to appeal to the right buyer. Since they are mostly second homes for wealthy buyers, they sell furnished to the nines. It needs to look like a top-of-the-line model home."

Her jaw dropped, and this time her eyes did fill with tears. For the first time in months, she felt washed with joy.

"Really?" she asked, breathless. "Staging a house like that could be the centerpiece for my portfolio. I'd...I'd *love* that."

Eli reached for Vivien's hand. "I know you will slay this place, Viv. I wouldn't want anyone else's creative eye on the interior."

"I fully agree," her mother said with a direct look.

While the rare compliment warmed, she still had to wonder what price would have to be paid for this prize.

Eli seemed to have no such qualms, whipping out his phone to tap his calendar app.

"Let's go down on Tuesday," he said. "I'd like to spend a few weeks there, or longer. I actually finagled with the county to give me the CO early, so we can put basic furnishings in and crash there while I finish up with the general contractor. Could you go or are you busy?"

She almost laughed, but was still in shock. "I'm free."

"Good, because I need to decide what to do with the apartment over the garage—it's not built out yet. Oh, and Destin's a design mecca, too, which you will love. With thousands of condos and short-term rentals that have exploded there, the décor business is solid. You'll find everything you need locally."

Good heavens, it sounded too good to be true.

"I only ask one thing." Maggie interjected.

Or maybe not.

On a sigh, Vivien turned to her mother, bracing herself. What demand, what parameter, what *condition* would she put on her love, which wasn't and never would be *unconditional*?

"I want to be kept out of it," she said. "For one thing, I'll be spending all of April in Europe, touring Keukenhof Gardens and the Loire Valley in France."

"I know you'll be gone," Vivien said. Her mother had planned the extensive tour with her closest garden club friends, so the fact that the elaborate vacation took precedence over this house didn't really surprise her. "But there are phones, and we can Zoom if you want to be involved."

Because even across the Atlantic, Maggie would have strong opinions.

"No," she said simply. "The memories aren't fond for me, and I have no desire to ever return to Destin again, physically, emotionally, or over a video call. You make all the decisions."

Vivien inched back at her vehemence.

"I wish you all the best with this property," Maggie continued. "And I hope you all make a sizeable amount of money. But I don't want to have anything to do with it except to sign the paperwork and toast your father's memory. Without him, this wouldn't have happened."

She had to give the woman credit—she'd defend Roger until the day she died, despite the fourteen counts of embezzlement, tax evasion, forgery and six different kinds of fraud.

After a beat of silence, Aunt Pittypat jumped into Maggie's lap and let out a little bark.

"There, darling," her mother cooed, stroking the tiny head and straightening the ridiculous bow. "I know it's time to work on the roses. Let's go change into gardening clothes."

With that, their matriarch stood and ended the discussion, glancing toward her prized flower bed. "We should have glorious color this year, don't you think?"

And just like that, the topic, as far as Maggie was concerned, was closed.

~

A FEW MINUTES LATER, Eli and Vivien headed back to their cars in the driveway.

"I told you it was good news," Eli said.

She looked up at him, searching his face for any sign of the skepticism that she felt. "You're not worried?"

"About what?"

"The long arm of Maggie Lawson, trying to control what we do, how much we spend, when we sell—all of it."

He chuckled and shook his head. "No. She's serious about staying out of it. You'll do whatever your keen designer eye wants to do. We have a generous budget, and we'll sell in November."

"It can't be that easy."

"Honestly, Viv, she hasn't made a single outrageous demand and gave me carte blanche on the plans and building process. And the same will be true of the interior, and the sale of the place. Don't worry."

Too late. She was worried. Happy about the possibilities, but too experienced opening gifts from her mother that were tied with strings attached to...something.

"Hey." He put a brotherly arm around her. "We're about to have a blast in Destin, Vivien *Lawson*. This is the fresh start you need."

She couldn't argue that. "How did you manage to keep this from me?"

"Please." He looked skyward. "She made me swear on her first-edition collector's edition of *Gone With the Wind* signed by Clark Gable himself."

Vivien laughed. "As good as a Bible to that woman."

"Not to me, but I didn't want to risk losing the job, so I didn't even tell Meredith," he added, referring to his daughter, an intern at his firm. "She just thinks Acacia Architecture has this great, mysterious client in Florida."

"That's amazing. Everything about this is amazing."

He gave her a squeeze. "What we call blessings, sis. Freely given and received with open hands."

"Is there such a thing with our mother?" she asked. "She really isn't capable of unconditional love."

"This is different," he assured her. "She doesn't want to have anything to do with that place. It's still tainted to her, though she won't say why."

"Why? The Others," Vivien said, adding a smile at their secret nickname for the Wylies stolen from a mutual love of the show *Lost*. "Whatever happened that summer before the hurricane and Dad's arrest is buried in the sand. But is that enough for her to—"

"Oh!" He snapped his fingers. "That reminds me. I have something for you I've been dragging around for months."

"For me? I think you've gifted me enough for one day."

He walked to the back of his sedan and popped the trunk, reaching in to produce something square, plastic, and the brightest fuchsia imaginable.

Vivien nearly choked at the sight of the shoebox-shaped container she once owned and loved.

"I found this in the attic of the old house when we started demo months and months ago," he said. "Not sure how it survived all those years and storms, but it did."

"Because it's a Caboodle," she told him. "Made of indestructible plastic and full of..." She frowned. "In the attic? How did it get there and, bigger question, is it safe to look inside? No critters?"

"No critters, but I don't know how safe it is." Holding the bottom with one hand, he turned the pink latch and revealed a collection of colorful notebooks.

"Are these..." Her heart squeezed as she looked up at him. "My *diaries*?"

He shifted the container from his hands to hers. "I do believe they are the yearnings of one teenaged Vivien Lawson."

"You *read* them?"

"I opened one and realized what it was, and never took another peek, I swear."

"Well, well. I'm not sure I even want to read these things," she said, snapping the latch closed as he opened the back door of her SUV so she could set the box on the seat. "But who knows? They might inspire my design."

"Everything about this might inspire you," he said, his voice serious. "I honestly think getting out of Atlanta will be good for you, Viv. You need to get away from Ryan, all the memories, and do something just for yourself."

Her heart softened as she looked up at him, the single dearest man she'd ever known.

"You're right," she said. "And I don't mean to look a gift horse or anything. I'm just stinging from the conversation I had on the way over here and my never-realized dream of being...free."

"Then it's time to realize that dream." He grinned.

"It'll be just like old times on that beach, the one thing about that town that hasn't changed."

"Only no Kate and Tessa."

He gave a wistful smile. "Can't have everything, can we?"

"But we have each other and a beach house in Destin," she said. "I call it a win."

"Amen, sister." He gave her a high-five and a wink. "See you Tuesday. If you don't mind, we should drive separately, because I want to take my truck and we'll both need cars down there."

"I'll drive, I'll stay, and..." She sucked in a breath and made a decision. "I'll introduce myself to all the new vendors as Vivien Lawson, independent designer. Emphasis on *independent*."

"That's my girl!"

Still smiling, Vivien drove home, making the decision to embrace her new job, her new adventure, and, yes, her new name. Ryan would think he'd won yet another battle without a fight, but the truth was, this was her victory. And she was going to enjoy the heck out of it.

Chapter Two

Eli

The hardest part about "the Destin job," as Eli called the most significant project in his current portfolio, wasn't that he'd been so hands-on—practically breathing down the GC's throat, making every decision, and deeply involved in every change order. He'd actually enjoyed that aspect, getting his hands dirty and doing some of the work himself.

Nor did he hate the five-hour drive from his Buck-head office to the Panhandle that he made a few times a month, since Destin offered a great break from the pace of life in Atlanta.

Without a doubt, the most difficult aspect was keeping the whole thing to himself. Eli had spent more time away from Meredith, his daughter, and the firm that he ran than he liked. He'd also built an invisible but very real wall between himself and his sisters, which he hated. Especially when Vivien was going through such a rough time.

Thankfully, that all changed yesterday.

And this Monday morning, as he sipped a cup of coffee at his desk and broke the news to his favorite employee and only daughter, more weight lifted from his heart.

Across from him, Meredith's green eyes widened and her dark brows lifted in surprise with each revelation. With every changing expression, she looked so much like her mother, with the same chocolate-colored hair and endearing smile that had made Melissa Lawson a favorite face on the local news.

"Dad, that property is *yours*? Ours? The family's?" She slapped her pink-tipped fingers on the desk in disbelief. "Get out of town!"

"I am, with Aunt Vivien, who's going to design and stage it for sale. I have to finish the punch list, plan the garage apartment build-out, and do something about the outside landscaping, which, as you know—"

"Is the icing on a house cake," she recited with a smile.

"You do listen to me, Meredith."

She grinned, the smile adding light to her eyes and making her look even more like Melissa. "I'm not doing my three-year Architectural Experience Program internship here for fun, you know."

"You? You don't do anything for fun," he teased. "In fact, if you weren't so close to finishing your AXP hours, I'd insist you come to Florida with Aunt Vivien and me so you could experience a little of the Destin magic."

She rolled her eyes. "I'm less than two months from being a licensed architect, Dad, and whoa, brace yourself for the raise I'm going to demand. Also, fun is for losers."

He gave a wry laugh at that, but really, his heart lifted. The fact that she wanted to stay at Acacia Architecture when she could have her pick of any firm in Atlanta or the whole country gave him a jolt of joy. But was he surprised?

Not at all. When their mother passed away fourteen years—and eleven months—ago, his two kids responded in utterly different ways. Jonah had been about to turn fifteen, the worst possible time for a boy to lose his mother. Well, there was no good time, Eli supposed.

His son had become distant, moody, and lost. He'd struggled to keep from failing high school. He dropped out of a community college after a year. Despite all of Eli's encouragement, he was downright disdainful about studying to be an architect like his father, grandfather, and now, sister.

At twenty-nine, Jonah lived in a van, traveled the country, and...

Eli had no idea how he made money, friends, or a life. They spoke so rarely.

Meredith, on the other hand, had attached herself to Eli in the wake of Melissa's death. She worshipped him, emulated him, and parlayed her extraordinary gifts and unparalleled work ethic into a fast-track architecture career.

He had no doubt she'd take over Acacia Architecture someday.

"So, this house is not only ours," Meredith said, her brain not on her career path for once but mulling over the news he'd just shared, "you vacationed there as a kid, right? How cool is that?"

"Pretty darn," he agreed. "We went for seven years—to a completely different, very small house. But we'd spent the summers there, from the time I was fifteen to twenty-one. Grandma Maggie would pile us into the car on Memorial Day and we stayed straight through until Labor Day. My father came down on the weekends."

She nodded. "I've heard about those legendary summers from Aunt Vivien. Wasn't there another family involved? Grandma Maggie's sorority sister from UGA?"

"Yes, Jo Ellen and Artie Wylie and their daughters. I always brought Peter McCarthy, since I was the only boy and was allowed to have a friend."

She smiled at the mention of his lifelong friend. "Wait—doesn't he live down there now? He's a cop?"

"A detective actually, and yes, he lives in Pensacola, which isn't far. I've seen him a few times this past year, but didn't tell him that I was working on the same house because..."

She snorted. "Grandma's a psycho."

"Well, she has her reasons for keeping things on the DL," he said, rising to his mother's defense. "For one thing, there was some serious legal wrangling to get this done, and it brought up some hard memories."

Meredith nodded. "My notorious grandfather."

He gave a tight smile, certainly not defending that parent. Roger Lawson's crimes still irked Eli in the most unreasonable way.

Thirty years later, Eli struggled with the memory of seeing his father arrested, arraigned, tried, and found guilty. He reeled when he thought of how Dad had used a firm much like this one to steal from clients, corporations, and no small amount of strangers.

Eli had almost decided not to become an architect, he was so angry at Roger. But then he'd met Melissa and she'd nurtured his love for the work, and encouraged him to prove to the world and himself that the profession was noble and respectable.

His father had been neither of those things. So when Eli struck out on his own and opened the doors of this firm, he certainly hadn't chosen the sullied name of Lawson Architecture to put on his door. Instead, he chose Acacia, the very wood God instructed Moses to use to build the Ark of the Covenant, a material recognized for its strength and integrity.

"Well, Roger did one good thing," Eli said. "He bought that house for a song—a *cash* song—and it withstood a hurricane. My mother was cunning enough to protect it from the government and now, thirty years later, it is rightfully and legally ours." He angled his head and took in the look on her face. "What? It is."

"I know it is," she said. "But you keep saying 'legally' over and over again, like *you* don't quite believe it."

"I believe it," he assured her. "I've seen the court stamp on the paperwork. I just..." He shook his head. "I never, ever want to do anything like my dad, Meredith. Everything must be legitimate and on the up-and-up."

"Just count it as a blessing, as I know you do, Dad."

He nodded. "I'm looking forward to the next few weeks in Destin to finish the project. That leaves you here on your own."

"With two other architects, three assistants, an office manager, and that cute guy who just opened up a mobile coffee station."

He drew back. "What cute guy?"

"I'm kidding. Kind of. But are you putting me in charge?" She clasped her hands and flexed, cracking her knuckles. "Oh, the whip is going to be snapped on these slackers."

He laughed. "Just be my eyes and ears while I'm gone for so long. Everyone knows their job, and of course, I'll be Zooming in for every important meeting. I just need you to make sure nothing falls through the cracks and there are no random unhappy clients floating around."

"Will do," she promised him. "Anything else?"

He shifted uncomfortably in his seat, knowing there *was* something else. "Have you talked to Jonah lately?"

"Speaking of slackers," she joked, but her smile faded. "No, Dad. My brother doesn't call me unless he broke up with his latest girlfriend and he needs an ear. When his life is cool, whatever that might mean to him, I don't hear from him."

He huffed out a breath, a cocktail of mixed emotions rolling around every time he thought about his son.

"I miss him," he admitted quietly. "I wish he wasn't... wherever he is."

How sad that he didn't know where his own son was.

"Call him," she said.

He grunted. "And get dismissed?"

"Hey, you have to keep trying."

Guilt punched when he realized how right she was.

"I will," he said. "I think he's on the West Coast, or at least he was the last time we talked, so I'll call him after lunch."

"And wake him up, no doubt." She made a face that showed her disapproval for her brother's lifestyle and stood, scooping up her notebook. "Hey, you're going to need something to sleep on in Destin. The house is empty. Should I order beds and frames to be delivered? I can get kings or queens for every room, and some sheets and towels for you and Aunt Vivien. A few basic life necessities and kitchen tools? I can have everything delivered for Tuesday."

He gave a grateful smile. "You're a gem, Mer."

"I'll also have the designs on the Southerland project to you before that, and then I wanted to go over the change orders for Markel & Markel. Oh, and I hope you don't mind, but I'm looking at a new version of Autodesk Revit, since the rep told me we could get a massive discount. Also, it's Gretchen's birthday tomorrow, so I ordered a cake."

He shook his head, marveling at her efficiency and drive. "I'm sure not worried about anything falling through the cracks with you at this office."

She flipped some dark locks over her shoulder. "And you think I don't know how to have fun."

"Work isn't fun."

"Is to me." She playfully stuck out her tongue, looking like a nine-year-old again, and then swept out of his office leaving a smile on his face and the remnants of her perfume.

Oh, Missy, he thought, closing his eyes to picture his late wife. *You'd have loved the young woman your little girl became.*

Now...the other child?

Eli turned to his monitor, wanting to work but the thought of Jonah weighed heavy on his mind.

He brought the screen to life, tapped a few keys, and found the plans for the Destin house, along with some new photos that had been added by his contractor over the weekend.

Eli had asked for outdoor shots so he could start getting serious about that icing on the cake. Peering at the image, he tried to imagine the landscaping it needed, and the boardwalk they'd have to build in the back to go over the sea oats to the beach.

He'd put in a gorgeous contemporary pool on the deck, but that backyard still needed so much work. The right "icing" could mean all the difference in the asking price.

He clicked on the shot that showed the view from the deck to the beach and gave a soft laugh. Talk about icing. That sure didn't need work—God had done the heavy lifting, creating a picture-perfect beach of white sand and turquoise water, tipped with frothy waves that stretched for miles in either direction.

There might be a billion condos and short-term rentals, just as many tourists, and traffic for days in Destin. But they were all there because of that pristine, blindingly beautiful beach.

That magical sand where he'd come of age and fallen

hard for beautiful, wild, enchanting Tessa Wylie. Where he and Peter and the girls had laughed around a bonfire until they darn near cried. The last summers when he was innocent...before Dad shattered his belief in mankind.

Melissa had restored it, then she was gone in the blink of an eye.

But the Good Lord had stepped in, saving Eli from a life of utter misery. But to be honest, some of his happiest and most exciting days had happened right there on that beach. The place could cast a spell, if he believed in that sort of thing. He didn't.

Still, he sat up straighter, and not because he could visualize the boardwalk he'd be installing in the next few weeks. Maybe Destin could work more magic. Maybe it could help another Lawson man.

He glanced at the clock and made the decision to call Jonah the minute he could.

SPRINGTIME IN BUCKHEAD was so lovely, Eli wondered why he frequently chose to eat a sandwich at his desk. Today, he opted to slip out of the office, mostly because he wanted complete privacy when he called his son. He didn't want to take a chance of Meredith coming in and trying to listen or, worse, talk.

Those two siblings certainly didn't have the connection he and Vivien shared, despite the fact that he and his sisters had lost a parent at a young age, too.

He crossed a street at the light, glancing at the chic storefronts and quaint restaurants that lined the busy streets of Buckhead Village. He spied a cafe that had open tables outside but was still a bit secluded, so he checked in at the hostess stand and then took a seat under an umbrella.

He ordered an iced tea and a BLT—all forms of procrastination. Why was he so hesitant to call his own son?

Because Jonah would be cold, distant, and disinterested in anything. He was, Eli thought with a wry smile, truly the prodigal son. And Eli would never stop hoping that boy would come home and accept the love this father wanted to shower on him.

If that happened, Meredith would probably act just like the prodigal son's brother had—resentful of having held down the fort and done the right thing.

Well, it didn't matter. He loved them both.

When his tea was served, he took out his phone, closed his eyes, and said a quick prayer before tapping the screen.

Meredith had shown him how to attach an image to a contact name, and the picture he had for Jonah always made him smile. With his long hair that darn near grazed broad shoulders, brooding hazel eyes, and movie star bone structure he'd inherited from his photogenic mother, Jonah Lawson was a force even in two dimensions.

He'd been born with a big personality, way too much

passion for one human, and a presence that couldn't be ignored.

Whoa, Eli missed the kid.

He pressed the call button and put the phone to his ear, bracing for the impact of Jonah.

"Hey, bro."

Or...a sleepy, irreverent greeting that lacked respect and caring.

"Jonah. How are you?"

"Eh. Hungover. 'Sup?"

"Hungover, huh? Were you, uh, partying?" He winced, wondering if that was going to earn him a verbal smackdown.

"Nah. We just had a few pops after work."

"Work?" The word was out before Eli could stop himself. "You're...oh. I didn't know..."

"Yeah, I just picked up a few hours at a local restaurant," he said, taking casual to a whole new level. "Line cook."

"Nice, nice. That's great, son."

Jonah snorted softly. "Not exactly the king of architecture like you hoped, but it pays for gas in the van."

Eli's eyes shuttered at the memory of their last massive fight, maybe five years ago, when Jonah accused him of putting more emphasis on money and work than anything else. It had caused the fracture that sent his son running, and he'd never come back.

"So, what's going on, Dad?"

In other words, get to the point so Jonah could go back to sleep.

"Well, I have a little family news," he said. "Turns out we own a beach house in Florida."

"Huh."

Yeah, about what he expected. But he powered on, telling the story to Jonah, explaining that he'd been working on the house and that Grandma Maggie owned it.

"Sounds cool, Dad."

Eli's sandwich arrived, but he pushed it away, ready to make his pitch. "So, listen, son, I was thinking..."

He waited for Jonah to lose interest, change the subject, or suddenly need to go. When none of that happened, he continued.

"I mean, I didn't know you had a job in California, but maybe you could mosey on out to Destin and hang with us for a while. It's a great place and I could use your input on the finishing touches."

"My input? Just because I hung drywall for Uncle Ryan for a few summers?"

"I mean your opinion. And we could have...some time together."

For a long moment, Jonah didn't say a word. Long enough for Eli to hope...then long enough for him to wonder if his son had hung up.

"You there?" he finally asked with an uncomfortable laugh.

"Yeah, yeah. I'm, uh, kind of locked in right now, Dad. San Diego's cool and I like this gig, so...maybe another time?"

Disappointment slammed his gut. "Oh, yeah, sure.

Door's always open. I mean, we'll be selling this place eventually, but summer's coming and if you wanted to hang..."

Oh, stop begging, Eli. You're his father. And Jonah was darn lucky to have one at twenty-nine. Eli lost his father when he was barely twenty-two.

"Well, I gotta go, man," Jonah said. "Early shift. But shoot me a pin of the address in case anything comes up."

"Sure, sure. Good to talk to you, son."

"See ya, Dad."

The phone went dead, and Eli stared at his sandwich, not seeing anything but that handsome face darkened with a shadow of sadness that had appeared when that boy lost his mother. A shadow that never went away.

He had a prodigal son and missed him so profoundly, he could taste it. But some things, he knew, were not in his hands.

He glanced toward the sky and inhaled a breath. *How much longer?*

Chapter Three
Vivien

With the bed covered in clothes, two suitcases open, and an exciting new project just over the horizon, Vivien couldn't help but hum a happy tune as she packed. Even though she had no idea what she'd need.

Work clothes? Beach attire? Was it chilly in Destin in March? Or would—

At the sound of the front door opening, she breathed a sigh of relief. Lacey was home from work and always packed like a pro.

"Hey," she called, taking a few steps to the door to make sure her voice traveled down the stairs. "I'm upstairs! Come on up and help me figure out what to take."

She waited a beat, expecting to hear her daughter's lighthearted laugh and the sound of her footsteps on the stairs. But there was nothing.

"Lacey?" she called. If she hadn't come in, then who—

"I'm here."

Vivien winced at the tone of utter despair. Oh, boy. Bad day at Ryan Knight Homes.

Abandoning her suitcase, she headed straight downstairs, a mother first and foremost.

She looked down the stairwell as she walked, noticing for the four millionth time that the flat, dull "builder's grade" gray screamed for color and the wall needed art.

Like the shoemaker's children, the interior designer's home was pitiful. Well, she had no connection to this rental and zero desire to hang even cheap wall art.

Coming around the corner, she found Lacey leaning against the back of the sofa that separated the living area from the kitchen, her face covered by her long sandy blond hair as she looked at her phone.

"Hey," Vivien said, slowing her step when Lacey didn't look up. "Everything okay?"

She sighed. "I screwed up an order for Dad and..." She tossed the phone on the sofa. "Now the client is unhappy because it's going to delay plumbing and electric for two weeks, which will push back...whatever comes next."

"Drywall," she said without thinking, coming closer with concern in her heart. "It's okay, Lace. Mistakes happen. They'll make up the time—"

She closed her eyes and inhaled so hard it flared her delicate nostrils. "Can I just say it? Can I speak some blasphemy? *I hate houses.*"

Vivien smiled, mostly because just looking at Lacey made her smile but especially when she got dramatic because, somehow, she made it funny. Her baby blues were never spiteful, her angel's smile was never really gone.

But, she had to admit, Lacey looked troubled tonight.

"Why is that blasphemy?" Vivien asked.

"Because I'm the daughter of a builder and an interior designer. The niece and granddaughter and cousin of architects. And now, you're leaving because of a house! I know girls my age have boy problems, but I have house problems."

Vivien knew the real issue that was bothering her wasn't that she hated houses...but she did hate that Vivien was leaving. Indefinitely, too.

Unlike most twenty-four-year-old women who might welcome the chance to be out from under the mother they lived with, Lacey didn't ever push Vivien away. Maybe because Vivien had learned a thing or two from Maggie about how *not* to be a mother.

She didn't judge, she didn't control, and she didn't keep secrets from Lacey.

Thanks to that, they'd always been crazy close, two peas in a pod who never tired of each other's company.

"How about some wine and we order pizza?" Vivien suggested, knowing it was a recipe for talk and healing.

"Yeah, whatever."

Uh-oh. Maybe this was more than wine and pizza could solve.

Vivien took a few steps closer, eyeing Lacey's expression. "You're upset that I'm leaving, aren't you."

"Upset?" Her eyes widened. "No! I'm thrilled for you, Mom. This whole thing—the beach house, the staging, the money it will bring it? You know I'm one hundred percent on board and happy for you."

Vivien nodded, waiting for the real reasons to emerge.

But Lacey sighed. "I guess I'll take that wine," she said, turning toward the kitchen. "We barely touched that white the other night. Think it turned to vinegar yet?"

"It's fine. I'll take a glass, too." Vivien perched on a barstool at the counter. "Which client got screwed up?"

"The couple from Chicago building in Peachtree Hills. Picky old biddy and her henpecked husband."

Vivien laughed at the description. "New since I was there. I don't know this lovely pair."

"Count your blessings." She popped the cork lodged into the chardonnay and poured into stemless wine glasses. As she handed one to Vivien, their eyes met.

"I want to quit," Lacey whispered.

Vivien froze in the act of reaching for her glass. "Excuse me?"

"I hate this job. I'm not crazy about my boss."

Vivien rolled her eyes, trying so hard not to say anything bad about Ryan to Lacey. Sure, she broke that rule frequently enough, but she tried.

"Mom, I really hate..."

"Houses," Vivien finished, taking the glass and offering a lackluster toast. "But we do all need them. And we need jobs, so...don't do anything rash."

Lacey sighed and started to take a sip, then put the glass down because she obviously needed to talk more than she needed wine. "People quit jobs, you know. You did."

And Lacey quit her last three—four?—but Vivien didn't have the heart to pour salt in her daughter's wound right now.

"I divorced the owner of the company," she said instead. "It was different."

"He's my father."

"Exactly. And he took you in as an admin when you left the...what was that last job?"

"See? You don't even remember. That's not a career, that's not a calling. It was..." She inhaled sharply. "A garden tool manufacturer and I worked in the accounting department."

Vivien made a face. "Yeah, that was rough. But, honey, you should talk to your father. Tell him what you want at the job if you're not getting it."

She gave a "get real" look. "I want a different job in a different business. I want to do something creative and exciting and... Oh, why am I so lost?" she whined. "Why can't I be more like Meredith, all focused and certain of her path?"

"Because you aren't your cousin," Vivien said. "But you can't just quit without a back-up plan, Lace."

"And I can't quit because I work for my dad."

Vivien flicked a brow. "It does complicate things."

Lacey sighed. "Yeah, okay. He does pay me well, so there is that."

"Good girl. We can talk about it. You can look. I promise you can." She took a sip and watched Lacey do the same, her shoulders softening with resignation.

"You're right," she agreed after swallowing. "It was just a bad day."

Vivien nodded. "Now, at the risk of suddenly changing the subject, can you help me pack? I'm clueless about what to take."

She curled her lip. "Pack *me*." At Vivien's look, Lacey clasped her hands together and added puppy dog eyes, pulling out all the stops.

"Please, Mom. I'll be your assistant. I'll be your best pal. I'll be quiet as a mouse and so much fun when you need it and...and... I need an escape. I want to figure out what to do with my life because, as God is my witness, to quote your namesake, Vivien Leigh." She grabbed Vivien's shoulders and squeezed. "I will never work in the house business again!"

Vivien laughed at the bad Scarlett O'Hara drawl, wishing she could just say yes and take Lacey along. But she had a job, and Ryan needed the admin support Lacey offered.

"Honey, you have to learn to stick with a job for a while. You've quit a few since you graduated."

"I know," she said glumly, grabbing her wine and jutting her chin toward the stairs. "Come on. I'll pack you. Hey, maybe I can be a professional packer."

Laughing, Vivien followed her, wishing she could help her daughter figure out her life, but knowing she had to do that for herself first.

AN HOUR LATER, Lacey was still nursing the same wine, laying on Vivien's bed, shooting orders about clothes and Googling everything she could about Destin.

"Apparently this place got so expensive it's not even a spring break destination anymore," she said, tapping her phone. "The college partiers mostly go to Panama City."

"It was big for spring break when I used to go, but we were only there in the summer."

"And you were young, right?" Lacey said. "Like, a kid?"

"Twelve the first summer, but eighteen the last." Vivien folded a cotton sweater, suddenly remembering the diaries. "It's all chronicled right there, I'm slightly embarrassed to say."

"What is?" Lacey sat up and peered at the pink box on the floor by the closet door. "What is that hideous thing? A makeup case? Please tell me you're not taking that."

"It's a Caboodle, darling, and I think you had one, too, to stash your girliest items in life. But what's inside is the real prize."

Lacey threw her a look. "Oh, I'm intrigued. What's in that...Caboodle?"

"My teenage diaries," Vivien said. "Uncle Eli found them before demo. I started the first year, filling one whole notebook for every summer."

Lacey's jaw dropped. "And you've been keeping this from me?"

"Please. I was a kid. I'm sure they're full of things

like, 'We made a bonfire,' and 'Crista cried when we wouldn't take her on the boat.'"

"Aunt Crista cried? Never!" Lacey joked. "And who's we? You and Uncle Eli? Didn't you tell me there was another family there, but Grandma Maggie had, uh, *issues*?" She rolled her eyes and laughed, already off the bed and headed toward the box.

"The Wylies—The Others, as Eli and I call them. The family that shall not be named."

"Why not?" she asked, twisting the pink latch to open the case and pluck out the top notebook. "May I?"

Vivien shrugged. "You may, but no judgment if I dotted every *i* with hearts and flowers. And I don't know why, but we lost touch with that family."

Lacey examined the spiral notebook splashed with shades of pink and purple. "Vintage Lisa Frank." She fluttered the cover, which, Vivien knew without looking at it, featured either a fluffy kitten or a unicorn. "These are worth a fortune on eBay now."

"Empty," Vivien said. "Which that one is not."

Lacey pressed the notebook to her chest and sat back on the bed, a gleam in her eyes. "This could be fun."

"Or mortifying. Please remember I was twelve in that first one. And it was 1989."

She stroked the colorful cover. "Of course you were. No one else bought Lisa Frank but middle-schoolers." She cleared her throat and flipped the cover, then snorted.

"What?" Vivien cringed, half expecting Lacey to

show her a large heart with *Vivien luvs Peter* scripted on the page.

But Lacey pointed at small lettering. "'Do not read under penalty of death'? Guess Aunt Crista isn't the only one with a drama streak."

"No, but I had a brother and his best friend poking around that beach house. No one could be trusted with a young girl's secrets."

Vivien packed another top, then picked up her wine glass and sat down next to Lacey, reaching over to stop her before she turned the page. "Wait. Maybe I should preview before you read."

"Are you embarrassed, Mom?"

"About what I wrote thirty-seven years ago?" She took a sip and leaned over, setting the glass on the hardwood floor. "Maybe. Give that to me."

Taking the notebook in her hands, she was instantly transported. The feel, the scent, the excitement of the first summer in Destin.

Suddenly anxious to read, she turned past the dire warning and looked at her round, clumsy, girlish words, written in a pink Flair pen.

MAY 25, 1989
  Today, my life changed forever.

SHE GLANCED AT LACEY, who was reading over her

shoulder. "Okay, maybe the drama streak runs through the whole family," Vivien acknowledged.

"What happened?" Lacey asked, pointing to the page. "Read on, young Vivien."

Giving her a look, Vivien scooted back to read alone, in case she had to edit on the fly. There could be something about Peter McCarthy on these pages that Lacey would surely use against her forever.

"'I officially have not one but two best friends!!!!'" She looked up. "With four exclamation points."

"Just read, Mom."

"'I have met Kate and Tessa Wylie and I totally LOVE them! They are only three months younger than me, and they came all the way from New York! Our moms were sorority sisters and I get to call their mom "Aunt" Jo Ellen. They are the coolest, most fun girls I've ever met and we are all sleeping in one room until school starts in September! They are twins but don't look anything alike. Aunt Jo Ellen calls them opposite twins. Tessa is soooooo pretty and funny. Everything she says makes us laugh. (Especially Eli!)'" She looked up again. "There's a heart next to that. He had it so bad for that girl."

"She was *twelve*," Lacey said, aghast.

"Not toward the end. Anyway, Tessa Wylie was never twelve. She was born nineteen and so pretty it was hard to look at anything else when she was in the room."

"Read on."

She scooted up, leaning against the pillows, packing forgotten for the moment.

"'Kate is the smartest girl I ever met and gets all A's. She knows everything but doesn't talk as much as Tessa. I love them both already. Tomorrow we go to the beach!!!!'" She snorted. "The amount of exclamation points and hearts is kind of incalculable. Can we stop now?"

Lacey had her phone out, tapping the screen. "For now, but only because I'm on Facebook looking for them. Tessa Wylie? Spell that. And is it Kate or Katherine?"

"Oh, honey, you'll never find them. I think her real name is Theresa, but no one besides Uncle Artie ever called her that." She closed the notebook and slipped down to get the wine she'd left on the floor. "They're probably not—"

"Could Kate be Dr. Katherine Wylie, a research chemist at Cornell University?"

Vivien laughed. "If anyone could be, it would be her." She inched closer to see the phone screen. "Cornell makes sense because her father was a professor there and they lived in Ithaca. How did you do that? Let me see."

"You said New York and they were born the same year as you." Lacey handed her the phone and Vivien squinted at the screen. The face peering back at her was...yeah, that could be Kate.

She flicked the screen to zoom in on a professional shot of a woman in her forties, with dark auburn hair and sharply cut bangs that brushed scholarly-looking dark-rimmed glasses. And that wide smile with dimples? Absolutely Kate Wylie.

"I think it is her," Vivien said. "How can I tell?"

"Check out her friends. Type 'Tessa' in her friends list and see if her sister comes up."

"Oh, you're so smart." She did and gasped softly as an image popped up. A gorgeous woman who could be on social media selling makeup products. Blond, stunning, dressed to turn heads and keep all eyes on her.

"Bingo," she whispered. "There you have the most fun person I ever knew in my life. She's a human party."

Lacey leaned in and whistled. "Yikes, she's attractive. I mean, she probably had some work done, but yeah. She looks good."

Vivien clicked back to Kate's picture, her heart aching in a way she didn't quite understand. "I loved Kate, you know. I loved them both, but Tessa intimidated me. Kate was so soft and smart and special. The last time I saw her we were sailing and promised to be friends forever, then, wham. It was over."

"You should message her, Mom. Tell her you're going back to the house where you spent all those summers together. Reunite with your old friends."

Vivien considered that. "After thirty years? What would I say?"

"Just say hi. Tell her you own the house. Wouldn't you want to know if the tables were turned?"

She sure would, except for one little problem. "My mother would have me put to death," she said, only slightly joking.

"What's Grandma's deal with these people?"

"No one knows or has the nerve to ask because she shuts it down." She angled the phone, thinking about long walks on the beach and the summer they graduated and all the years in between. "Send me this link so I can find Kate again, okay? Now, I want to finish and get some rest."

Lacey pushed off the bed. "I still think you should take me."

"And I think you should be a grown woman and go to work tomorrow," Vivien replied. "Go face your boss-father, and knock his socks off by being the best admin Ryan Knight Homes has ever had."

Lacey made a face. "I don't want to be the best admin they ever had."

"What *do* you want?" Vivien asked.

All her daughter could do was sigh. "I don't know but I do know that I'll recognize it when I find it. But how can I figure it out when I'm trapped in that office doing change orders?"

She heard the plea in Lacey's voice, but didn't give in. At least there was one person she could say no to—but only for her daughter's own good.

"I'm just your mom, trying to guide you to do the right thing, Lace," she said. "And if you really, really want to quit, then I'll help you work on your resume. I promise."

"Fine." She groaned the word. "Are you taking the diaries? Because I'd inhale them."

"Which is exactly why, yes, I'm taking them," she quipped.

"You are no fun, Mom." She blew a kiss, and took her phone, leaving Vivien to fold her last few items and organize her cosmetics. But the entire time, she was thinking about Tessa and Kate, the opposite twins.

They'd even grown up to be exactly that way, it seemed.

When she climbed into bed, she went back to Facebook and looked at both pages again. Kate hadn't posted in four or five years and the page was essentially dead. Tessa posted a few pictures of Ritz-Carlton hotels, giving the impression that was where she worked.

It was sad that they'd lost touch, and for no reason she ever really understood.

On a whim, she tapped "messages" on Kate's page.

When the box came up, she stared at it, knowing that sending a message would absolutely infuriate her mother. What would she do? Cut her off from this new inheritance?

Maybe.

But *why*? Why did Maggie hate the Wylies so much? And why should she have the power to keep Vivien from reaching out to an old friend? And should Vivien automatically submit to that demand?

She started to type and when she finished, she closed her eyes and hit Send.

Take that, Maggie Lawson.

Chapter Four
Kate

Ten thirty? Kate finally lifted her head from the laptop where she'd been transcribing her notes, peering at the clock on the lab wall in dismay.

How did she lose track of time the way other people lost track of their glasses? Speaking of, where were hers?

She glanced around the small desk, then turned toward the long testing tables, only now aware that all her colleagues had gone home. Had anyone even said goodbye?

Probably, but she'd been so busy inputting the results of the lithium-sulfur battery test she'd created that she didn't notice. She was certain that, this time, the results would support her hypothesis that the capacitor change her team proposed would improve the energy density and life cycle for large batteries.

That meant more efficient electric cars. Which meant a cleaner environment. Which resulted in a better world.

And wasn't that why Dr. Kate Wylie spent the vast majority of her life under the oh-so-not energy efficient fluorescent bulbs of a Cornell University science lab, improving the world one supercapacitor at a time?

The phone in her pocket vibrated softly, reminding

her that she had a life outside of her work. And a good one, too.

For one thing, she had two kids—and this was surely one of them—and her angel of a mother, Jo Ellen, still grieving the loss of Dad six months ago. Plus, even though they were divorced, she remained friends with Jeffrey, co-parenting Emma and Matt into their teenage years.

And she had her kitchen, stocked full of every imaginable tool and utensil so Kate could lose herself in another form of chemistry—the culinary kind.

So, yes, she insisted to herself as she fished out her phone, she had a life outside of this lab. All she had to do was actually leave this place and live it.

She glanced at the blurry screen and remembered her glasses. Where were they? As she turned, they slipped from her head and dropped onto her nose, making her smile.

It wasn't a call from Matt or Emma, both of whom were with their father this week. A notification? From Facebook? Good heavens, she hadn't been on that in forever.

Who was Vivien Knight?

Curiosity won and she tapped the screen, opening the message.

Hey there. This is your old friend from Destin, Vivien Lawson.

She gasped audibly. *Vivien Lawson?* Vivien of the Destin summer vacations? It had to be, what? Decades—several of them. The year she graduated from high school was the last time they'd gone down to Florida for a whole summer and that felt like a lifetime ago.

Why would she write now? Maybe something had happened to someone in her family. Or maybe she'd somehow heard about Dad passing away last year. Settling back, she read the rest.

Long time no talk. I hope you are well, Kate—happy, healthy, thriving, all the good things. And that you remember me, your pal from our summers in Destin as teenagers. I'm reaching out because it turns out that the old Destin house has unexpectedly come back into our lives after all these years. Apparently, my mother owned it (who knew?) and then my brother—you remember Eli?— has spent the last year remodeling it. (He's an architect.)

She stopped there, catching her breath while staring at the words "you remember Eli." She almost laughed. *Yes, Vivien,* she mused. *I remember your adorable brother and the crush I had on him from the first day to the last.* Not that he noticed—not when Tessa was in the room.

But the Lawsons owned that house? The thought was bittersweet, since the place had been humble and understated and packed with good memories.

Anyway, Eli and I are headed down there tomorrow for a few weeks. He has some work to finish with the contractor and I'm going to stage it for sale (that's what I do for a living). But I couldn't help meandering down memory lane to think about our happy summers and then, voila! Found you on Facebook! No surprise you're a scientist! I'd love to hear about your life, Kate. Or...okay, hear me out. Want to come see us in Destin? The house is huge now—unfurnished but we'll get the essentials while I stage it. And the beach is still the best in the world. Anyway, please think about it and know that I remember you and Tessa so very fondly. Best, Vivien

For a moment, Kate couldn't move except to have her mind transported back.

It had been thirty years since she'd been in Destin or anywhere near it, but she could still smell the salty air and feel that incredible sugar sand in her toes. The cool tickle of the surf on her legs and the hot, hot July sun bringing out some freckles on her nose.

Just thinking about it gave her a dopamine kick. What would it be like to be there?

Closing her eyes, she let herself drift back to a place and time she'd often thought about—a world with everyone she loved all together, bathed in sunshine and high hopes. A place where logic and common sense took a back seat to playfulness and freedom and good, good times.

A place that got wiped away in what felt like an instant, never to return.

She'd tried, over the years, to figure out a way to go back to Destin. Jeffrey hated Florida's humidity, and vacations with her kids were on the Finger Lakes or up to Canada. Then she'd thrown herself into work and life as a single mom and a researcher, and forgot that dream.

She re-read the note, focusing on the invitation at the end. Could she possibly—

"Dr. Wylie?"

She turned at the sound of her name to see a cleaning woman rolling her bucket into the room.

"Oh, Ivette. I'm always in your way, aren't I?"

"I work around you, ma'am," the older woman replied, her Brazilian accent lilting. "Is no problem."

"Actually..." She stood, grabbed her phone and straightened her glasses. "I'm done for tonight. The table's clean, my team is gone, and I must head home and make some dinner."

Home to think about this invitation, she added mentally.

Ivette beamed. "You try the shrimp, Dr. Wylie?"

"I did!" She gave a happy clap, remembering her latest success, thanks to this woman's amazing recipe. "The coconut milk was the answer! Thank you!"

"Of course, of course. Now, you go home." She waved a rag, dismissing her. "You work too much."

"Only the weeks my ex has the kids," Kate said, gathering her purse. "But I'm leaving now, and thanks again for the ingredient advice."

"Of course, of course. Bye now!"

But she wasn't thinking about Ivette's recipe as she drove the short distance from campus to her brick ranch house in Cayuga Heights. Kate barely noticed the dark, cold, wintry night in northeast Ithaca or the chilly, empty home that greeted her when she walked in.

Instead, her mind was back at the beach, in a weathered cottage with paneled walls and Formica counters and sandy floors that "Aunt" Maggie tried and failed to keep clean.

She was fourteen, fifteen, sixteen, seventeen. Young and free and becoming a woman. Spectacular days, moon-spun nights, and some of the most fun she'd ever had in her life.

Vivien's invitation was so tempting. Utterly illogical —which made it out of the question—but tempting.

LATER, after a bite, a shower, and a few trips through her house searching for Marie Curie, she poured some kibble for and called the always hidden kitty.

Almost immediately, her orange tabby appeared from the den—she'd been under the sofa, no doubt about it— giving a stretch and a high-pitched mew, then sauntered to the bowl like she was doing Kate a huge favor by eating.

While she nibbled, Kate stared at her phone on the kitchen counter, picking it up to read Vivien's message for the fourth time. *Oh, be honest.* The twentieth.

Had she contacted Tessa, too?

At the thought of her sister, Kate's heart dropped. It had been weeks, more than three, since she'd had anything but a cursory text from Tessa. That could mean one of a few things with her sometimes flighty, always unpredictable twin.

Either she'd met a new man who took all her attention, or she was deep in an event-planning project for the Ritz at some glam locale.

But more likely, she was just blue, grieving the loss of the late, great Artie Wylie.

It was nearly midnight, but time meant nothing to Kate's sister. Concepts like time, home—she lived at different Ritz-Carltons around the country—logic, structure, and discipline were meaningless to her oh-so-capricious sister.

Would memories from the past matter to her? They should. Tessa had been as much a part of those long-ago summers as Kate had been.

Suddenly longing to hear the voice of a person she loved almost like no other, Kate called Tessa, disappointed but not surprised when she got voicemail.

She listened to her sister's instructions to leave a message, somehow imbuing the order with her magical laugh and that sense of pure fun that Tessa oozed in every sentence.

She didn't leave a message, but closed her eyes, missing that fun-loving Tessa who'd checked out when Dad died after a shockingly short battle with pancreatic cancer six months ago.

Like their mother, Tessa was mired in mourning. Kate was far better at compartmentalizing the grief, focusing on her work and family, only taking out memories of Dad when she was alone and able to process the pain of his passing.

As she walked to the stove to make a chamomile tea, she heard her phone buzz with a call and pivoted instantly, practically diving in anticipation of talking to Tessa.

The smile was already on her face when she picked up the cell and read the name on the screen. Mom? Why was she calling at nearly midnight?

Because Jo Ellen hadn't even tried to compartmentalize, and grief had her in its grips.

"Hey," Kate said as she answered. "You okay? It's late."

"I'm...I'm sorry to call at this hour. I figured you were still up." Her mother's voice was thick, like maybe she'd been crying.

And it felt like Kate's heart folded in half. "Of course I'm up. What's wrong?"

Her mother gave a dry, humorless laugh.

"I mean, other than the obvious," Kate added, hoping these conversations would get easier with time. They had to. But right now, six months after burying the man she'd been married to for more than fifty years, Jo Ellen Wylie was one sad, lonely widow.

"I just wanted to hear your voice," her mother said. "Make sure you got home from work okay. The roads are a little icy."

Putting the phone on speaker and leaning it against the backsplash, Kate got her kettle and filled it with water.

"I didn't hit any ice," she said. "But I do have some interesting news. Would you like to hear?"

"Of course." She heard a glimmer of happiness in her mother's voice, picturing her smoothing her long silvery hair and tucking herself under a blanket in Dad's recliner.

She'd sat in his beloved chair ever since he died.

"I got a message from—brace yourself now—Vivien Lawson. Do you remember her?"

Mom was quiet for so long, Kate glanced at the phone to be sure the call hadn't dropped.

"What did she say?" she finally asked, her voice surprisingly flat. "Did...her mother die?"

What a strange question. "No. On the contrary, she told me her mother *owns* that beach house in Destin. Where we spent those summers."

"Huh. Really."

Whoa. Definitely not the response she expected. "I don't know when she bought it, but Kate said her brother's an architect and he remodeled or rebuilt it or something. Anyway, she invited me to come and stay there with them."

Again, a weirdly drawn-out silence before she asked, "Are you going?"

"Of course not," Kate said instantly. "I've got work and the kids and...aren't you shocked, though?"

"I guess."

Kate frowned. "You never heard from Maggie Lawson, did you? I mean, I know Roger went to prison, but you two were tight as tics. What happened to break all that up, anyway? Just Roger being an actual criminal?"

She didn't answer immediately, but Kate could hear movement, like her mother was shifting in her seat or trying to get comfortable.

"I don't know, honey. There was a hurricane and, oh,

I haven't thought about those people in forever. Maggie was..."

"A control freak."

She heard her mother give a soft laugh. "That's one way of putting it."

Intrigued, Kate poured steaming water into a cup and dropped a bag in. "Can you tell me what happened? Like, did you know her husband was... What was his crime, exactly? Fraud?"

"I don't know," she said, sounding exhausted. "I shouldn't have called this late, honey. I'm going to bed now. I just needed to say good night to someone."

Poor thing, Kate thought. She was an absolute wreck without Dad.

"All right. Oh, have you heard from Tess?" she asked. "I tried calling but..."

Another sad sigh filled the air. "Not for weeks," her mother said. "Last I heard she was in...somewhere in Florida for an event. Naples, maybe."

"Well, you know Tessa. Can't pin that girl down." But the truth was Tessa had never been close to Jo Ellen like Kate was. Tessa was a daddy's girl through and through, which was another reason she was so broken this past six months.

"Mmm. G'night, dear. I'm tired now."

"Good night, Mom."

She slipped onto a stool behind the counter and blew on her tea, not even slightly surprised when Marie Curie leaped up to the surface and gave a green-eyed stare.

"Hey, Madame Curie." She stroked the kitty's head,

holding her gaze. "Was it my imagination, or was your grandma keeping something from me? Not like her to avoid a good gossipy topic like I handed her."

But it wasn't a happy topic. They'd talked about the Lawsons over the years, but Mom and Dad always changed the subject, as if the falling out hurt too much. And they never discussed why it happened.

She wondered if Vivien knew.

Picking up her phone, she thought about writing back, but didn't have the energy and honestly didn't know what to say. She'd wait until she talked to Tessa. Tessa would know what to say—and it would be witty, bright, and perfect.

Right now, Kate wasn't feeling any of those things. She felt a little blue, distant from loved ones, and chilly.

Nothing a trip to Destin wouldn't cure, she thought with a wry smile.

She scoffed at the totally ridiculous thought and finished her tea.

Chapter Five

Eli

The traffic was just this side of wretched on 98, but the moment Eli turned onto Gulf Shore Drive and saw the blue-on-blue horizon of the beach, everything was good in the world.

Maybe not everything, he thought, glancing into his rearview mirror with no sign of Vivien behind him. They'd gotten separated just past Santa Rosa Beach, but she couldn't be too far behind.

Shame they couldn't drive together because he'd love to hear her reaction to how much this little slice of paradise had changed in thirty years.

To his right, as he drove east along the Gulf, the neighborhoods spilled off into a warren of streets and canals. The houses were shoehorned along the roads, a mix of older but remodeled Florida ranch homes, newly built modern coastal beauties, and an endless sea of town-houses and condo complexes.

But on his left, beachside, was a whole different story. One lot after another, each featuring a unique dream home with a Gulf view that offered residents a panorama of sand, sea, sky, and the most breathtaking sunsets imaginable.

The homes were two or three stories, with a smattering of widow's walks, balconies, and picture windows. A few were utterly gorgeous, some were contemporary eyesores, but almost all had long driveways, stunning views, waterfront swimming pools, and private boardwalks over the sea oats and sand dunes to the glorious waters of the Gulf.

He slowed his truck when he reached the orange construction barriers and black plastic temporary fencing that outlined their lot. Only one truck was on the street, which had to be Jorge, the tile guy who was replacing a few cracked porcelain tiles in the back.

Eli pulled into the paver-covered driveway and stopped the truck, looking up at what he had to admit was an absolute masterpiece on the beach.

Not the most expensive home on the block, but certainly one of the most beautiful. And, at three creamy stories trimmed with modern balconies and huge windows, it sure was a far cry from what it once was.

He sat there a few minutes, part of him taking in the beauty, another part already creating the latest punch list. The apartment above the garage had windows installed now, but he knew that inside there was a gaping hole of nothing. On the house, the shutters weren't all hung yet. The second-floor railing still had to be painted, and...wait a second.

Was that an open window on the third floor? Not good. He'd have to have a talk with the GC, Don Eveland. In fact, he'd—

He turned at the sound of a car, spotting Vivien's Highlander pulling in behind him.

Climbing out, he couldn't help smiling at the look of astonishment on her face behind the steering wheel.

"Eli!" She leaped out of her SUV, her dark blond hair blowing back as she stared at the structure. "No! This cannot be the same place."

"It isn't," he assured her. "We flattened the old beach house, I'm sorry to say. I saved the front door, which is in the garage. And a few of the interesting knobs, and remember the wavy glass windows in the old sunroom where Peter and I bunked? I saved the glass and some floorboards that could be repurposed into shelves. Other than that, this is the Summer House, two-point-oh."

"Two-point-oh, baby!" she joked. "You should get a little sign on the mailbox that says 'Summer House,' and make our family name for the place official."

He shrugged. "Whoever buys it might call it something else." He put an arm around her and guided her past the oversized garage door toward the stairs up to the entrance. "Come on—"

"Wait, wait." She held up both hands and stood firmly on the pavers, pushing her sunglasses up on her head to take another look. "Let me process. First of all, are you sure we're in Destin and not, like, Southern California? This can't be the same town."

"It's huge and pricey and crowded," he acknowledged. "But it's got a vibe, doesn't it?"

"I'm glad we got to experience the old Destin," she

said. "But I'm excited about having a house to sell in *this* Destin."

"Right? I've talked to enough locals to know that the last year we were here was kind of the beginning of the change."

"The hurricane?" she guessed.

"Yep. After they cleaned up from Opal and started rebuilding, people discovered this place and came in droves." He ushered her toward the stairs. "Come on. First floor—beach and pool level with a rec room, two small bedrooms and a bath. And above the garage, what could be a two-bedroom apartment for rental income. But let's start on the main living level. That's the wow factor."

"The whole thing is a wow factor," Vivien gushed. "This place is going to be a blast to decorate."

"It's a clean slate." At the top of the stairs, he entered the code on the front door lock. "I had to make some decisions without you—tile, floors, the basics. But beyond that, you can go nuts. We'll need window treatments, built-ins, decorative trims, and, of course, paint, furniture, and art. It's all yours, Viv."

With that, he swung open the glass and wood door and backed up so she could go in first, laughing as she squealed and gasped.

"Look at that view!"

The entryway led into a large living area, open to a glistening gourmet kitchen, all facing a patio that ran the length of the house. And beyond that a water view that was, of course, the main event.

Despite the popularity of Destin, this beach was

almost always deserted. It wasn't technically private, but if a visitor didn't live in one of the houses on the beach, it was next to impossible to get to the sand. And that only added massive value to the property.

"This is the heart of the home," he said, his voice echoing in the empty house. "I laid it out for living, cooking, gathering. Right down that hall is an office, an extra bedroom with an ensuite, a powder room, and a huge laundry room—washer and dryer are already installed."

He took a breath while she walked slowly over the pale wood floors, enjoying the enraptured look on her face.

"Upstairs there are three bedrooms, all main-suite quality," he added. "Six bedrooms total counting the two on the first floor. And, of course, the unfinished apartment over the garage. It can be a vacation getaway, a dream home, or money-generating high-end rental, all of which are in major demand in this market."

She stood in the middle of the living room, put her hands on her cheeks, and spun around, taking it in. "It's perfection! Eli, you are an absolute genius."

"Aw, thanks, Viv." He never wanted to be prideful, but it was almost impossible not to get a boost to his ego seeing this house through another person's eyes. And hers were trained to know excellent construction, so Vivien's opinion meant more than most. "It really needs your touch."

"I can't wait," she said on a laugh. "The light is incredible. The view, the openness—oh, the fireplace, too!

Look at that stacked stone!" Her golden-brown eyes danced with enthusiasm. "I can't believe we own this!"

"Right? Well, Maggie does. But cha-ching, sister. This place is going to go for a hefty price."

"Yeah, I guess." She sighed, sounding as if that hefty price didn't thrill her at all, which was weird.

She wandered into the kitchen, her fingers grazing the granite countertops, lingering over the beveled edge. "Went for the waterfall island, I see. So elegant."

"We'll want to attract high-end buyers, who want top of the line in everything."

She didn't answer, and he eyed her, definitely picking up...something. His sister was usually an open book, but he wasn't quite reading this reaction.

"You like it, right?"

"You're kidding, I hope."

"You seem...wistful."

She laughed. "Only because we have to sell it." She turned from her examination of the walk-in pantry. "I never want to leave."

"You can stay here, Vivien. All summer, if you want."

She wrinkled her nose. "That would be...a question-able career choice. I can't build a business in Atlanta on one job in Destin."

He acknowledged that. "Well, it's yours until..."

"Until it's not," she said, sounding a little sad again. But she pressed her hands on the pantry door. "Did you say you kept the front door to the original house?"

"Yeah, it's in the garage."

"It had leaded glass," she said. "I remember you could

peer through one diamond in the middle and see who was coming up the driveway."

"It still has the same glass," he told her. "I kept it because I knew you'd love it."

"Yes! I could use it right here on the pantry, or..." Her expression changed. "Wait. You knew? Like, you've known all along I'd stage this place?"

"I hoped," he said. "But I couldn't say anything because..."

"I know why. I totally get it and I'm beyond grateful for your faith in me." She turned again, checking out the oven and gourmet gas stove. "I love this look with the gold accents." She pulled the refrigerator door open and gave a soft laugh. "Goodness. Your workers have expensive taste."

"What?" He came closer, spying a few cans of some fancy flavored sparkling water.

She pulled out a narrow can. "Pellegrino Essenza. Not your usual painter's drink."

He made a face. "I don't care what they drink, but they shouldn't store it in a brand-new multi-thousand-dollar fridge. Why don't you make yourself at home while I go talk to Jorge, my tile guy? I'd like to know who's been in here last and he might have a clue."

"All right. I'll nose around upstairs."

She took off and Eli scowled at the offending cans of water. Turning, he eyed the kitchen, suddenly noticing that it didn't look entirely...perfect. Was that a crumb on the counter?

Pulling the handle of the trash drawer, he inhaled

sharply at the sight of a plastic supermarket bag hanging inside in the place of a container he hadn't yet inserted.

A bag holding an empty Starbucks coffee cup.

Fighting the urge to swear, he yanked out the bag and rumpled it up, heading outside by way of the construction Dumpster, where he tossed the trash.

He'd have to stay here until the project closed. If that meant doing some things himself, then so be it. His general contractor was never around—nor did he expect him to be. But the subs had to get under control.

He wandered down the side of the house to the pool deck, another masterpiece of design.

The expansive 30-by-30 square pool was dramatic with bright teal waterline tile and a contemporary edge. When the pool was filled—hopefully in the next few weeks—it would drop off an infinity side opposite a sun shelf and be a huge selling point in this house.

"Hey, Mr. Lawson." Jorge Masa looked up from where he crouched, replacing a porcelain square that had chipped during the initial install. "What do you think?"

"I think it's amazing," Eli said, walking around the perimeter to greet the other man.

They chatted about the job for a few minutes, ironing out the details of some artificial turf that would be installed along one side.

After a moment, Eli tucked his hands into his pockets, and asked, "Have any of the other subcontractors been in the house recently, Jorge?"

He looked up, his dark brows pulling. "Not that I've seen, sir. It's been all outside work this week and last. I suppose Mr. Eveland might have been in and out, though."

But would his GC leave water in the fridge and a Starbucks coffee cup in the trash? Maybe, but it seemed out of character.

After saying goodbye, he walked back into the house, passing through the family room and jogging back up to the main living area. Not seeing Vivien, he turned and walked up the stairs, his architect's eye admiring the landing four steps up and the window behind it, the whole design both beautiful and functional.

"You up here?" he called as he jogged up to the top floor.

"In the primary suite, although they'd all qualify for that honor."

He followed his sister's voice to the biggest bedroom in the house, which featured a gas fireplace, a walk-in closet, and a full wall of windows leading out to a balcony.

Vivien was standing out there, braced against the railing like a sun worshipper who'd been starved for the light.

"This is the money shot," he said when he walked out.

"Oh, Eli. I can't."

He came closer, smiling at how she lifted her face and let the sun shine on it. She didn't look like a woman about to turn fifty, he mused, although this past year had given her a few lines and some silver threads in her burnished gold hair.

"You can't what? Wait to start your design?"

"I can't stand that people get to live like this and I'm in a townhouse in Brookhaven with a view of the parking lot on one side and the next-door neighbor on the other."

"Your neighbor is right there," he said, pointing to the three-story stucco home about thirty feet away.

"Completely different, and you know it," she said, that same melancholy in her voice. "I'm just...achy. I love it here. The smell. The sounds of the sea. The way the clouds move and the waves come in and, oh, that sand. I'm painting the walls that color in every room. Destin White."

He chuckled. "Sounds perfect. By the way, did you see a window open up here?"

"I think in the bathroom," she said.

"Heads will roll," he muttered, heading back inside to check it out. In the ensuite, he spotted the window, open wide enough to let rain in.

As he closed it, he heard Vivien come in.

"This is a magnificent spa bathroom," she said. "I love the finishings you picked."

"I did my best, but really wanted your input on the pulls."

She grabbed one of the handles of the vanity. "The gold is stunning," she said, sliding the drawer open. "And —*whoa*. What do we have here?"

"Now what?" he asked, coming closer to look in the drawer and spy—

"A *toothbrush*? What the heck?" Ire marched all over him. "First water, then coffee remnants, now this. I have to go call the GC. Don's guys are not supposed to be using this place as their own private residence. Who would do that?" He scowled at the offending toothbrush.

"Um, a finishing carpenter with good oral hygiene?"

"Not funny," he said, pulling out his phone as it vibrated. He glanced at the text and looked at her. "Oh, good news. The bed delivery will be here in a few minutes. And Meredith said all the sheets and towels are on their way, too. And 'a bunch of other stuff you guys will need.'"

"That girl is a gem," Vivien said with a smile.

He couldn't agree more, but the toothbrush got his attention again. "I'll get it out of here for you, Vivien."

"For me? I don't get the big room. You're the oldest."

He smiled at her. "You're the one who wants to live in this place so bad it's written all over your face."

"Who wouldn't?" she teased. "But, seriously, I can have this room? All by myself?"

He pointed to the toothbrush. "You and the squatter."

She jabbed his arm. "I thought you said it wasn't funny."

It wasn't. While they waited for the beds to be delivered and set up, he called Don Eveland, his general contractor, who swore it wasn't his guys.

Yeah, right.

By the time sunset rolled around, Vivien and Eli were on the upstairs deck, parked on two folding canvas chairs

Vivien had wisely packed in her SUV. While he dealt with some house issues, she'd gone to Publix and got them stocked up with a few essential food and drink items, including the makings for a couple of gin and tonics that hit as nice as the sun on the water.

She bought a small plastic table they'd placed between them, where they had chips and guac, happy as clams with this setup.

After toasting Solo cups and sipping, Vivien took out her phone, trying to capture the sunset.

"For Lacey?" he guessed.

"Yes, but I'm trying not to make her too jealous." She lowered the phone and glanced at him. "She begged to come with me on this trip. And by begged, I mean pulled out all the stops, even making an announcement that she hates everything that has to do with houses, and that includes her job at Ryan Knight Homes."

He drew back, surprised. "I didn't know she hated working there."

"She just hasn't discovered her career path. I know she thought a business degree would be the ticket, but she hasn't found the right business. Every job is entry-level, which is fine, but just not exciting enough for her. Still, she's twenty-four and it's time to get in the groove."

"Tell that to my nearly-thirty-year-old son who's living in a van and picking up line cook gigs."

She grimaced. "Poor Jonah. He'll come around."

Eli waved off the conversation, not ready to ruin the moment with a walk through his abject failure as Jonah's father.

"At least Lacey has a job," he said, not wanting to make the conversation about him.

"With Ryan." She curled her lip.

"I'm sorry for being so absent these last few months, Viv. I know you understand why, but I honestly thought this was a fairly amicable divorce. I mean, you accepted it."

"Because that's what I do," she said dryly. "I accept. Need a doormat for that pretty front entry? I'm your girl."

"Stop it," he said. "You are not a doormat. You are not confrontational, that's all. You like harmony and peace, and were raised by a controlling woman who taught you that life is just easier when you agree to what others want."

She pointed one finger at him. "Nailed it."

"I was raised in the same house by the same mother," he said. "It's just not the same when you're the oldest and a son. She needed me in a different way when Dad died."

"I've spent my life being a Yes Man to my mother and my husband. I would really, really like that to be over."

"It is."

She shot him a dubious look.

"I mean it. Forgive the worst cliché imaginable, but today really is the first day of the rest of your life."

She snorted on her next sip. "Stick to the Bible, bro."

"Fine, I will. 'His mercies are new every morning.'"

"And that means..."

"You're starting over," he said. "For one thing, you are truly launching your brand—Vivien Lawson Designs—

and you don't even have a client breathing down your neck. You're free."

She let out a sigh and stared straight ahead at the horizon. "Here? I can almost believe that," she said. "There's something in the air in this place that is like a great big whiff of freedom and joy and not answering to anyone. It's summer on steroids and we had such good ones here."

"We sure did," he said.

"And don't worry about Jonah," she added. "He'll roll back, you'll see."

He appreciated the thought, but had doubts. Lots and lots of doubts. "He never recovered from walking into the principal's office one day to be told his mother was dead. He was a superstar up to that point, just like Meredith—maybe even more motivated, if that's possible. But that moment, a switch flipped and..." He sipped his drink, hurting and hating the tightness in his throat. "He changed. We all did, obviously. I recovered. Meredith rebounded. But Jonah?"

Vivien reached over and put a hand on his arm. "Let's not talk about it. Let's just bask in the Destin sunset and the monumental accomplishment of this house and the fact that we own it."

He tipped his cup to hers and they toasted again. "Here's to a great future for a piece of land that has a great past."

"It sure does." She repositioned on the canvas and studied him. "I messaged Kate."

He almost choked on his drink. "Kate Wylie?"

"Blame yourself. Those diaries, dude."

"Did you read them?" he asked, reaching for a chip to dip.

"Just a few pages from the summer we met. But it moved me enough to want to reach out to a girl I once thought of as another sister."

"Don't let You Know Who find out," he said after he swallowed his bite.

Her eyebrow rose again. "Told you there'd be conditions."

"Well, the Wylies are blacklisted, for whatever reason."

"It's been thirty years, Eli," she said.

"Yeah, but Maggie cut off ties with some friends who judged Dad too harshly, remember? The Wylies were collateral damage."

"I guess."

They sipped quietly for a minute, giving him a chance to think about the fact that she'd reached out to Kate. And what about Tessa?

"Anyway, Kate never responded," Vivien said, breaking the silence. "It was an old Facebook page, and she probably didn't see it. Or she's ignoring it. Either way, I invited her here."

"You what?" He sat up so fast he nearly toppled the folding chair. "Are you kidding?"

"What? Maggie won't find out. She made it perfectly clear she wouldn't ever step foot in Destin. God forbid she tell us why."

"God forbids a lot of things," he said. "Lying to your mother is one of them."

"Wouldn't you like to see Kate again?" she countered. When he didn't answer, she leaned in. "Or is it Tessa you'd like to see?"

He narrowed his eyes at her. "Man, you can slide into obnoxious little sister territory in a hurry when you want to."

She grinned and leaned back. "I brought the diaries, you know. I may read some more tonight. Refresh my memory and all."

He just laughed, safe in the knowledge that anything he'd shared with Tessa didn't make the pages of Vivien's diary—it had happened moments before they left and they never spoke again. Still, just thinking about Tessa could put him in a bad mood.

Yeah, he should let that go, but some things stay with a man his whole life. And like his mother, he would be just fine never laying eyes on Tessa Wylie again.

He'd never met a woman like her, that much was true. Not before and not since. And that was probably a good thing. His heart would always belong to Melissa and no woman, past, present or future, could ever change that.

June 2, 1989

It's official. Destin is the best place IN THE WORLD! Today, we went out on a boat from this cute marina across the street. Mr. Wylie—now he's officially "Uncle Artie"—drove it out in the middle of the water so we could go snorkeling!

The 'rents (that's what Tessa calls our moms and dads) stayed on the boat (well, Mama took Crista in the water but she got scared by a jellyfish). But we got to put snorkeling stuff on and go underwater and see everything. It was so cool!

Eli is acting so different. Like he's Mr. Cool cuz he and Peter McCarthy are fifteen—big whoop—and us girls are only twelve. I was so mad that he got to bring a friend and I didn't but now I have Tessa and Kate, so who cares?

All Eli does is try to show off. He bet Tessa a dollar that she wouldn't touch a barracuda and SHE DID. Eli got all freaked out and practically lost his snorkel mask but when they came up all she did was laugh because I guess barracudas aren't dangerous. (Dad says that's true.) But Eli didn't know that and he must have thought she was going to die or something. She's not afraid of anything.

For lunch we found this completely empty beach near the marina and had a picnic and, of course, Tessa went off exploring all by herself and came back with a coconut she got from a tree! Nobody believed her, so when we got home, she climbed a big tree across the street to prove she could climb anything, or so she said. Eli tried and couldn't get halfway up, which made me and Kate laugh so hard.

Peter didn't try because he's not a complete jerk like Eli.

Kate is kind of shy and quiet, but I like her so much. She's reading The Hobbit, which is like a million pages long. She wants to be a scientist or doctor or a professor like her dad, who teaches college at some school that Dad keeps calling "an Ivy" like that's really impressive.

Tessa said she wants to work on cruise ships and see the world! I don't know what I want to be, but I hope it's here in Destin because it's a bazillion times better than Atlanta.

I guess I'm a little jealous of Tessa because I never knew a girl my age who was that pretty and made everybody laugh. She even has boobs, too. Eli just acts stupid around her. Peter isn't like that, though. He's really sweet and I think someday I want him to be my first kiss. (If Eli reads this I will kill him with my bare hands.)

Goodbye for now from the Summer House, the best place in the world!

Vivien

Chapter Six

Vivien

Pulled from deep sleep, Vivien blinked into the darkness, swamped with the unsettling feeling of not having any idea where she was.

Oh, Destin.

The best place in the world.

The words from the childish diary entry she'd read before going to sleep floated around in her brain, weirdly fresh but also feeling like they'd been from a lifetime ago.

Because they had.

She turned, inhaling the scent of crisp new sheets and the hint of briny air from outside. Barely conscious, she reached to the nightstand, then remembered that there wasn't one. Her phone rested on the floor, plugged into the charger.

Rolling over, she spied the little black rectangle and lifted it, bringing it to life to discover that it was only two-thirty. It felt like she'd slept for hours. Deeply and with no dreams.

There was a text from Lacey, sent at midnight. It was long and Vivien wasn't awake enough to digest it all, but she got the main points. She hated her job, Dad was a pain, the townhouse was lonely, and could she please, please, *please* come to Destin?

How long until Lacey won that argument, Vivien wondered. Maybe she should just say yes and get her here.

Uncertain of what to do, she stared at the main page of her screen, scanning the apps. She knew what she wanted to press, she knew what was pushing at her heart, wondering and waiting.

Giving in, she went to the Messenger app and checked for an answer from Kate Wylie...*again*.

Nothing.

But then she sucked in a soft breath as she saw a tiny picture from Kate's profile at the bottom of her note. Didn't that mean she'd read it? That made the lack of response hurt a little more than it should.

Which was ridiculous. After thirty years, did Kate Wylie owe her a response? Of course not.

Still, Vivien remembered the witty, wise, and generally wonderful eighteen-year-old girl as a class act. She had an underlying sense of decorum in the way she moved and talked, in her regard for other people's feelings, and her sense of right and wrong.

Tessa? Not so much regard for feelings or decorum, and her moral compass pointed one way: toward fun.

But now that she knew Kate had seen the message and ignored it? It stung.

Why? Did the Wylies hate the Lawsons as much as her mother hated the Wylies? Did Kate know more than

Vivien, or have some deep knowledge about why the two families had parted so unceremoniously?

And if she did, would she hold a grudge for thirty years?

Honestly, Vivien didn't know how anyone—other than Maggie—could hang on to something so utterly unproductive for three decades.

Sadly, she'd hoped Kate would be better than that. Apparently, she wasn't.

On that disconcerting thought, she tried to swallow, but her mouth was bone dry. No bedside table, and no bedside water. She hadn't even grabbed a Solo cup for the bathroom.

Sitting up, she peered into the shadows of the room as a breeze wafted in from the open sliding door. Eli said it was fine to keep it open up here on the third floor, and promised her there was no alarm activated yet.

She'd never close it. The air smelled too good—like saltwater-infused happiness.

Even unfurnished and unlit, this room was magnificent. She would do it in shades of cream with pops of black and white, all neutrals, turning this into a true adult oasis. She tapped the flashlight and let the beam slice through the room, moving it like a spotlight over imaginary chairs and a table, maybe an understated built-in, and some dramatic pieces of art.

Wide awake now, she threw off the sheet and light blanket that superstar Meredith had thought to order for them. Her dry throat won the battle over whether or not to go downstairs and get something to drink, so she let her feet hit the cool plank-wood floor and stood up.

Dressed in her sleep pants and a T-shirt, she used the phone light to find her way through a small vestibule, pausing as she passed Eli's closed door in the hall.

Eli is acting so different.

The line from twelve-year-old Vivien's observations of life floated in her head. She'd forgotten that from the summer they'd all met. Her brother, based on what she'd written, had undergone a huge personality change in those months.

Maybe his hormones had kicked in. Maybe the freedom of being at the beach with his buddy had brought out a new Eli, one who'd blessedly disappeared in the ensuing years.

Maybe, she thought as she tiptoed down the stairs into the moonlit living area, something else happened that summer and every single one after—or some*one*. Someone named Tessa Wylie.

That made her smile as she reached the bottom, slowing to make sure she didn't miss the last step and face-plant in the darkness. She'd have to tease him about it tomorrow, she mused. Mercilessly, in fact.

Taking a few steps into wide-open living space, she looked beyond the glass doors to the deck. A full moon illuminated the sky and water, shining like a beacon into the house and kitchen.

It was profoundly lovely and...comforting.

To Vivien, that was a very good sign for this house. She always liked to visit a home late at night, before and after she'd decorated them. To her, the real definition of "home" was found in the dark of night, without benefit of people, good lighting, or noise.

That's when you knew if a house would cuddle and protect you...or make you feel like a stranger in a cold, unfamiliar place.

Not here. Not on this sacred ground in this beautifully built home. Here, Vivien was wrapped in the peace that came with warm touches and the smooth, matte finish of the wood floors under her feet.

Even the high ceilings seemed welcoming and secure, and the kitchen beckoned like a friend waiting to put arms around her.

"Well done, Eli," she whispered as she crossed the living room. Yes, she'd tease him about the past, but she also had to praise her brilliant brother for his talent right now in the present.

She turned off the phone flashlight, since there was enough moonlight to easily find her way, rounding the counter into the true heart of the home, the gourmet kitchen. They'd had take-out on the deck last night, and she'd thoroughly cleaned every bit of evidence that they'd eaten, wanting to keep the new build as pristine as possible.

Not that they'd be able to do that if they stayed for weeks, but she'd try to respect the newness of the house that they would eventually stage and sell.

She grunted as she opened the fridge and grabbed a bottle of water, twisting the cap and taking a deep drink for her parched throat.

No question about it, she already hated whoever would be lucky enough to own this house. Yes, that sale would make her far more secure—maybe she could buy a little place of her own, or really invest in her business by building up some staging inventory.

But, wow. To own and then sell this place? It was bittersweet.

Holding her cold water bottle, she wandered through the living room, visualizing the size and scope of the furniture, getting ideas for colors, textures, and a way to dress this utterly magnificent model.

Not for the first time, she was struck by what a shame it was that her mother was so weird and stubborn and strange that she'd kept this secret from them all these years. Even the old cottage, as humble as it had been, would have been an amazing place to visit. Lacey would have loved it so much, and she and Eli and Crista could have given their kids a taste of their special memories of childhood.

She still could.

Glancing at her phone, her heart dropped at the thought of how Lacey longed to be here. Vivien should just tell her to come. Life was so short, and their time left with this house was fleeting.

And this was a big house to stage! She could use the help. She should just text Lacey and—

She froze at a sound—a soft rustling or a movement of some kind. Had that come from the other side of the house?

At the far end of the living room, past the stairwell,

was a wide hallway she'd only been down once today to wash the sheets and supervise the bed delivery. There was a small office and a bedroom and ensuite, too, with a door to the back deck, if memory served her correctly.

Eli hadn't opted to sleep down there, had he? She could have sworn she'd heard the sound of...something. Or some*one*.

Her heart stopped. Maybe there *was* a squatter.

Chills crawled up her back, her whole body suddenly numb. All the comfort, peace, and good vibes evaporated as she stood paralyzed, looking into the darkness of the wing off the living room.

Eli had dispelled the squatter possibility, certain it was just a thoughtless construction worker.

But she'd definitely heard a noise.

One more step and she peered into the wide hallway, which didn't have the benefit of moonlight to remove the darkest shadows. She'd gone back there when the beds were delivered to show the men where to put the queen-sized mattress and frame. One of them, she recalled, had commented several times about the view.

He'd probably opened the sliding glass door to step out and look at the Gulf, then forgotten to lock or even close it. The breeze would rustle the plastic she'd left on the mattress, which was exactly what that sounded like.

Certain of this theory, she took one more step into the hall, hearing nothing but silence.

Tamping down any qualms, she passed the door to the laundry room, and walked toward the bedroom. Reaching into the doorway, she flattened her hand on the wall to press the switch, bathing the room in blinding light.

"Oh! Hey!"

Vivien shrieked at the feminine voice, freezing in abject horror as she stared into the room, speechless at the sight of a woman scrambling up from the bed in shock.

"What are you doing here?" Vivien yelled out, backing away as terror washed over her at the sight of the stranger.

Sitting straight up, crunching the plastic that covered the new mattress, the woman stared right back, pushing long blond hair over her shoulder.

Swearing under her breath, she grunted. "I fell asleep."

She fell asleep?

"Who are you?" Vivien demanded, instinctively sensing the woman wasn't going to hurt her. "Why are you here?"

The woman let out a groan of utter disgust, using two hands to pull up her pale hair and get it out of her face. She didn't look like any squatter Vivien could have conjured up, that was for sure.

She huffed out a breath and pushed up. "I had nowhere else to go."

Vivien choked. "Well, sorry, Goldilocks, you can't just break into a house and—"

"Vivien! Was that you? Vivien, are you okay?" Eli's voice echoed from the stairwell, his footsteps moving fast and hard.

"In the back bedroom, Eli! I found the squatter."

"*What?*"

"I'm not a *squatter*," the woman said, having the absolute audacity to sound indignant. "I used to live here."

Eli came tearing into the hall, wearing nothing but boxer shorts, slamming to a halt at the doorway.

"Who the hell are you?" he shouted.

She pushed off the bed and Vivien inched behind Eli. Not that the woman looked very threatening. She was petite and thin, dressed in jeans, a T-shirt, and pretty darn expensive Nikes.

Was she lost? Mentally unstable? Hiding out or on the run? What was she doing sleeping in their house?

"Look, I thought the place was..." Her voice trailed off as she looked from one to the other, her jaw dropping a bit. "Wait a second. Wait just one ever-lovin' second. Did you say *Vivien* and *Eli*? As in *Lawson*?"

Vivien glanced at her brother, who was staring at the woman like she was a literal apparition.

"Who *are* you?" Vivien asked on a whisper.

She didn't answer, but Eli took one step closer, his shoulders rising and falling. "I don't believe it. I absolutely don't believe it. It's really you."

The woman laughed, a familiar, haunting, lyrical sound. She put her hand on her hip and angled her head. "Tessa Wylie, in the flesh." She flicked a hand with a gesture of self-deprecation. "Such as it is at the moment."

"*Tessa?*" Vivien croaked her name. "What are you doing here?"

"Now that, my friends..." She closed her eyes and gave a soft sigh. "...is a long story."

"Then why don't you tell it?" Eli asked.

She crossed her arms and gave that sly, all-knowing smile that Tessa once used to torment and tease. "Does that mean I can stay?"

"Let's meet in the living room in five minutes," he said, pivoting and walking out, presumably to get dressed.

Vivien just stared at Tessa, who lifted a brow. "Well, hey, old friend. Nice to see you."

Nope, she hadn't changed, not one bit. She was the same fearless, sassy, too beautiful for her own good girl who'd touched a barracuda and climbed a coconut tree.

And now, Vivien knew, everything about this little adventure had changed.

Chapter Seven

Tessa

One of Tessa Wylie's superpowers was the simple fact that nothing really embarrassed her. She'd learned at a young age that anyone who looked as good as she did—or certainly had in her peak years—could get away with just about anything.

But that power had disappeared tonight. In fact, shame crawled all over Tessa's body, like hives that caused a miserable, itchy rash. She felt it on her skin, in her bones, pressing on her heart.

Anyone else and she'd have lied and laughed, squirmed out of a sticky situation, and slipped away, leaving her audience teetering between smitten and amused. But this wasn't anyone else. These people were part of her past and had, at one time eons ago, felt like family.

Did they own this place? Were they renting...a completely empty home? Or were they just here like she was—drawn by nostalgia and an ache for a better time...a better life?

How and why had they ended up here?

Guess she was about to find out.

Waiting for them, Tessa stood on the deck outside the

main living area, her arms crossed in front of her chest as she stared out at the moon over the dark waters of the Gulf. Awkward didn't begin to describe how she felt, half dreading a prickly confrontation, half hoping they could just dive right back into the past.

At the sound of the sliding glass door opening, she turned from the railing to see Eli and Vivien coming out to join her, both dressed now, looking much calmer but no less curious.

"Would you like anything?" Vivien asked. "We have water or...a drink."

"I wouldn't mind one of my Pellegrino's, which I so carelessly left in the fridge."

"And a toothbrush upstairs," Eli said with zero humor.

Tessa cringed. She had made herself a little too comfortable here, she supposed.

"I'll get your water," Vivien said, the picture of class in this super bizarre situation.

Kate would act that way, too, she thought. It was no wonder those two had always been thick as thieves when the families were together.

"It's a little chilly out here." Eli walked to two canvas folding chairs—the only furniture other than the new bed in the entire place. "I'll bring these in. We can talk inside."

She searched his face, which looked less harsh in the moonlight than it had under the beacons that had blasted her from a deep sleep.

Eli Lawson was, what? Fifty-two or fifty-three now.

Even without seeing him for thirty years, she might have recognized him. The blue eyes, of course, but he had a distinct smile—relaxed and warm. Back in the day, that smile was generally aimed at her.

Not that he was smiling now. He was furious, she guessed, and having a tough time hiding it as well as his sister.

"Okay," she said, not wanting to argue with anything, since they could, by all rights, call the cops and have her hauled out of here.

Inside, he placed the chairs in the living room, which was lit only by the soft under-cabinet lights in the kitchen. He nodded for her to take one.

"The witness stand?" she joked.

"I'll sit on the floor," he replied, folding down as Vivien walked back and offered her a can of overpriced sparkling water.

"Relax, Tessa," she said softly. "We're old friends."

The words were like a balm on her ragged heart, and she darn near hugged the woman. Instead, she lowered into the canvas chair and thanked her for the water.

"So, are you renting here again?" she asked. "Or... what?"

"I think we'll ask the questions," Eli said, waiting a beat for Vivien to sit in the other chair. "Starting with, what exactly are you doing here, Tessa? This is quite literally trespassing. Breaking and entering, even."

She looked from one to the other, considering all the ways she could go. An embellishment of the truth. A total and complete lie. Or honesty?

"Tessa." Vivien reached over, gently touching her arm. "Are you in trouble?"

Against her will, she nearly melted...and chose honesty.

"I guess it depends on how you define trouble," she replied. "I was, uh, let go from my job about two weeks ago, and with that went my lavish lifestyle as a permanent resident of the Ritz-Carlton."

"So you just broke in here and...and made yourself at home?" Eli asked, giving none of the gentleness that his sister had offered.

"Not...exactly." At his unconvinced look, she laughed lightly and shifted in the ridiculously uncomfortable canvas seat. "I mean, yeah, I brushed my teeth a few times and might have left a coffee cup, but I'm not *living* here, if that's what you mean."

"Then what are you doing asleep in a guest room?" he asked, his gaze narrow with suspicion.

"I didn't mean to crash, but..." She took a sip, knowing he wanted specifics and facts and a reasonable explanation. Nothing that she actually had on hand. "Long story, like I said."

"Well, considering we found you trespassing on private property, we'd kind of like to hear it," Eli replied, his gaze icy.

Vivien inhaled sharply, clearly wanting to give Tessa more of a chance than her brother. "You said you worked for the Ritz-Carlton," Vivien said. "Why don't we start there?"

Tessa regarded her old friend, remembering her as a

teenager. Much about Vivien hadn't changed, other than the usual softening and a few laugh lines. She still had thick, gorgeous dark-gold hair. Curtain bangs framed friendly eyes that were just a few shades darker than her hair.

There had always been something trustworthy— innocent, even—about Vivien, and Tessa had liked her very much all those years ago.

"I live—well, *lived*—at various properties," Tessa finally continued. "I was one of the top event coordinators for the Ritz. I plan huge parties, conferences, weddings, whatever. I move from property to property, and that's where I stay, residing in-house for the duration of a major event."

"Don't you have a home?" Vivien asked.

She shrugged, used to the question. "No point. I would never be there. My job requires me to be on-site for long periods of time and as soon as one event ends, I head to another Ritz and start the next one." She curled her lip. "Put all of that in the past tense, since it's over now."

"And what brought you here?" Eli asked.

"I was down at the Ritz in Naples, about ten hours south, working on a massive event, when..." She shifted in her seat.

When she got used, betrayed, lied to, and possibly set up for failure. But that might be a little *too* much truth.

"When I, uh, left the company rather suddenly. I packed up and got on the highway and headed to my next event, in Dallas, because I was certain my name would be cleared—"

"Cleared of what?" Eli sat up straighter. "Charges?"

The way he said it brought that kick of shame back, but it was the look of total disgust in his eyes that really hurt. Then again, hadn't their father been arrested for something work-related? She couldn't quite remember, only that after that last summer, the Wylies never heard from anyone named Lawson again.

There was plenty of explaining to go around, but since she was in the hot seat, she tried to appease him with a smile.

"No, I wasn't charged with anything, unless stupidity is against the law. I trusted a man I shouldn't have. A tale as old as time, I'm afraid."

Her smile didn't get one in return, but the short speech did take some of the ice out of his eyes.

She took a sip of water, wanting to get this grilling over with. "Anyway, by the time I was a few hours away, I found out I was good and gone at a job I had slayed for quite a few years and didn't even get severance."

"I'm sorry to hear that. So what brought you here? To this empty house?" Vivien asked.

Closing her eyes, she remembered the moment when she made the decision, teary-eyed and sad, desperately missing the only person in the world who would have been able to help her. And the fact that it happened on February nineteenth only added to her bone-deep misery —a date that always reminded her that she'd made some questionable decisions in her life.

Alone, unemployed, and longing for comfort, she made what might have been another one.

"I was on I-10 when I saw the sign for Destin and I..." She blew out a breath and turned to Vivien, sensing she might get this. "I just had to come back."

From the smile she got in return, she instantly knew that her old friend—once one of the best she'd ever had—understood.

Relief washed over Tessa. "I'd never been here again since that last summer and I had nothing else to do, so I zipped on down here," she continued. "I remembered the street was Gulf Shore Drive and came from memory to where I knew the house was."

"How did you know?" Vivien asked. "Everything's different."

"Eight hundred and two steps," she said.

"From the harbor to the house," Vivien finished, a smile lifting her lips. "We used to count them in a song."

"Right!" She laughed, inexplicably overjoyed that Vivien shared that silly childhood memory. "It's more like a marina than a harbor, but I figured it out. When I got here, that oak tree I liked to climb was still across the street. I knew I had found...our summer cottage. Except it's a cottage no more, huh?"

"So you just walked on in and brushed your teeth?" Eli asked without the humor she'd so hoped the situation would get. Maybe it wasn't funny, but he didn't have to act like she broke the law.

Okay, maybe she had.

"I, um, got chatting with the contractor, Don," she

said. "He mentioned that the owner might be looking for a buyer, so...I might have pretended to be house shopping."

He dropped back in his chair. "Yeah, he mentioned you. Said a woman was sniffing around a few weeks ago."

"That's me. The sniffer."

"And squatter," Eli muttered.

"No, not that very moment, no. On that first visit, I was just...blown away." Tessa heard the awe in her voice, and didn't try to hide it, looking around. "Not only is it beautiful, it's..." She searched for the word. "It's Destin. It's a part of my childhood. No, not this actual house, but the beach and atmosphere and the very essence of this place is just..." She pressed her hand to her chest and closed her eyes. "It *called* to me."

"I get that," Vivien whispered in a tone that said she'd had the same response.

"I simply had to stay," Tessa told them. "I got a hotel that night. The next day, the contractor was here again, and he thought I was really interested, so he let me walk around by myself for a while. I noticed there wasn't an alarm, so..."

She wet her lips and looked directly at Eli, who would surely disapprove of what she was going to say next, but she'd committed to the truth now.

"I unlocked the door to that bedroom. I saw the spiral steps that led up from the pool level, so I knew I could come back when no one was here. And I did. A lot. Like every night, and a few times, yeah, I fell asleep, usually upstairs in the main bedroom. Then when I came tonight, I saw the bed and I knew someone was either here or had been. I came by way of the beach, so I didn't see any cars, but I didn't want to take a chance. I just put my head down on that new mattress for a second and wham…here we are at the Grand Inquisition."

"It's not an inquisition," Vivien said quietly.

It kinda was, but she deserved it. "I parked my car with all my earthly belongings at the marina, and…" Oh, good heavens, she *was* a squatter. A homeless, jobless, almost fifty-year-old *drifter*. She groaned at the thought, mortified.

"It's fine," Vivien insisted, as though she felt Tessa's pain. "I understand why you would come here. I do. This place has called to me more than once over the years."

Tessa smiled, loving the other woman for the empathy. She knew in her heart why this place felt like home and comfort, but wasn't sure she could explain it. Would they care that it reminded her of happy times with her father and soothed her grieving soul? Maybe. Or maybe not.

"Anyway," Tessa continued, "Destin in general and this slice of heaven in particular has my heart and I needed somewhere to feel good and…I'm sorry." She looked from one to the other, never meaning the words more. "It was wrong and I'm sorry. I'm happy to leave and never come back—"

"No." Vivien leaned forward, and Tessa could have sworn she saw tears in her eyes. "You're in a bind, we have a ton of room, and you should stay."

A few feet away, Eli bristled, no such sympathy on display.

"Unless that's a problem for you," Tessa said to him.

"No, of course it's not a problem," he said, casting his gaze away as if it caused him actual pain to look at her. "It's just...a big surprise."

"That's an understatement," she said wryly, praying for a change in the direction of this conversation. "Now, enough about me. What are *you* doing here?"

Vivien and Eli shared a look, their brother-sister connection palpable even to a virtual stranger.

They'd frequently been at one another's throats, Tessa recalled, but they'd watched out for each other—and their little sister whose name she couldn't recall at the moment. But these two always had each other's back in various scrapes and binds that the crew had gotten into those summers. Usually because of some wild scheme of Tessa's.

"Hasn't Kate told you?" Vivien asked.

"Kate? My sister?" Tessa blinked. "You talk to her?"

"No. But I messaged her," Vivien said. "I told her we'd rebuilt a house on this property, and I actually invited her down. It was sort of on a whim."

They'd rebuilt it? Did that mean they owned it? And, wait—they'd invited Kate? Yet Eli acted like Tessa had brought the plague into this place. How was that fair?

"I'm sure that's why she called me the other night," Tessa said. "I haven't talked to her for a while."

She'd ignored Kate's calls because there was nothing Tessa hated worse than being the family disappointment.

And without Dad to charge to her defense for whatever dumb decisions Tessa had made, it was easier to avoid Kate and Mom. But she missed them with every fiber of her being, just like she ached for her father.

"I haven't heard back from Kate," Vivien said. "Is she doing well?"

"Oh, yes. She's a superstar researcher at Cornell," Tessa said.

"And your parents?" Vivien asked.

Tessa swallowed. "My mom's okay, but my dad died six months ago."

Vivien reached for her. "I'm sorry, Tessa. I always loved Uncle Artie."

"We all did," she said softly. "His loss was a tough one. One day he went to the doctor for something routine, they found a tumor, and he was gone less than two months later. It's probably part of the reason I..." She caught herself and shook her head. Nope, not going to go there. "Anyway. How are your parents?"

Vivien blinked at the question, and again, shared a look with Eli, both of them obviously surprised by the question.

"Oh, no," she said, sensing she'd stepped in it. "They're gone?"

"Our father died about a year after...after we last saw you," Vivien told her.

She drew back. "I never heard that. We didn't know. How could we not know that?"

"Our parents stopped speaking to yours," Eli said. "Don't you know that?"

She turned to him, digging into her memories. "I knew they'd lost touch, but...oh, he died young. I'm so sorry. How did it happen?"

"He was in prison for fraud," Eli said. "He had a heart attack."

A chill covered her skin, mostly at the emotionless tone in his voice. There was some pain and unfinished business right there. Yes, she'd heard from her parents that Uncle Roger had trouble with the law, but nothing more. Nothing this dark. Prison? Yikes.

"I'm so very sorry," Tessa said again. "And Maggie?"

"She's alive and well," Vivien said, seeming happy to get off the subject of their father. "She lives with Crista—"

"The baby," Tessa said as soon as she heard the name.

"Not a baby anymore," Vivien told her. "She's married with a daughter now. We're all still living around Atlanta and see each other frequently."

"I'm glad to hear that. Kate still lives in Ithaca near my mom, but I'm..." Tessa lifted a shoulder. "Making myself at home in unfurnished beachfront mansions."

"Stop," Vivien said, the kindness in her eyes evident even in this dim light. "You know, I had hoped to hear from Kate and was sad she didn't respond."

"Want to call her now?" Tessa asked, reaching to her back pocket for her phone. "She'd love to—"

"It's three in the morning," Eli said, pushing up to a stand. "And I'm going to bed. Feel free to stay in that room, Tessa."

"Thank you, but I'm so confused. You built this new house—do you own the property?"

"My mother does," he said. "I'm just the architect and I've been overseeing the construction. Vivien can fill you in on the rest."

She sure hoped somebody would. "Well, it's awkward, but thank you for being so understanding. I'm sorry I intruded and..." She laughed. "I guess I'm really glad you don't have a gun."

He looked down at her and gave the first vague hint of a smile as he studied her. "It's good to see you, Tessa. Night, all."

He gave a nod and walked out, heading up the stairs, leaving Tessa to stare at his back until he disappeared around the landing.

"He's still ticked at me," she muttered, rising to her feet.

Vivien stood, too, and slid an unexpected arm around Tessa. "I'm not," she said. "I love seeing you again. Eli's a stickler for following the rule of law, that's all."

Probably because his father was a white-collar criminal, Tessa mused, but she covered that thought by wrapping her arm around Vivien, who'd made this whole thing so much easier.

"You grew up beautifully, Vivien," she said. "Are you married? Have kids?"

"In the middle of a divorce, but I have a fabulous twenty-four-year-old daughter. You?"

"Never married, no kids. Just free as a bird," she added.

"Lucky you," Vivien gushed.

"It sounds better than it is," Tessa quipped. "Do you work?"

"I'm an interior designer," Vivien said. "In fact, I'm here to stage this house for sale."

"So your mother owns it, your brother is the architect, and you're decorating it. All so you could *sell* this gem?"

Vivien exhaled, sinking deeper against Tessa. "It's a long story, but, yeah, that's the gist of it. My mother's required by law to give the profits to us, so that's a tiny silver lining."

Tessa had a million questions about what had happened to Uncle Roger, but didn't want to pry. At least, not yet.

"So...Tess." Vivien gave her a squeeze. "Would you rather sleep or talk?"

"Are you kidding?" Tessa scoffed. "Come to my plastic-covered bed and let's talk until the sun comes up, just like old times."

Next to her, Vivien let out a girlish giggle that took Tessa back three decades to a place she never wanted to leave. She had no idea how long they'd let her crash here, but she'd take as much time as she could to bask in this escape from reality.

THE SUN HAD INDEED RISEN by the time Vivien blew a kiss to Tessa and headed back upstairs to her own room. They'd talked for three hours, sharing details of life, laughing about old times, and bonding like it was the start of just one more summer in Destin.

Before she'd left, Vivien brought down a towel and some soap so Tessa could shower, and she was just stepping out of the steam, thinking about Kate.

Her sister had to be here. *Had to.* For one thing, it would be like old times. For another, she'd have a Wylie on her side and it would level the playing field. And maybe they'd let Tessa stay for a good long time.

It might take some convincing, but there really wasn't anything her sister wouldn't do if Tessa asked, so she decided to call her right then and there.

Kate answered on the first ring, always wide awake at six in the morning. "Tessa! Oh, my goodness, it's been so long! I've been worried. Are you okay?"

"Fine, more or less. Katie, you are not going to believe where I am."

"What do you mean, 'more or less'?" The concern was clear in her voice. "What's wrong?"

She'd find out sooner or later—especially if she did exactly what Tessa wanted her to do.

"I lost my job."

"Tess! What happened?"

She didn't want to go into detail, at least not on this call. "Doesn't matter. But I ended up in Destin, of all places."

"Seriously? Wow, that's a coincidence," Kate said on a laugh. "I just—"

"Heard from Vivien that she and her family still own this property and are building a mansion on it."

"Wait. *This* property? Are you *there*?"

"I am looking at our beach right this minute, Lady Katie."

Her sister laughed at the old nickname. "Did Vivien find you on Facebook, too?"

If only it were that simple. "Not exactly. I sort of found them. Well, I..." She bit her lip. "I'll tell you the whole story, but only in person."

"Are you coming home?"

Home? It had been a long time since Ithaca was home. "No, you're coming to Destin. Today, tomorrow, soon. I don't know how much time we have here because they are going to sell this house, which is nuts because it's beautiful, but we have a chance to be together again. Please come down, Kate. I don't want to do this without you. I actually don't think I can."

The response was dead silence, as expected.

"Can't you just put your experiments on hold and let the kids stay with Jeffrey?" Tessa pressed. "Mom loves when you let her take care of Marie Curie. Vivien really wants you to come, too. Please throw caution and your schedule to the wind and come down. We'll stroll the beach and take out a boat and make bonfires and—"

"Yes."

Wait, had she heard that right? "Did you say yes?"

"I did. Vivien invited me in a message, and I was waiting to talk to you because I really want to go."

With a soft hoot of joy, she fell back on the mattress, free of the plastic covering that she and Vivien had ripped off so they could get comfy and talk until dawn. "And I didn't even have to tell you that Eli is here."

"Oh, shut it."

"Never. But he's not nice like he used to be," she added. "He's the architect who designed this house. And it's stunning with a capital stun."

She laughed. "I told you I'm coming, Tess. You don't have to sell me any more."

"When can you be here?" Tessa asked.

"Give me a couple of days to pull it together. There's an airport in Destin, right?"

"Heck if I know. I drive everywhere."

"I'll figure it out. Send me an address and I'll let you know when to expect me."

Tessa popped up and did a little dance in her towel. "Best news ever! And let me tell you, Kate, Vivien is an absolute doll. The same cool kid you remember, too. Oh, did you know Uncle Roger died in prison, like a year after he was arrested?"

"No! I wonder if Mom knows."

"I doubt it, because wouldn't she have told us? Vivien said her mother won't even mention the Wylie family name. We are *persona non grata* to Maggie Lawson."

"Huh. I wonder why," Kate murmured. "Mom said they lost touch, then Uncle Roger got arrested, and Maggie cut out all her friends to save face."

"I think there's more to it than that," Tessa suggested, picking at a thread of the terrycloth wrapped around her. "But whatever. Just come down here and let's have some fun."

"Tessa," she said. "What about your job? What happened?"

"Oh, long story. And I'll figure my life out soon enough. But this week? This house? This unexpected adventure? We need to recapture the magic of a summer in Destin."

She waited for her uber-commonsense scientist of a sister to launch into a lecture on maturity and responsibility. But Kate just gave a happy sigh. "I fully agree."

And that was the best and most unexpected surprise of all.

After they said goodbye, Tessa floated out to the balcony, clutching the towel around her torso. She felt like calling out to the seagulls and diving into the ocean and running up and down the sand.

Hearing a sound, she looked down the length of the house to the other end of the deck, and spotted Eli leaning against the railing, sipping coffee.

Just then, he turned, and even with the distance of the whole house between them, she could feel... animosity.

Despite her attempt to give a truly honest explanation, he wasn't thrilled about her being here. Maybe it had to do with why his mother had such beef with the Wylies. Whatever. She'd win him over eventually. She hoped.

Chapter Eight

Kate

This was *Destin?*

From the backseat of an Uber, Kate peered at the endless lanes of traffic, the streets flanked by high-rises and townhomes, the strip malls and hidden neighborhoods. How could one sleepy beach town have changed so much?

Destin had always been bathed in shades of sunny yellow and seaside blue, but now it was vibrant, a vacation paradise that turned relaxation into a business.

"Can I open my window?" she asked the driver, who gave her a nod.

Taking a breath of clean, clean air, she instantly realized it hadn't changed at all. It still smelled like Destin. Like salt and sandcastles, sunshine and summer freedom, like mangroves and coconuts and sweet hibiscus.

Yes. This was still Destin, only now the rest of the world had discovered it.

Not only this town, though, since she of course had done her research before leaving. The whole Panhandle had blossomed, with some places known just by the highway number—30A—and full postcard towns built from the ground up in the last twenty or thirty years.

There were still state parks along the shore and plenty of palm fronds silhouetted against skies so blue it kind of hurt to look at them.

Wait a second. Was that AJ's?

She peered at a colorful neon sign over a large waterfront building, high above what used to be a tiny harbor with one popular restaurant and a massive landmark magnolia tree.

She could practically smell AJ's fried clams from here.

Smiling at that and the many memories of big family dinners there, a mantle of familiarity fell over Kate as she rode through the town, leaving the window wide open to inhale the dreamy air.

Escaping the dreary cold of Ithaca had only been one of several incentives to take this unexpected sojourn. Another had been spending time with Tessa who, no matter how "fine" she said she was, sounded like she needed her other half right now.

And, of course, the chance to tiptoe into the past with Vivien and Eli was a cherry on top of this delightful sundae.

After her strange conversation with her mother the other night, Kate had added another good reason for coming to Destin—unfinished business.

Or at least a bit of a mystery that had her intrigued.

For thirty years, her mother—and her father, for that matter—had just shrugged off the end of their friendship with the Lawsons. When the subject came up, which it hadn't for probably fifteen years, both Jo Ellen and Artie said that Roger Lawson had been arrested for white-collar crimes without ever specifying what he'd done.

Because of that, Maggie had terminated all her personal relationships and put a wall of protection around her family. Knowing Maggie, who always struck Kate as a woman who lived by strict guidelines and deeply valued her privacy, that explanation made perfect sense.

It was sad to lose their friends from the Summer House, but Kate and Tessa—and Vivien—had been headed to three different colleges that last year.

Then a massive storm hit Destin just months after their last summer and wiped out the beaches—or so they thought. This was long before email, text, or social media, and people did lose touch back then.

It never seemed like much of a big deal...until last night when her mother had responded to Kate's update and news in a way that had been totally out of character.

Jo Ellen Wylie *didn't* live by strict guidelines or build walls of privacy. In fact, her mother was an open book. And she'd literally blanched last night when Kate brought Marie Curie over to her house and told her she planned to go to Destin. Jo Ellen had insisted—practically made Kate *promise*—not to discuss the past with Eli or Vivien.

She said it was because Roger's jail time was surely a source of great embarrassment for them, but Kate sensed it was more than that. Her mother and Maggie Lawson were sorority sisters and lifelong best friends. There had to be more.

When pressed about why she'd lost touch with Maggie, Mom had gone quiet, pretended to be tired, and curled up in Dad's chair with Marie Curie on her lap. She swore she didn't know Roger had died, but Kate wasn't completely sure she was being honest.

That bizarre response had done nothing but pique Kate's interest in the parents' mysterious falling out. Still, out of love and respect, she'd promised to go easy on the questions and only pursue the topic if they did.

Would they? She had no idea. She hadn't talked to Tessa again, except for texts these last two days, so she had no idea what had been said among them.

She couldn't wait to find out. She couldn't wait to see her sister and her old friends. Especially...

Yes, she admitted to herself, especially her old crush, Eli. No doubt he was happily married to some lucky woman—a loving father, a good man, a great catch. She'd known that at eighteen, and still believed it at forty-nine.

The driver turned and slowed at Gulf Shore Drive, giving her a new perspective on the beachfront homes, which were nothing like she remembered.

One was bigger and more beautiful than the next, all facing the water, which actually couldn't be seen from the road. Their houses and fences blocked it, unlike thirty years ago when there were just shacks and cottages and even beach parking lots.

"This it?" the driver asked as they reached the orange cones and construction fencing. The house was done, right?

"I think so."

He turned into a long driveway, and she sucked in a shocked breath at the sight of a house that was completely different than the one in her memory.

Three gorgeous stories as white as the sand with teal shutters and trim perched on the beach.

Was it different from the three-bedroom cottage with a Florida sunroom where the boys bunked? Oh, yes. But to Kate, this house made sense here—it belonged.

For some reason, that made her happy. If it couldn't be the windswept rental with weathered decks and chipped railings, then it should be this breathtaking showplace that stood like a queen on the dunes of Destin.

The driver parked behind a pickup truck with Georgia plates. She climbed out and the driver got her bags, then was gone before she could actually confirm that she was in the right place.

Clunking her suitcase over the pavers, she left it at the bottom of the steps to the front door, which looked like it was on the second level. Walking up there, she rang the bell and leaned to the side to peer in a long window next to the door, but all she could see was the Gulf on the other side of a wall of glass. The rooms that were visible were completely empty.

Good heavens, she hoped she was in the right place. Maybe getting an Uber and surprising Tessa with her arrival hadn't been such a great idea, she thought. Pivoting, she walked down the stairs to get her phone from her purse, but as she reached the bottom, she heard a noise at the side of the house. Turning the corner, she saw a man in shorts and a filthy white T-shirt, using a shovel to dig at dirt and sand.

The landscaper, wearing a hat, earbuds, and sunglasses, didn't even notice her. Would he know the whereabouts of the people living here? Possibly.

"Excuse me," she called, carefully navigating the unpaved dirt, her cable-knit sweater and jeans suddenly feeling very heavy in the Florida sun. "Sir? Excuse me."

He turned around, popping an earbud.

"Hi," he said, tipping his hat back enough that she could see sweat-soaked hair and suntanned skin.

"I'm looking for someone named Tessa Wylie," she said, guessing that if he'd seen Tessa, he'd noticed her. "A blonde. Very charming. Probably flirted with you."

The man laughed easily. "I think I've met her," he said, a dry note of humor in his voice.

"Do you know if she's here?" she asked. "Or maybe you know Mr. Lawson, the architect?"

He slowly took off his hat and used the side of his hand to push his sunglasses up, squinting at her in the late afternoon sunlight.

"You don't recognize me, Kate?"

For a moment, she couldn't speak as she realized who she was talking to. "Oh, my gosh!" she exclaimed, locked on eyes the very same color as the sky above him. "Eli!"

She automatically reached to hug him, but he lifted his hands, inching back and gesturing toward the dirt-covered white T-shirt. "You'll be covered in dirt, but...hi."

She beamed at him, punched by the bone-deep joy of

seeing someone who'd always held such a special place in her heart. "Hi to you," she said on a laugh.

The years had taken away all his boyish good looks and left a handsome man in their place. Some crow's feet around his eyes, plenty of silver in his hair, but the same strong jaw and huge smile.

Suddenly, she was eighteen, standing in this familiar blistering sun, all ready, willing, and able to give her heart to a boy who simply didn't want it.

Time took the sting of that away, but the memory was shockingly vivid.

"You look amazing," he said, the compliment so genuine and enthusiastic that she nearly lost her footing again. "Exactly like the last time I saw you."

"Better put those glasses back on, Eli, it's been thirty years."

He laughed and nodded, giving his silver temples a brush with his knuckles. "Don't I know it. I was really happy when I heard you were coming, Kate."

She remembered Tessa saying something about how he hadn't been friendly, but that couldn't be right because he was absolutely the personification of warmth right now.

"Not as happy as I was to leave chilly Upstate New York and come to the land of sun and fun." She glanced at the house. "This cannot be the same house."

"Except for a few pieces saved for nostalgia and design, it isn't," he told her, leaning on his shovel to follow her gaze to the house. "We demolished the old place down to the foundation, which, I have to say, hurt a little bit."

"I bet it did," she agreed. "So many memories. All good ones, too."

His smile wavered a bit. He lifted a shoulder, surprisingly broad in the dirty T-shirt. "Anyway, the gang's all here again, huh?"

"Most of us," she said. "Is Crista coming down?"

"Nah, she's still a mommy's girl, and Maggie..." His voice faded out. "Anyway, it's just us, but we've got plenty of room. Beds for everyone, but not much else, I'm afraid. That's where Tessa and Vivien are, by the way. Shopping for some insta-furniture to hold us over while Vivien undertakes the official interior design of the place."

She glanced at the house again. "I can't wait to see it. You were the architect, I understand?"

"Yep. And I've done a lot of the construction and..." He angled the shovel in the dirt. "Now the outside. Jack of all trades, as they say."

"But you're an architect as a profession? Like your father?"

The smile completely disappeared. "Nothing like my father except the letters after the name."

"Well, you've done an amazing job here," she said quickly, hearing the echo of her mother's warning to avoid the landmine of a subject. "And how are you, Eli? Still in Atlanta? Are you married? Have kids?"

"I have two great kids. My son Jonah is twenty-nine, and Meredith, who's a year younger. My wife..." He paused as a shadow crossed his expression. "Um, Melissa passed away almost fifteen years ago."

"Oh." She breathed the word, surprised and saddened. "That's terrible. Was she ill?"

He shook his head. "Actually, she was in a private plane for work and, um, there was an accident."

Without thinking about it, she reached for his arm, not caring about the dirt but hurting for her old friend and his children. "I'm so sorry. I can't imagine how difficult that must have been for you, and your kids."

"Thanks." He nodded. "We coped. Barely," he added with a humorless smile. "My son...well, he's still coping, I think. But I've made my peace with it."

She regarded him for a moment, easily seeing the older but very distinct features of a boy she once dreamed she'd marry. He'd endured so much, but you could never tell from the air of stability and calmness about him. A light even, despite what he'd suffered.

"You've clearly made a good life, Eli," she said, gesturing to the beautiful house. "And I can see your architectural skills even from out here. I still can't wrap my head around the fact that I'm standing right here at the site of the old Summer House."

"Right? It's hard to believe we've all come back."

"I thought about it so many times," she admitted. "I loved those summers, and I even tried to get my family down here for a vacation, but it never happened."

"Tessa told me you have two teenagers," he said. "Emma and Matt?"

She smiled, touched that he'd asked about her and

then remembered her kids' names. "Yes, and they aren't thrilled that I came here without them, but it isn't their spring break yet. They're with my ex-husband, Jeffrey."

Just then, a horn honked noisily as an SUV pulled into the driveway.

"And I think I hear the girls now," he said, looking over her shoulder.

She laughed at that. "Girls?"

"Sorry," he said. "I guess some things never change. Come on, let's go see them."

He smiled at her, the old Eli smile that always made her go weak in the knees. She wobbled a little right then, too, but only because she was on soft dirt in slippery loafers.

She hoped. If not, then some things never did change...like her illogical and totally frustrating feelings for a man she hadn't seen in thirty years.

"Lady Katie!" Tessa's voice floated over the warm breeze, and instantly, Kate knew she wasn't going anywhere.

Like everyone else on the planet—and that counted the man standing next to her—she fell under the spell cast by Tessa Wylie.

"Tessa!" She found her footing and jogged to the outstretched arms of her twin sister, always the missing piece in her puzzle of life.

～

THE REUNION WAS a blur of updates and laughter, hugs and questions, and a few things that had Kate wondering if she'd heard them right.

Tessa had been *living* in the house?

In true Tessa fashion, she glossed over that little detail. Keeping everything light and happy, they'd all chatted briefly while they helped Vivien and Tessa unload some household items, many for the kitchen, she was happy to see.

It did look as though they got enough to move in and throw a party, but Tessa was involved, so that made sense.

A roofing inspector showed up to meet with Eli, and Vivien had to run out for a meeting with a window treatment company, so Kate announced she'd like to make them all a special dinner that night.

After unpacking and accepting a spacious room on the third floor, Kate asked Tessa to drive her to the supermarket, finally giving them complete privacy. She didn't waste a minute, diving into her questions before they turned onto Gulf Shore Drive.

"You crashed there? In an empty house?"

"What? It's not a big deal," Tessa said, shooting her a glance from the driver's seat. "I never dreamed it belonged to the Lawsons. Like, what are the chances of that happening?"

"That's not the point," Kate said coolly as she studied her sister's always beautiful profile. "Whoever lived there could have had you arrested. And you'd have no defense except..." What had she said? "It called to you."

"Loudly," she retorted. "Called to you, too."

"No, you called me. Yes, I did want to come back and experience Destin again, not going to lie. Although..." She peered into the lanes of endless traffic. "It ain't what it used to be."

"I know. I love it," Tessa proclaimed. "There's a nightlife we certainly didn't have the last time we were here."

"We were eighteen," Kate said. "Our nightlife was bonfires and you pilfering gin from Uncle Roger's stash."

"That you didn't drink."

"Someone had to keep their head on straight," Kate said, knowing full well that had always been her job.

"Anyway, there are bars and restaurants now," Tessa said. "Tons of people. Want to go out tonight?"

Kate's eyes shuttered. "I guess you forgot you're almost fifty years old and jobless. And—"

"If you say homeless, I'll cry."

Kate reached over and put a hand on her shoulder, even though she was pretty sure her sister wouldn't cry. Except for the dark, dark days around Dad's funeral, Tessa never cried.

"You want to tell me about it?"

"Not particularly, but I will." She accelerated and passed a car on the left, then pulled at the seatbelt on her chest as if it made it difficult to breathe.

"Let me guess," Kate said. "There was a guy."

Tessa closed her eyes and groaned. "Oh, how I hate being predictable, clichéd, or dumb. But, yes, sister of mine, it was all of the above and then some."

"Oh, Tess. What did you do?"

"I broke one of Dad's golden rules: 'don't fish off the company dock.'"

"This guy worked at the Ritz?" Kate asked.

"A client—a huge one. He's the CEO of a billion-dollar transportation company, good-looking, loaded, and charming as all get out. All my weaknesses."

"Married?" Kate asked, wincing and waiting for the worst.

"No! I make mistakes, Kate. I make bad choices, but not that one—I've never made that one—and you know it."

Her voice was just hurt enough that Kate could have kicked herself for the comment.

"I'm sorry," she said quickly. "I know you don't go near married men."

"No. I'm just a serial dater who goes through men like paper towels."

"Tess," Kate said gently.

"But sometimes *I'm* the paper towel," she said on a sad sigh. "But don't get the wrong impression. I didn't fall in bed with the guy, just went out with him a few times."

Kate gave her a sympathetic look. "What happened?"

"This client, a local Naples gazillionaire named John, was hosting a three-day summit for his company execs and wanted everything first class and over the top. That included an absolute banger of a black-tie event—which, as you know, is my party planning specialty."

"Did something go wrong at the event?"

"I'll say," she scoffed. "After weeks of flirtations, evenings on his yacht, and some pretty serious claims of attraction, he brought a *date* to the event...and it wasn't me."

"Eesh. What did you do?" Kate looked at her.

Tessa lifted a brow. "Not a thing, and that's the beastly part. I was disappointed, but honestly? We had only gone out a few times and it was not a relationship, per se."

"Well, then, how did you end up getting fired?"

"Someone set me up," she said. "I think it must have been someone who might have known I'd been seeing the guy and wanted to get me in trouble. I don't know. Anyway, his date's weekend went south. And by south, I mean poor Tiffany's reservation got lost, she couldn't get into the spa, and all of her luggage went missing until Monday." She made a face. "And the room she did get? In the low-rent annex? There was a shower flood."

Kate gasped. "And you had nothing to do with that?"

She held up her hand like a Boy Scout. A beautiful, contrite, irresistible Boy Scout. "I did not, I swear on our sisterhood, our last name, and...anything else worth swearing on. I did not have anything to do with Tiffany's travails. Someone pulled some ugly strings, but it wasn't me. You have to believe me."

"I do," Kate assured her.

"Well, sadly, *he* didn't. And who knew Mr. Naples CEO was old college pals with one of the highest executive VPs of our parent company? Not me. You'd think he'd have mentioned that, but no. Then, wham. I was canned without warning or severance or a letter of recommendation."

"Oh, Tess. That's awful."

"They kicked me out faster than you can say false accusation." She pushed out a breath. "Can you blame me for falling into the arms of Destin?"

As Tessa turned left at a light, Kate thought about how things like that always happened to Tessa. Wrong place, wrong time, wrong guy, and no one to rise to her defense. Especially now that Dad, Tessa's number one cheerleader in life, was gone.

Pulling into the lot, Tessa found a spot and put the car in Park. As she turned off the engine, Kate put a hand on her arm. "How can I help you, Tessa?"

"Don't fight me if I want to move here."

"Move *here*?" Kate choked. "And do what?"

"I guess plan parties, since that's what I do," she said, looking around. "I'll call local resorts and see if they need an on-site event manager. The place is packed with tourists and surely people have parties, weddings, whatever. I'll figure it out."

"Do you have money saved?" Kate asked, always the more practical of the two. "It's an expensive place to live."

"I have some. Enough. Okay, a little." Tessa patted her shoulder. "I'll be fine, Lady Katie. The wind carries me where I need to go, you know? I'm free and having fun. What else matters, really?"

As always, Kate marveled at her sister's talent for making instability look like an asset in life. It made no sense to Kate, a woman whose world was ruled by structure, planning, and scientific accuracy. But Kate loved her twin sister and would do anything at all for her.

"And who knows?" Tessa twisted the key and whipped off the seatbelt as though she hated anything that constrained her. "Maybe I'll win the heart of Eli Lawson, convince him not to sell that gorgeous property, marry him, and live in the Summer House until the day I die."

Kate just stared at her, her jaw opening as all that sympathy and tenderness evaporated into...hot, raw envy and fear. She wouldn't! She wouldn't use him for—

"I'm kidding!" Tessa poked her arm. "I knew it, though. He *still* makes your little heart go pitter-pat, doesn't he?"

"He does not." She turned away so her twin sister didn't see something in her eyes that would be forever used against her. "But that does," she said quickly, rooting for a subject change. "That beautiful, awesome, amazing place called Publix. Oh, how I've missed it."

"A supermarket?" Tessa scoffed.

"The world's best."

Laughing, Tessa threw the door open and turned back to Kate. "Nice try, Kate. I know how you feel about Eli. Always loved that guy, am I right?"

With that, Tessa climbed out, leaving the echo of her pronouncement in the car.

Yeah. Kate did once love Eli. But he always loved Tessa more. That was the rule of nature in Destin, and in Kate's scientific world, nature didn't change her rules.

Chapter Nine

Eli

Eli had been less than thrilled to discover Tessa Wylie doing what Tessa Wylie always did—using her sorcery to get what she wanted with little regard for rules, protocols, or, frequently, the feelings of those around her. However, the sting of her uninvited invasion was eased by the arrival of her sister.

He wasn't sure why, but Kate's warm smile and even warmer personality allowed him to come to terms with the two unexpected guests. Why fight it? The old gang was gathered again, and there was a cool nostalgia about the reunion that he didn't hate at all.

In fact, after passing the roof inspection that afternoon, Eli's mood was so good that he'd taken Vivien's Highlander for a trip to Walmart. Since Kate wanted to cook, he decided to bring the table—picking up a long folding table, some chairs, and a few more household items they'd need to live comfortably for the short term.

At least they wouldn't be "camping" or sitting on the floor.

Judging from the aroma in the air as he came down the stairs after showering and changing, they would be eating well at his folding table. *Wow.* What was Kate cooking?

He paused on the landing, taking in the sights, sounds, and scents that had already transformed this big empty box into the earliest stages of a home.

Tessa had produced a mini speaker that had her flitting about the table, setting it with paper plates and Solo cups, singing about the rains in Africa, taking him right back to the eighties.

Vivien had set up a small bar on the island, lining up bottles of tonic and a handle of gin and limes. So G&Ts would be the drink of this spontaneous vacation, he presumed.

Kate was at the stove, her back to them as she stirred something that smelled like spices and heaven, moving with the music, tossing comments over her shoulder to Vivien.

Here are the girls, he thought with a smile, still watching, since no one had noticed him yet.

He and Pete McCarthy had so many names for them. The Three Amigas, the Three Blind Mice, the Three Stooges—the names varied depending on their moods and ages. But mostly, Tessa, Kate, and Vivien were just "the girls," and their presence all summer long simply made things more fun.

The song ended and, after a second's pause, a few drumbeats and snares came from the speakers. Instantly, all three of them squealed so loud, Eli jumped back in shock.

As the drums got louder, so did the shrieks as Tessa

shot around the island and grabbed Vivien, who abandoned her bar prep. Kate whipped around from the stove, the three of them suddenly dancing in a circle.

In perfect time to the music, they each threw a hand in the air and yelled, "Ow!" as they rocked side to side. The song kicked into high gear and so did they—belting out every lyric to "Walking on Sunshine" to each other as if they'd sung it together a million times.

And they probably had, since Tessa had proclaimed that song the "Summer House anthem" a lifetime ago.

Each one took a line, mimed with exuberant hand gestures and ridiculous faces—singing, laughing, dancing, and looking at each other with so much love he could feel it across the room.

He was transported, too, back to when he and Pete would roll their eyes while the girls sang and danced to this catchy tune all summer long, every single year.

In the early years, they were young middle-schoolers, acting obnoxious and stupid. In the in-between years, they were mostly amusing. But in the end, that last summer, when they'd been eighteen...he loved nothing more than watching them perform their favorite song.

Well, watching Tessa.

Back then, he'd try not to stare until she'd point her pink-tipped finger and belt out the words right to him.

I feel a love that's really real...

Except, boy, she hadn't.

That line—the whole song, really—captured everything about those summers. Fun, sun, girls, and...love. Of course, he knew better now. He knew what love was—

and what it wasn't—because he had basked in it with Melissa.

As a college kid, he'd had a debilitating ache for Tessa Wylie. But now, she was relegated to "merely amusing" status again. Yes, she was a woman who no doubt turned heads, but not his. Not anymore.

So why was he still ticked off at her for something it was painfully obvious she didn't even remember? Something from all those years ago? Eli wasn't the grudge holder his mother was, but his last encounter with Tessa back in 1995 occasionally haunted him even today.

As the song built to a noisy, frenetic crescendo, his gaze slipped to the right and landed on Kate.

Had she always had such elegant beauty that was overshadowed by the explosion of Barbie doll perfection that was her sister? Kate's dark hair was up in a ponytail that swung behind her, and she'd left her glasses near the sink, giving him a chance to really see her fine features and how gracefully she'd aged.

In leggings and a loose white T-shirt, she was fit and strong, but not in a "fifty-year-old killing herself at the gym to look thirty" kind of way. She exuded health and intelligence and a far more appealing grace than her twin sister, who once owned Eli Lawson's heart.

And with that thought, he let go of the bit of age-old resentment he felt for Tessa. What a waste of emotion, being mad about her careless abuse of his heart. She didn't know better.

Feeling a little freer, he jogged down the last few steps and belted out the final lyrics with the girls.

"'I'm walkin' on sunshine, whoa-oh!'" he hollered, utterly out of tune.

They all shrieked again—sounding exactly like teenagers—and clapped, waving him over as they finished with a noisy, enthusiastic group hug.

"Hey, the eighties called and they want their song back," he joked as the tune ended.

"Well, they can't have it," Tessa announced. "That's the Summer House anthem—lead caps, please!—and it shall forever belong to the Wylies and the Lawsons." She dropped her head back and let out a hoot as if adrenaline had rocked her whole being. "Wow, that was fun!"

"G&T, big brother?" Vivien asked.

"Yes, please, and Kate, what are you cooking that smells so insanely good?" he asked as he came around the island to inspect the sizzling pan.

She smiled at him from the stove, reaching to the right and then the left. Instinctively, he picked up her dark-rimmed glasses from near the sink and handed them to her.

"Thanks," she said, smiling up with a spark in her eyes and flushed cheeks from the impromptu performance. "Shrimp scampi on angel hair pasta with a side of tomato and burrata—drizzled with oregano-infused olive oil." She lifted a colander of raw shrimp, ready to pour it into a pan full of an aromatic butter sauce. "It'll be ready soon, so enjoy your cocktail."

"Where'd you learn to cook?" he asked, accepting the drink Vivien gave him with a nod of thanks.

"Self-taught," she said. "I started just making the

usual for my kids and soon realized cooking was exactly like chemistry, which I love. And before I knew it, my time at the stove was the most relaxing thing I did. I am what they call a stress-cooker."

He laughed at that. "Not stressed now, I hope."

"Not at all," she assured him. "I just talked to my kids, who are staying with their father, and doing well. And I chatted with my mom, who's happy because she has Marie Curie."

His brows lifted.

"My kitty," she told him.

"Ahh." He lifted his Solo cup toward her. "Here's to famous female scientists, like our chef."

"I'm not famous," she said, picking up her own drink and making the toast real. "I just hunker down in a lab in Cornell."

"Cornell, just like your dad."

"Yes," she said, sighing at what must still be a raw memory. "We both followed in our father's footsteps, more or less."

"Less, in my case," he said coolly. "Your father was a law professor, right?"

"He sure was. He taught legal ethics to forty graduating classes of Cornell Law School," she said with unabashed pride.

What would it feel like to be that proud of your father, he wondered.

"Truly a great man," he said. "Again, I'm sorry for your loss."

"And yours," she countered.

He managed a shrug. "Speaking of ethics...or not."

"Oh, Eli." She looked up, over the glasses that slid down her nose, a world of sympathy in her brown eyes. "It's never easy to lose your dad, no matter your age or the circumstances."

His chest softened a little at the tender comment, which did actually make him feel better.

"I have another Father," he said quietly, then pointed upwards. "He never lets me down."

Her eyes flickered in surprise. Of course, she'd have no way of knowing he'd found faith later in life. He didn't wear a cross or scream it out to people, and none of the Lawsons were particularly religious.

"What are we chit-chatting about over here?" Tessa somehow managed to slide into the conversation, a drink in one hand, a saucy smile on her face.

"Our fathers," Kate said.

"Ah, the elephant in the room."

"Tess." Kate shot her a look.

"It's fine," Eli said, inching back. "We all know the history."

"Actually, we don't," Vivien said, joining them with her drink.

"About your father?" Kate asked. "We know—"

"About our parents," Eli said, knowing exactly what Vivien meant. "And the great falling out of 1995."

For a moment, no one spoke as only looks were exchanged.

"Did they...fall out?" Kate asked with a confused expression. "Or get frozen out?"

"What do you mean?" Vivien asked.

Kate looked from one to the other. "I mean, it was always our impression that your mother just closed herself—and you guys—off to people who knew your family. Because..."

"Because of your father going to jail," Tessa finished, sounding a little exasperated. "I mean, I'm sorry that happened, but it was thirty years ago, and I don't see how it should keep us all apart. More than it already has, that is."

Eli shook his head. "I just don't think it's that simple," he said. "Maggie is notoriously private, that's true. But we've always thought something specific happened."

"Like what?" Kate asked.

"Like they had a huge fight," Vivien said. "Eli's right —our mother didn't separate from *all* people in those years. She was protective of us, yes, and she is a controlling woman. But she didn't stop talking to all the other people they knew. Just...the Wylies."

"What did the Wylies do?" Tessa asked, indignant. "We didn't even know he'd died."

Eli let out soft grunt, troubled by the conversation.

"Something doesn't add up," he said. "They must have had a disagreement or some big issue. It might not have had anything to do with my father's...situation. I mean..." He stole a look at Tessa, wondering if what he was about to say might jog her memory of that night. After all, the events coincided. "Your family did leave in a big hurry that last night."

Tessa threw her hands up. "Who even knows, but can we just let it go?"

Nope, no memory of what had transpired between them. For that, Eli was relieved. So he raised his Solo cup for a toast, but really, in his heart, it was a prayer of gratitude.

"Out with the old and in with the new," he said, grabbing the first cliché he could think of.

"Absolutely!" Tessa tapped her cup to his and the others joined in. "We're walking on sunshine!"

Laughing, they all took a deep drink, then Kate turned to the stove and the mouth-watering sizzle of her shrimp.

The conversation shifted as they moved to the table and enjoyed every bite, easily spending the next hour learning about each other's lives while the sun, and the past, set behind them.

AFTER DINNER and a quick group cleanup, Kate pulled on a hoodie and checked her watch.

"Are you headed out?" Eli asked.

"I like to walk after dinner." She tapped her watch. "And this beach sure beats the streets of Ithaca. Who wants to join me in walking off the carbs?"

Tessa was lounging comfortably at the table, nursing the end of her wine. "I like my carbs to load in peace after dinner, thank you very much."

"I'm going to do some online shopping for the house

and look at design sites," Vivien said, opening her laptop on their makeshift dining room table.

"I'd love to go," Eli said, hoping she'd meant to include him in the invitation. "Plus it's almost dark now. You shouldn't go alone."

"It's not safe?" Kate asked, surprised.

"I'm sure it is, but there's no boardwalk to the beach yet and I don't want anyone twisting an ankle on my construction site."

"Awesome. I'd love the company," she said. "And we could bring a phone light to get through the sea oats."

"For a few more weeks," Eli said, grabbing his phone from the island. "Then the boardwalk will be built, and we can just cruise to the beach."

"If you haven't sold it by then," she said, making a sad face as they walked toward the door.

Outside, he waited until they were down the steps to respond. "We can't," he told her. "There's a legal clause that says the profit can't be distributed until thirty years after my father's passing. Which means it's ours until November."

"Oh, wow." She slowed her step, zipping up the hoodie. "Really? I had no idea."

"Well, to be fair, none of us even knew my mother owned this place." At her "I'm not surprised" look, he laughed. "Yeah, you're right. She's...private."

They climbed the dune in silence as he lit the way with his phone, not that they really needed it with the full moon. At the top of the rise, they stopped to look up and down the deserted beach.

"I can't believe how crowded this town is and how empty this beach is," she observed. "How is that possible?"

"It's essentially a private beach," he said. "There's no public access for half a mile or more in either direction. So, unless you're willing to sneak through someone's yard, the beach is ours. Come on, let's walk."

They took a few steps along the sand, then he paused, holding out his hand to stop her. "You hear that?"

"The waves?" she asked.

"The way our sneakers sound on the sand. It's such a distinctive Destin noise—it takes me back. I've never heard it on any other beach."

She moved her foot, making the squeaky sound. "Yes, I remember."

"I don't know why it's just Destin," he said. "But it evokes memories. Like magic."

She laughed softly. "Not magic," she said. "I hate to give you the far less romantic and mystical explanation, but that's probably quartz particles, which are the same reason the sand here is so white. The sediment flows from the Appalachian Mountains, which have a ton of quartz."

"Oh, that's...not..."

"Magic," she supplied, taking her gaze from the view to look at him. "Sorry. Ask a scientist a question, get a scientist's answer."

He laughed and nodded. "Fair enough. But how about the view?" He gestured toward the moonlit surf. "Now that's magical."

"Indeed it is," she agreed. "You are literally sitting on a goldmine, Eli. At least, if you sell it."

He looked down at her, appreciating how that same moon lit her in the most attractive way, with her bangs fluttering over her eyes in the breeze. She adjusted her glasses, looking suddenly self-conscious, and he turned back to the water view.

The waves were a little rougher than normal, breaking in layers that created rows of white froth over the dark water, all of it illuminated by a giant moon.

"There really isn't an 'if' involved in selling it," he said. "Unless..."

"Unless you change your mind?" she guessed.

"Unless something weird happens," he replied, putting a hand on her shoulder to guide her toward the flat sand so they could walk alongside the surf.

"Something weird? What do you mean, Eli?"

"I mean...some things *can* be too good to be true, and I'm a cautious guy. The truth is, my mother found a legal loophole, but technically? She hid the fact that she owned this house when she put it in a trust, keeping it from the authorities. I know it was thirty years ago, but I guess I'm just traumatized by how they took everything we had when my dad was found guilty."

She gave a soft grunt. "Oh, goodness. That had to be rough for your family. Your home? Your assets? Everything?"

"Everything but what my mother could scrounge and squirrel away. She and Crista moved into a tiny apartment. I was in my last year at the University of Georgia and Vivien was a freshman at Georgia State. We both had scholarships and got jobs, and my mother worked in a dentist's office to make ends meet."

"Oh, my. I admit, I have a hard time picturing Maggie Lawson as the receptionist in a dentist's office."

He laughed. "She's tough as nails, Kate. God put her on a very difficult path, and she walked it as only Maggie could—like she owned that path and everyone else was just a bystander."

"I always admired her so much," she said. "So did my mother...until..."

"Until she didn't," Eli said.

"You're bothered by their falling out," she guessed. "I can tell it's a sore subject."

"I'm bothered by everything my father did," he admitted. "And now, I worry that there's another surprise that will come back to bite us."

"What kind of surprise?"

"I don't know," he said. "Yes, we are free to keep and sell the house, but you never know what could happen. I have nightmares of some government official knocking on the door with a seizure warrant and a forfeiture order."

"Eesh." She thought about that for a moment, silent as they fell into step on the hard-packed sand, then asked, "When exactly did they buy the house that used to be here?"

"That last summer in 1995. My dad bought it—probably to hide or launder money. I don't know and don't want to know. But he paid cash for the little house and the land —essentially for a song back then. Not long after that, he was arrested and then Hurricane Opal hit and decimated most of this beach and much of the town. In the melee that ensued, Maggie managed to hide the house in a trust. I don't know how." He threw her a look. "Once again, I apologize for the shaky ethics of the Lawson family."

"No apologies." She smiled. "Anyway, I get the impression your ethics are rock solid, Eli."

"Thanks. I try, but the sins of the father and all."

She stopped mid-step and looked up at him as if a thought occurred to her. "What if the reason for our parents' falling out was the house, or the purchase of it? Maybe my mother knew about the house and Maggie was worried she'd tell the authorities, so she cut ties."

He nodded slowly, considering that. "Maybe, but was that enough for the big fight? I mean, do you remember that night?" He certainly did, and not because the Wylies were packing up and leaving in a hurry.

She took her glasses off and slipped them into her pocket, as if they distracted her while she thought.

"I don't remember much," she said. "I remember I'd gone sailing that day with Vivien and when we got back, my mom was packing to leave. Dad was looking for Tessa. Where were you?"

With Tessa.

"I was out," he said instead, which wasn't a lie but sure wasn't the whole story. "And y'all were gone when I got back." He'd been relieved at the time, not having to face Tessa, but looking back? It had been beyond weird, and he never got to say goodbye to any of them.

"Yeah, it was a lightning-speed exit," she said. "I remember Mom had some excuse about my father having to get back to Cornell. I recall it was a long and quiet ride back to Ithaca, but you know, I don't think any of us ever dreamed it would be the last time the Wylies and Lawsons would ever be together." She elbowed him. "And guess what? It wasn't."

He sighed, still uneasy over the history and timing. "I'd love to know what happened, Kate. Wouldn't you?"

"Yes, but we all know Maggie's not talking. And when I told my mother I was coming to Destin and Tessa was already here?" She wrinkled her nose. "I have to say she acted odd, at least for Jo Ellen. Shut down, changed the subject, and reminded me not to ask about your father's problems with the law."

He searched her face, considering that. "I wonder why."

"Because she knew it embarrassed Maggie, and assumed you would be uncomfortable."

"Yeah, it's not my favorite subject," he admitted, looking to the right, realizing how far they'd gone. "We should head back, Kate."

As they turned, Kate put a hand on his arm. "Eli, what if they're not the only two people who know the whole story?" she asked.

He frowned. "Who else would know?"

"They had friends here," she said. "You said someone managed the whole thing?"

"A lawyer, who's dead. His son, who took over his

accounts. He was the one who found the loophole that allows us to sell it."

"Does he know what happened?"

Eli shook his head. "No clue, but he's Maggie's lawyer and I'm not sure I want to overstep that boundary. Not just to satisfy personal curiosity, anyway."

"What about neighbors and people they knew?" Kate suggested. "I'm sure many of those folks are gone, but we can dig around."

"We can," he said, smiling at her. "I have low expectations, but thank you, Kate. For caring about it. And for coming down here. It's really, really good to see you."

They looked into each other's eyes, the connection, the history, and the friendship feeling very real right then.

Turning away, she looked out into the water, then squinted and tapped her head.

He gestured to her jacket. "Pocket."

Laughing, she slipped her hand in and produced her glasses. "How'd you know?"

"You're easy to read."

She made a face. "I hope not."

He wasn't sure what she meant by that, but he let it go.

Chapter Ten
Vivien

S tanding back as the last chair was brought into the dining room, Vivien felt a familiar thrill as her "organic coastal" vision started to take shape with this first but very critical furniture delivery. Choosing mostly shades of cream and sand with touches of blue and the occasional gold accent to mirror the outdoors, she could slowly feel her vision taking shape to bring this unfinished house to life.

Although, to be fair, the four "residents" who'd lived here for nearly a week had contributed plenty of vitality to the place.

Despite the "camping in a mansion" atmosphere they'd created, the house had become—well, not a home, exactly, but what Lacey might call a "vibe."

For one thing, Tessa always seemed to have music playing from her portable speaker, creating playlists that blended their youth with a modern sound and kept the spirit high. She'd dubbed her favorite "The Sounds of the Summer House" and the name stuck.

It didn't matter what the eventual owner would call this place, to them it was and would always be the Summer House.

In addition to the music, Kate's cooking meant the kitchen was always active, hopping like a well-oiled diner. And Eli's constant crew of construction workers buzzed around outside, starting the boardwalk, filling the pool, and generally making noise and progress.

It was a unique experience for Vivien, actually surrounded by "life" in an empty house she was staging. It helped her create spaces that functioned, and use light, sound, and traffic patterns to plan the furniture layout.

When the delivery crew completed their work, the noisy sound of a circular saw from the outside project floated in from the open sliding door.

"What's all this?" Tessa came out from the hallway, dressed in shorts and a tank top and carrying bright orange running shoes, her hair pulled up in a ponytail.

Good heavens, Vivien thought, she did not look like a woman about to turn fifty.

"Furniture!" Vivien announced, pointing to the corner for two men carrying an oversized club chair.

"And barstools, I'm happy to see." Tessa's topaz eyes flashed with approval as she cruised through the room, making both men look up fast enough that Vivien thought they might drop the chair.

Clueless of the attention, Tessa zoomed in on the cream leather seats lined up in the kitchen. "Amen and hallelujah, now we can sit at the island and watch Kate work while we drink our G&Ts. Well done, Vivien."

"Thanks, Tess. I'm happy with the way this looks."

Tessa came closer, slipping an arm around Vivien's

waist. "I have ideas for my bedroom. You want to know them?"

Vivien slid her a look, always walking that fine line between delighted and dismayed by this woman. *Her* bedroom? Should she remind her that they would be selling this house...or ask the question she was starting to think about a lot—would Tessa ever leave?

She studied the other woman, marveling at her glowing complexion, her tumbling blond hair, and, of course, a nearly flawless figure. For all that beauty on the outside, though, Vivien frequently sensed someone very lost on the inside.

Kate had confirmed those suspicions during some long walks with Vivien on the beach. Tessa had taken their father's death extremely hard, Kate had told her. She'd basically rolled up in an emotional ball and hadn't begun to climb out of her grief.

Kate was certain that losing her job was as much a result of mourning as it was making bad decisions. The last thing Vivien wanted to do was hurt Tessa or remind her that all of this was temporary.

"Absolutely," she said instead. "I'd love to hear your ideas."

"Okay, but fair warning. There's pink involved."

"Why am I not shocked?" Vivien joked, stepping away. "Kate asked me to tell you she went to Publix. She wanted to ask you to go with, but your door was closed."

"Beauty rest and now I'm going for a run," she said, strolling back into the living room, her sock-covered feet sinking into the off-white area rug. "Wow, you nailed this room."

"It needs accessories," Vivien said as one of the delivery crew came with a tablet for her to sign.

"All set," the man said. "You can sign right there and add your title at Vivien Lawson Designs."

"Title?" She smiled up at him, still getting used to using her maiden name. "That would be president, CEO, and employee of the month." She scratched her signature on the tablet and handed it back, reaching into her pocket for a well-deserved cash tip.

"Thank you," she said, following him to the door and slipping him the money. "You guys did a great job."

When she turned, she found Tessa strolling around the edges of the living room, examining the new sectional with a loving fingertip.

"That must feel good," Tessa said.

Did she mean giving them a tip? Or the fabric? "What's that?" Vivien asked.

"To be president, CEO, and self-employed."

"Ahh. Well, it would feel a lot better if I actually made money."

Tessa eyed her, strolling into the kitchen, because the woman *never* stopped moving. "Why don't you look for another job like the one you had?" she asked. "Why try to go solo?"

Vivien shrugged. "Because the one I had was for my husband. I don't really want to step back into a firm. I'm not even sure I'd know where to go and, frankly? I don't like working for someone else."

"Who does?" Tessa scoffed, glancing over her shoulder. "But there's security in it—a paycheck, I mean."

Vivien slipped into one of the new barstools and watched Tessa fill a Solo cup with water from the fridge.

"Is that your plan?" Vivien asked. "To get another job like the one you had at the Ritz?"

"I guess. I've been eyeing some of the bigger resort chains, but no one is hiring for what I do. I'll probably have to devise Plan B. Ugh, that's my least favorite word."

Vivien frowned. "Devise?" she guessed.

"*Plan*. They make me itch." She sipped, her eyes smiling over the rim of the cup. "I'll keep looking, but I can't count on my old employer for a reference, so I'm not feeling super optimistic."

"Perfect time to go out on your own," Vivien said.

Tessa snorted, but didn't say anything, surprising Vivien.

"It's not impossible, you know," Vivien continued. "You can work from home."

Tessa launched a brow north. "Home? You forget I don't have one of those."

"That's temporary."

"Until I get a job, so, vicious cycle, isn't it?"

"I'm serious, Tess. You could easily start an event or party planning business."

"Easily?" She sounded doubtful as she picked up one of Vivien's business cards. "I mean, look at this. How did you know you needed a cute logo? And a website? I could never."

Vivien leaned back, surprised by the sudden lack of confidence in a woman who seemed to ooze it.

"There's a website that'll make you a logo for nothing if you order cards from them. I was able to create a new business card with the Lawson name in about six minutes, and they overnighted the pack to me. As for my site? Well, it did help to have a Gen Z daughter who knows her way around something called Squarespace, and we made my site in an afternoon. And Lacey updates it for me—even changed the name and got me a new URL."

Tessa rounded the island and settled into one of the barstools. "Well, I don't have a Gen Z daughter and I'm not...business-oriented."

"Tessa!" Vivien exclaimed. "You can do anything. You're smart and resourceful."

Tessa shot her a "get real" look.

"I'm pretty and fast on my feet," she said with no irony or humility—as if she knew the truth. "That doesn't help with..." She fluttered the card. "A business? With tax liabilities and employees and a website that doesn't crash? Please. I do not have my sister's IQ."

Vivien was stunned. "You can't be serious, Tess. You're very bright. No one can be as witty as you and not be smart."

"Street smarts," she said. "The book stuff?" She tapped her ear. "Goes in one, goes out the other. There's a reason they call them airheads."

Vivien just shook her head. "Not buying it. Let me

show you my website and the spreadsheet I use to run my business—or will when I have multiple clients."

"So I can be intimidated?"

"As if Tessa Wylie has ever been intimidated by anyone or anything," Vivien quipped as she opened her laptop and brought it to life.

"I'm not kidding, Vivien. Want to see a grown woman cower in the corner? Make me read a spreadsheet."

Vivien blinked at her. "Are you serious?"

"What I am is seriously dyslexic, but most people don't know that about me."

"I didn't," Vivien said.

"Because I didn't have to read in the summer," she said easily. "Now I just deal with it. But numbers and spreadsheets? I might as well be reading Latin. And, trust me, you don't want to see the inside of my checkbook. I haven't balanced it since that thing we called Y2K."

Laughing, Vivien tapped the keys. "Spreadsheets are easy now—the computer does it for you. Calculators do the hard stuff, and the bank balances your account. You're making excuses."

Tessa leaned in and whispered, "Hey, Kate got the brains and I got the looks. Sadly, one of them fades over the years." She touched her face. "Tick-tock, you know?"

Vivien's heart twisted with sympathy as she put her hand on her friend's arm. "Tess," she whispered. "You're wrong."

She looked like she was digging for a quip, but couldn't find one.

"You just need one client and you're off to the races," Vivien said. "That's all you need."

"And I need *that*." Tessa looked past her to the computer screen as the clean lines of vivienlawsondesigns.com appeared. "Holy moly, that's gorgeous!"

"Thank you," she said, smiling at the reaction to her beautiful site. "It really was surprisingly easy. I bet I could help you get started."

"Maybe." Clearly intrigued, Tessa reached over and turned the laptop to get a better look at the crisp tones and modern font. "Show me around your little corner of the internet, Viv."

"Of course," she said. "This is the main page, with my mission statement."

She dropped her head back with a grunt of disgust. "See what I mean? A mission statement? My mission is to have a good time."

"And that," Vivien said, pointing a finger at her, "is not a bad mission statement for a party planner."

Tessa cocked her head, thinking. "Maybe that could be the company name? Good Time Girl?"

"Um, if you're running an escort service."

Tessa snorted and nodded. "Point taken. Go ahead, tell me more about this mythical business I'm going to start."

The door to the garage opened and Kate walked in, laden with bags. "Morning, all! Need arms and assistance."

Tessa pushed away from the counter. "I'll help you."

"You stay right here," Vivien insisted, putting a hand

on her arm. "Click through the site and get ideas." Without waiting for an argument, Vivien pushed the laptop closer and followed Kate down the few steps to the garage. "How was shopping?" she asked.

"Like a supermarket dream. We're having chicken parm with my homemade red sauce tonight."

"Really? That's Eli's absolute favorite meal. He orders it everywhere."

"I know," she said, reaching into the trunk for one of about ten bags. "That's why I'm making it."

Vivien tried to hide her smile, and fought the temptation to make a comment about how much time the two of them had been spending together.

Teasing Kate about Eli had been fine thirty years ago when her friend had a very secret crush on her brother.

Now? Vivien didn't want anyone to be uncomfortable. And she really didn't want to jinx what she hoped might be something more than friendship.

"Can you get the rest?" Kate asked, taking her armload of bags.

Just as Vivien reached for a bag, she heard a vehicle pull in behind her, making her grunt in annoyance. When were the construction guys going to stop using their driveway?

She frowned as she turned and saw the car which was...really familiar. It looked exactly like Lacey's little blue Mazda.

Because it *was* Lacey's little blue Mazda!

"What?" She let go of the six-pack of soda and rushed into the sunshine just as her daughter stopped the car and threw open the driver's-side door. "Lacey, what are you—"

"Don't be mad, Mom. Please don't be mad." She came forward, arms open. "I absolutely needed to see you."

Mad? All Vivien could do was wrap her arms around her favorite person on earth and squeeze, overwhelmed by joy.

"I'm so glad you're here," she whispered and realized she'd never meant anything more.

They stood in the sun long enough to hug and squeeze and for Vivien to look hard in her daughter's eyes and see...trouble.

"Are you okay?" Vivien asked.

"Yeah, I just...had to come."

"How long are you staying?" she asked as Lacey pulled two—make that three—bags from the hatchback. "More than just this weekend?"

Lacey gave a tight smile. "Listen, Mom, I—"

"Oh, hello!" From the garage, Kate called out to them.

"One of the sisters?" Lacey asked, looking at her. Vivien had told her that they'd arrived, but they had talked so briefly over the last few days, she hadn't filled Lacey in on any details.

She guided Lacey toward the garage. "This is Kate Wylie," she said, gesturing to the other woman. "Kate, this is my daughter, Lacey, who has knocked my socks off by showing up unannounced."

"Lacey." Kate beamed at her, extending a hand. "What an awesome surprise! I'm so happy to meet you."

"Hi, Kate." Lacey shook her hand, smiling at her. "Great to meet you. And I hope there's room for me. I know I didn't give any warning. I made the decision to come rather, um, impulsively."

"We'll fit you in," Kate assured her, taking the last bag from the trunk and using it to gesture toward the stairs that led up to the kitchen. "We certainly have plenty of food. Get your bags and come on in and meet Tessa."

"Are you having fun with them?" Lacey asked Vivien as they went back to where she'd left her suitcases.

"I am, and I'm staging the house room by room, which is a blast. Uncle Eli is finishing the outside and…" She frowned, searching Lacey's face for the honest explanation. "What's going on with you?"

She exhaled, hauling a bag. "It's a long story and…not a great one."

Vivien's heart dropped. "You quit, didn't you. Did you—"

"Lacey!" Suddenly Tessa rushed out, arms extended. "I just heard you're joining the party! Welcome!" She threw her arms around Lacey and squealed. "I can't believe Vivien's daughter is here!"

A little surprised by the welcome, Lacey hugged the other woman right back, then leaned away. "You must be Tessa."

"The fun one," Tessa confirmed, taking Lacey's chin and moving her face side to side, checking her out. "Oh, Vivien Junior," she announced. "You look exactly like your mother when she was a few years younger than you. Welcome to the Summer House. We're walkin' on sunshine and happy to include you."

Lacey laughed and glanced at Vivien. "They're so different—just like it said in your diaries."

"In your *what*?" Tessa's voice rose two octaves. "There are *diaries*? From when we were kids?"

"I kept journals," Vivien admitted. "And they are as juvenile and embarrassing as you would imagine."

Tessa's eyes flashed. "Juvenile, maybe. Embarrassing? Never. Did you bring them? Please say yes, because I'm already thinking about a bonfire and a dramatic reading tonight. You in, Lace?"

Lacey giggled, already infected by...the Good Time Girl.

But all Vivien could picture was Eli throwing that diary in the fire before he subjected himself to the public humiliation of his childhood crush on Tessa.

"Let's just get Lacey settled first," she said, purposely vague.

"One of the first-level bedrooms?" Tessa asked, taking one of Lacey's bags by the rolling handle.

"No beds in those rooms," Vivien reminded her. "I'm in a king in the main suite and I'm swimming in space. Lacey can bunk with me."

It took a while to get upstairs, since Lacey had to tour the house, greet her Uncle Eli, and swoon over the mini mansion. But an hour after she arrived, Lacey and Vivien were finally alone as she unpacked.

Vivien plopped on the bed, nursing a bottle of water,

watching her daughter unzip a bag, waiting for the right time to ask...well, everything.

"Tessa's amazing!" Lacey cooed as she flipped open the suitcase to what looked like a very hastily packed assortment of clothes.

"Kate's really sweet, too," Vivien said, feeling a decades-old urge to defend and support the quieter and less attention-grabbing twin. "Just more low-key."

"Yeah, Tessa is...high key," Lacey agreed as she pulled out a cotton dress and looked over it. "I didn't have any idea what to pack, so..."

"Lacey." Vivien leaned back and wrapped her arms around a throw pillow, hoping the non-confrontational body language would get her some answers. "You going to tell me what happened?"

"I quit." She headed to the walk-in closet, disappearing into it as Vivien squeezed the pillow with a growl. She *knew* it.

The only sound in the suite was a hanger sliding over the bar in the closet. After a few seconds, Lacey came back out, her expression ominous.

"Please don't try and make me go back there, Mom. Because I'm not. Not after...no."

"Not after what?"

Letting out a soft groan, Lacey sifted through the mess of packed clothes. "It's not...good."

"Well, quitting a job never is." She searched Lacey's face, taking in a measurable amount of pain in those pretty blue eyes. "Honey, what happened? Did you mess up another construction schedule? Get into a tiff with the picky old biddy from Peachtree Hills?"

"There's a new, uh, person at the company."

Vivien waited for more, but Lacey just lifted a T-shirt and looked around. "Is there a dresser I can—"

"In the closet. Lacey. What kind of new person? Did Dad hire a new admin who's moving in on your job?"

She looked up. "A new designer."

Vivien swallowed a wallop of disappointment, refusing to let it buckle her. "Well, that was bound to happen. Who is it?"

"Una Tatum."

"*Oof.*" Vivien flipped the pillow away at the name of a woman who ran rings around her design-wise. Her clients were the wealthiest in the whole Atlanta area, and her work was stellar. "I'm surprised she'd deign to work for a home builder, considering her client base."

Lacey bit her lip and turned to go back into the closet. "Yeah, well, it's...complicated."

Frowning, Vivien sat up a little straighter, a bad, bad feeling creeping through her. Complicated? "How so?"

"Just...complicated," Lacey said from inside the closet.

It wasn't what she said, it was how she said it, making Vivien slide through all she knew about the well-regarded, painfully successful designer. Vivien had heard her speak at a home show once, although they'd never met.

Una Tatum was talented, creative, reliable, and...

really attractive. Tiny, gorgeous, and weighed down by flowing blond hair.

"Well," Vivien said, fighting a lump in her throat as she stood to help Lacey unpack. "It's Ryan's business and she's very good."

Lacey stepped out of the closet, tears glistening in her eyes. "Very good," she said, her voice rich with meaning, disgust on her face.

Vivien dropped right back on the bed, crushed by the weight of this revelation. "Are you telling me they..."

Lacey didn't answer. She didn't have to. She just curled her lip and shuttered her eyes, and Vivien knew the hard, cold facts. Ryan was looking for "more" and, boy, he'd get it and then some with Una Tatum.

Lacey crossed her arms and stared at Vivien. "Now, do I have your permission to stay for a while, reexamine my life, try to figure out what I want to be when I grow up, and never, *ever* go back to that place? 'Cause our family is completely broken and I am choosing sides—yours."

"Lacey..." Her voice cracked.

Instantly, Lacey reached for her. "Mom, I'm so sorry to tell you. I know it hurts. I'm sorry."

She hugged harder than she should have, channeling all her disappointment and pain into squeezing this sweet angel who she loved so much.

"I hate him, Mom."

"No, no. Don't hate him. We're divorced and—"

"Not officially. It's not final. He shouldn't be with someone, if you ask me."

But Vivien was certain Ryan hadn't asked anyone. She eased back, waiting for a tear that didn't come. But, oh, this was hard. This pretending to easily accept the end of a marriage, decades of dreams and a lifetime of... partnership. No, this was not for the faint of heart.

"Are you jealous, Mom?"

Jealous? No. She was...broken on the inside. But she certainly didn't want Lacey to know that. She had to be strong for her daughter.

She gave a careless shrug. "Not jealous. But I'm wondering if he's going to like being with a woman who won't roll over to his every command." She gave a soft laugh. "Hard lesson for Ryan Knight to learn."

Lacey put her arm around Vivien. "I don't care what he learns," she said softly. "I'm here to be your precious daughter, best friend, and beloved roommate. I literally am choosing you over Dad. Period, end of story."

Vivien hugged her, more emotional about the sweet speech than whatever Ryan was doing with another woman. "To the victor goes the spoils, huh?"

Lacey inched back, narrowing her blue eyes. "But I still hate houses."

"I understand," Vivien said. "But this one? You can't hate it."

She nodded and looked around. "You're right. It's got a vibe."

Vivien tilted her head back and chuckled. "I knew you'd say that."

"So you knew I was coming."

She sighed. "Yeah, I guess I did." She planted a kiss on Lacey's cheek. "And, honey, the vibe just got better with you here."

Chapter Eleven
Tessa

S o much for a morning run. By the time Tessa had chatted with the breath of fresh air that had blown in from Atlanta, the sun was high and hot. She wanted to run—*had* to—but she was sure to have two new age spots on her shoulders and at least one fresh wrinkle from the assault of UV rays.

Oh, the battle raged on, didn't it? What would Tessa Wylie be when she wasn't...pretty?

As alone as she was now, she presumed.

Tugging the brim of her baseball hat lower to protect her face, she started with a slow trot once she reached the hard-packed sand. And then she started to jog as fast as possible—waiting for the dopamine hit, longing for her runner's high.

But all she felt was...discomfort. Maybe worse.

"Come on, Tessa!" she chided herself.

With each step, she tried to do her usual mental review of her body, which was feeling okay for fifty.

No, no, no! Not fifty yet. Forty-nine...and a half. She had to smile because that sounded like a three-year-old trying to age up, not a midlife woman trying to age down.

But she had to face facts: fifty loomed and she was... doomed.

Doomed, she thought. *Really?* Just because she was homeless, jobless, and...fatherless?

The old sting squeezed her chest, so she slowed to a walk, feeling the sun beating her down like the grief she just couldn't shake.

Turning from the rays, she looked toward the row of spectacular houses that lined the beach. Homes for successful, smart people who weren't afraid of spreadsheets and logos that always looked backwards and sideways to her dyslexic eyes.

But did that really have to stop her? Where was her confidence?

Buried in a plot in Ithaca.

She whimpered at the thought, looking up to the blue sky and imagining him—Arthur Wylie—up there in the ether, gazing down from above. Far, far away.

"Oh, Dad, why aren't you here anymore? I need you," she whispered. "I need you to tell me Excel isn't the enemy, that my own head is getting in the way. I need to hear it from you, Dad."

Burning in the sun, she walked toward the shade of the longest boardwalk over the dunes. It was one thing to have a crisis of confidence and a grief attack, but she sure wasn't going to ruin her skin while she did it.

As she navigated the soft sand, she imagined her father right next to her. He would be, too. He loved exercise and fresh air, and he loved sneaking time with Tessa to just talk and talk and talk. He'd take her fishing, hiking, skiing. They loved to be outside together.

She'd never had that kind of friendship with her mother—not that she felt any animosity with Jo Ellen. They just weren't close. Her mother never really understood her and always drifted toward Kate, who was the more logical, brilliant, and far less complicated of the two. Those two liked to stay in and read—Tessa and Dad just wanted air and their long, long conversations.

He knew her heart and her weaknesses. He knew her highs and lows. He certainly knew her secrets, she thought with an ancient pang in her chest.

Always, he generously gave her advice, help, and a shoulder when she needed it.

It had been Artie who'd helped her navigate the job at the Ritz from the beginning to almost the miserable end. She would have never gotten involved with that guy if her father had been alive.

She could just imagine what the ethics professor would have said: "Fraternizing with a client might not be illegal, but it is unethical. It's a fine line, but one you never want to cross, Theresa."

She smiled at the name only he was allowed to use. Truth was, if it hadn't been for Dad, she might have quit —or been canned—a few years ago. But she took every challenge to her father, and he helped her through the whitewater.

Now she was bouncing around without a rudder or an oar or whatever one needed not to drown.

She slipped underneath the boardwalk, able to see

that it connected to a glorious house, easily one of the biggest on the beach. The faux weathered clapboard gave off hints of New England, with a massive deck, shuttered windows, and a bay of French doors. Would the people who lived there think she was trespassing if she just sat in the shade of their boardwalk?

She didn't care. She didn't care about anything, to be honest.

Closing her eyes, she folded onto the sand, abandoning her attempt to run away—literally—from the punch of pain she still felt when she thought about her father.

What she wouldn't give to talk to him right now. Anything. Anything at all. And he'd tell her what to do. He'd love the idea of her starting a business. He never saw her shortcomings as flaws.

Who cares if you have trouble reading, Theresa? You're charming and funny and beautiful! Find someone to read for you!

She could hear every word right now.

You just go out and find that client! If not you, then who?

He'd *always* said that to her—it was his motto for her. *If not you, then who?*

Artie Wylie systematically built confidence in a little girl who had trouble reading and cried in math class—somehow understanding how hard it was to be the twin sister of the student who won every academic honor and got a nearly perfect SAT score.

She sat up straighter at the sound of a man clearing

his throat, which reminded her of Dad. A million goose-bumps exploded on her bare arms despite the heat. Was he here? Watching over her?

She heard noisy footsteps on the boardwalk, too loud to be the spirit of Artie Wylie. Great. She was about to be caught *squatting* again. This time literally, in the sand.

Cringing, she stayed perfectly still and listened to a man's voice, deep and strong.

"Of course I can do that, but dragging him all the way here? That could easily be a complete waste of time, and my time is valuable."

Valuable enough to buy this multimillion-dollar house, she mused.

As the footsteps came closer, she cocked her head, waiting for a response, but there was nothing except silence and more footsteps.

"Yes, yes. Anything can be done for a price. So now I'm wasting time *and* cash."

Ah, he was on the phone, she realized.

"Fine, I'll call someone. But who? I don't know a soul in this God-forsaken town."

His voice was low, confident, and just a little irritated with whoever was on the other end.

"Okay, okay. I'll throw myself a stinking birthday bash and invite the guy. If that's what it's going to take to get him and close the Bank of Boston deal, that's what I'll do. How hard can it—"

He stopped right over her. So close she could look through the slats of the boardwalk and see the bottoms of his feet and muscular legs in khaki shorts.

Oh, *man*! Why was she always in the wrong place at the wrong time?

"Invite fifty people, Brian? To my own party? Jeez. Okay. Fine, if you think that'll get him where we want him, but I absolutely do not have time for this."

Wait. Did he say fifty people...for a party? She sat up a little straighter, closing her eyes to hear every nuance in the guy's voice.

"All right, all right. I'll figure it out. Just get the paperwork ready to get him on the board. I'll call the lawyers and...a caterer." He punctuated that with a dark curse.

Could this be possible? Could Tessa Wylie have been in the *right* place at the *right* time for the first time in her forty-nine-and-a-half years?

Or...*did Dad just send her a client?*

Of course he did, because even from his angel's perch in heaven, he was the greatest guy who ever lived. And he wouldn't let her be stopped by a spreadsheet or a logo.

Suddenly, the man pivoted and marched back toward the house, leaving her to finally exhale one long breath.

Now what? How could she get this job without making it painfully obvious she'd been trespassing *and* eavesdropping? *Would that be unethical or illegal, Dad?*

Well, her father had clearly pulled some saintly strings to help her get a client, so she had to believe Artie would look past a transgression or two.

Stepping out into the sunshine, she pushed back her hat and peered toward the house. She spotted the man instantly, leaning on the deck railing, looking at his phone. She couldn't quite tell his age from this distance, but guessed over forty and under sixty.

An age she could definitely work with.

Squaring her shoulders, she started to jog toward the dune, like any runner out on the beach. In a few hundred feet, the rise put her right at the same level as his deck. As she got closer, he looked up from his phone and did a double-take—always a good sign—and she flashed him a smile and a wave.

"Don't tell me," she called as she stopped to jog in place. "It's a private beach and you're going to have me arrested."

He lowered the phone and adjusted his sunglasses. "It depends. How do you feel about handcuffs?"

Oh, puh-lease, honey. Don't even suggest it.

But she just gave an easy laugh because that's what he expected, and she wanted a client. Not bad enough to do anything stupid, but she could humor him.

For a moment, they just looked at each other, both of them eyeing one another, waiting for someone to say something. If she didn't, Mr. Bank of Boston Deal would go right back to his phone, and she'd be forced to admit to eavesdropping.

"Nice house," she said, gesturing toward his mansion. "Reminds me of Newport or Nantucket."

He slid a quick glance over his shoulder. "Then there would be a widow's walk, but thanks." He studied her for another few seconds, probably deciding if she was worth the effort of a conversation. "You live near here?" he asked, giving her a shot of relief.

"In the new one about a half a mile that way." She pointed toward the Summer House. "Where they're noisily building a boardwalk." She made a fake grimace. "Sorry about that."

He abandoned the phone, interested. "Don't be. I was happy to see that ramshackle cottage was finally condemned and a decent house went up. You built it?"

"No." She shook her head. "My friends did. I'm staying with them."

He came a few steps closer, allowing her to see he was probably mid-fifties, maybe sixty—hard to tell with his shades on. In decent shape, good bones, and light brown hair. He had a short, salt-and-pepper goatee that might have just been a refusal to shave, but it looked okay.

"How long are you here?" he asked, giving her just enough of a crack in the door to push her way in.

"Hard to say. I'm doing a little work for some clients..." *Sorry, Ethics Professor Wylie. Little white lie. Very little, very white.* "I'll be here for a few weeks, at least. Are you full-time or a snowbird?"

"I'm from Boston," he said. "I just came down for business. What kind of clients?"

All right now, here we go. "I'm an event coordinator."

"What?" he choked, taking off his sunglasses. "You are kidding me."

She raised her hands in feigned innocence. "It's what I do."

"You're...like a party planner?" His voice rose with disbelief.

"I'm not *like* a party planner, I'm the best darn one around." She carefully navigated the sand of the dune, walking closer to the boardwalk. "My name's Tessa Wylie." She extended her hand as she reached the railing. "President, CEO, and employee of the month at..." She echoed what she'd heard Vivien say, but hesitated as his large hand closed over hers, ready to say *Good Time Girl*.

But suddenly, she didn't want that to be the name of her pretend company. Not this time.

"Tessa Wylie Events," she finished. "So, if you are planning a, uh, St. Patrick's Day bash later this month, I'm your girl."

"Holy..." He finally let go of her hand, crossing his arms and shaking his head. "If I didn't know better, I'd think Brian sent you here but even he isn't that good."

Someone sent me but his name isn't Brian.

"I don't know anyone by that name," she replied. "Are you looking for an event coordinator?"

"Can you throw a cocktail and dinner party for fifty people in less than three weeks?"

She gave a dry laugh. "With my eyes closed and my hands behind my back."

His lips kicked up in a half smile that she instantly recognized, bracing for a sexual joke about tying her hands. Because if he did, then she was going to say no. She would not, under any circumstances, encourage that. This was *business*.

But he just nodded. "I may want to hire you, Tessa." He reached into his pocket, pulling out a wallet. "I'm

Garrett Fischer and this is my cell. Text me your number and we'll set up a meeting. How's tomorrow?"

She nearly toppled over, fighting the urge to throw her hands in the air and yell hallelujah. Instead, she took his embossed business card and slid it into her back pocket with her phone.

"Let me check my calendar, Mr. Fischer, and I'll text you."

"Perfect." He put his sunglasses back on, but she knew he was checking her out. *Well, you can look but you can't touch, Garrett Fischer.*

She'd just started her new business and nothing—especially not a man—was going to derail it.

With a super-professional nod and a crisp goodbye, she stepped away and headed down the dune back to the beach. She didn't turn and look to see if he was watching. She didn't take out his card to check out his title. She didn't do anything unprofessional, flirtatious, or dumb.

She just ran like the wind and thanked her dearest, darling father for helping her from heaven, where she knew he was.

"VIVIEN, where are you? Lacey, I need your help! Kate, you're not going to believe this!" Tessa called out as she ran up the back stairs to the second level to find...no one. "Where is everyone?" she whispered, let down that they weren't there waiting to celebrate with her.

"I'm here." Kate stepped out of the pantry, holding a

bag of flour. "Just making homemade pasta. Want to help?"

"No. I want to make a website and a logo and I need a client work order and—where are Lacey and Vivien?" She marched through the house. "Where's my new business team?"

"What's all this?" Vivien came down the stairs with Lacey behind her, both looking far too serious for this big news. "What are you talking about?"

"I did it, Viv! I found my client ı I'm starting my business and I'm not calling it Good Time Girl—"

"Cute name," Lacey said.

"If you're a hooker!" Tessa shot back, making them laugh. "It's Tessa Wylie Events. Can you do a website for me? Also some forms? And I want one of those logos—maybe a T and W intertwined with a—"

"Slow down!" Vivien exclaimed, laughing. "Start from the beginning. Who lit a fire under you?"

"You did." She pointed at Vivien, then turned to Kate. "And Dad. I know this happened because of him, I just know it."

"What happened?" Kate asked, joining them.

"Well, I met a man."

Kate huffed out a breath and rolled her eyes. "Of course you did."

"No, no, this is different."

But her sister just gave a dubious tilt to her head, and honestly? That hurt.

"Come on, Kate," Tessa said, taking the excitement out of her voice. "Give me a chance. Give me the benefit of the doubt. I'm done with men like that and this guy, who happens to live down the street, needs a party planner for a fifty-head event, dinner and cocktails, possibly music, in two weeks."

Vivien gasped. "Can you do that?"

Tessa looked from one to the other, her gaze landing on Lacey. "With a little help."

"I'm in," Lacey said without a nanosecond of hesitation, making Tessa instantly love the girl. "Who is this guy?"

She pulled out the card from her back pocket and finally read it. "Garrett John Fischer, no title. Company is Fischer Holdings. Some guy named Brian wants him to have a birthday party so he can close a Bank of Boston deal and I'm going to make that happen."

"The deal?" Kate asked on a laugh.

"The party," Tessa shot back. "And, hey, maybe the deal, too, if he pays me enough."

Kate's gaze softened, still too doubtful for Tessa, so she turned away and looked at Lacey.

"I'm meeting with him tomorrow. I'd love to show him a website, wow him with some...thing, and close the deal. I'll need a list of local caterers, rentals, florists, DJs, the works. I can do that if you work on something that will make me look...real. Can you do any of that and do you take compliments and gin for pay?"

Lacey threw her head back laughing. "Done and done!"

Vivien stepped closer, taking her hand. "I'm so happy for you."

"Well, I'll be happy when I get a check and a reference and four more clients. Then Tessa Wylie Events will be official. I just hope I can face a spreadsheet."

"I love spreadsheets!" Lacey said, her eyes bright.

Of course she did. "And I love you!" Tessa threw an arm around her. "How long are you staying, kid?"

She gave a questioning look toward Vivien. "How long am I staying, Mom?"

Vivien lifted a shoulder. "Lacey and I are in no hurry to get back to Atlanta," she said to Tessa. "You can count on both of us. In fact, one of the design shops I've been working with has a side rental business. I'll get you the number for tables and décor."

"Woo-hoo!" Tessa raised her hands, snapped her fingers, and did a happy dance. "We are in business now!"

But as she turned, she came face to face with her twin sister, who simply hadn't caught the fever at all.

"Hey, buzzkill, what's your problem?"

Kate didn't smile, but sighed. "Just be careful, Tess."

"I'm careful." She frowned. "Why? You think he's a serial killer?"

"No, but he could be...looking for more than a party."

"Yes, Kate, he could be. And I don't care because I don't want to go out with the guy, I want his business. Don't you think I can separate the two?"

"Of course you can," she said, but Tessa heard the note in her sister's voice. She heard the doubt, the protective and oh-so-wise twin sister who'd spent a lifetime reining in her wilder sibling and watching out for her.

But they were grown now, and Kate didn't have to protect Tessa or do her math homework or pick her up when a boy got too pushy at a party.

She loved Kate for all that, she truly did. But this time, she didn't need her sister to save her. She'd do it all on her own. Well, with Lacey, who loved spreadsheets.

Thank you, Dad. Thank you.

July 1, 1989

I love Destin!!! I have never had so much fun. I cannot—simply CAN NOT—ever go back to boring old Atlanta after knowing that Destin actually exists.

All we do is have fun, even on rainy days. Kate and Tessa are the best friends I ever had and I love them both so much. Last week we went to this cool beach camp and made matching friendship bracelets. Each one had three beads with the letters V, K, and T. Of course Crista cried her fool head off when we came home so now we have to make her a bracelet and put a C on it. As if she's one of us!

Okay, tonight. Mom and Dad and Aunt Jo Ellen and Uncle Artie went out to dinner with their friends, the Cavallaris. They are the people who own a little grocery store we always go to, and Mom and Aunt JE got to be really good friends with Mrs. Cavallari. Anyway, no babysitter since they put Eli and Peter in charge. We had so much fun!

Peter made a bonfire on the beach and brought his boombox down so we could sing and dance. Of course we were "Walkin' on Sunshine!" until Eli told us all to shut up. Crista fell asleep on a blanket and then we played this really fun game called "Never Have I Ever."

Everyone had to hold up ten fingers and drop one if they've done something weird or funny like gone someplace or eaten bizarre food. (Peter's had FROG'S LEGS – eww.)

Of course, the boys said gross things like "never have I ever made out with a girl" and Peter HAS DONE THAT. Anyway, we played that for a long time and laughed so hard my face hurt.

Mom and Dad got home really late and we were still on the beach. I thought they'd get mad but they were as silly as we were. Mom and Aunt Jo Ellen kept saying some weird word in Italian then howling with laughter and doing their Tri-Delt secret handshake. Mom is so cool down here in Destin. Nothing bothers her. Daddy has to go home to Atlanta tomorrow but we have two more months!!!

Love, Vivien

P.S. Never have I ever told anyone how cute PM is!!! I secretly like him a lot.

Chapter Twelve

Kate

From where she sat at the bonfire, Kate could see there was a PS at the end of that entry, but Vivien didn't read it out loud. She'd been selectively reading passages, probably saving herself—and all of them—from a little embarrassment.

But mostly, the diary entries brought back lovely, warm memories and non-stop laughter.

When she finished, Kate noticed that Eli was quiet, closing his eyes and not laughing with the others. No doubt because of the mention of their father, which seemed to make him withdrawn.

"Read more," Tessa insisted, maybe a little blind to that dynamic.

"I need a break from my exclamation points and capital letters." Vivien snapped the diary closed. "And I'm not sure I can bear another word written in pink glitter gel pen."

"Oh, to be able to write in pink glitter again." Tessa sighed and added a wink to Lacey. "Some things a girl shouldn't have to give up, you know?"

"Plus, Never Have I Ever?" Vivien rolled her eyes. "Embarrassing."

Eli leaned closer to the fire and used a long twig to stoke the flames. "As I recall, Never Have I Ever didn't get truly embarrassing until the later years."

From her lounging position on the sand, Kate regarded him, remembering one of those later-year games all too well—the one where, with the simple lowering of one finger, Eli outed himself for having a crush on someone in the circle.

And that someone she—and everyone else—knew, was Tessa, who hadn't even noticed Eli's admission. But Kate had noticed. She saw that index finger drop and, with it, her heart.

Silly game, but a tough memory.

Eli certainly didn't seem to be under her sister's spell at all now. He was cordial to her, of course, and laughed when she was around because her sister was surrounded by a cloud of fun that all mortals breathed in her space.

Kate shifted her glance from Eli to Tessa, who was in a high mood tonight. Fresh off a day of creating a website for an endeavor that didn't even exist when she woke up that morning, Tessa was humming with happiness.

And that, Kate decided, was a good thing. Her sister hadn't been happy, not truly happy, since Dad died. Mostly, she'd had that defeatist undercurrent that Kate always hated. Her mother could have that, too, and, in fact, sounded that way when Kate had talked to her earlier today.

"So now we know why we didn't get in trouble that night," Tessa mused, nursing the dregs of a gin and tonic.

"They'd been slamming down chianti with the Cavallaris."

"And we should have gotten in trouble," Eli said. "As I recall, we didn't have a permit for a bonfire and Artie Wylie was a rule-follower who did not take well to unpermitted bonfires." He grinned. "I always liked that about your dad," he added, glancing at Kate.

"Tessa's right," Kate said. "Every time they got together with those people—which was frequently—they came home tipsy. Mom and Aunt Maggie channeled their inner 'Tri-Delts at a Dawgs game' and that Betty Cavallari was an enabler."

Lacey choked. "Grandma Maggie got drunk? Not possible, nope. I won't believe it. She'd die of Southern lady shame."

"*Puh-lease.*" Tessa rolled her eyes. "I remember that night we got caught playing Never Have I Ever at the bonfire. They were so many sheets to the wind, they could have sailed out to sea. Who cares? They were young married couples who had a few pops with their closest friends. No harm in that."

"You *remember* that night?" Vivien asked. "I don't and I wrote the diary entry."

"Hey, no one forgets their first Never Have I Ever. In fact..." Tessa clapped her hands and looked around. "Who's up for a good round right now? But no fingers at our age—if you've done something, you take a drink like an adult."

"I don't hate that idea," Vivien said. "After all, we've

missed thirty years of details in each other's lives. What better way to fill us all in?"

Lacey made a face. "Not actually sure I want to play Never Have I Ever with my mother."

"She could say the same about playing with you," Tessa fired back. "Everyone remembers the rules, right?"

Eli, Vivien, and Kate laughed. "The truth, the whole truth, and nothing but the truth," they all said way too loudly.

Tessa pushed up. "Then I'm going to need a refill. A light one, of course. I have a new business to run."

"I got you." Eli stood faster, taking her cup. "Never have I ever trusted you with a bottle of gin and a bonfire."

"I'll help you," Kate said, standing. "I need to go in for a sec anyway."

She let the others think she had to go to the bathroom, but she really wanted a minute alone with Eli.

"Do you remember the Cavallaris?" she asked as they climbed the dune to the house.

"Sure," he said. "Betty and...Frank, right?"

"Yes! Frank Cavallari ran an Italian market—I remember I loved going into it and Mrs. Cavallari would give me green olives. She said I was the only little girl she knew who liked green olives. Tessa used to just stick them on the tips of her fingers and call them 'beauty shop rings' for reasons I will never know."

Laughing, he let her go ahead of him up the stairs to the main level. "Funny the things we remember from back then, right? The Cavallaris. I wonder if they still live around here—or still live at all."

"Well, that's what I wanted to talk to you about. We should talk to them." She paused at the top of the stairs, turning toward him. "They might know something."

He frowned but almost instantly, his eyes widened. "About what happened with our parents? Great thinking, Kate." His expression softened as he looked down at her. "Still the smartest girl in the room, as always."

She felt a soft blush rise to her cheeks at the compliment. "You'd have thought of it eventually," she said. "But you're right. They could be moved or...gone."

He opened the slider to the softly lit kitchen. "They were a little older than our parents, if I recall, so that puts them deep into their eighties."

"Still, it's worth a try to look them up," she said. "Although I know the Italian deli is gone because I searched for it already—longing for olives. That strip center is all different now, and there's a Starbucks where Cavallari's used to be. Sad, huh?"

"Ah, Destin, how you've changed." At the sink, he poured out the cups and refilled them with ice, thinking intently for a moment. "You know, I just remembered something."

"What's that?" she asked, lining up the cups that she'd neatly initialed with Sharpie when they first started cocktails.

"My parents saw Frank and Betty after you all left that last summer."

"They did?"

He nodded. "I remember those last few days pretty clearly," he said. "Your family left and...there was a lot of tension. A lot of conversation behind closed doors that I'm certain they didn't want us kids to hear. But I distinctly recall they went out again with the Cavallaris, so you are absolutely right. They could know what caused the fight."

"Yes, Maggie might have, you know, spilled some tea with Betty."

Eli laughed at the expression. "Which would be totally out of character," he said. "My mother doesn't 'spill tea'—literally or metaphorically."

"Well, we won't know until we try. Let's dig through the internet and get an address or phone number."

"Or obit," he deadpanned.

"If that's the case, so be it. But if either or both are alive and nearby, I'll go with you to see them."

He looked up from the drink he was pouring, his blue eyes as warm as his smile. "That would be awesome, Kate. I would really love to know what caused that falling out. Now more than ever."

She searched his face, wondering exactly what he meant. "Because you're still worried something might happen...legally? With this property?"

"Not really, but..." He sighed and held her gaze, looking right into her eyes. "I don't like that it hangs over us."

"Over...us?" Why did her throat catch at that?

"Over these two families' friendships," he said quickly. Maybe too quickly. "I mean, this time we've spent together is...great. Don't you think?"

She felt a smile pull. "Yes, I do. Beyond."

"Well, how sad to think that we can't hang out and share memories and...well, be friends just because our mothers are mad at each other. Like, how dumb is that?"

Not quite as dumb as how easily she was falling back into fifteen-year-old Kate Wylie with a crush the size of the Gulf on Eli Lawson. Not as dumb as the unwelcome and uncomfortable sensations that still tortured her when she was alone with him.

And really not as dumb as hoping he might feel the same.

Kate Wylie wasn't dumb. So she just nodded in agreement and took the last cup from his hand, careful that their fingers didn't touch.

"Speaking of dumb..." She lifted the drink. "G&Ts and Never Have I Ever, grown-up style. There's a recipe for disaster, huh?"

He just laughed. "And fun, Lady Katie. Plenty of fun."

She melted when he called her that, a nickname no one but Tessa still used.

On the way to the beach, she thought about the rules of the game—the truth, the whole truth, and nothing but the truth. And Kate, like her father, was a rule-follower.

She stared at Eli's back. Oh, boy. What had she gotten into?

She lifted her drink to her lips and took a generous gulp.

THE FIRST ROUND started off fairly harmless—never have I ever been to Greece, seen a World Series Game, forgotten a sibling's birthday, broken a bone. They laughed, shared a few tales of their lives, and took plenty of sips.

Then it got slightly more personal and deep—never have I ever lied to a boss, caused a car accident, smoked a joint. That one caused a stir when Kate was the only one who didn't take a drink.

At the friendly teasing about her provincial lifestyle and how she'd hardly had to take a drink in the game so far, Kate shrugged.

"What can I say? As you all love to point out, I've lived an unexciting existence in the science lab."

"Unlike you, Tessa," Lacey said, giving her a friendly jab. "Your life is wild."

"Just...interesting. But we'll get her to take a drink, you'll see." Tessa lifted a brow, a challenge in her expression. "We just have to get more specific and personal in the next round."

Kate gave a nervous laugh and Vivien leaned in, clapping her hands lightly.

"Okay, okay, it's my turn." She looked around, zeroing in on Tessa. "Never have I ever let a random group of guys drive me to McDonald's at three in the morning."

Tessa hooted and lifted her glass. "They were harmless young gentlemen from Spring Hill College in Mobile, Alabama, and I was already out of high school that summer. And, whoa, the French fries were good."

No one else drank for the three a.m. drive to McDonald's, only Tessa.

"My turn," Kate said. "Never have I ever..." She looked around the group, settling on Vivien and a very distinct memory that would make her laugh. "Set my hair on fire on the Fourth of July."

Vivien shrieked. "I forgot about that!"

"The wayward sparkler!" all three women shouted at the same time, then howled with laughter, making Eli and Lacey exchange looks at not being in on the joke.

"I literally had to wear a hat until the end of August." Vivien sighed and sent a toast to Kate before taking a sip. "Good times, Kate. Good times."

"And still Kate is clean," Eli noted, smiling at her. "We must have *something* on you."

"Well, it's your turn, Eli," Tessa said. "Give it all you got to get her to take a drink."

He frowned, looking at Kate with just enough intention that her whole body betrayed her and made her feel like she'd had a drink even if she hadn't.

"Well, I never did know which one of you did this," he said. "Never have I ever broken a boogie board in half."

For a moment, no one moved. Then Vivien slowly lifted her cup and winced. "Sorry about that. I was trying to do a front flip, and I was still mad that clown you hung around with named Dustin broke mine the summer before."

"*You* did it?" he choked. "My own sister?"

She looked at him over the rim of her cup, her eyes dancing. "It's your turn, Tess."

She situated herself on the blanket, pinning her gaze on Kate, her eyes glowing gold in the firelight. Completely unrelated to the game, Kate was struck for the zillionth time in her life how gorgeous her sister was.

"Never have I ever had a crush on someone around this bonfire."

Tessa's statement was like a gauntlet thrown into those very flames, and a bit of a shock, especially when Kate had just been thinking about how beautiful her sister was. That wasn't...beautiful.

But it was Eli who lifted his Solo cup, a look of wry resignation on his face. Kate knew she didn't have to take a drink—neither of these two women would out her. Would they? For a long moment, she didn't move, just held her sister's gaze.

And after a lifetime of knowing each other's every expression, she could see what Tessa was doing.

Let him know, Tessa's gaze said. *It's your turn, Kate.*

For some reason, that sisterly encouragement touched her. She knew exactly what Tessa was doing and she loved her sister for that sweet nudge.

Tessa was right. Kate should let him know.

She glanced at Eli, who looked a little sheepish at his crush admission, which wasn't a surprise to anyone except maybe Lacey, who was quiet during the whole thing.

Silently, she lifted her cup and took a drink.

"Finally!" Tessa whispered under her breath.

"She drinks!" Vivien clapped.

Lacey laughed, probably having no idea of the tiny little drama unfolding.

But Eli looked at her with a sense of surprise and wonder in his eyes, confirming that before this very moment, he really had no idea how she'd felt all those years ago.

The game wound down not long after that, and they cleaned up from the fire. The four women took all the blankets and cups and bonfire paraphernalia back to the house to store it in the garage. While they did, Eli stayed on the beach to put out the fire and shovel the sand back into the pit, because that's what responsible firepit makers did, Kate thought with a smile.

"We're going to bed," Tessa said as Vivien turned out all the lights but the kitchen. Then she leaned over the counter. "You can stay here, though." She glanced toward the beach and flicked a brow. "I'm sure Eli wouldn't mind."

Kate gave a fake dirty look. "Go to bed, you little troublemaker."

"Hah! That's the thanks I get."

Kate blew her a kiss and continued to slowly wipe down the counter that was already well and truly clean, waiting until Eli came up the stairs.

"I appreciate all you do to keep this kitchen looking brand new," Eli said as he walked in and closed the sliding door behind him.

"As the resident cook while I vacation here, I feel like it's my responsibility."

He didn't respond, but walked around the island and pulled out the trash container, dropping in some paper towels and used matches. The whole time, he had his eyes on her, and she just looked right back at him, the undercurrent of unspoken words humming between them.

"So," he finally said, taking a clean plastic cup from the stack they all used, filling it with water from the fridge. "You had a crush, huh?"

He wasn't wasting any time, was he. She leaned against the counter and crossed her arms, smiling at him.

"Little one, yeah." She exhaled the confession, weirdly nervous and inexplicably excited to finally have this conversation. No surprise there—Eli Lawson had always defied logic for her. Nothing about her feelings for him then—or now—made sense.

A slow smile pulled on his face, instantly reaching his eyes and somehow making them even bluer in the dim kitchen light. "I'm flattered."

"Well, we were kids."

"Not at the end," he said. "I was twenty-one and you were eighteen."

"When it started, we were kids," she clarified.

"When did it start?"

She gave a soft laugh. "Are we still playing the game of truth-telling? If yes, it started...day one."

He chuckled as he regarded her. "And when it ended?"

She considered saying it hadn't, but there had to be a limit to these admissions.

"When Destin ended," she told him instead.

"Really? The whole time?"

She lifted a shoulder. "Don't embarrass me."

"I'm the one who's embarrassed," he said. "Clueless-ness will do that to you. I'm just...wow. Why didn't you tell me? Why didn't someone?"

"Because you couldn't take your eyes off my sister," she said flatly.

His smile faded and he exhaled, putting the cup on the counter. "Kate, I'm sorry." The apology was simple, direct, and stunningly sincere.

"Why? For what?" She gave a soft laugh. "You're a human male and she was—*is*—Tessa. No need to apolo-gize for anything. She's captivating. Always has been and always will be."

"She was a distraction," he said. "And that was my mistake." He crossed his arms and looked hard at her. "Fact is, I had my eye on the wrong Wylie girl."

Heat crawled up her chest, prickling her skin. "Well, this is ancient history, Eli," she said, trying to sound as light as they all did down at the bonfire. "There are no hard feelings."

"But are there...feelings of any kind?"

The question made her feel like swaying a little. Was he asking her if she had feelings *now*? For a moment, she couldn't think straight. But wasn't it always that way around Eli? The woman who did nothing but think straight simply...couldn't.

No one else had *ever* made her feel that way, she real-ized on a sharp breath. No one, not her whole life.

Certainly not Jeffrey, who'd been a rational, safe, practical choice for a husband. No passion, no swaying—just good old-fashioned friendship and that hadn't been enough to sustain a marriage.

With Eli? All feelings, and not a nanoparticle of common sense.

"I will say..." she whispered, choosing every word with the same care she'd use when mixing two volatile substances. Except in the lab, she'd have protection on her eyes and hands. She needed something for her heart right now as she powered through this particular experiment.

"What's that?" he urged.

She finally looked him right in the eyes. "That I have thought about you a lot over the years."

"You have?" He took a step closer. "That's—"

A loud knock on the door made them both startle.

"What the heck? It's almost midnight." He glanced over his shoulder toward the door, then held up a finger. "Don't move, okay? We need to...finish this."

Or start it, she thought, realizing just how hard her heart was slamming against her ribs.

He left the kitchen and walked around the wall that blocked the entryway just as someone banged on the door again.

"Dad? Dad? Are you home?"

Dad? She heard the latch unlock, not sure she'd heard right. Whose Dad—

"Good heavens, Jonah! What are you doing here?"

Jonah? Eli's *son*? Kate took a few steps around the

corner, catching sight of a tall young man with long hair and handsome features.

"I can't believe you're here!" Eli's arms were already outstretched toward the other man. "I'm speechless."

His son gave a wistful smile and hugged him, closing his eyes in a way that made Kate think the embrace meant more than Jonah wanted to admit. "Hey, you invited me, remember? Pinned the location and everything."

He tried to sound cavalier, but the hug had given him away. This visit meant something. She didn't know enough about him to understand, but her maternal sense told her this was very, very important.

Far more important than that playful conversation in the kitchen. So Jonah had either saved her from a tender admission of feelings...or wrecked the moment she'd been dreaming about most of her life.

Oh, well. They'd pick up that conversation again. She hoped.

Chapter Thirteen

Eli

In the distance, Eli heard rushed footsteps and voices, but the thump of his own heartbeat drowned it all out.

"Who's here, Eli?"

"Everything okay, Uncle Eli?"

"Do we have another squatter?"

At the cascade of concern, Eli drew back from the embrace, but it wasn't easy to let go. He'd hardly seen this boy for the last several years and all he wanted to do was hold him, gaze skyward, and thank God for this moment.

"It's Jonah!" he called out with maybe a little too much enthusiasm, since his son flinched at the over-the-top announcement.

"*Jonah?*" Vivien came rushing to the entryway, her hair up, pajamas on already. "I don't believe it!"

"Hey, Aunt Viv," he said with that sheepish smile that gave the impression he knew he was kind of a big deal in the family. He always had a bit of celebrity status in the Lawson clan for no reason except he was tall, great-looking, funny, opinionated, and the kind of person who attracts attention without trying.

"I can't believe you're here!" She came closer and reached for a hug, which he gave like a dutiful nephew, then looked over her to see Lacey next in line.

"Hey, Spacey."

She laughed at the childhood nickname he'd given to his little cousin years ago. "This is a surprise!" She took her hug next, flattening her hands on his face and staring at him. "Dude, I haven't seen you since I graduated from college. Maybe it was high school."

He nodded, silently acknowledging his absence from the family.

"I had no idea you were here," he said. "I might have stayed away," he added, giving her shoulder a playful poke. Then the smile faded, and he glanced past her. "I don't think I can handle it if Miss Perfection is here, though."

"Meredith's in Atlanta," Eli said quietly, then gestured to Tessa and Kate, tamping down a shot of regret that he had to end that oh-so-stimulating conversation in the kitchen. But everything—old crushes, new feelings, and life in general—took a back seat to Jonah's unexpected arrival. "This is Kate and Tessa Wylie, old family friends."

He shook their hands and greeted them with just enough interest and class that pride rose in Eli—he hadn't raised a complete loser. Just a lost soul who'd come home.

"Come on in, come on in," Eli said, bringing him into the main living area, then glancing through the front window to see a van bathed in a floodlight. The filthy vehicle looked like it had two hundred thousand miles and a few wrecks on it.

"Did you *drive* from San Diego?" Eli asked, incredulous.

"Of course. Have wheels, will travel. I slept a little on the way, but..." He looked around at the dimly lit house and let out a whistle. "This is a pretty sick set-up. You built this place, Dad?"

"I designed it, yes," he said with another swell of pride. It was a small comment, but it might have been the most interest Jonah had ever shown in any of Eli's projects in a dozen years.

They gathered in the kitchen, with Vivien explaining that the sofa in the living room was strictly for looks, which made Jonah laugh.

Eli poured him a soda, Kate made him a sandwich, and Vivien fussed over him like a good aunt. Somehow, he managed to get the explanation of what they were all doing at the house.

Through it all, Eli didn't say much but just let his heart beat with an unexpected joy at the sight of his son.

Jonah didn't offer a ton in the way of information— did he ever?— just said he got the location pin that Eli had sent and was ready for a break from Southern California, so here he was, following the jet stream and a whim.

"You just go where the wind sends you, huh?" Tessa asked, leaning on the counter, clearly amused by this new arrival. "I can certainly relate to that."

He studied her, then looked at Kate. "Wylie?" he frowned, not answering Tessa's original question. "Why is there something in my memory that says...that's a name that isn't spoken?"

They all shared a quick look, silent.

"Ancient history," Eli said, his gut tightening a little because everyone knew the Wylies were "off limits"—yet there he'd been, a minute from confessing feelings for Kate. Could that history come back to haunt him?

He couldn't think about it now. He had to concentrate on Jonah, who still looked confused.

"So, what's the deal? Grudge match? Family feud? What are we playing here?" Jonah asked, lifting up the diner-quality roast beef sandwich Kate had made with a look of overwhelming gratitude. "Thanks, Kate Whose Last Name Shall Not Be Said."

And even that joke gave Eli an uncomfortable feeling.

Kate laughed easily. "You're welcome. And you missed the games tonight," she said. "As far as we know, there are no grudges held on the Wylie side."

"And for us? Only by Grandma Maggie," Eli added.

"*Only?*" Jonah scoffed. "Trust me, no one wants to get on her bad side. The woman scares the daylights out of me, personally."

"You?" Lacey rolled her eyes. "You can do no wrong in Grandma Maggie's eyes. You *always* get more money at Christmas than Meredith or me. You're her favorite by a long shot. Well, besides Nolie, but she's seven."

"Probably not a favorite anymore," he murmured, sending another brief silence over the group.

"We'll have to figure out where you're going to sleep," Kate said, breaking it with something less personal. "You must be exhausted."

"Fried. I sleep in my van."

"No, no," Eli said. "There are two empty bedrooms downstairs. You'll be more comfortable inside."

"Great, I have an air mattress," he said, obviously not bothered by the idea of camping anywhere.

"Then let me help you get set up," Eli offered. "We can scare up some sheets and towels."

"I'm self-contained, Dad, but anything clean would be a luxury." He looked around the room again. "Which seems to be the operative word in this crib."

After a few more minutes, everyone said goodnight again and Eli followed Jonah out to his van in the driveway. Inside, he was surprised by how neat it was, and set up for actual living. A small slab for a bed, a simple stove, fridge, storage, and a portable toilet. No shower, but Jonah explained that he stayed in campgrounds and truck stops, and...managed.

It sure seemed like a tough way to live, from Eli's perspective.

Inside, Jonah plugged in his air mattress and Eli went upstairs to get extra sheets and towels that Meredith had thoughtfully sent for backup when she learned they had more people at the house.

How, he wondered as he jogged back down the stairs, could two children turn out so differently?

He found Jonah sitting on the inflated mattress, dead center in the middle of the room, staring ahead. When Eli walked in, he looked up, a world of pain in his haunted hazel eyes. So much that Eli stopped dead in his tracks.

"Are you okay, son?"

He threaded his large fingers through his nearly shoulder-length hair, pulling it off his face.

"Aunt Vivien doesn't want you to sell this place," he said, the words making Eli shake his head a little—so unexpected and out of the blue.

"You think?" he asked.

"Oh, I can tell. She's always been easy to read, and she just coos about it when she talks. Every time you mention selling, her whole face changes."

Eli considered that, and the fact that his son was always more observant regarding people than anyone ever gave him credit for.

"You might be right," he said. "But she's here now and we're having our last hurrah, so to speak."

When Jonah didn't answer, he came into the room with the pile of sheets and clean towels, a bar of soap he'd grabbed from his bathroom sitting on top. "Not sure what you need, but—"

"Help," Jonah interjected softly. "I need help, Dad."

Eli practically folded on the floor, but managed to set the linens down and ease himself next to Jonah on the bouncy mattress, wanting to choose every word carefully.

"Are you in trouble, Jonah?"

He huffed out a breath. "I haven't been living in the van," he said. Again, the non sequitur threw Eli.

"Okay..."

"I've been living in an apartment in La Mesa, near San Diego State."

Eli blinked at this news. "Are you...in school again?"

"No," he said. "And that seems to be the problem."

Frowning, Eli didn't say anything, waiting with a breath caught in his chest.

"I can't hold a job, Dad. I've been fired from my last two line cook positions and, well, that's another problem."

"Maybe you just haven't found the right place," Eli said, surprised by Jonah's honesty, and wanting so badly not to blow this rare opportunity to connect. "What happened to cause...termination?"

"I can't follow rules." He scoffed. "Probably not news to you."

"Did you clock in late? Or miss work?"

"No, I committed the cardinal sin of a chain restaurant line cook—I tinkered with the recipe, which is, apparently, created in something holy and absolute called a *corporate test kitchen* and is not to be messed with."

"Did you ruin the food, or did someone get sick?" he asked, having a hard time understanding how this was a huge problem.

"No," he said with an eyeroll. "I added spices and twisted ingredients and changed the cook time and made garbage taste like delicious food."

Eli leaned back, laughing softly at how very Jonah that was. He did the same thing on the football field when he was young—changed the coach's plays and they always worked better.

But then Melissa died, and Jonah—a gifted high school quarterback who could have gone far—never walked onto the gridiron again.

"Well, it's their loss, son, and you'll find another place. You'll find a job or a—"

"I *have* found something," he said, turning to look Eli in the eye. "I found a woman I love."

"Oh." He eased back, once again shocked by words he wasn't expecting. "That's awesome, Jonah."

He nodded, the first smile since they'd walked in the room lifting his lips.

"Her name's Carly," he said. "Carly Danes. She's twenty-nine and is the manager of a restaurant—not either of the two I got fired from," he added. "She's a graduate of San Diego State's hospitality management program and really smart and so beautiful and fun and amazing and...pregnant."

"What?" Eli gasped the word, not sure he'd heard right.

"Yep. Imma be a daddy." He slid Eli a wry look. "File that under things you thought you'd never hear."

"Jonah." He covered his mouth with one hand, trying not to smile or let his jaw drop and hit the floor or anything. "That's...awesome. And terrifying, I know, but really." He couldn't hide the smile any longer and put his hand on Jonah's back, fighting the urge to hug the life out of him and cheer. "A baby! That's...wow."

Please, God, please say they're getting married. Eli managed to hold that thought in, though.

Jonah sighed. "There's only one problem. She kicked me out of our apartment in La Mesa. She says I'm too unstable to be in the baby's life and she thinks it's better to have a kid alone, at least until I get my act together."

"Oh, man." Eli dug his hand into his hair, vaguely aware that he was mirroring Jonah's gesture—a move they both made in moments of great stress. And this surely was. "How far along?"

"Seven and a half months." Jonah grimaced. "But that little nug is real to me."

Eli's heart nearly crumpled at the words. "So, what do you think's going to happen, son?"

"I don't know. But I know this—she's right. She's right about everything, which is why I love her, but she's dead-on about me. I'm in no position to be a father and I...I... I'm scared that I'll never figure it out." He groaned and turned back to Eli. "So when she booted me, I got in the van, drove east and came to the only person on the planet who can help me figure out what to do."

Of all the astonishing statements his son had made tonight—including the news that Eli was going to be a grandfather—that last one? That took the cake, answered all prayers, and nearly brought Eli to his knees.

Jonah needed him? Respected him? Wanted *help* from him?

Then he would get it, and more.

"Is this something you want to keep between us?" he asked.

Jonah looked at him, thinking. "I don't care if people know, Dad, but I don't want to talk about it in great detail with strangers." He gestured toward the upstairs, presumably meaning Kate and Tessa.

"What about Meredith?" Eli asked.

Jonah rolled his eyes. "Miss Perfection?"

"Your sister loves you," Eli said. "She cares deeply about you. But I won't say anything—"

"It's fine, Dad. I'm not ashamed of the baby. I don't consider it a mistake. I love Carly and I want to raise this kid with her, but I have to..." He moaned like he was in physical pain. "I don't even know what I have to do. Grow up really fast, I guess. Get my act together and do all kinds of things I've been avoiding."

"Oh, Jonah." Eli dropped his guard, no longer caring about saying or doing the right thing. In one move, he wrapped both arms around Jonah and gave him another bear hug.

"I'm scared, Dad," he whispered.

"You came to the right place, son," Jonah said through a thick throat. "I'll help you. Whatever you need. If you want to figure out what's next and how to do life, I am here for you."

Jonah's shoulders shook with a nearly imperceptible sob. "I don't want to lose her or my kid, Dad. I want them both so bad. I can't lose them. I'm scared. I've never been so scared—of losing them or, if I don't, that I won't be a good father."

"Don't be afraid," he said, saying the words he personally knew appeared three hundred and sixty-five times in the Bible for a reason. "You're going to be fine, I promise."

He had no earthly idea how he'd keep that promise. But it wasn't in his hands.

Closing his eyes, he did exactly what Jonah had done —cried out to his Father for help. It would come, Eli thought. His Father never let him down—and Eli wouldn't let his own son down, either.

FINISHING up an early morning meeting at the contractor's office, Eli was still mulling over Jonah's situation as walked to his truck. He moved quickly because it was past nine and he wanted to get home before Jonah got up and did something totally *Jonah-ish* and mysteriously disappeared. Just as he backed out, his cell rang with a call from Peter McCarthy.

Well, it was about time, Eli thought as he reached for the dashboard speaker. He and Pete had seen each other a few times since he'd been working on this project, but, per Maggie's parameters, Eli had been vague about what had brought him to Destin.

The facts were "public"—at least within the family— now. And Pete, as a part of all the seven summers they'd spent in the cottage, qualified as family, in Eli's mind.

It had been at least two months since they last hung out, and Pete hadn't even answered Eli's text telling him that he and Vivien had come down and that Tessa and Kate showed up.

"Hey, man," Eli said with a warm laugh in his voice. "Been a while."

"I haven't been ignoring your messages," Pete assured him. "I've been head down on an investigation."

"Did you get the bad guy?" he asked, always fascinated by Pete's job as a detective for the Pensacola Police Department. It was way cooler than being an architect, and a little more dangerous, too.

"I always get the bad guy, although in this case, it was the bad wife."

"Eesh." Eli grimaced. "That sounds...not good."

"Good now that she's in custody," he said with a cool laugh. "But I finally have a little time. So what's this in your text about Vivien and the Wylie girls? They're all in Destin?"

"Not just in Destin, but on the very same beach," Eli said. "What I didn't tell you for arcane legal and family reasons is that the project I've been working on is a complete rebuild of the old house where we spent all those summers."

"No way! Are you *kidding* me?"

"Long story, but the gang's all there," he said, pulling into traffic. "Also some kids, since my son showed up unexpectedly last night and Vivien's daughter's here. How about you come over one of these days? I know they'd all like to see you."

"The same place? On the beach? I can be there tomorrow night."

"That's awesome, man. It's not exactly the same, though. We have room if you want to stay a few days and soak up the beach. Might have to sleep on the floor, though."

He chuckled. "Not the bunk beds in the Florida room?" he joked.

"The Florida room is long gone." But they had great memories of being the only two summer residents who hadn't had a bedroom. They'd had some great memories in that room along the back that wasn't much more than an enclosed screened-in porch.

"Well, I don't do floors at fifty-three," Peter said. "And I'll have to get back for work. But I can be there around four tomorrow. Will that work?"

"Perfectly."

They finalized the plans, and Eli was smiling when he pulled into the driveway at nine-thirty. Certain Jonah was still asleep, he jogged up to the front door and pushed it open, not surprised to smell something amazing wafting from the kitchen.

Kate was up to her culinary tricks.

But he was surprised by the loud burst of laughter—male laughter that was definitely Jonah. He was *up*?

"Gruyere!" Jonah exclaimed. "Gruyere makes the world go round."

Eli took a few steps into the entryway, coming around the privacy wall to take in the scene, unnoticed by the others. Tessa and Lacey were sitting closely at the dining room table, hunched over a laptop, deep in discussion. Vivien was on the living room floor, surrounded by what looked like fifty patches of fabric.

And Kate and Jonah were both in aprons—where did

those come from?—in the kitchen, cooking. Jonah was at the stove, sliding something around in a pan with the finesse of an Iron Chef, while Kate stood next to him waving a bottle in the air.

"Found the truffle oil!" she sang.

"That's what I'm talkin' about, Katherine the Great!"

Katherine? He already knew her real name?

"I don't care if we're camping in an unfurnished house," Jonah said, taking the bottle.

"Almost furnished!" Vivien called out.

"Truffle oil is the essence of surprise that every dish needs." Jonah drizzled some oil over the pan. "*Voilà!*"

"Just put it in now while the oven's hot," Kate said, whipping off her glasses and tossing them on the counter, where she'd surely forget she'd left them.

Opening the oven door, she took a deep whiff of whatever he was sliding onto the rack.

"Jonah! You're a genius! That looks perfect. And the chives? Brilliant." She added a chef's kiss.

He bowed—seriously—and made a formal flip of thanks with his hand. "A team effort, my lady." When he straightened, he grinned at her. "And to think I was fired from my last job for climbing out of the culinary box. I should—" He whipped around, just then noticing Eli. "Oh, hey, Dad. Just in time for a gruyere frittata in truffle oil dusted with sea salt and served with..."

"Arugula salad with segmented oranges and a drizzle of honey lemon vinaigrette," Kate said.

"That." Jonah grinned. "Want some?"

"More than my next breath," Eli said, dropping his

keys on the counter and dividing his gaze between Kate, who looked bright and beautiful that morning, and Jonah, who looked...blissful.

Had he ever seen his son so...playful? Probably not in fifteen years, he thought with a silent gasp.

"This lady is a beast!" Jonah said, placing a casual arm around Kate. "Dr. Chef, Katherine the Great, the mad scientist of the Summer House."

He even had the house name correct.

Eli just laughed, not even having words to respond to this. Clearly, they'd been getting to know each other.

"Hey, Eli, give me your male opinion on this color palette for the upstairs suites," Vivien said, waving a fabric swatch. "Men do sometimes buy houses."

He turned to her, but his gaze was snagged by Lacey and Tessa, both whispering madly, punctuated by laughter.

"You, kid, have got it going on!" Tessa gave a high-five to Lacey. "Why are you not my daughter?"

"Because she's mine," Vivien called out in warning, looking up with a scowl. "You can't have her, Tessa Wylie."

Tessa threw her arm around Lacey. "She's mine now, he he heeeh," she teased, giving a bad impression of a villainous laugh.

For a moment, Eli stood stone still, dead center in the middle of it all, soaking up the sensation of...family. Of love and support and good times and relaxation.

It felt exactly like the old house in Destin, when the Lawsons and the Wylies would make a meal or play a board game or just co-exist in utter peace as the summer months and the Gulf waves rolled by.

The realization hit him in the gut, in the old memory bank, in the heart. He'd been so right about getting Jonah here for the magic of Destin. There was something about this place that changed people—whether the physical structure was a tumble-down beach house or a mansion.

It was sacred ground with an aura of goodness in every corner—and *that* was something no architect could build or design.

"Hey." Vivien snapped her fingers. "Earth to Eli. I need an opinion."

"Oh, sure." He walked to where she sat on the living room floor. "You know I'm no expert in color."

She widened her eyes as if to say this was not about colors. Flicking her fingers to beckon him closer, she whispered, "Jonah seems really good, Eli. Did he tell you what's going on?"

"Yeah." He inched back. "Did he tell you?"

She shook her head. "Nothing specific. But he's not... a mess. Is he?"

"Just a little," Eli said, knowing his whole family was stymied by the enigma that was Jonah. "I'll fill you in later."

"Okay. How was your morning?"

"Excellent. And guess who's coming for dinner tomorrow night."

"I have no idea."

He gave her a playful look. "Peter McCarthy."

"Really?" He could have sworn her color deepened ever so slightly. "Wow, I haven't seen him in thirty years."

"He's single, you know."

She whipped a small fabric swatch at his ankles. "Shut up."

"Still a good-lookin' guy."

"Stop it." More ankle whipping.

"And I will say that I haven't heard from him in weeks, but five minutes after he finds out you're in town? Bam. He's making dinner plans."

She narrowed her eyes. "If you say one embarrassing word you will regret it, Eli Lawson." The glint in her eyes said she was teasing. Then she slid her gaze to Tessa at the table. *Maybe* she was teasing. But she *could* blackmail him with those stupid diaries of hers.

"Don't worry," he said. "Your childhood crush secret's safe with me."

"It better be."

"Frittata is up!" Jonah called. "Come and get it."

Eli turned to the kitchen to see Kate taking a chef's taste on the edge of a spoon, her eyes flashing. "Oh, my... Jonah! You are the best!"

His son beamed at the compliment and suddenly Eli was rocked by a moment of déjà vu, seeing a ten-year-old Jonah running off the pee wee football field after throwing the game-winning touchdown.

Melissa was screaming, arms in the air, cheering for her boy.

Jonah! You are the best!

And Jonah, young and innocent and unaware that

he'd lose his mother just five years later, tossed his helmet in the air and threw both arms around her and hooted with joy.

"Dad?" Jonah asked.

"Eli?" Kate looked just as uncertain. "Are you okay?"

He looked from Kate to Jonah and nearly swayed on his feet at the impact of that unwelcome but beloved memory.

"Yeah, yeah. Just hungry. I'll take that frittata, chefs."

Chapter Fourteen

Tessa

She'd have preferred a Starbucks or even a meeting at one of their homes, but Tessa drove to The Wine Bar off 98 to meet Garrett Fischer later that day at his request. As she stepped inside, she hoped this wasn't a mistake. It was not light, bright, or professional, but small, intimate, and smelled like oak barrels and lavender.

Whatever, she told herself. All that mattered was that she got this assignment and a fantastic reference she could put front and center on her new website.

The muted hum of conversation filled the room, punctuated by clinking glasses and the occasional burst of laughter rippling through a crowd that liked their lunch served with a flight of red or white. Although, in Destin, most of these people were on vacation and these weren't business lunchers.

But she was.

She paused in the small foyer, looking past the bar to the tables, smoothing the lapels of a linen blazer she'd dug up from the bowels of her suitcases. Lacey—that little angel—had insisted it be ironed.

212 Hope Holloway & Cecelia Scott

No surprise, the Summer House didn't have an iron.

But Kate, always great in the clutch, had packed a steamer, and Lacey made the jacket look tailored and professional. In fact, Lacey had sent Tessa off with a kiss on the cheek like an encouraging momma wishing her good luck on the first day of school.

Well, it was her first solo gig as an event planner with no corporate office to back her up. This had to go perfectly. No distractions. No charm offensive. No flirtation.

Just professionalism.

Scanning the room, she spotted Garrett sitting at a corner high-top table, engrossed in his phone. When he looked up and saw her, his face broke into an easy smile, and he stood, gesturing her closer.

"Tessa," he said warmly, extending a hand for a nice, professional shake. "Glad you could make it."

"Hello, Mr. Fischer," she replied, responding with her most firm grip. "Of course. I'm happy to get to work on this party."

She slid onto the stool across from him, setting her tablet on the table alongside her handbag. She'd commit everything to memory and hope she didn't need to use the tablet, but it helped to look professional.

Her eyes landed on the glass of rosé already waiting for her.

"I took the liberty," Garrett said with a glimmer in gray-blue eyes. "You seem like a sparkling rosé kind of woman."

Dang it—she was. But not today. Tessa gave him a polite smile. "Thank you, but I would have ordered a club soda."

"Then we'll just toast to the party, and I'll order one," he said, raising his glass of red wine, using his other hand to brush back some slightly too long hair, at least for a man his age. A cropped cut would be more attractive, but she wasn't here to give him a makeover.

"To an amazing night," he said.

Reluctantly, Tessa clinked her glass to his. "To a wonderful event," she said, keeping her tone crisp. She set the glass down without taking a sip, then leaned back. "So, let's talk about this party. Menu? Décor? Theme? Settings? Where do you want to start?"

"Maybe get to know you just a bit."

Oh, no, we don't.

"All you need to know is that I take my work seriously," she replied, meeting his gaze. "Just because it's a party doesn't mean it's all fun and games. I promise you an event that will go flawlessly and if it doesn't?" She lifted a brow. "You won't know that because I will fix it. You have my word."

A slow smile pulled, making him look a little better. Not that he wasn't a decent-looking guy. He reminded her of someone who might have been told by a woman in a bar that he looked like Brad Pitt and he'd been trying to live up to the compliment ever since.

He didn't quite make it, but A for effort.

"Let's start with your party goal, Mr. Fischer."

"Just Garrett," he corrected.

She nodded and made a mental note to call him... nothing. "I understand the event is to celebrate your birthday."

The minute she said it, she realized her mistake. His eyes flashed with a nanosecond of surprise.

"I didn't mention that to you," he said, and it wasn't a question. "How did you know?"

She wanted to lie. She wanted to make this easy on herself so much and say she'd done research on him and saw the date and had a hunch and...

Truth, Tessa. Always the truth.

She could hear the ethics professor whisper in her ear.

"I happened to be under your boardwalk while you were on the phone. I overheard you."

For a second, he just stared at her, and that look could have gone either way—from *get the heck out of here, you little eavesdropper,* to *wow, how clever you are.*

"What were you doing under my boardwalk?"

"Protecting my skin from the sun," she said, gesturing toward her face.

"Understandable with a complexion as beautiful as that," he said.

She wasn't sure if she was relieved—she hadn't been fired for eavesdropping—or on guard for the big flirt.

"What all did you hear?" he asked.

"Very little except that you are reluctant to have this party, but need to impress at least one guest. And I am not reluctant to coordinate an event that will impress *all* your guests."

His brows rose in surprise. "Far more than I expected from your average party planner."

"I'm not average."

"You can say that again," he lobbed back.

Darn it! They were flirting.

"So, give me an idea of what you see for an ideal evening," she said, deftly bringing the conversation back to where it belonged. "Then I'll figure out how to make it happen."

He studied her for a moment, and she braced herself for...*Oh, honey, my ideal evening ends with you...*

But he nodded. "I want something elegant, simple, and low-key. Why don't you describe that to me?"

Finally. The interview section of the meeting.

"Okay," she said, dragging out the word as she summoned her memories of a million Ritz-Carlton events. "I imagine a comfortable gathering hour, one small bar, mostly champagne and wine, maybe a signature cocktail."

"I like it," he muttered.

"Hand-passed hors d'oeuvres, of course," she added.

"Such as?" he asked, inching closer.

"We're on the beach," she said. "Let's keep a seafood theme. Maybe mini-lobster rolls on brioche buns or seared scallops on a crostini with a truffle oil drizzle." She recalled the banter in the kitchen that morning. "One of my favorite local chefs says truffle oil is the essence of life."

"Oh? Who's that?"

Dang. He would ask that. "An up-and-coming young culinary talent named Jonah Lawson," she said, getting a kick out of the moment and already looking forward to sharing it with Eli's son.

He nodded. "And you can make it all outdoors at the beach house?"

"Absolutely. We can hold the entire event on your patio deck, which looked like it could easily handle five round tables for ten and space for mingling over cocktails."

"It could."

"But only with acrylic chairs," she said, already picturing the setting. "White linen exclusively, and very understated floral centerpieces with a touch of coral and shells to bring in the sea."

"Perfect," he said, his eyes alight with interest on the topic, not her, giving her that boost of confidence she needed. "Keep going."

She nodded. "An elegant dinner with an understated dessert and absolutely no cake or singing."

He threw his head back and laughed. "Thank you, God, she gets it."

Encouraged, she continued. "Throw in some music—"

"Live?"

She made a face. "Might be too much. An excellent soft jazz playlist on what I'm going to guess is a state-of-the-art sound system."

He angled his head to acknowledge that, of course, there was one.

"And professional servers, candles everywhere, and picture-perfect weather," she added.

"Oh, is that all?"

"Well, if you're adventurous, you can end the night with fireworks on the beach, which would require a permit—and I know exactly how to get it."

He stared at her, nothing but admiration in his eyes. Admiration for her *work*. That was...new. "Can you do all that?"

"All but..." She laughed. "Oh, why not? The answer is yes, including the weather." She grinned. "It's March in Florida. How much of a gamble is that?"

He lifted his wine glass. "No gamble and no risk in hiring you. Tessa Wylie, you have the job."

She resisted the urge to give a victorious air punch, nodding once as if she'd fully expected that response. "Then I have one question."

"Budget?" he guessed.

"Oh, please, no." She flicked her finger, not remotely interested. "You don't have a budget."

He chuckled. "She knows me too well already. What is your question?"

"The name of your important guest." She'd learned a few other tricks at the Ritz and intended to use them. "It's possible to do a little research just so I know his—or her—very favorite dishes and drinks, and add that extra personal touch that will make this VIP feel very important indeed."

"Wow. That's…" He nodded, pure respect in his expression. "That's next level."

"That's what Tessa Wylie Events is known for—next-level service."

"Amazing," he said. "The man's name is Sai Gupta, and he is an executive vice president of the Bank of Boston. He has a winter home in Rosemary Beach and will be staying with me the night of the party. I need him to feel as comfortable as a king."

She opened the tablet and carefully tapped his name into the tablet, not wanting to misspell it while he watched. "Indian? We should take that into consideration with the menu."

"Yes and no. For one thing, he's quite cosmopolitan and has probably eaten in more Michelin-starred restaurants than we have. Moreover, I don't want him to feel singled out, nor would he want to be."

She made a mental note to add a few vegetarian items to the kitchen list, just in case. But she didn't say that—she hadn't been hired to challenge the client.

"All right, then. I think I have everything and we're on for March 31, correct? Isn't that the date you texted?"

"Yes." He took a slow sip of wine. "I can't believe my good fortune in finding you. I had no idea how I'd do this alone."

She searched his face, tempted to ask if there was a wife, a woman, a girlfriend…even an administrative assistant. Why was he alone? But if she asked, it would look like she cared, and she did not.

"We had good luck, great timing, and some help from above," she said.

His brows rose. "We did? How so?"

She smiled. "My guardian angel."

"Oh, I'm intrigued."

She held up her hands. "No details. This isn't about me, just your party."

He reached across the small table and put a hand on hers, the touch warm. She fought her instinct to snap her hand out from under his because it would be rude. But she didn't want to welcome him, either.

"You can relax, Tessa," he said. "I'm sure you're so used to men hitting on you that you have to put ten-foot walls around yourself. You're safe with me."

She felt her shoulders soften as she very slowly inched her hand away. "I'm only trying to make sure this event is a huge success, that you are a completely happy client, and that you give me a glowing reference for my website."

"I have no doubt all of that will happen. Can I see it?" He jutted his chin toward her tablet. "The website?"

"Oh, of course."

With true pride, she tapped the link and instantly the creamy linen background and rose-gold letters appeared. Thanks to Lacey's magic, the clean lines of the Tessa Wylie Events website they'd made and uploaded together was contemporary and crisp, simple, but utterly gorgeous.

"And to think this didn't exist yesterday," he said.

Swallowing, she lifted her gaze to meet his. "No, it didn't," she said very slowly. "How did you..."

"You're not the only one to do research on people, Tessa. Of course I looked you up. As far as I could tell, there is no Tessa Wylie Events, but you did work for the Ritz-Carlton."

Yikes. How much did he know? Who did he know? Those smarmy execs ran in tight circles, and with her luck and timing? It would turn out he was a frat bro of her former client and boss.

"I did, and recently left," she said, lifting her chin and refusing to cower from the truth. "I just started this business, and I happened to be—"

"Stop." He held up his hand. "I am a sucker for raw ambition, am inspired by entrepreneurs, and I always support new and independent businesses. You are exactly the right person for this job."

She didn't answer, searching his face, just a tiny bit lost in eyes the color of a stormy sky. Maybe he did look like Brad Pitt.

She tamped down the thought and smiled. "Thank you for trusting me to handle your party," Tessa said, her voice firm.

"The trust is mutual," he replied, standing when she did and offering his hand to shake. "I'll expect regular status reports," he added.

"Then you shall have them. Thank you again."

As she walked out of the wine bar into the sunshine, Tessa smiled to herself. Not just because she got the business. And not just because he hadn't flirted with her. But because he'd taken her one hundred percent seriously... and she'd delivered.

She glanced up to the sky and hoped her dad had been watching.

LATER THAT NIGHT, Tessa sat at the dining room table at the house, leaning back and dictating while Lacey tapped her laptop and pulled up floral samples and tablecloth options.

Already invaluable to Tessa, Lacey was not just adept on the computer, she had a good eye and a sharp brain.

"You're good at this job," Tessa said, always free with compliments when she liked someone this much. "You have a real sense for it."

"You think?" Lacey asked, a spark in her blue eyes. "Because, wow, this doesn't feel like work. I had no idea there was a whole business simply picking out flowers and place settings. What's more fun than planning a party using rich people's money?"

Tessa laughed, leaning forward. "It's fun until the napkins are missing, a server calls in sick, the shrimp isn't fresh, and the wrong wine shows up. The biggest thing you have to plan for is for something to go wrong. Because, trust me, it will."

"Maybe, but I don't mind stress," Lacey said. "In fact, I thrive on it. Every job I ever had was boring, nine-to-five, and the biggest challenge was changing the toner in the copy machine." She tipped her head. "And forgetting to send out change orders and getting yelled at by my dad."

Tessa made a face. "Yeah, that's boring and not fun. This is anything but. And if you think this guy's low-key birthday party is enjoyable to plan, you should see a black-tie wedding. With a crew, headsets, timing, staging, and, of course, a bridezilla. I don't know why, but oh, I loved the big weddings."

Actually, she did know why. Because Tessa was a "think on your feet" kind of girl, not a "think on the computer" type. But Lacey could be the secret weapon she needed to do both.

"You love weddings, but you never got married?"

Lacey's question made her laugh. "Direct, aren't you?"

"Curious," she said. "I didn't mean to..."

"No, it's fine. No wedding *pour moi*. But I don't see that as a flaw in my character. Or...maybe it is." She trilled a laugh. "Honestly, I simply never met the right guy."

"Did you try?"

Tessa thought about it, looking off as she remembered a few men over the years who seemed sincere in their feelings for her, who weren't just trying to get physical.

But something was always wrong with those men. They were...not good enough.

"You want to know the truth? My father was amazing. He was smart, funny, and loved me more than any guy ever could. No man could possibly live up to him, so..." She shrugged. "No man did."

Lacey sighed. "You're lucky to have had a dad like that. Mine is... He's not awful. But the way he left my mom with zero legit reason except he wasn't 'feeling it' anymore? And now he's 'feeling it' with another woman? Another designer?" She rolled her eyes. "Yeah, not Father of the Year material."

"Don't let that keep you from finding the right man." Tessa reached over and squeezed Lacey's hand. "You're too awesome to spend your life alone. Or changing copy toner for work."

Lacey smiled. "Thanks. And honestly, I'm having way too much fun to call this work."

Tessa eyed the younger woman, thinking about how frequently Vivien joked about Tessa stealing her daughter. And why wouldn't she? Vivien had a winner with this girl and Tessa...

Her heart dropped, but, out of habit and time, she ignored the sensation. The parenting ship had sailed, and she hadn't been on it.

When Lacey looked up, Tessa realized she was staring at her. "We make a good team," Tessa said to cover the beat of an awkward moment.

Lacey grinned. "Yeah, we do."

Out on the deck, a burst of laughter from Vivien, Kate, and Eli got their attention. The three of them were setting up new patio furniture and an outdoor dining table that had arrived that afternoon.

"So, who is this Peter guy coming over for dinner tomorrow night?" Lacey asked, forgetting her laptop screen to watch the exchange outside. "My mom has mentioned his name a few times."

"Peter? Oh, you should look in those diaries." Tessa

leaned in on a playful whisper. "There will be plenty of mentions, I'm sure. Vivien had a mongo crush on him during all those summers here."

"Mongo?" Lacey lifted a brow.

"Yes, mongo. I'm a child of the eighties and you get the idea."

Smiling, Lacey glanced out at her mother again, then back to Tessa. "Is this Peter a good guy?"

"I remember he was nice, which tells you absolutely nothing, I know," she acknowledged. "He and Eli were thick as thieves. They were boy besties, so Peter always came along like a family addition. Eli says he's a cop now, a detective. Divorced. Why? He's too old for you, you know."

Lacey snorted. "I was thinking of my mom."

Tessa chuckled, knowing that was exactly what Lacey was thinking. "Yeah? You think she's ready?"

"I think she needs to accept that my dad has moved on."

Tessa followed her gaze, regarding Vivien, who was such an attractive, easygoing, and talented woman. "She certainly deserves love."

"Like no one in the world."

Tessa got a little jealousy jolt, thinking how lucky Vivien was to have this loving daughter.

"Why don't we help things along with old Peter the cop?" Tessa suggested.

Lacey looked over the laptop screen at Tessa. "How can we make that happen?"

"Hmm." Tessa sat back, considering the challenge.

"First of all, we'll need to agree he meets our standards. So, let's have a code word. If he's up to par—and you are fully on board—then we'll have a code word like..." She looked around, her gaze landing on the water. "Turquoise."

"Turquoise?"

"Well, it can't be a word we know we'll use in casual conversation, but something we could slide in unnoticed." Tessa grinned. "A casual, 'My, the water looks turquoise,' or 'Lacey, did you order those turquoise tablecloths?' kind of thing."

She snorted a laugh. "Okay, turquoise it is, to agree he meets our standards. Then what?"

"Then we get them alone. Leave that to me."

Propping her elbows on the table, Lacey rested her chin on her knuckles and stared at Tessa. "Where have you been all these years?" she asked. "We've needed you in this family."

The compliment warmed her. "You know, I was just thinking that about you, kid. Consider me an auntie. I used to call your grandmother 'Aunt Maggie,' so it makes sense."

Lacey's eyes widened for a second.

"What?" Tessa asked. "Aunt Maggie is too much?"

"No, no, it's just that...she doesn't talk about the Wylies. Like, my mom and Uncle Eli cannot mention your family. Why do you think?"

"I don't know. Eli and Kate are mulling that over, but I honestly don't care. Past is past, you know. Let's move on and have fun, that's my motto."

Lacey nodded. "I hope she gets over it because I want to be friends with you forever."

"Aww." Tessa angled her head. "Sweet."

The smile was still on her face as they went back to work, returning to the party they were planning.

But as Lacey jotted notes, made suggestions, and found an absolute gem of a florist, a tendril of an idea tugged at Tessa's heart. No, Lacey couldn't be her daughter...but that didn't stop her from wishing.

July 22, 1989

Not to be, like, totally dramatic or anything, but it feels like my skin is five thousand degrees and it's all going to peel off and leave me looking like Freddy Krueger. Yes, I got sunburned. UGH. I had been sooo good about not getting fried all summer. I mean, I'm practically best friends with Coppertone, not the baby oil and iodine that Tessa uses to get the most beautiful tan. But yesterday, we were hanging out on the beach and I fell sound asleep. Big mistake.

Eli is being SUCH a jerk, as usual. He called me a lobster and "Tomato Face" like it was the funniest joke in the world. Newsflash: it wasn't. And Tessa noticed he was being mean, so take that, butthead. She said my pink skin "complements" my hair, which made me laugh, and that hurt my face. Kate promised it'll heal quickly and brought me an Advil from her mom. At least some people around here are decent.

Mom said I shouldn't go outside today even though it's a perfect beach day. Fine. Uncle Artie went to Blockbuster a couple nights ago, which was great since I was stuck inside like a loser.

I tried to watch The Goonies but got bored halfway through (why does everyone love that stupid movie?). Then I put on Ferris Bueller's Day Off (PG-13 but Uncle Artie said it was okay for us) and laughed until my sides hurt, which made me forget about my lobster legs for a while.

But then something really weird happened. I was lying on the couch with cold cloths on my arms and legs, feeling very sorry for myself, when Peter came in and sat down. That's not the weird part—I figured he wanted to watch the movie. I didn't mind (ha ha) but not just because he's so cute. He's so much nicer than Eli. Less dumb. Actually tolerable.

Anyway, he said I needed aloe vera for my sunburn. Duh, I know, but we didn't have any in the house. But then Peter got up and disappeared. Like, gone. I thought he went back to the beach, but about an hour later, he came back holding a bottle of that bright vera goo and said, "Here you go." Just like that.

And OH MY GOSH, it did help. I felt soooo much better.

When I asked where he got it, Peter said he walked to the drugstore a mile away. A MILE. In this heat. For me. That's when it hit me—Peter McCarthy is, like, genuinely kind. Every single person was on the beach today, but Peter noticed how miserable I was and walked a mile to help me feel better.

We decided to start Ferris Bueller from the beginning and watched the whole thing—Peter laughed so much. I really like his laugh. It sounds like those bells on an ice cream truck in the summer—a happy sound that you want to hear over and over again. And unlike Eli, he wasn't laughing AT me!

So now I'm upstairs listening to the mixtape Tessa made from the radio and I keep playing that new song "Lost in Your Eyes." Love Debbie Gibson!! Good thing Tessa and Kate aren't here to tease me about why I'm playing it.

But I can't stop singing it and thinking about Peter getting me that aloe vera.

When he smiled at me and handed me the bottle, I swear...I got lost in his eyes. They're dark, dark brown, like Hershey's chocolate syrup and he's just really sweet. And cute, I guess. But sweet mostly. Anyway, he's fifteen and would never notice a kid like me.

I hope I don't look like a lobster tomorrow. Or a tomato. Or a tomato-covered lobster. I'll wear a hat and sleeves!

Vivien

Chapter Fifteen
Vivien

Peter McCarthy's eyes, were, in fact, the color of Hershey's chocolate syrup, as only a twelve-year-old with a crush could describe them. Now, they were aged slightly by sun and laughter. And his laugh, which, Vivien had to admit, was deeper than the bells on an ice cream truck, but just as sweet.

A few minutes after he arrived at Summer House, Vivien's phone blew up with texts and voicemails from Ryan, forcing her to slip away while the others caught up and shared a cocktail.

Upstairs in her room, she dropped on the bed and stared at the phone. Whatever her almost-ex wanted, whatever was wrong, she would not be used, walked on, or taken advantage of. That determination would not waver, she swore.

With that vow in place, she tapped his name and the call button, only a little surprised when he answered on the first ring.

"Finally! I've been killing myself to reach you."

"I'm busy," she said dryly. "Still am, as a matter of fact, so what's wrong?"

"The Hoffmans," he said as if that meant something to her.

She had to think for a moment. "Miranda and Sam? In Johns Creek?" She closed her eyes and pictured the blueprints of a five-bedroom mid-century-meets-farmhouse estate home they'd contracted Ryan to build in Atlanta's ritziest area.

"The design went sideways."

She gave a quick laugh. "And that's my problem... why?"

"They took bad advice," he said, clearly not answering the question.

"Then bring Una Tatum in to save the day."

He was dead silent, and she knew why. Because he hired the woman to take her place and not because he was seeing her romantically? Nope.

She laughed again, getting a jolt of satisfaction. "Oh, *she* was the designer that took things sideways."

"It went a little too edgy for their tastes," he said. "I mean, it's gorgeous, but they wanted a little more, uh, classic. More your style, so I was hoping you'd meet with them at the house."

Well, if this wasn't the perfect test for her new backbone, she didn't know what was. "I'm sorry. I'm too busy to help."

"Come on, Viv," he said, his voice soft and, yes, a little sad. "This job is so in your wheelhouse. I wanted you on it from the beginning."

"But I'm *not* on it, Ryan. I'm doing my own work,

building Vivien Lawson Designs. I can't run back to Atlanta and get you out of hot water."

"I know you aren't here. And I know Lacey went flying to wherever you are and left me high and dry with no admin, and I probably deserve that bit of family desertion."

Probably? No doubt he considered those words contrite enough to qualify as an apology—and now he expected her to say yes. She stayed silent, listening to bursts of laughter coming up from downstairs, where she really wanted to be right now.

"They asked for you specifically," he said, sounding defeated. "Miranda is a fan of your work and...well, I think she thought it was a package deal when they picked us as the builder last year. So..."

"So tell her the package is getting divorced."

"Vivien, this is an important client, and I will pay you very, very well. Double your rate and they'll give you a glowing reference for your new website. Which is really nice, by the way."

She bit her lip. Double her rate was also nice, a glowing reference and images from that fantastic residence would be nicer, but...but...but...

She couldn't think of a reason to say no except to prove she could. Was that wise?

"I have to think about it," she said, fighting a grunt of disappointment. "It would be very hard for me to get up there and leave this job. I'm five hours away by car."

"What are you working on?" he asked, sounding genuinely interested.

"A beach house in Destin." And that was all she would say about it.

"How'd you get that?"

"Mad skills and close contacts," she quipped, standing up. "And I have to go, Ryan."

"Okay, but the Hoffmans will be at the house on Thursday morning. If you drive up Wednesday night, you could do the meeting and be back Thursday night in...Destin, is it? Where you used to go as a kid?"

She just sighed. "Yeah."

"Okay, well, I'll be waiting to hear," he said, not really that interested in Destin. "Thanks, Viv."

With that, he hung up and she took a minute to inhale deeply and try to figure out what was right. Maybe she'd talk to Lacey. But not now. Now, she wanted to spend time with Peter McCarthy and enjoy a beautiful evening with friends and family.

A few hours later, she'd almost forgotten about Ryan. With the new furniture set up, they ate al fresco on the deck in the waning light of the day, taking in the sights and sounds of the beach.

To Vivien, it felt very much like old times, when the Wylies and the Lawsons—and, of course, Peter—would eat on the small back porch of the house at a long picnic table after a day in the sun.

As they finished Kate and Jonah's best dinner yet— crab cakes and risotto—the words from the diary Vivien had peeked at last night kept echoing in her head. The entry was so childish she'd cringed reading it, but seeing

Peter right here, in person, it was like those long-ago hazy days were suddenly in sharp focus.

Truth was, if Vivien had bumped into this man on the street far from Destin, she might not have recognized him.

His hair, once a wild mess of sandy brown curls, was now streaked with silver, cropped close, and thinner than she remembered. His dark brown eyes were gentle and earnest, despite a low-key swagger he must have picked up when he'd done a stint in the military, or maybe as a cop.

He asked pointed questions, looked right at the person talking, and regaled them with plenty of stories about being a cop that had them all in stitches and awe.

She'd seen him once or twice over the years, the last being almost fifteen years ago at Melissa's funeral. They'd all been in mourning and shock over the death of Eli's wife, so she hadn't really talked to him.

But now she could see that the boy who had walked a mile for her had turned into an attractive man with a fascinating life and career.

"You know I can't tell you that," Peter said, his expression serious as he pointed at Jonah in response to a question about an investigation. Then he broke into that easy laugh. "Because I have no idea where that dude hid the murder weapon! But he didn't know that. I got the confession, and he got twenty to life."

As they reacted to that, he looked around the table and held up his hands. "Okay, enough cop talk. This meal was too amazing to sully with homicide investigations." He glanced at Vivien with interest. "You haven't told us about your business, Vivien. Interior design? Based on what I see here, you know what you're doing."

"Oh, this place is a work in progress, but it's a dream assignment, thanks to my brother." She beamed at Eli.

"I will say you two certainly get along better than you did back in the day."

Eli and Vivien laughed. "We only fought in the early years," she said. "As we got older, we learned to appreciate each other."

"And Crista?" he asked. "Your baby sister?"

The whole table cracked up and Peter looked a little lost at the joke.

"It's just that everyone here calls her that," Lacey explained. "I don't think of my Aunt Crista as a baby."

Tessa gave an exaggerated eyeroll. "That kid was the ultimate tag-along," she said, "so at this beach? She's still the baby sister."

"Remember the time she ran away and we had to find her?" Peter asked. "That guy who owned the deli found her way down on the end of the jetty pretending to be a mermaid."

"Frank Cavallari," Eli said, giving a look to Kate. "He and his wife still live around here."

"You looked him up?" Vivien asked.

"Kate and I wondered about them," he said. "I asked Meredith to do a little digging and all she could find was an address in Santa Rosa Beach, no phone number or cell listed. No obituary, either, which is nice, since they must be well into their eighties."

"Are you going to contact them?" Tessa asked.

Kate shrugged and she and Eli shared another look as if they'd talked about it. "We were hoping to call or email rather than just show up on their doorstep, so I don't know."

"They were nice people," Peter said. "They loved to party with your parents. And you know, I heard an old rumor that Frank Cavallari ran numbers from that deli."

"He did?" Eli blinked at him.

"What is 'running numbers'?" Lacey asked.

"Old school gambling," Peter said. "Wiped out by the internet."

They shared a few Cavallari memories as the dinner ended and the cleanup started while Eli, Peter, and Jonah went outside to check out the nearly finished boardwalk.

Lacey and Tessa were side by side at the sink, whispering, when Vivien playfully muscled her shoulder between them.

"You're determined to steal my daughter," she teased.

The two of them shared a look, then laughed.

"And why is that so funny?"

"Because Lacey has beautiful blue eyes. Almost... turquoise."

Lacey threw her head back and laughed. "As turquoise as that...flower arrangement we liked today?"

"Turquoise like..." Tessa looked past them, to the patio. "That horizon, which would be even nicer from the beach. Why don't you take a walk with Peter, Viv?"

She looked from one to the other, then back again, inching away. "What are you two up to?"

Kate came in from the pantry, smiling at them. "They want to set you up with Peter. Turquoise is their code word for 'he meets approval.'"

Lacey's jaw dropped as she gave an accusatory look at Tessa. "You told her?"

"She's my sister. No secrets. Well, not many."

But Vivien was the one sputtering. "Your approval? Set me up? What is this all about? Turquoise and... Peter?"

"Oh, *puh-lease*. Don't act like you never thought of it!" Tessa waved a little sponge shaped like a face.

"Not in the last thirty years," Vivien fired back.

"Not in the last thirty minutes?" Kate prodded more gently. "Because he's a sweet, successful, good-looking man and he's single."

Surprised at how hot her cheeks were, Vivien just shook her head. "I'm not going to make a fool of myself because some guy I liked as a teenager shows up."

"Mom." Lacey stepped away from the sink, coming closer. "He's nice and good-looking, I mean for fifty-something, and you guys have a history."

"First of all, the *history* is that he came on vacation with my brother. Not exactly an emotional connection. And second?" She narrowed her eyes at her daughter because she *knew* this. "The divorce isn't even final yet. I'm not single."

Lacey angled her head, sympathy in her baby blue—not turquoise—eyes. "But it's close. It'll be final in a month and, Mom, Dad's seeing someone."

"I don't know about that," she said. "He just informed

me he's throwing her off the Hoffman job and asking me to step in—at double my rate."

Lacey's jaw dropped. "They haven't been happy with her," she said. "I'm not totally surprised he needs your help."

Vivien felt a stab of guilt since she'd just about decided not to take the job—as much out of spite than not wanting to be used.

"Who cares?" Tessa interjected. "Revenge is sweet. And so is Peter. Personally, I think you should at least talk to him."

Vivien let out a long sigh of defeat and glanced out the sliders to see the three men on the boardwalk, laughing as the sun spilled into the Gulf behind them.

"Once," she said softly, "when my friends and family neglected me with a sunburn, Peter McCarthy walked one whole mile in the summer heat to get me aloe at the market."

"I remember that," Kate said.

"Me, too," Tessa said. "It launched your Debbie Gibson obsession." She shuddered. "So painful."

Vivien laughed, looking at these wonderful women— who did have a real history and emotional connection with her—and realized they only had her best interest at heart. Someday, she'd have to move on. But was that...today?

No. Yes. *Maybe.*

"I can't just go...ask him to walk with me."

Tessa snorted. "As if he wouldn't jump at the chance."

Would he?

"I'll go with you," Kate offered. "I always walk after dinner and Eli frequently comes with me. Let's go down together and tell them we're taking a walk."

"And I'll tell Jonah I need him back up here," Tessa said. "He's helping with the menu descriptions Garrett expects tomorrow. He had some awesome ideas."

After a beat, Lacey crossed her arms, looking more like a mother than a daughter. "Go. This is an order."

"Lacey..."

"Come on, Mom. What's the worst that could happen?"

Vivien stared at her and Tessa inched closer, fighting a smile.

"She'll get *lost...in his eyes*," she sang, cracking them up.

"You"—Vivien pointed at the sassy blonde—"shut it. And you." She turned her finger to Lacey. "Don't get your hopes up. And you." She pivoted to Kate. "Get your sneakers and let's go, uh..."—she gave a playful wiggle of her eyebrows—"talk to the boys."

SOMEHOW, with zero awkwardness and lots of laughs, Vivien found herself walking the beach with Peter, well behind Kate and Eli, who were marching like they had actual calories to burn or a place to go.

She and Peter, on the other hand, stopped and looked

at shells, took a few pictures of the sunset, and continued talking as they had before and during dinner.

"Amazing how this beach hasn't changed," he noted, staring out at the horizon as the sky deepened to twilight purple.

"Only in that direction." She gestured toward the houses, the harbor, and the town of Destin. "Big changes over there."

"But the beach is forever. And this one? It's one of the reasons I live in Florida."

She frowned, thinking of the life and career trajectory he'd mentioned. "I guess I thought you were in Pensacola because of the military. Isn't there a base there, too? Like Eglin is here?"

"The Naval Air Station is there, but I was in the Air Force and spent most of my time at Lackland, in Texas. Never went overseas or saw combat."

"What did you do?" she asked.

"From day one, I was on a law enforcement path. Got a base patrol position after about eighteen months and then I ended up in what they call Security Forces on bases. Basically a military cop. I loved Texas and I loved being in the Air Force. We were right outside San Antonio, and it was a great place to live."

"Why did you leave?"

He gave a wry tip of his head. "For love."

"Really? Your...wife?"

"Ex," he said with a sad sigh. "She did not want to be a military wife or raise military brats, so I got out. She wanted to live in Florida on the beach, and Pensacola seemed like the closest place to Texas that's still a Florida beach town. And it was the Panhandle, which had such good memories for me."

"The Destin summers," she said, knowing that's what he meant.

"Yep. I didn't have the greatest family up in Atlanta, as you might recall, so I wanted to come back to the place where I had...a real family."

"Ours?" For some reason, that surprised her.

"Absolutely. My parents were divorced—not sure if you remember that—and when I came here with the Lawsons and the Wylies, I could..." He slid her a sly, maybe even a sad, smile. "Pretend I was one of you."

"Oh, Peter. I don't think I really knew that."

He shrugged and bent over to pick up a broken shell, tossing it after a quick inspection. "I didn't talk about it much, and Eli's too much of a guy to share stuff like that. Anyway, I went through police training and got a job with the Pensacola force, and I've been there ever since."

"Raised your boys there," she said, remembering him talking about his sons, Cameron and Connor. "And is your ex-wife still there, too?"

"She is, but..." She heard the pain in his voice, sharp and clear.

"Bad divorce?" she guessed.

"Is there such a thing as a good divorce?" he asked, then his expression softened. "Eli mentioned you're in the throes of one now."

"Yeah," she said. "I am, sadly."

"I'm sorry. Mine was years ago and I still hate talking about it."

"Really?" Her heart dropped. "You mean it doesn't get easier?"

He shook his head and snagged another shell. "There's nothing about divorce that's easy, but I guess if I could go back and do things differently, I would."

"You'd try to work it out?" she guessed.

"No," he said on a dry laugh. "There was no working it out. But I would try not to..." He cringed. "Hate each other. Turns out, when marriage isn't forever, divorce is. If there's any advice I can give you, it's stay friends with your ex. Be civil, be nice, and make it easier on your daughter."

"Oh." She slowed her step, the words hitting hard in light of the conversation she'd had earlier than evening with Ryan.

"I'm sure you're at that point where it could go either way," he said, accurately interpreting her reaction.

"It could," she agreed, dragging out the word and standing still to process what he was saying. "But I'm really trying not to, you know, be a pushover."

"Big difference between being a pushover and being a good human being," he said. "I always hate the trip up there, but the view from the high road is better." He added a self-deprecating laugh. "Not that I took it when my marriage ended, which is why I'm offering this unsolicited advice. It will make it all better—not easier, but better—if you can remain on good terms."

Sighing softly, she closed her eyes because she knew

in her heart he was right. "He asked me for a favor earlier," she said. "And I thought I'd take a stand and say no."

"Yeah, I totally get that. But what feels good now might not serve you well in the future," he said, giving her a long look that had old pain openly on display.

"Hey, this is a walk!" Eli called, yanking them from the conversation as he and Kate came plowing back from the other direction. "Not a stand-around-and-chat. A walk!"

They both gave hollow laughs and simultaneous thumbs-up.

"We'll be right there," Vivien said as they headed toward the house. Then she turned back to Peter, looking up and seeing honesty and friendship and a man who'd given her good advice. "Thank you," she said. "I really needed to hear this tonight."

"Look, I don't know the soft underbelly of your marriage, Vivien, or how you think or what he's like or... anything really. But I'm an investigator, so I can read people pretty well. I think you might be confusing being kind with being weak. They're not the same."

"Oh." She reached for his arm. "You've always been very kind, Peter, and put other people first. Clearly, you haven't changed that much."

He smiled, then looked up when Eli whistled at them.

"Sir, yes, sir!" Peter called with a sharp salute, then he gave Vivien a friendly nudge. "Let's get back before we're on KP for violation of beach code."

Laughing, she jogged with him, ready to follow his advice.

Chapter Sixteen

Kate

"This was certainly not here thirty years ago," Kate said to Jonah as she looked around at what was once a quiet harbor with a handful of local seafood joints.

Not quiet anymore. Today, HarborWalk Village was a bustling hub packed with shops, restaurants, and street entertainment, its vibrant energy a stark contrast to the sleepy charm of the past.

They'd borrowed Tessa's car for today's errand, and as Jonah locked the door and slid the keys in his pocket, he grinned with the knowing look of a local.

"I found this place the other day. It's a tourist trap, of course, starting with a restaurant called Jimmy Buffet's Margaritaville—isn't that supposed to be in the Keys?— and ending with mini golf. But it's also home to a seafood shop that Reddit says has the best and freshest shrimp in town. Perfect for that Brazilian specialty you're teaching me tonight, Kate."

"I hope I can do my lab's cleaning lady justice," she mused.

"Just don't forget the coconut milk," he joked, the two

of them having discussed the recipe for way longer than necessary—but they'd bonded over food and enjoyed every minute of their "role" as the cooks of Summer House.

The walked together to the crowded wharf and dock, warmed by the sun and salty harbor air.

She frowned, getting her bearings from the past and spotting the distinctive roof of AJ's, which had been a new and very hot restaurant thirty years ago. But something was definitely missing. "Where's the magnolia tree?"

"Is that a shop?" Jonah asked.

"No, it's a literal tree and it was huge and right... there." She pointed to the dead center of the whole place where an information sign stood next to a brightly painted ceramic pelican. "There was a monstrous magnolia tree—probably the biggest landmark in Destin —right there, over a tiny wharf."

Walking up to it, Jonah bent over to read the plaque. "Yep. The magnolia tree died and was cut down twenty years ago. And in its place, I give you..." He gestured toward the blindingly teal and tangerine pelican. "Peli, the outrageously painted bird who stands as a beacon of progress."

She snorted, always amused by his mix of cynicism and humor. "Hey, your father took down a beach cottage jam-packed with memories and built a mini-mansion, so progress isn't always bad."

"Touché, Katherine the Great." He shook his long hair back and donned a pair of sunglasses. "Shall we brave the sea of *touristas* and find these legendary jumbo shrimp—the world's best oxymoron—sold at this harbor?"

"We shall."

Together, they walked down a set of steps, threading the crowds as they strolled among the shops and restaurants on either side of a wide wooden boardwalk. The harbor wafted briny air, putting her in the mood to buy fish.

The planning, shopping, and cooking had become a bit of a ritual over the past week. The days slid into happy evenings around the table, with the ad hoc "family" gathered to feast on whatever Kate and Jonah wanted to try that night.

For Kate, the break from life in the lab was beyond welcome. She'd had a few Zoom calls with her team at Cornell and, somehow, the testing of energy density and life cycle of large batteries was proceeding without her hands on the experiments.

She missed Matt and Emma terribly, and their pleas that they spend their spring break in Florida with her were starting to sound...possible.

Their break started at the end of next week and she certainly didn't expect to still be here...but she didn't want to leave.

And then there was the matter of her mother, who never sounded great when they talked.

The fact was, *life* beckoned Kate home to Ithaca, but she just didn't want to answer that call yet. She was having too much fun.

And a big part of that was this easy and unexpected friendship with Jonah Lawson.

The two of them had spent a good deal of time together over the past week, and he'd let his guard down just enough that Kate could see glimpses of the man he might be if life hadn't been so unkind and taken his mother when he was a teenager.

He was broody, sure, and his rough edges showed themselves in bursts of self-effacing humor or sarcastic comments. But when he was in the kitchen with her, experimenting with spices or slicing vegetables with a practiced hand, he seemed at ease.

Eli had filled her in on Jonah's situation—the cross-country drive, the van, the girlfriend, the baby. They all knew, but no one had really brought it up or put him on the spot. As they walked, she decided it was as good a time as any to see if he'd talk to her about it.

"So, your dad sort of filled me in on what's going on in your life," she started. "Feel free to tell me to shut up if this is out of line, but...how are you feeling about it all?"

Jonah didn't react immediately, but he didn't look annoyed, either. Finally, he shrugged.

"It's not out of line," he told her, then pointed to a small crowd standing outside what was essentially a shed with a sales window at the end of a dock. "But there *is* a line at the seafood shack. Do you mind waiting?"

"Of course not," she said, smiling up at him. "Do you mind talking?"

He chuckled. "Sure, let the therapy begin."

"No therapy," she assured him as they joined the

crowd. "I'm just curious and, well, maybe you need someone to talk to. Here I am, in line for jumbo shrimp."

He regarded her with a wistful smile that she couldn't quite interpret, then slid his sunglasses off as if he didn't think they could have a heart-to-heart while his eyes were covered.

Kate did the same, taking off her glasses as she often did to have face-to-face conversations so she could really see into someone's eyes.

"I don't even know how to describe it," he began. "Honestly, I'm freaked out. I mean...I'm about to have a kid."

Kate smiled softly, a pang of longing tugging at her heart as she thought of her own babies and how much joy they gave her—and still did. And the possibility of grand-children someday? She got a shiver of anticipation just thinking about it.

"That's really exciting, Jonah," she said. "Becoming a parent is the best thing that ever happened to me."

Jonah gave a faint smirk. "Yeah, but you were married, I'm sure. Likely very financially stable with good jobs and a nice house and a station wagon and probably a picket fence of some sort, right?" His tone was teasing, but Kate could sense a little fear and self-loathing beneath it.

"Well," she replied with a laugh. "Stability is impor-tant when becoming a parent. But nothing is perfect, obviously. My ex-husband and I split up when the kids were only three and five, so...our picket fence collapsed."

Jonah looked surprised as he stepped back to let someone carrying a bag of fresh fish on ice walk by.

"Huh. Well, still. I'm sure you were way better suited than I am. You've got degrees for days, a terrific job, and, except that you can't keep track of your glasses, you're pretty together."

She laughed. "You're together, too."

"Oh, now I know you're lying," he said. "I can't keep a job, and I don't have a mailing address. Not exactly dad material."

Kate glanced at him as they finally stepped into the cool dark shack and were smacked with the smell of fresh fish. "Those are easy fixes, Jonah."

He shot her a look that said he didn't agree, but zeroed in on the shrimp, launching into a conversation with the fisherman behind the counter.

"I'd like two pounds of your best white shrimp, preferably sixteen-twenties, if you have them," Jonah said, impressing Kate with his knowledge of seafood.

The man grimaced in disappointment. "I got colossals, which are ten-to-twelves. What are you using them in?"

"A Brazilian stew but no sixteens, huh? The smaller ones could get lost in the sauce."

The man leaned closer and lifted a brow, crinkling his forehead. "Gimme an hour, tops. The boat just radioed in that they've got a ton of those jumbos and they're on their way back to the dock. They'll be so fresh, you'll have to name those suckers."

He turned to Kate. "Mind waiting?" he asked. "We could hit Jimmy Buffet's, search for that lost shaker of salt and...direction."

Lifting a shoulder, she angled her head toward the restaurant. "When in Margaritaville..."

A few minutes later, they were at a table in the air-conditioned coolness of Jimmy Buffet's Margaritaville bar.

He lifted his drink for a toast. "To therapy."

She narrowed her eyes. "To good conversation," she countered and tapped his glass with hers.

"So, where were we?" he asked after a sip, surprisingly open and ready to talk.

"You were telling me that you're not dad material." She rolled her eyes. "Not sure I know what that is, but go ahead."

"It's...my dad—that's who and what 'dad material' is," he said with a dry laugh. "I'm not responsible, which is Carly's beef. I'm not like you, or my dad, or—oh, please, the queen of overachievers, my sister, Meredith. I don't have that stable, life-together kind of mindset. I feel like no matter how hard I try, I'm just gonna end up screwing everything up. Carly's probably right to want me as far away from the baby as possible."

Kate's chest tightened at the hopelessness in his voice. It sounded familiar to her—like young Tessa being forced to read a thick book for an English class. It had been so hard for her and, like Tessa, Jonah covered his hopelessness with humor.

"That is absolutely not true," she said, her voice firm. "And I think the only reason you haven't discovered a career path is because you haven't taken yourself seriously enough to give something a real chance."

He dropped his head back and closed his eyes. "No one has ever taken me seriously except..."

When his voice trailed off, she felt her heart shift in her chest. "Your mom?" she guessed.

He smirked again. "Right you are, Dr. Freud."

"Jonah." She reached across the table. "I'm trying to help, and I know you deflect serious emotions with humor, like my sister. But, honestly, I think your dad takes you very seriously."

He considered that and took a deep drink before answering. "He took me being an architect seriously. When I made it clear that wasn't in the cards, he stopped thinking I was legit. We ended up in this huge fight and... and..." He flicked his hand as though the topic were an annoying mosquito. "Anyway, I know I'm a disappointment to him. And now, to Carly. And in six months, or sixteen years? I'll be a disappointment to...Junior."

"That's only true if you make it true," Kate said. "It's in your control. And Eli is not disappointed in you, trust me."

Jonah ran a hand through his unkempt hair, the gesture reminding her so much of Eli when he was thinking hard about something. For reasons she didn't really want to examine right then, she found it utterly endearing.

"I'm completely unqualified to do anything, Kate," he

said. "And I sure as hell am not qualified to be a dad. I don't even have any money."

"The money will come if you find something you love and put your heart and soul into it," she said simply.

"I don't have something I love," Jonah shot back. "I didn't want to be an architect."

"When did that become the only job in the world?" she asked with a laugh.

"When you're a Lawson."

Kate put both elbows on the table and leaned in to make her point. "Do I have to spell it out for you, Jonah? Isn't it obvious? You're a *chef*!"

Jonah barked out a laugh. "I'm a line cook who gets fired every two months and barely scrapes together enough hourly pay to fill my gas tank. I'm not exactly the next Bobby Flay."

"But you *could* be," Kate insisted, determined that he see what she did. "You have serious talent. There's a reason you can't stand doing a restaurant's boring burgers the same way over and over again. You have a passion for food and flavor, and a really, *really* good culinary instinct. I cook like a chemist—you cook like an artist. Big difference."

Jonah stared at her, his expression torn between disbelief and something she couldn't quite place.

"I mean...I just like cooking," he said finally. "Experimenting with stuff. I don't know if that's really a career that's gonna put my life on track. I need to get, like, a suit. And sit at a cubicle in some office. That's the only way Carly will see real change."

"Is that what *you* want?" Kate asked, unable to believe it was. "A suit and a cubicle?"

Jonah made a face. "Of course not! If I could mess around in the kitchen all day long and get paid to do it, I would. Obviously. But real chefs go to school for years and have all kinds of education and training. I have nothing."

Kate shook her head, seeing how deep his insecurities ran, once again reminded of her sister.

"Those are just obstacles, Jonah. They're not permanent. And you're so much more capable than you give yourself credit for."

Jonah didn't respond right away. He turned to look out to the harbor, quiet for a long moment before whispering, "I'm terrified to be a dad. I want to fix things...so badly, but I don't even know where to begin. I've never asked my father for help before, but I didn't know where else to turn."

"You made the right call by coming here," Kate said gently. "And, really, no one is ever ready to be a parent. It's a one day at a time thing. For now, as you prepare for it, you have to figure out some plans and logistics, and the rest will follow. I promise."

Jonah looked over at her, something vulnerable and raw in his expression. "You really think I could do the whole cooking thing as an actual job? Not just a line cook, but, like...for real?"

"Absolutely. I have zero doubts about you. None."

He let out a sigh, and his hazel eyes softened as all the

edge left his handsome features. "I bet you're a helluva mom. Lucky kids."

She drew back at the compliment. "Thank you. But this mom is day-drinking in Destin after leaving her teenagers for two weeks in the cold harsh winter of Ithaca." She wrinkled her nose. "Maybe you *shouldn't* take parenting advice from me."

He chuckled at that. "Nah. You're really good at it. You remind me of..." His smile faded. "She believed in me, too. Like no one else."

She lifted her glass again in a toast. "And to honor her, Jonah, you should believe in yourself."

He closed his eyes as the words hit. "You're right," he admitted on the softest whisper. "But what do I do? Where do I start?"

She lifted a shoulder. "Why don't you get that degree? How about a culinary school?"

"How about I win the lottery?" he asked without humor.

"How about you talk to your dad?"

"And say what? Give me money? Nope. Not happening."

"Let him know what you're thinking about, Jonah. He loves you and would do anything for you."

His eyes shuttered. "It's been an hour. We should go get our jumbos before they sell out. And stop for that coconut milk. I think a little mango salsa, too, which would bring together the tropical flavors."

"See? You know what you're doing."

"Yeah. Changing the subject."

They both took one more drink and headed back to the seafood shack, talking about Brazilian shrimp recipes instead of his life.

LATER THAT AFTERNOON, any serious conversation was set aside for the equally serious business of making dinner. Tessa's beloved speaker blasted out her latest playlist, "The Kate and Jonah Show"—a mix of eighties and nineties classics and the much, much newer rock that Jonah preferred.

"Try this," Jonah said, holding out a tasting spoon as Kate finished chopping Thai chilis and green peppers.

She leaned forward, taking a bit of the salsa he'd been working on—mango, lime, cilantro, and just a hint of jalapeño.

"That's amazing," Kate said, her eyebrows lifting in surprise. "Jonah, this is perfect. How did you think of the lime zest?"

Jonah shrugged, trying to play it off. "Just felt right."

"I told you," she sang the words. "Inspired."

As if on cue, Eli strolled into the kitchen, his T-shirt and shorts wrinkled and speckled with dirt as he made finishing the landscaping his top priority. He paused midstep, sniffing the air like a man who'd been starved all day.

"Holy...what are you two making tonight?" he asked, wandering closer but holding his hands up. "I'm not clean yet, but, man, am I hungry."

"Grab a chip and taste this mango salsa, Dad." Jonah eased the bowl over the island. "I'd love your opinion."

The words made Eli smile—not the food, Kate knew, but the words—*I'd love your opinion*. Was there anything better for a parent than to feel valued?

She held his gaze as she slid another bowl of tortilla chips his way. "Here, it beats a spoon."

Taking a scoop on a chip, he ate it in one bite, closing his eyes and moaning. Kate took the chance to just look at him and...feel things she couldn't explain. She was starting to get used to the sensation, though. Maybe a little too used to it.

Her crush on the man was alive and well, she knew in her heart of hearts. This crush—far scarier than the old one she had as a teenager—was still a secret. Although if anyone suspected, it might be Eli himself, since their long walks on the beach had grown progressively more personal.

"This is *unbelievable*," Eli said as he finally opened his eyes. "You made up this recipe? The two of you?"

Kate pointed to Jonah. "He's the man," she said with a burst of pride. "I'm nothing but the sous-chef in this operation."

Jonah actually blushed a little. "Yeah. Just...threw it together."

"You've got some serious skills, kid," Eli said, reaching for a second chip. "This is...yeah. Top-notch taste. I've never had anything quite like it."

"It's just salsa," Jonah muttered, clearly uncomfortable with the praise, but Kate caught the way his shoulders lifted slightly, like her words at the restaurant had planted a seed that was just beginning to sprout.

Before she could say anything, Tessa and Lacey strolled in, with Vivien right behind them, all three laughing about something Kate didn't catch.

"What's for dinner?" Vivien asked, grabbing a chip and scooping up the mango salsa. "We're famished."

"Brazilian jumbo shrimp with coconut milk and Thai chili peppers, mango salsa and chips for the appetizer, and chocolate mousse for dessert," Kate announced as she set her glasses on the counter. "Jonah's taking the lead tonight."

"I'm experimenting, really," Jonah said.

"It's perfect," Vivien cooed.

"We are your willing and hungry guinea pigs," Lacey said, taking a big scoop of her own. She barely finished chewing when her eyes went wide. "Whoa!"

"Too much jalapeño?" Jonah asked, sounding worried.

"No, no, it's perfect. This is it!" She gave Tessa's arm a jab. "This is that perfect bite you wanted for the party apps. Can you put this with seafood, Jonah?"

He gave her a look like she was crazy. "Abso-stinking-lutely. It goes beautifully over salmon or mahi."

"It goes beautifully in my belly," Lacey crooned, taking another scoop. "Yikes, this is good. Everything you make is, Jonah."

Kate beamed at him, catching his eye and giving her best "I told you so" flick of the eyebrows.

But her phone buzzed from her back pocket before

she could say anything. She pulled it out and read the screen, seeing that it was Jo Ellen calling.

"I need to take this," she said. "It's my mom. Save me some salsa, please."

"No promises." Lacey waved another chip.

"Slow down, Spacey," Jonah teased.

"Make more, Chef," she countered.

As Kate walked out, she got to see those shoulders square even more at the title.

Happy about that, she left the banter behind to slip up the stairs and take the call.

She let it ring again as she paused in the afternoon sun pouring on the landing, knowing deep in her heart what she was about to hear.

Come home, please.

Sighing, she took the steps slowly, soaking in the place that had become her home these past few weeks. Everything was so bright, airy, fresh, and bathed in blinding Destin sunshine. She'd already made new memories to pile on top of old ones, and just like those bittersweet late August days so many years ago, she didn't want to go home.

But she had to. And this call was just one more reminder why.

In her room, she tapped the phone. "Hey, Mom. How's everything going?" she asked as she softly closed the door. "You okay?"

"Well, Katie, honey, I'm just having a really hard time here with Marie Curie," her mother's voice came through, sounding more fragile than she should, even for a woman in her late seventies. Before Dad died, Jo Ellen had been vibrant and dynamic.

Now? Sad and frail.

Kate pinched the bridge of her nose. "What's the matter?"

"Oh, you know. She's meowing a lot. She keeps looking at the front door. I think she misses you."

Kate sighed softly. *Someone* missed her, and it wasn't Marie Curie. "Mom, I'm coming home soon, okay? Try giving her those squeezable tuna treats."

"We're all out of tuna treats," Jo Ellen said with a sadness that tugged at Kate's heart. "When do you think you'll be coming back? I mean, I'm sure you're having a good time. Are you?"

She dropped on the bed and braced for a tough call.

"It's been great, Mom. Such a wonderful place—it's like old times."

"Who all is there? Not Maggie, right?"

"Oh, no. Just Eli and Vivien, and their kids, like I told you. Oh, and Tessa, of course."

"Yes, yes. That's nice. But...are you coming back soon? I mean, I'm sure it's warm and lovely there. So there's no rush, but..."

But she was lonely, and still grieving her husband. Guilt smacked Kate in the face, and it hurt.

"It won't be too much longer, Mom. I don't want you to get tired of Marie Curie."

She gave a soft laugh. "The cat who now sleeps on the empty pillow next to me?"

The empty pillow. Ouch.

"That sounds like my Marie," Kate said, trying to keep her voice light. "She's not bad company if you don't mind a little kitty snoring."

"I love snoring," her mother said. "I miss the sound of it."

Kate closed her eyes, the ache in her chest deepening. "I know, Mom. I know how hard it's been for you. I promise I'll be back soon."

"How is Tessa doing?" Jo Ellen asked. "She hardly ever calls."

Because she knew her mother would talk about their father, and Tessa couldn't take it.

"She's busy starting a business," Kate said, purposely brightening her voice and tamping down any of her worries about Tessa's latest adventure.

"Oh? She is?" Jo Ellen sounded interested. "I thought she worked for the Ritz-Carlton."

Kate winced, realizing Tessa hadn't told their mother she'd lost that job. "Well, you know Tessa. Always on the move."

Her mother sighed. "I just ache for... I need you, Katie. Well, Marie and I both do. She's staring long-ingly at the door right now, hoping you'll walk through it."

Kate tried to chuckle, but her heart tugged hard. "I know, Mom. And I promise I'll be home soon."

After they said their goodbyes and hung up, Kate leaned back on her hand, looking around the empty room. Vivien would fill it soon, with texture and color and style, but Kate wouldn't be here to see it because she couldn't keep making that promise to her mother and not follow through.

Reality felt like a storm cloud inching closer, ready to pour down on her idyllic escape. As much as she wanted to stay here, she knew she couldn't.

As she stepped out into the hall, Eli was coming up the steps, an expectant look on his face.

"Everything okay?" he asked as he slowed at the top stair, searching her face.

"It's fine, but..." She lifted a shoulder, not wanting to say the obvious.

Real life was waiting, and these dreamy days had to come to an end. Not tomorrow. Not the next day. But very, very soon.

"Well, you left these." He held out her glasses and smiled. "Which surprises absolutely no one."

She laughed softly and slid them on. "Thanks."

"I'm going to shower," he said, thumbing over his shoulder. "You'd better get into the kitchen before you lose your job to Jonah."

She opened her mouth to share some of what they'd talked about, but it all felt like too much right then. Too much emotion after the call with her mother and she just didn't want to delve into it.

"What is it?" he asked, always reading her so well.

She just shook her head. "Just...well, I had a great day with Jonah," she said. "He's an awesome kid, Eli."

His smile grew. "Thank you for being so good to him." He reached for her hand. "If you need anything..."

She held his hand for a moment, letting the sensation

dance over her. Then she withdrew her fingers from his and smiled, knowing this time was coming to an end and not wanting to make the parting any harder on her heart.

"Just some mango salsa," she said lightly. "Which is probably gone by now, huh?"

"He's making more."

"Good boy." She slipped by him down the steps and heard him sigh behind her. A sigh that echoed exactly how she felt.

Chapter Seventeen

Eli

After an epic dinner, Eli stepped out onto the deck, which felt exactly like he'd hoped it would when he'd first drawn out the elevation of this house. Thanks to Vivien's keen eye, they had a full outdoor living space that offered air, light, and warmth but was still an extension of the main floor.

She'd nailed the furnishings with a collection from Frontgate grouped around a firepit coffee table, a comfortable sofa, two reclining chairs that looked out over the water, and a white egg-shaped swing for a touch of whimsy.

Resale value? Oh, yeah. Cha-*ching*. The problem was, what price do you put on paradise and the incredibly special time they were enjoying?

Ignoring the new furniture, he leaned on the railing, his gaze pinned on the now-finished boardwalk to the beach, but he wasn't thinking like an architect or home-seller at the moment.

He was thinking like a father.

Listening to Jonah's chatter with "the girls" in the kitchen, Eli's heart soared. That was more laughter than he'd have ever dreamed he'd hear from his son when he'd arrived broken, scared, and lost.

Maybe he was still a little lost—Eli frequently saw a distant look in his son's hazel eyes, his gaze revealing an all-too-familiar pain. They were the eyes of a young man who'd suffered, but today? Tonight?

He didn't seem nearly as broken, and the only thing that scared him was too much seasoning or an over-charred shrimp. And that wasn't fear—it was pride in his work.

Which was yet another character trait he hadn't seen in a long time—maybe since his football days before... before Melissa.

Something was working on Jonah. Yes, Destin was magic—but not *that* much magic. This might not be a case of where, but *who*. His brief conversation with Kate at the top of the stairs came back to him, a reminder that—

"Hey, Dad."

"Hey, there." He turned at the sound of Jonah's voice.

"Want company?" he asked.

Eli almost laughed. Did he want to spend time with his only son? Was that a rhetorical question? With another person—like Meredith—he'd make that joke about how dumb that question was.

But he always treaded lightly with Jonah, so he just smiled.

"Sunset's just starting," Eli said, beckoning him closer. "It's gonna be a beauty."

Jonah nodded, then threaded his fingers through his long hair. He stayed quiet for a moment, lost in thought at the railing next to Eli, his gaze fixed on the waves.

Once again, Eli sensed something different about his passionate, expressive son.

There was something in his son's posture—a calm he hadn't seen in years.

"That dinner tonight was something else," Eli said, breaking the silence. "Seriously, Jonah. You've got a gift."

Jonah smiled faintly, the corners of his mouth tugging upward. "Thanks, Dad."

"No, I mean it. Kind of inspired, if you ask me, which..." He laughed. "I know you didn't. But I've been to a lot of restaurants and never had anything that good."

Jonah gave him a side-eye. "Funny you should describe it that way."

"Why's that?"

"Well, I've been thinking about...maybe getting more serious. About cooking, I mean." He rubbed the back of his neck, his voice hesitant. "Kate's been...kind of pushing me to think bigger. Like, not a line cook, but a...chef."

He whispered the last word so softly, Eli wasn't sure he'd heard it.

"A...*wow*." Eli raised his eyebrows, a mix of surprise and gratitude flooding him. "Yeah?"

"Don't get jealous that I listened to someone else's encouragement," he said with a teasing smile.

"Jealous?" Eli scoffed, because it was the last thing he was. "No, that's not how I think, son." At Jonah's questioning look, he added, "You know how I look at the world. God puts people in your path for a reason—for change or enlightenment. Kate could most certainly be that person."

She could be that person for Eli, too, he thought fleetingly, but wanted to keep his focus on this rare father-son talk.

"She's just...hopeful, you know?" Jonah said.

Eli knew. He was a big fan of hope, and the descriptor just made him adore the woman even more.

"She's been teaching me a lot in the kitchen," Jonah continued. "She's got this uber-chemist point of view. Which kind of helps me when I go off the rails," he added with a laugh. "But more than that, she's kind of persuading me to believe I might have...something."

For a flash, he remembered Jonah Lawson in the early days, before he lost his mother. Confidence hadn't been an issue—in fact, they used to joke about the size of Jonah's ego.

Had that been a result of Melissa's gentle but constant praise and support? Something he'd needed, maybe especially from a mother figure?

"What you have," Eli said, "is talent. In spades."

He brushed back his hair again. "I don't know about... well, yeah. Maybe. I sure do like it, and it feels natural. Is that talent? I don't know but I'd like to maybe explore the possibility of being a..." He chuckled as if he couldn't even say it. "A chef."

Eli felt a surge of optimism he hadn't felt in years. Jonah, a chef? Why not? He loved the idea. "You could.

No doubt about it. Have you thought about culinary school?"

He braced for the disdainful look, the dry laugh that said "school's for losers."

But Jonah merely nodded again, slower this time. "Yes, I have. Carly got her degree in hospitality, so I've seen what a difference having that piece of paper makes in getting a good position in a restaurant or whatever. So, I have been thinking about it, yeah. But..."

Eli studied him, imagining what might be stopping his son. Fear of failure? No encouraging mother? Maybe something as simple as he didn't think he could get in.

"I'm broke," Jonah said simply, going to the most obvious place that Eli should have seen. "Culinary school isn't cheap, and I've got, like, zero savings."

Eli had to fight his urge to figuratively whip out his wallet and get rid of that obstacle. Instead, he placed a hand on Jonah's shoulder, squeezing gently. "Jonah, would you let me help you?"

Jonah shook his head, pulling away slightly. "I can't let you do that. I'm not a kid anymore. I'm turning thirty and I'm not taking money from...Daddy."

Eli chuckled softly, not able to remember the last time Jonah called him "Daddy." Twenty-five years ago, at least.

"How about a loan?" he suggested. "Pay it back after you're done with school and working. No interest."

"Dad, that's not a loan, it's a gift."

"It's a loan if you pay it back," Eli said. "And I fully intended to cover your entire education anyway."

"Then I dropped out," he said glumly.

"Well, now you'll drop back in."

Jonah turned to him, his eyes softer than Eli had seen in years. "I could work for you. I don't know how, but if I did something and didn't get paid, that might...work."

Eli had no idea what Jonah could do, but he wasn't going to let that stop him. "I'd hire you in a second."

"Not as an architect or intern or anything like that," Jonah said quickly. "But I did a few summers of construction for Uncle Ryan, and I know how to hang drywall and basic finishings."

Eli inched back. "The apartment over the garage?"

Jonah shrugged. "I know you weren't sure you were going to be able to get the same subs for the job and it might take me a little longer—"

"I could help," Eli said quickly, already imagining hours in the small apartment, talking, laughing, doing finishing work and being a father and son again.

"That kind of defeats the purpose of me doing the work, but I'm sure I'll need some supervision."

Eli exhaled, taking the small opening and being content with it. "And...culinary school?" he asked.

"There are some community colleges around here, various programs. I'll start doing research, but I have to know I have an income and a flexible job."

"You have both," Eli said without a second's hesitation. "I'm so glad you're..."

"Growing up," Jonah finished with a laugh.

"I was going to say sticking around, but yeah. Growing up is good."

"I guess having a kid'll do that to a person," Jonah said. "Kind of hard to embrace the 'live in the moment' lifestyle when you have a responsibility like that."

Eli turned and smiled at him, overcome with an indescribable emotion.

"Still getting used to that idea there, Grandpa?" Jonah asked, searching his face and probably trying to read that emotion.

"I was just thinking..." Eli took a breath. He was so deeply private about his faith, and he was never one to thrust it on others. But he had to say this. "You know, sometimes God's plans are nothing like what we expect. We might pray and pray and when He answers, you kind of want to look up and say, 'Huh? *That's* your idea?' But it's always good."

"You've been praying for me to grow up?" Jonah asked.

"I've been praying for you, period. I left it in God's hands beyond that."

Jonah studied him for a long moment, any traces of sarcasm gone. "Thanks," he said softly. "Don't stop. Praying, I mean."

Eli's heart swelled. All he could do was nod, then reach for his son's broad shoulders. He hugged hard, then patted his back. "Welcome to the construction crew."

Jonah sighed into the hug, his body relaxing. "Thanks, man. This means the world."

As they parted, Eli stole a glance skyward, thanking God for this miracle. Next, he had to find Kate and thank her, too.

KATE WAS FINISHING up in the kitchen while Lacey and Tessa set up a game at the dining room table.

"You want to play Wits and Wagers with us?" Tessa asked. "The math is light, and you get to place outrageous bets, which is why I like it."

"Sure, after a walk," Eli said, glancing at Kate. "Join me?"

"Of course." She dropped a used paper towel in the trash and looked at him with a question in her eyes.

And, wow. Eli could actually read it, communicating clearly with her while not a word had to be spoken. *How was your talk with Jonah?*

She understood him—and Jonah, it seemed.

"Let me get my sneakers," she said, slipping out of the kitchen and up the stairs.

As she did, Vivien came in from the garage. "I'm taking off, you guys. Just put my overnight bag in the car."

"You're leaving?" Eli asked. "How did I not know this?"

"I'm headed up to Atlanta, just for tonight. Ryan, um, has a problem."

He lifted his brows. "What kind of problem?"

"He's in a design bind," she said. "And I'm going to... how did Jonah put it? Do him a solid. Peter called it taking the high road. I call it...a five-hour drive to Atlanta."

"Why?"

"My question exactly, Uncle Eli," Lacey interjected.

Vivien glanced at her daughter, then back to Eli. "I just told you, I'm doing him a favor and being kind. Isn't that what's taught in that Good Book you like so much?"

A splash of shame wormed through him. "Of course, yes. That's the right thing to do. But why tonight?"

"Because there's a meeting with the client in the morning and I don't want to get up at four a.m."

He nodded. "Okay, Viv, just...be careful."

"Driving? Roads'll be easy at night."

"I mean Ryan. Don't let him take advantage of you."

She shuttered her eyes. "I'm aware enough that I won't let him," she said. "But thank you for caring."

Lacey came into the kitchen and wrapped her arms around Vivien. "Mom, you might be doing the right thing, but we don't have to like it. And Uncle Eli's right. Don't get bulldozed by him."

"I won't."

When Kate came back down, they gave Vivien a group hug and plenty of love and support.

A few minutes later, Eli and Kate headed downstairs, past the pool and out to the newly completed boardwalk.

When their feet hit the wood, Kate paused to run her finger over the freshly varnished railing.

"This is beautiful, Eli. Top-quality work, perfectly constructed. And the palm trees you planted outside the downstairs deck are a great touch. Is there anything prettier than a palm tree silhouetted against the sunset while you're sitting in the pool?"

Eli smiled, so grateful she appreciated the thought he'd put into the design.

"That's exactly why I placed them there," he said. "From the pool or the first-floor patio, you'll see the water and sky through the fronds when those palm trees grow."

She glanced at him, sliding off those glasses as she frequently did when they were face to face. "You're worried about Vivien," she said softly.

"How can you tell?"

"You run your fingers through your hair, like your son. It's a stress tell for both of you."

He chuckled, thinking of all the ways that comment made him feel. Delighted by how observant she was, touched that she knew Jonah so well, surprised at how accurate the assessment was.

And the fact that she paid such close attention to him? That was the best feeling of all.

"Well, as far as Vivien, I'm concerned, as any brother would be. She has a soft heart and Ryan Knight has kicked it around enough for one lifetime."

"I think she has her head on straight over this trip," she replied as they reached the end of the boardwalk, pausing to drink in the vista that never got boring or old.

One hundred and eighty degrees of water and sand, waves crashing, gulls squawking. The sky was a deepening blue, stars just beginning to peek through as the sun's last light faded.

But Eli couldn't help but look down at the woman next to him who, right that moment—most moments, to be honest—was more beautiful than the view.

"So, Kate," he whispered, leaning his shoulder lightly

into hers. "How can I thank you for whatever fairy dust you sprinkled on my son?"

She trilled a laugh. "He's quite a kitchen buddy."

"He's more than that—he's a different person," Eli said. "I mean, he's still himself with his sarcasm and his 'I don't care' attitude, but change is in the air."

"You think?" Kate smiled. "Well, we had a good talk today. It might have gotten him thinking."

"No might about it," he said. "He wants to go to culinary school, and he mentioned that you had a little something to do with that."

"Oh!" Her whole face lit up. "He did? He's going? He...oh." She pressed her fingers to her lips, her eyes dancing. "I'm so happy, Eli!"

"So am I," he admitted. "Beyond happy."

"I'm so glad he listened to my advice. Not that I told him what to do but..."

"You encouraged him." He put his hand on her back, needing to have some physical touch so she knew just how much this meant to him. "You made him see himself differently and with confidence. You gave him the gift...a mother's gift."

Kate's cheeks flushed. "No, no, Eli. He just started opening up to me about his insecurity and how he's worried that Carly is right, that he's unfit to be a dad, that his life is a mess. He was very vulnerable, actually. I think I just helped point him in the right direction."

"And I think he's going to stay here and find a program that he'll pay for by working for me—building out the guest apartment above the garage."

Her eyes widened as she gasped. "Oh, that's amazing! I'm so sorry I'll miss all that."

The words gave him a quick punch and a reminder that any day, she'd be headed back to Ithaca.

Without giving it too much thought, he stopped walking and reached for her hand. The touch was light at first, tentative, but when Kate didn't pull away, he gave her fingers a gentle squeeze.

"You've blown me away with your kindness, Kate," he said. "You are as good-hearted as you are brilliant, and I don't think I've ever met anyone like you."

Even in the waning light, he could see a faint blush deepen her complexion. "Oh, Eli..." she began, her tone tender. "That means more to me than I can say."

They stood there for a moment, the sound of the waves filling the silence between them. Eli's chest tightened with a mixture of emotions he hadn't allowed himself to feel in years—hope, admiration, maybe...something more.

He was falling for her, and he knew it.

She sighed and let out a soft laugh to break the silence. "And to think of all the days and nights—seven summers of them—I dreamed of you saying something like that to me."

"Ah, the secret crush I didn't know was happening."

"You could have known if you weren't so enamored with Tessa," she teased as they started walking, but didn't let go of each other's hands. "I was right there the whole time, just not as blond and dynamic."

Eli groaned, looking skyward. "I was such an idiot."

"You weren't an idiot," she assured him. "Just a human male under ninety."

He laughed but felt the smile fade as he looked down at her. "A dumb kid with no clue what I was doing. I'm sorry."

"Don't be sorry," she said quickly. "Please. Dad always said she got the beauty, and I got the brains."

"That's not true," Eli said firmly. "You're stunning, Kate. Always have been."

"Well, thank you for that, but I adore my sister, beauty and flaws and everything."

Still holding hands, they turned to head back to the house, walking for a while in silence as Eli rooted for the right words to make yet another confession.

"Can I be honest about Tessa?" he finally asked.

"To a point," she countered. "She is my twin sister, after all."

"I know. It was weird seeing her here at first," he said. "I was definitely annoyed."

"She told me you didn't seem thrilled. Why would you be? She was legally and technically a trespasser, and you had every right to be bothered." Kate raised an eyebrow, curiosity sparking in her eyes. "But even after you found out who she was?"

"More after I found out," he said with a laugh. "But that's because of our history."

"Your history?" She looked up, curious. "I didn't know you had one, other than, well, the family vacations."

He considered how much to tell her, and if it would make him feel better or worse.

"Is it history if only one party remembers?" he joked. "Like a tree falling in the forest and no one's there to hear it?"

She stopped and studied him. "What do you mean? What doesn't she remember?"

They were back at the boardwalk, so Eli tugged her down to sit on the bottom step and look out at the water, not quite ready to go inside.

"It happened the last night of the last summer," he told her. "At the very same moment your parents were packing and rushing out of the house. Do you remember that night? That scene?"

"Of course I do," she said, her brow furrowed. "What happened that Tessa doesn't remember?"

"When the arguing started, she and I bolted and took a walk down to the marina," he said. "We ended up staying for a while, all alone down there, and of course Tessa climbed on a random boat and draped herself over the sun loungers like she owned the thing."

Kate didn't smile, but stared at him, paling slightly. "Did you get in trouble?"

"Depends on how you define that. I did. She didn't."

"What happened?"

He swallowed, realizing that he'd never told anyone this story. Not Melissa, not Peter. And certainly not Vivien.

"I kissed her."

"Oh, okay." But it didn't sound okay. She sounded a little surprised. Disappointed, too.

"That's all. One kiss. But then I, uh..." He gave a mirthless laugh. "I told her I loved her."

She drew back, eyes wide. "You...did?"

"I didn't—love her, I mean. I was such a kid and a dork and smitten. I didn't know what love was and once I finally did, I just looked back on that night with a big fat cringe."

She considered that, quiet. "What did she say?"

He closed his eyes. "She laughed in my face, flicked her hand like my love was a bothersome gnat, and said we needed to get home." He heard an ancient ache in his voice and from the look on Kate's face, she heard it, too.

"She rushed back to the house alone and I just sat there and...hated myself. When I got home, the Wylies were gone, and we never said goodbye."

She nodded. "I remember looking for you. I told Vivien to tell you I said goodbye, but..."

"But I was too wrapped up in my own issues," he said sadly. "Where were you during the big fight?"

"Vivien and I had gone sailing," she finally said. "And the whole time? I was crying over my unrequited love for...her brother."

He dropped his head back with a grunt of frustration.

"Hey, Eli." She put her arm around him. "It's history. Ancient, unimportant history."

"If it was, I'd have forgotten it," he said.

"Maybe. But have you forgiven her?" she asked.

He considered the question, holding her gaze. "Obviously not, since just seeing her that first night brought back a flood of bad feelings. Suddenly, I saw Tessa Wylie as a user again, an interloper on boats and beach houses that don't belong to her, a woman with no regard for other people's deepest secrets and feelings."

"I get that," Kate said softly, looking out toward the darkening horizon as the moon rose over the water. "But that's not who she is at all. She's just adventurous and fun-loving. She was eighteen and every boy in Destin was circling like a seagull over a picnic lunch. She was heady with the realization that she could have anyone she wanted, and you were much more like a brother than a boyfriend."

He nodded slowly, knowing she was right.

"And as far as trespassing in the house?" Kate shrugged. "What you might not realize is that despite her humor and flippant remarks, she's utterly broken over the loss of our father. She was searching for comfort, which she associates with Destin. Dad always defended and supported her, no matter what, and she needed that."

"Did she? Tessa seems like she doesn't need anyone rising to her defense when she can handle it on her own."

Kate gave a sad smile. "It's easy to think Tessa had no struggles in life—just a beautiful girl who loves a good time. Her dyslexia gave her the wrong impression that she wasn't that bright, when I'm sure she could meet me IQ point for IQ point. But she had to learn to manage it."

"I've heard her mention dyslexia in passing—I got the impression it was mild."

"Define mild to a seven-year-old who simply can't

read," she said. "My mother didn't know what to do about it, but my father was a natural teacher. He took up the job that a professional tutor or child learning expert would do today. He was quite brilliant at it, and it made them very close."

"A good father," he said.

"A great one," Kate agreed. "He worked tirelessly with her, but it always sounded like they were having a blast. Somehow, he guided her through reading and writing, teaching her shortcuts and creative ways to identify backwards letters and do simple math while I was..." She gave a tight smile. "Winning science fairs and academic awards."

"Oh." He nodded. "I know what it's like when one kid's a superstar and one is struggling."

"Imagine twin girls," she said on a laugh. "Tessa did learn. And she realized quite young that she's charming and creative. She's actually quite a big-picture problem solver and, obviously, she's gorgeous. That has helped her get by more times than I can count. It's also meant a lot of men have fallen for her."

He laughed softly. "And she barely noticed some of them."

Kate shook her head. "And maybe she did notice, but that night, hell was breaking loose at this place. You said the two of you left to escape the arguing. She probably didn't have a chance to think about it."

"I guess I never saw it that way, but I can see that under her quips and easy-breezy attitude is a woman who's mourning her father." He let out a sigh. "I know it's hard to lose a father, at any age. I'm sure you're all still reeling."

"I compartmentalize my grief, so I've managed better than Tessa or Mom."

Eli glanced at her, sensing the weight of what she wasn't saying. "Your mom isn't doing well?"

"Well..." Kate hesitated. "Physically, she's fine. But emotionally? She's been wrecked. And she leans on me a lot. I...I have to start thinking about going back to New York soon."

Eli's heart dropped and he search for something that could make her stay. "But we haven't visited the Cavallaris yet."

"And we should," she agreed. "We know they're in Santa Rosa Beach. Let's at least do a drive-by at the address."

He nodded. "I think if God wants us to talk to them, He'll open that door."

She gave him a slightly dubious smile, one he'd seen many times in his life when he put his faith on display.

"But after that," Kate said, "I need to go home."

He felt his whole body sink at the news, though it didn't shock him.

"This has been a wonderful vacation, Eli, but vacations aren't meant to last forever."

The words hung between them, heavy with unspoken emotion. He held her gaze, inches apart, close enough for a kiss he ached to share.

But then he remembered the last time he gave in to his longings with a Wylie girl, and he just didn't want

that kind of rejection again. She'd be kinder, but it might hurt even more.

He stood, reaching for her hand to bring her up next to him. "I wish this one vacation could last forever."

Kate's lips parted, but she swallowed whatever she was about to say. Instead, she reached out, her fingers brushing his arm lightly.

"Me, too," she said finally, her voice barely above a whisper.

Chapter Eighteen
Vivien

Despite the long drive and late arrival at her townhouse, Vivien woke early the morning of her meeting with the Hoffmans. Coffee in hand, she prowled her two-story unit, trying to imagine coming back here for good after the days in Destin.

And all she could conjure up was a deep sense of sadness and loss.

"I kind of hate this place," she admitted to the empty rooms.

Hated it enough that she not only dreaded coming back, she couldn't wait to leave. So much that she took a shower earlier than necessary. After she did her makeup, she stepped into her closet, which seemed small and unfamiliar after the massive one she had in Destin.

She picked an outfit and stepped to the dresser to open her jewelry box, inhaling softly at the sight of her engagement and wedding rings tucked into velvet slots. She'd cried when she'd taken them off, she remembered.

Very slowly, she lifted the wedding ring, which always meant more to her than the solitaire diamond Ryan had given her when he asked her to marry him. It was this ring that said *forever*, this circle of gold that meant they were well and truly one.

She slipped it on her finger, getting a hard punch at her heart. She tried to remember how it felt the first time she wore it—blissful—and the million times she'd looked at it since then. Mostly happy, always satisfied, and never sorry she'd put this band of gold on her finger.

It was loose now since she'd lost a little weight over the past year, and looked...wrong. That was a win, she supposed. That was—

She startled at a loud bang on the front door. Turning, she hustled downstairs and peeked out, seeing her neighbor, Lorraine.

"Oh, hey, there," she said, opening the door.

The other woman held out a packet of mail, smiling warmly. Lorraine was a very chatty retiree guaranteed to turn five minutes into fifteen—or more. Right now, Vivien was not up for small talk.

"Hi, Vivien. Your daughter asked me to grab your mail while she was gone and I saw your car, so here you go. How was your trip?"

"Thank you," she replied, taking the letters. "It's actually not over. I just had to run up here for a meeting today."

"Oh, I love Florida," the other woman said. "Have you been to Sanibel Island? So pretty there, if you like—"

"I'm so sorry, Lorraine, I'm just running out the door for my appointment." She reached to her right and grabbed her purse and tablet from the entry table where she'd left them last night. "Thank you for getting the mail. We might be gone a while longer, so I'll stop the mail and you won't have to be bothered."

She stepped out and pulled the door behind her, tapping the electronic keypad, chatting about nothing and then cutting short what could have been a long conversation.

With a friendly goodbye and some more thanks for the mail, she climbed into her Highlander, gave Lorraine a warm wave, and headed up to Johns Creek.

Traffic wasn't bad at all, and she pulled into the Serene Hills development along with plenty of construction trucks. The entry gate that would keep out solicitors and intruders when construction was complete gaped open now, allowing subcontractors to get in and out while the new neighborhood was built.

She drove carefully, praying she didn't get a flat on a random nail, passing lots in various stages of build-out. Ryan had contracted almost half the homes in Phase 1, a coup at the time. Back then, things had been good between them.

He had, in fact, credited her astounding design of the model for his success in the early days of bidding on lots. Buyers walked through that finished home and were ready to sign for one of their own.

Thinking of that design and realizing she had forty-five minutes to kill, she turned at the first road, heading off the main drag to the sales office and model homes.

She'd totally forgotten how spectacular that model had been, with a fabulous "organic modern" timeless style. If it was open now, she could get some pictures for her website, and a few of the main bedroom's built-in entertainment center that she wanted to duplicate in the Summer House.

She parked and walked right into the two-story model, hearing some voices as she entered. A woman popped out from the guest suite and smiled, her crisp jacket bearing the logo of one of the real estate firms handling Serene Hills, but Vivien didn't recognize her.

"I'm with some customers right now if you want to grab a brochure and peek around," the woman said. "Then I'll be right with you."

Vivien nodded thanks, not bothering to explain why she was there.

She bypassed the brochures and walked upstairs, past the loft that she'd styled as a combo study-room and hangout area for teens, with a wall of storage that worked for toys for younger families. She'd put touches like that everywhere, offering lifestyle flexibility that buyers loved.

She made a mental note to get a picture and use that on her website, too.

Walking around the corner, she stepped into the main suite and smiled, still in love with the blend of neutrals, the textured grass wallpaper and thick columned drapes, and that jaw-dropper of a chandelier.

As she took her phone out to take a picture, she heard the Realtor coming up the stairs.

"It's well over four thousand square feet," she said. "And every inch has been made more beautiful by the keen eye of Una Tatum, a master designer."

Vivien froze. *Excuse me?*

"Una works very closely with Ryan Knight Homes creating stunning designs," the Realtor continued. "He can work the cost of a professional designer—absolutely the best in the Atlanta area—into your contract. Ms. Tatum can make your home look as beautiful as she made this one."

"What?" she croaked the word in disbelief.

"Excuse me one second," the woman said. "Take a good look at this study-TV combo. That storage works for toddlers with toys and can be transformed into an entertainment area for teens. That makes this house one you'll stay in for years. That's how Ms. Tatum designs."

With fury surging up her spine, Vivien whipped around, coming face to face with the woman who entered the room.

"I'm so sorry, ma'am, but I'm with a very serious buyer right now. Can you come back—"

"Una Tatum did *not* design this house," she ground out the words, not wanting to take her anger out on the stranger.

The woman drew back, clearly not expecting that. "Yes, she did. She works closely with Ryan—"

"No, no." Vivien rooted for calm professionalism. "There's definitely been a mistake, but I'm sure they'll fix it. Actually, I designed it. Quite...lovingly, I might add."

The woman cocked her head, as if she were uncertain if this could be true or if Vivien was just a delusional snoop poking around model homes.

"You see, I'm married to Ryan Knight—well..." She held up her hands, noticing the ring she'd forgotten to take off when the neighbor arrived. "I mean, I was, or am about to not be..." She gave an awkward laugh. "Anyway, not important. I just...you know. Pride and all. I picked everything in this house. Even that chandelier. Me. I'm Vivien Law—Knight. Well, Lawson..."

She closed her eyes and sighed, hating the look of disdain and pity on the other woman's face.

"It's on the brochure," the lady said. "Designed and staged by Una Tatum. With her logo. So...I don't know..."

But *she* knew. Vivien knew exactly what was going on.

"Of course. Not your...problem. Thank you. I'll just..." She gestured toward the steps, walking past the couple who stood looking even more confused in the hallway. "Good luck," she murmured to them with a tight smile, unable to make eye contact.

She was vibrating with emotion as she strode downstairs, her hands shaking when she snapped a brochure from the pile and stuffed it into her bag.

Do Ryan *a solid*? Take the *high road*? Be friends because divorce is longer than marriage?

Oh, *hell, no.*

This was cheating. This was fraud. This was wrong on every level, and no one knew that better than a woman whose father went to jail for that kind of crime. It would *not* be perpetrated on her.

～

Vivien almost called Lacey on the short drive to the other side of the neighborhood just to vent, but decided her time was better spent calming down. Taking deep breaths, she got her heart rate to something resembling normal and managed to stop trembling.

She'd gone through a litany of opening lines from, "How dare you!" to, "I'll sue you!"—none of which truly captured just how indignant she was over this egregious breach of ethics.

If she was going to sue anyone, it would be Una Tatum, who surely knew she was being given credit for Vivien's designs. But first, she was going to rip Ryan Knight from one end of Serene Hills to the other and if the Hoffmans were there to witness it, all the better.

She pulled up to the address he'd sent when she'd texted him that she'd be up today, seeing only one car—a two-seater Lexus convertible. Either that belonged to Miranda and Sam, or Ryan got a new car, which would be a classic midlife crisis move.

Maybe it was Una! Surely she wouldn't have the nerve to show her face to Vivien!

She threw open the SUV door with way more force than necessary, grabbed her purse and yanked out the crumpled flyer.

She shook it out and angled it to the sun, fighting back a very dark word when she saw the scroll-like logo for UTD, which sounded more like a disease than the Una Tatum Designs acronym.

Huffing out a breath, she slammed the door and marched to the front patio. Which, she noticed with a cringe, was painted black. Ouch. She hated that trend. Very popular but, in her opinion, very ugly, and the owners would be repainting it in two years.

In front of the door, she glanced down and saw the UTD logo again, this time woven on the doormat.

She took it as a reminder *not* to be a doormat. Not this time. No matter what he said, she would not let him get away with this.

She didn't knock, but squeezed the oversized—too big for the door—knob and pushed into the entryway. She took a moment to inhale one more time, getting a whiff of fresh paint and that overpriced sandalwood cologne that Ryan loved.

So *he* bought a Lexus convertible. What a cliché.

"Ryan!"

"Oh, Viv, you're early!" She heard his voice from above, drawing her eye up a set of open tread stairs that screamed mid-century modern but had no warmth and no grandeur.

He appeared at the top, wearing a white shirt, a tie, and dress pants—the picture of a successful builder meeting with wealthy clients. Also the picture of someone whose eyes she wanted to scratch out.

"Hey," he said, jogging down the stairs. "I didn't think you—"

"You didn't think at all." She spat out the words, making him do a double-take.

"What's wrong, Viv?"

"What's *wrong*? This!" She came closer and waved

the creased brochure at him. "Designed by Una Tatum? The model I sweat blood to make perfect?"

He shuttered his eyes like she was a whining child who needed to be put in her place.

"It's called *business*, Vivien, and it's how people make money. Money that will, ultimately, be shared with you under the generous divorce settlement I have agreed to."

She took another breath, this one so full of vitriol she felt her nostrils flare. "You will *not* let her take credit for my work."

"Yes," he said simply, sliding his hands into his pockets. "I will. Because it's my company and I can do what I want and all she has to do is switch out a pillow and it's no longer yours."

Was he serious? "How...what...why..."

He gave the slightest smile at her loss of words, pure condescension and victory.

"Come on, Viv. Don't get your panties in a bunch. It's about money and I told you, if you'll give me some great pointers for this place, I'll pay you well. Very well. Now, let's look at the living room. I think we went a little over-board with the black paint on all the woodwork, so I was wondering if you—"

"No."

He gave her a blank look, like he didn't understand the simple two-letter power word that she hadn't used enough in her marriage.

"I mean it, Ryan. I will not do this for you, and you will not let her take credit for my work."

"No one is getting hurt by it, Viv. It sells houses. Her name is a brand—a strong brand—and putting it on the house gets us all more money." He breezed by her and gestured toward the back of the house. "Skip the living room, I know what you're going to say. Too edgy. I like it, but the Hoffmans are old school, you know? Come and look at—"

"Ryan." She ground out the word, not moving. "This is going to end right here, right now."

He stopped without turning, letting out a frustrated breath. "I knew this was a mistake."

"Then why did you call me?"

He didn't answer and still didn't turn.

"Because no one else would help you," she guessed, knowing she was right. Design was a small world in Atlanta, and this was a smarmy thing to do.

She took a few steps across the marble floor so she didn't have to raise her voice.

"Because everyone knows that you are going to give credit to your new girlfriend and not the real designer."

"Oh, so you're jealous?"

She snorted and rolled her eyes.

"Look, Vivien, overlapping designs and sharing credit is common in your business, just like—"

"It's called *stealing*," she fired back, feeling a punch of clarity as she realized just why this made her so deeply distraught. "It might be common, but it is exactly what put my father in prison thirty years ago. You might think it's no big deal, but I happen to know it's a *very* big deal. And I have no qualms seeing you pay the price for it."

He finally turned. "You'd do that to your husband?"

"My *ex*-husband," she reminded him.

"Not yet," he said, walking toward her. "Please don't forget I still have the power to change that divorce decree quite easily. I don't have to pay you a red cent if you turn on me. We're not divorced, so—"

"You're *not*?"

They both whipped around at the words, delivered with sharp precision and disbelief from a woman who'd just silently pushed the unlatched front door wide open. She strode in, five-foot-one inches of big hair and skinny jeans and really expensive boots.

"Convenient that you never mentioned that, Ryan."

"Una! I didn't expect you..." His voice faded as he looked from one woman to the other. "Who called you?"

"The new admin at Ryan Knight Homes that I got to help you out? She's my niece and she got a heads-up from a Realtor at the model. I happen to be working down the street." She crossed her arms and stared daggers at him. "You're still *married*?"

"That's not...relevant."

"It is to me," she scoffed, sliding a coffee-brown gaze to Vivien. "I'm Una Tatum. You must be the *not* ex-wife. Vivien? I really like your work."

She blinked at the unexpected compliment. "Thank you," she mumbled, resisting the urge to say something far less polite.

"And I thought I liked your husband," she added dryly. "But that's when he told me he was divorced."

"The divorce is almost final," Ryan said.

"Really? Because your *wife* is wearing a *wedding ring*."

Vivien sucked in a breath and touched the ring she'd completely forgotten she was wearing.

"I do have a line in the sand," Una announced. "Although it might not seem like it under the circumstances. I don't do married men—never have, never will. Obviously, she didn't leave you high and dry and take money from you like you told me she did when you oh-so-smoothly persuaded me to put my name on that model. Fraud isn't 'in her blood,' like you said it was, but it might be in yours."

Vivien spun, tearing her attention from the woman to Ryan as a flash of white-hot anger rocked her. "You told her *what*?"

"Look, listen, I'm just..." He held up both hands, clearly the one drowning now. "I'm sorry. Both of you."

"Keep your apologies," Vivien said, the need to get out of this house and away from these people stronger than anything she'd felt in a long time. "I'm leaving. Just fix the name and give my work the credit it's due."

"Come on, Viv."

"Do *not* 'come on, Viv' me. We're done." She turned her back to Ryan, her sights on the open door and her escape.

"Vivien."

Ignoring him, she brushed past the other woman and walked to the door.

"Vivien Knight!" he yelled.

She pivoted to stare at him for one dark, raging second.

"It's Vivien *Lawson*," she said, barely above a whisper. "As in Vivien Lawson Designs. As in your very-soon-to-be ex-wife. As in a free, strong, single woman who doesn't need you and never did."

Stepping out, she looked down at the doormat, giving it a little kick as she stepped on it, spinning it to a satisfyingly crooked angle.

You are a doormat no more, Vivien Lawson.

She strode to her car, relieved that Una had parked on the street. She couldn't get out fast—

"Ms. Lawson? Can I talk to you?" Una rushed out of the house after Vivien.

"No." *Ooh*, she was starting to really like the sound of that word on her lips.

"Please."

She put her hand on the door handle but stopped, waiting for the other woman to trot over in her red-bottomed boots.

"Listen, he painted an entirely different picture! He said you stole other people's work and that's why he—"

"Stop," Vivien said, pointing right in her face. "I don't want to hear your excuses or his lies. Una, that man in there is all yours. But..." She leaned a little lower to get closer to the petite woman. "My work is not."

"I didn't—"

Vivien shoved the crumpled flyer at her. "If you ever so much as claim a paint color I picked as yours, I will sue you from here to eternity. I will ruin your name and wreck your business and take you down. Is that clear?"

Una took the flyer, holding Vivien's gaze, a flicker of surprise in her brown eyes. "Huh. Weird. He said you were kind of a pushover."

Vivien smiled as she yanked open the door and slid into the driver's seat.

"Well, Una, he was wrong. Now, unless you want me to run over those two-thousand-dollar boots, you better move. I have a beach house to get to."

Chapter Nineteen
Tessa

Maybe it was a mistake, but Tessa felt her guard slipping ever so slightly toward the end of her meeting with Garrett at his beach house. To be real, this session hadn't been anything they couldn't cover on the phone or even with emails, but he'd invited her over that afternoon to touch base on some final details.

With business complete, they now sat on the expansive deck that would be the site of his dinner party for forty-four guests at final count, enjoying the sunshine, warm Gulf breezes, and a very easy conversation. He'd made her a tall iced tea and drank something a similar color in a much smaller glass—scotch, she imagined.

He'd taken the time to give her some fascinating details about his guests, holding nothing back. He told her about the private pilot who flew charter jets for exclusive clients and had dirt on everyone who was anyone. He shared a few stories about the entrepreneur who'd started the first online grocery app and sold it for millions, buying several hotels in Destin.

There was a widow who ran her husband's property

management business, an independent war correspondent just back from a secret trip to Taiwan, and a few locals he knew casually.

Most important was Sai Gupta, the executive VP from the Bank of Boston who was the reason Garrett was having this party.

"So our goal with Mr. Gupta is to lavish attention and impress him?" Tessa asked.

He tilted his head, the sunlight catching a few silver whiskers on an unshaven face, which, for Tessa, was a good look on a handsome middle-aged man.

"Don't let him know I've singled him out, but yes. Make Sai happy."

She searched his face, noticing once again that he was an attractive man with strong features and a warm smile. Beyond that, he had the kind of quick wit and listening skills that made her want to linger a little while longer and chat.

And there went her guard, slipping like the ice in her tea under the hot Destin sun.

She leaned in, propping an elbow on the table, determined to keep the conversation on business. "So, can you tell me why Gupta is so important?"

"I'm trying to get him on the board of my REIT," he said, then quickly added, "are you familiar with that term?"

Familiar enough to know that a Real Estate Investment Trust managed high-end properties that could range from hundreds of millions to a few billion in assets, depending on its size.

"How many properties?" she asked. "Commercial or residential?"

He lowered the glass he was about to sip from, regarding her with amusement and admiration in his gaze. "So you're not just another pretty face, Tessa."

She lifted a shoulder. "I worked with oodles of professionals at the Ritz and that exposed me to a lot of businesses."

And, having battled a reading and writing disorder her whole life, she had a freakish memory, which she used to her advantage.

He nodded, accepting her explanation. "I specialize in high-end office space in major metro areas around the world, and luxury mixed-use developments. My partner handles the premium residential side of the business, like this"—he waved his glass toward the house—"which is one of ours."

"So, you don't own this house?" she asked, a little surprised.

"My corporation does," he explained. "It's usually a long-term rental but since it was empty, I decided to stay here while I pursued Gupta, who is, I think I mentioned, over in Rosemary Beach."

"What else can you tell me about him?" she asked, glancing at the guest list on the table. "Or his wife...Priya, correct?"

"Correct. I know nothing about her, but he doesn't drink, likes soft jazz music, and has three daughters, all under eleven."

That was news to her. "Are the daughters coming?"

"I have no idea, but they aren't on the RSVP list, so you don't have to worry about them."

"I do if you want to impress Mr. Gupta," she replied. "I'll have chicken tenders just in case, and a streaming version of *Wicked* at the ready."

His jaw dropped. "I would never have thought of that."

"I take it you don't have kids."

"No," he said, lifting his glass again. "I wasn't that, uh, fortunate."

Something in the way he said that made her drop that guard even more. Could this handsome, wealthy, successful man really have a tender heart? Oh, how she'd longed to meet someone exactly like that.

"Do you, Tessa?" he asked after taking a sip.

"Have children?" She took a breath, hating the question almost as much as she hated when someone asked her to read something. The answer never felt right. "I never married," she said.

He studied her intently, looking right into her eyes. "Someone missed out," he said softly, the words giving her an unwanted thrill.

She managed to wave off the compliment. "Oh, I don't know about that."

"You're young," he said. "Still plenty of time to fall in love, right?"

"Not that young. Not that much time." She smiled. "I'm very picky."

"As you should be." He leaned forward and put a

hand over hers. "You could find someone worthy of you. Although he'd have to be extraordinary."

She held his gaze one second too long, then common sense rose up and took over. She gave a tight smile and eased her hand free, pushing back her chair.

"Thank you," she said, purposely vague so that she'd sufficiently thanked him for the compliment and the meeting, but didn't encourage anything more. "I'd better go and get to work."

Smiling, he stood slowly, his eyes telling her he knew he'd gone one little bit too far, which actually made her like him even more.

"I fear I'm not paying you enough," he said.

She drew back. "You're paying exactly enough."

He reached into his pocket, and she half expected him to whip out his wallet and throw some money at her. But keys jangled as he handed them to her.

"I'm taking off in an hour for a trip to Miami and will be gone until the morning of the party. These will get you into the house, the downstairs storage in case those acrylic chairs are delivered, and this one..." He plucked an oversized key and held it up. "Is very special."

The key to his heart? She held her breath to see where he was taking this.

"There's a twenty-nine-foot Sea Ray inboard docked at the harbor across the street in slot fifteen-A. It comes as part of this house, and you should feel free to take it for a spin. I am going out on a limb and guessing a woman as capable as you can drive a cabin cruiser."

"Actually, I can."

He dropped the keys in her hand. "Have a blast, and I'll see you the day of the party. Text me if anything comes up."

She nodded, gathering her tablet and bag. "Awesome. I may take you up on the boat ride."

"I hope you do."

He guided her to the gate that led to the dunes, since she was walking back to the Summer House. Opening the latch, he put a light hand on her shoulder.

"I really enjoy your company, Tessa," he said softly. "Am I making that too obvious?"

She slid him a look, swallowing hard, clinging to the last shreds of that wall of protection and caution she was so desperate to keep up when she was around this man.

"I'm not looking for anything except new clients," she said, giving herself an internal, silent fist-pump for the response. "But I appreciate...the interest."

"Let me know if you change your mind," he said. "And if it's clients you want, I'm happy to be a reference for you after our soirée. Assuming everything goes...as planned."

Something in the last two words shot that wall right up again. What was...*planned*? Other than a party, of course.

"I'm sure we will have a spectacular event," she said, stepping back. "Goodbye, Garrett."

As she walked away, she could have sworn she heard him sigh and something in that sound put a smile on her face.

She must have been wearing that smile the whole time she and Lacey pounded out the final lists, chatted with the caterer—ordered the chicken tenders for the kids —and signed off on the flowers and table décor delivery times.

That's when Lacey leaned over the dining table that had become their de facto conference room and pointed at her. "You seem happy," she said.

"I'm always happy," Tessa replied.

"Happi*er*. Is it because we got so much done today in this empty house?"

"It is empty." She looked around, rooting for a response that wasn't the truth...she was thinking about *a man* again. "With Eli and Kate off to hunt down the Cavallaris, Jonah touring that local college, and Vivien in Atlanta, we got so much done today."

"You weren't this happy before your meeting with Garrett," Lacey observed, narrowing her eyes. "Or am I imagining it?"

Oh, no. She wasn't imagining it. And why was Tessa so danged transparent? Was that why Garrett flirted with her? Did she make it obvious she found him attractive?

"Well, he is very complimentary of our work," she said. "And he offered to be a reference for my business and— Oh! He also gave me the keys to a twenty-nine-foot boat, so anytime we want to—"

The front door smacked open, and Vivien marched in dragging two large suitcases behind her.

"Mom." Lacey instantly forgot her interrogation and looked at Vivien. "What's all this?"

"It's my clothes for the summer."

They both stared at her as she gave in to a slow grin.

"I found my backbone, kicked Ryan to the curb, threatened the competition, and decided I'm staying here until we sell this place in November. It's officially another summer in Destin. What should we do to celebrate?"

Tessa snagged the keys resting on top of her bag. "I know exactly what we're going to do."

TESSA HAD TRAINED on a fifty-two-foot yacht, so this little cabin cruiser didn't intimidate her in the least.

Much to Vivien and Lacey's amazement, she settled into the captain's chair, took a few minutes to memorize the dashboard and walked her two passengers through the process of untying the lines so they could undock.

Shortly after, they were motoring through Destin Harbor, a four-mile-long waterway that separated the east-west residential peninsula where their house was from the main part of "downtown" Destin. Well-protected by land, the entire harbor was a no-wake zone with very little boat traffic.

All in all, it made for a perfect late afternoon cruise with gorgeous views of the marina on one side and the expansive docks and shops along HarborWalk Village.

"How did you get so confident driving a boat?" Lacey asked in amazement.

"I had to do a yacht wedding once and the captain liked me." She grinned. "He gave me free lessons."

Lacey laughed. "Men just give you things, don't they? Boats, lessons..."

"Headaches," she said dryly.

Vivien snorted from her seat on the bow. "Amen to that, sister."

She'd dished the details of what happened in Atlanta on the way over, so Tessa understood exactly why Vivien sounded bitter right then. Bitter but wildly victorious, and the mood was infectious.

"I just can't believe he lied to Una," Lacey said, and not for the first time. "I mean, he knows I talk to her when she comes in the office. Did he think I'd cover for him? That I'd lie about your divorce being final? And you being a fraud? What did he think?"

"He didn't think," Vivien said.

"Not with his brain," Tessa muttered.

They were quiet while Vivien filled three plastic cups with the G&Ts they'd mixed in a large Thermos before leaving. While she did, Lacey spread out some cheese and crackers on the bow table.

Tessa kept her eyes on the water, planning a slow spin through the harbor that would end with them facing west so they could watch the sunset.

"Let's toast to freedom," Vivien said, holding up two Solo cups. "And not being...what did she say he called me? A pushover."

"He couldn't push over a feather," Lacey said, taking the drinks and bringing one to Tessa at the helm.

Tessa accepted the cup with a smile of thanks, sliding it into a holder so she could keep two hands and a clear head. "Drink to the worst part of it being over, Viv," she said. "Then put this divorce in the rearview mirror. That's my advice."

"The worst part was that he used my father against me."

Tessa curled a lip. "Agreed. That's unforgiveable."

"So are you seriously staying here, Mom? You're not going back to Atlanta until November?"

Vivien took a sip and looked from Tessa to Lacey. "Yes. But that's not all."

They waited, the only sound the rumble of the inboards and the water splashing on the hull.

She reached over and gave the brim of Lacey's bright blue sunhat a playful tug. "So are you."

"What?" Lacey whispered.

"And you." Vivien pointed at Tessa.

"What are you talking about, Mom?"

"The three of us are going to live at this house from now until it sells in November. We're happy, we're starting our lives over, and we're excellent caretakers."

Tessa rose from the leather chair, guiding the throttle down to quiet the motor. She couldn't have heard that right.

"What did you say?" she asked.

Vivien smiled. "You heard me. We have the place until November, when it goes on the market. You know we can't sell until then."

Tessa checked the surroundings, switched the engine

off, and let the sun-bathed world go quiet, the only sound the thrum of her heartbeat at what Vivien was suggesting.

Very slowly, she lifted her cup from the holder and crossed the deck to the bow seating area.

"You can't be serious," she said.

"Why not?"

"Because Eli would have a cow, for one thing. He's barely over my squatting in the first place."

"Not true," Vivien countered. "He's not a grudge holder. Plus, let's all say it out loud—he's got it so bad for Kate he can't see straight. If you're here, she has a much higher chance of visiting."

Tessa had known that for a while, but hadn't said a word to anyone except Kate. "I could probably start a business in Destin. There's a ton of social events and some wedding venues."

"And I'm going to launch a full-court press to find new clients," Vivien said.

"And..." Lacey looked from one to the other. "I'm going to..." She gave an expectant look, not able to finish.

"You, my little lamb, are going to work for me." Tessa put an arm around her. "I might not be able to steal you as a daughter, but I'll take you as my right hand and good eyes and brain."

Lacey let out a little squeak of delight. "Mom, what do you think of that?"

"I think you may have just found the elusive fun job you've wanted for years."

Tessa lifted her glass. "I will toast to that!"

"Wait! Wait!" Lacey stood, pushing back that

turquoise hat. "Are we doing this? Are we staying in Destin until November and starting businesses and living in that dream house together? Is that really happening?"

"Yes!" Tessa shrieked. "We are!"

They all jumped up and squealed and hugged, rocking the boat with their joy.

"Woo-hoo!" Vivien flung her hands in the air. "This is so— Oh, no!" She gasped noisily, then let out a shocked squawk, grabbing one of her hands with the other.

"What's wrong?" Tessa asked, seeing the blood drain from her face.

"My ring!" she mouthed the words in disbelief. "My wedding ring! It just went flying into the water!"

For a moment, they stood in utter shock, three jaws wide open in incredulity.

"Why did you have it on?" Lacey finally asked.

Vivien blinked, staring at her empty hand, then looking at the harbor water. "I forgot I tried it on. It was loose and I got distracted..."

Tessa slid her arm around her. "And now it's at the bottom of the deep blue sea, where it belongs."

Vivien gave a quick laugh, then closed her eyes, suddenly fighting tears.

"Oh, Mom, it's okay," Lacey insisted. "You didn't ever wear it. You didn't need it. I certainly didn't want it."

"It's not the ring," she said softly. "It's the fact that... it's over. My marriage is over and..."

"Your new life begins today," Tessa said. "In Destin."

Vivien wiped a tear, stared at her bare hand, and swallowed hard. "Yes, it does."

Still holding each other, the three of them lined up at the bow, looking out at the water, ready to plan the rest of their lives.

Well, the rest of the summer in Destin. And that, Tessa knew, could be the best season of a girl's life.

Could Garrett Fischer be part of that summer? She wished she didn't care so much, but she did.

July 31, 1989

Last night was so much fun!! I ate soooo much spaghetti I thought I might explode. It was Aunt Jo Ellen and Uncle Artie's anniversary, and Kate had this super genius (natch) idea that we could make them dinner as a surprise. Like a real fancy dinner. With candles and cloth napkins folded—Tessa knew how to make them look like flowers!

All of us kids—even Eli and Peter—got in on it. I couldn't believe Eli wanted to help, but I think Peter talked him into it. We didn't know how to make anything nice at first, but we all walked to the Cavallari's deli and Mr. Frank told us how to make the best spaghetti and meatballs ever. Eli wrote everything down, and we walked to Publix together to get the stuff. It felt super grown-up.

The parents were out on the boat all afternoon, so we had hours to cook. Good thing too, because we totally burned the first batch of meatballs and Kate said the spaghetti turned to mush. We laughed so hard I almost dropped a pot.

Kate made the red sauce, and I swear it tasted exactly like the fancy stuff from the Italian restaurant we go to back home. She's kind of amazing at cooking. I was scared to mess anything up, so I just helped roll the meatballs. It was kinda like playing with Play-Doh...but grosser if I thought about it too much. I tried not to.

Tessa and I pretended we were waitresses and made a whole menu and everything. We even dressed up and called it "Ristorante Destin." They let us pour the wine, too! I only spilled a little.

The best part? The parents loved it. Aunt Jo Ellen even said it was one of her favorite anniversary dinners ever. We all sat outside with candles and the sun was setting, and it felt so cool to watch them enjoy something we made. Even Eli smiled a lot. (Until he smeared sauce on my nose, but whatever. He's Eli.)

I guess I didn't realize how fun it could be when we all worked together like that. It felt like...we were a team, even if we don't always get along.

Peter was really nice to me the whole time. I think he stayed near me on purpose. I liked it but...I also got nervous sometimes when he talked to me. I don't know why! Ugh.

Anyway, the whole thing made me wish summer wasn't almost over. I want to stay here forever.

Vivien

Chapter Twenty
Kate

Kate accompanied Eli on a few errands around Destin, the two of them laughing and talking and enjoying the day before they finally got down to the business of driving to an older neighborhood in Santa Rosa Beach, about a half hour east of Destin.

They rumbled along in his truck, taking the scenic route along the water as far as they could, and as they turned inland to get back on the main highway, a text from Jonah buzzed her phone. After she read it, she let out a little groan.

"Don't tell me," Eli guessed, glancing from the traffic to look at her. "Your mom needs you home...tomorrow."

She almost smiled at the bit of dread and disappointment in his voice. Not that she wished either on this dear man, but she knew it meant he didn't want her to leave, and that touched her.

"No, this was from your son." She held up the phone. "Hitting brick walls on the culinary arts search."

His brows lifted. "Really? What's the issue?"

"Well, he's only found three decent programs anywhere near Destin," she said, glancing at Jonah's text. "There are some cooking classes in the area, but the only real degree he can find is at Pensacola State, and that's a haul for daily drives. Plus, it's a year-long program and he'll want to get back to California before his baby is born in six months."

"Words I never thought I'd hear," he said softly. "But that does present a challenge for him, especially if he wants to work while he goes to school."

"He has to," Kate said, leaving no room for argument. At Eli's look, she added, "He wants to earn this himself, Eli. Not mooch money from you. Respect that."

"Oh, I do. And I respect that he wants a legit degree. But Pensacola State is far. There's nothing else anywhere nearby?"

She re-read the text, seeing the subtext even more than the actual words. "He's frustrated."

"And that's when he gives up," Eli said on a sigh. "I'm praying God opens a door, and fast."

She eyed him for a moment, used to his references to God and faith by now, but still not entirely comfortable with them. "Can I ask you a question?"

"Of course."

She cleared her throat, not wanting to be condescending or disrespectful, but she had to know. "Do you really believe there's a man up in the sky looking down and worrying about Jonah's degree?"

He gave in to a slow smile, looking like he'd expected the question or at least was used to it.

"In a word, yes. I don't think He's in the 'sky,' but I do think He is the Highest Power, and I have a good relationship with Him." He let out a slow breath before continuing. "I have built my entire life on Him, Kate, and that will never change."

The power of the statement rocked her. "Oh, well. Huh. I'm a scientist, so I don't believe in...that."

"I know."

"And *that* will never change," she added.

"If you're worried about me cornering you and forcing you to read the Bible, you can stop. My faith is private and I'm not very good at evangelizing, sadly. But I do try to live with complete trust that God has the steps planned."

She thought about that. "I can only imagine how broken you must have been after Melissa died..."

"And you think my faith was a crutch to get me through the pain."

She nodded, hoping that wasn't offensive.

But he just smiled. "Actually, she had become what they call 'Christian curious' about six months before she died. We both began exploring the concepts together, reading books but we hadn't given ourselves to Christ. Then...then...yeah, then she was gone."

She heard the rasp of pain in his voice, surprisingly fresh. "I'm so sorry, Eli," she said, putting her hand over his on the console. "For your loss, of course, and for the question. I don't mean to belittle something so important to you."

"You didn't," he assured her. "I understand doubts more than I understand faith, to be honest. It's a lot easier to doubt or simply refuse to believe."

She considered that, trying—and failing—to understand such, well, ridiculous beliefs. "I just want you to know that I built my life on science, and it doesn't co-exist with faith."

"I'm not sure I agree, but..." He smiled and threaded his fingers through hers. "Why don't you stick around for a long time, and we can discuss it?"

She took in a slow breath, allowing herself to just feel the gentle thrill of his touch and the sentiment.

"I wish I could," she said just as the dashboard lit up with a call from Meredith Lawson.

"Do you mind if I take my daughter's call?" He gave her hand a squeeze. "I'm kind of enjoying our conversation."

"So am I, but yes, talk to her. She's basically running your company and you're..."

"Having fun with a beautiful woman." He winked, then pressed a button on the steering wheel. "Hey, Mer."

"Hi, Dad. How are you?"

"I'm with Kate Wylie and you're on speaker," he said.

She gasped softly. "Oh, wow. A Wylie girl! I feel like I'm meeting a secret celebrity I've only heard whispers about."

Kate laughed at that. "Not a girl, not a secret, and certainly not a celebrity. Hello, Meredith."

They chatted about the house and some business, then he filled her in on Jonah's decision to stay, the excitement in his voice palpable as he told her the news.

"Wow!" Meredith exclaimed. "This is huge, Dad! I'm stunned. Culinary school? Does that mean he'd go back to California?"

"He wants to stay here so he can do some work on the house, but it seems the closest good program is at Pensacola State," Eli said. "And that's well over an hour away, closer to two with traffic."

In a few seconds of quiet, Kate could hear a keyboard clattering on the other end.

"Let me do some poking around," Meredith said. "If I know Jonah, he hit one obstacle and gave up."

Eli chuckled. "Not quite, but...yeah. Can you work some of that Meredith Magic? I want him to stay. It's honestly the best thing that's happened in a long time." He slid Kate a look and smiled. "Well, one of them."

The words warmed her as much as the sun beating on the windshield from a sky so blue, it hurt to look at. A sky and a man she would miss very much when she got on that plane to Ithaca.

"She sounds amazing," Kate said after they'd said goodbye to Meredith, thinking of all Eli had told her about his high-energy, overachieving daughter. "And she obviously loves Jonah."

"She does, but they've had plenty of conflict over the years," he said, peering at the GPS on his phone. "We turn up here into what looks like a small community. Hope it's not gated."

"If we get in, do you think we should knock on the door?" she asked. "I don't want to give them a heart attack. They could be old or sick or...not remember us."

"I hope they do, and I really hope they remember what happened that year," Eli said as he turned off the main road into a residential area. "It's become more important, actually."

"Why?"

He blew out a breath. "It could affect...things," he said. "I mean, I don't like the idea of my mother having an issue with...you."

"Or Tessa," she added.

He gave her a look. "Don't be coy, Dr. Wylie."

"Coy? Me?" She laughed, aware of a tendril of heat curling through her chest, a longing she'd first felt as a teenager, hoping that Eli Lawson would someday kiss her.

"Oh, we're here." He slowed at a small brick one-story with impeccable landscaping and a cheery red door.

"And there's someone." Eli pointed to an old man coming around the side of the house in a giant sunhat, overalls, and with a shovel in his hand. Eli stopped the truck and stared at the man. "Think that's Frank?"

"I do," she said. "Just much, much older."

He put the truck in Park and turned off the ignition. With one silent look at each other, they opened their doors and climbed out.

"Can I help you?" Frank croaked the question, stabbing his shovel into the earth and leaning on it.

"Frank Cavallari?" Eli asked as he met Kate at the front of the truck.

"What's it to you, son?"

Eli smiled and came closer, extending his hand. "My name's Eli Lawson. This is Kate Wylie. I believe you—"

"No!" For a moment, he did look like he might fall

over. "Not a chance you're those young teenagers from Destin all those years ago."

He remembered! Kate beamed at him while he and Eli shook hands first.

"Not teenagers anymore," Eli said, sounding as happy as she felt. "But it's good to see you, Mr. Cavallari."

"You, too, young man." He pushed back his straw hat and squinted at Eli, then Kate, then back to Eli. "Holy smokes, you're the spittin' image of Roger."

She could have sworn Eli blanched. She knew him well enough by now to know he did not enjoy comparisons to his father.

"It's good to see you, sir," he said. "I hope we're not intruding on you and, uh, Mrs. Cavallari. Is she here?"

"She better be or we're all in trouble. She promised me ice-cold limoncello if I turned over her garden bed. It's my own homemade. Come on in and have some, now." He ushered them toward a side door, taking a moment to study Kate. "Artie and Jo Ellen's girl, huh? You had a twin sister, right? Li'l wild thing, if I recall correctly."

Kate laughed. "She still is. Tessa. How nice that you remember our families."

He reached for the kitchen door, looking from one to the other. "We lost touch, you know. And it 'bout broke Betty's heart. I think she'll be very glad to see you. Come on in. Betty! Brace yourself, woman. Don't keel over from a heart attack. The Lawsons and the Wylies are back."

Kate and Eli shared a look, both of them laughing

softly when a woman squealed like a teenage girl, nothing but delight in her voice.

For some reason, Kate sensed this was going to go very well.

THE LIMONCELLO WAS COLD—AND strong—and so were the opinions of two people who might have been married for sixty years, but had extremely different memories of the past.

Betty thought the Summer House property had been on the old Scenic Highway; Frank remembered it as right off Henderson Beach. They were both wrong.

Betty recalled a night they went to AJ's and Maggie had too much to drink and lost a shoe in the harbor. Frank insisted it was a different restaurant and it was Artie who got food poisoning that night. But they did agree it was fun and they all drank too much.

Betty was especially animated when she talked about meeting Jo Ellen when the family had first come shopping in Frank's Italian Deli in Destin. Betty had hit it off with her because the Wylies were from New York.

"We just liked each other right away," she said, her smile revealing yellowed teeth. "She was a good woman, and a fine mother."

"She still is," Kate said.

"That's not how we met them," Frank interjected. "It was Maggie. She came swooping into the deli like a true Southern belle looking for something 'Eye-talian' and I let her have her first taste of *prosciutto*." He pronounced it 'pro-jute' and gave a soft hoot. "Oh, she was a fan after that. That Georgia peach never had good Italian cold cuts."

Betty gave him a side-eye. "That is not how we met them, Frank. That was another time. Oh, what does it matter? We were friends way back in the day and we had a lot of fun going out together those summers."

Frank's bushy brows moved. "We, uh, heard Roger had some problems in the end."

Eli shifted uncomfortably. "He did, but we all like to remember him as you do, Frank. A man in his prime, a good father, and a loving husband."

Frank lifted a brow as if that last one might have not hit quite right. And he shared a look with Betty who Kate could have sworn gave an infinitesimal shake to her head.

"Oh, Roger," she said on a sigh. "He was always so..." Her voice trailed off.

"So...what?" Kate asked, leaning forward and sensing they'd just hit the gold they'd come to mine.

The older couple looked at each other again, this time with a question behind both sets of bifocals.

"It's not important," Frank finally said.

"It is to us," Eli replied, bracing his elbows on his knees and leaning to look hard at them. "Our mothers are still alive, but they haven't spoken to each other in thirty years, and they won't say why. Kate and I—and our siblings—are trying to figure out what happened to cause that falling out. We were honestly hoping you'd shed some light on it."

Betty huffed a breath and stood up, moving remarkably well for a woman deep in her eighties. "I need something in the kitchen."

Kate stood and followed her in, sensing she might get more from a woman-to-woman chat.

"I think I left the shed unlocked." Frank pushed up. "I better check. Come with me, son."

When the door closed behind the two men, Betty turned and let out a long sigh. "I knew it would come to this someday," she said. "People have to pay the piper."

"What do you mean?" Kate asked, a sickening sensation crawling through her. "Please, Betty, tell me what happened."

She thought for a moment, then her shoulders sank as if they couldn't stand the weight of this anymore.

"I don't know how far it went," she said. "I don't know if it got, you know, physical, but..."

Kate tried to swallow, already knowing she was going to hate this. "But what?"

"He's dead and I don't want it to change your opinion of your father, dear—"

"Tell me," she said through gritted teeth, bracing for... she didn't know what.

"It was Maggie!" she said. "She had...power. She was beautiful, of course, but she could just reel a man in with one little finger. Have you ever met anyone like that?"

Yeah, she thought. *My twin sister.* "What did she do?"

"She made Artie love her!" Betty announced. "He fell so hard for that woman, he...he couldn't see straight."

And neither could Kate right then. Her father...*loved Maggie*? She felt every drop of blood drain from her face.

"I'm not a hundred percent sure of course. I barely remember what I had for lunch yesterday let alone what happened thirty years ago, but..." She tsked repeatedly, shaking her head. "I'm sure that's why Roger bought Maggie that house, which they never told us about. But it would be like him to try to win her back after it all came out."

"So...everyone knew about...this?"

"I don't remember who knew what. Honestly, I don't want to gossip, but I never liked Maggie Lawson and couldn't imagine what Artie saw in her. I couldn't find common ground with her like I could with your sweet mother. Tell me more about how Jo Ellen is, dear."

Kate blinked at her, not sure she could make small talk after that...revelation.

Her father loved Maggie? And that caused the breakup? Her parents hadn't ever given her any indication that there was a rift like that in their marriage, and they often spoke of the Lawsons without rancor.

But they never did speak *to* the Lawsons again, did they?

"She's...all right," Kate finally said, barely remembering what Betty had asked. "Sad, though. She misses my dad."

"I'm sure she does. She was a sweet soul, so much kinder than Maggie, as I recall. But then..." She gave a dry laugh. "I'm eighty-six and I don't recall all that well."

The back door opened, and Eli came in first, his face

as pale as Kate's must have been. So Frank had told him this dark news, too.

"We better let these people get on with their lives," Eli said, bringing the reunion to an abrupt halt. "I need to get back to Destin."

She nodded, beyond grateful and anxious to leave.

After a rather rushed goodbye, some light hugs and quick waves, Eli and Kate hustled to the truck, climbing in, silent.

He turned on the ignition but didn't move, staring straight ahead.

"He told you?" she guessed. "My dad and your mother."

"What?" His head whipped to the side to look at her. "What are you talking about?"

She stared at him. "Betty said that my father fell for... Maggie. He was in love with her."

He looked stunned. "Frank said that my father had an affair with Jo Ellen. And that he bought my mother the house as a consolation prize because she was so mad, she threatened divorce."

She inched back, frowning. "No, not Roger and Jo Ellen. It was...Artie and Maggie."

He shook his head. "Frank was clear. Roger wooed Jo Ellen hard, and Maggie went ballistic when she found out."

They stared at each other and then, without really thinking about it, they both gave quick, short laughs.

"They don't know what they're talking about," Eli said. "Neither one of them can agree on a thing."

324 Hope Holloway & Cecelia Scott

"I'm not sure they remember any of it," Kate said, the hurt that had her heart in a vise-grip loosening a little bit. "She doesn't like Maggie, and this could have been in her imagination. Oh, I hope so."

He nodded, letting out a breath it seemed like he'd been holding since they left the kitchen. "Frank despised my father. Honestly, if anyone had a little crush on Maggie, I think it was him and he made up the whole thing."

"I'd like to think that," Kate said. "Otherwise, one of them might be recalling correctly."

"But there was a falling out," Eli reminded her. "There's no denying that. Or the fact that we don't know any more than we did when we got here."

"No, we don't. Some doubts, some questions, and the same dearth of information we came with." She reached into her bag for her phone as he drove down the street. "Let's see if Jonah responded."

"That's funny," Eli said. "You're waiting for a text from my son."

She smiled. "We have a nice connection, Jonah and me. We— Oh." She stared at the message on the screen and her poor heart fell again.

"What is it?" he asked.

"Mom took a tumble. Nothing serious, but her ankle is sore. My daughter is staying with her but..." She dropped the phone on her lap and closed her eyes.

"Really? Are you sure she's okay?"

"Yes, but...you know what it means."

He let out a grunt of disappointment. "You have to go back."

"I do. I'm sorry, but..."

"Hey, you do what you have to do. I...I just..." He struggled for the right words then reached over and took her hand. "I'll miss you so much."

She clutched his hand, fighting tears that made no sense at all. Of course, this was Eli, who sent her logic flying away, replaced by confusion and longing and... faith.

"I could use some of those prayers of yours," she said with a smile. "Even if I don't believe in them."

"You don't have to." He lifted her hand to put a soft kiss on her knuckles. "Because I do, and I'll be saying the prayers."

"For what?"

"That you stay in my life."

She leaned her head back and smiled, letting a tear roll down her cheek. That was a prayer she hoped was answered.

Chapter Twenty-one

Eli

Eli had slept fitfully and woke the next day with a heavy heart. He came downstairs hoping to find Kate and Jonah making a breakfast feast, but the living area and kitchen were still, quiet, and empty.

He made a pot of coffee, taking a cup to the deck to drink in daybreak on this, his last day with Kate.

When had this happened? He'd thought they were friends—barely—and suddenly, all he wanted to do was wrap her in his arms and make her stay. Stay here? He didn't even live in this town.

But Vivien, Lacey, and Tessa did...at least, they were planning to for the next seven months.

He fought a smile as he settled into a comfortable seat and took his first sip of coffee, remembering what had unfolded last night.

The three of them had been out on a boat ride and came in smelling like salt spray and giggling like, well, like the girls he remembered on this beach so many years ago. Clearly hopped up on a plan, they took no time convincing him that they should live in the Summer House until it went on the market in November.

He'd never even considered saying they couldn't—
but, dang, he wished he could figure out a way to stay,
too. With Kate, of course.

But after the way Ryan treated Vivien in Atlanta, he
fully encouraged her to stay, and Lacey, too. He loved the
idea of having caretakers for the property getting it ready
to sell.

As for Tessa? Well, he was happy that she no longer
held sway over him. Especially after Kate's insights, he'd
fully forgiven Tessa for past hurts and could now see her
as a woman still searching for her place in the world. If he
could help her find it, then that was a good thing.

He and Vivien had privately agreed not to mention
the addition of Tessa Wylie as a temporary resident to
Maggie, since their mother did *technically* own the place
and would undoubtedly freak out.

He and Kate told Vivien and Tessa about the visit
with the Cavallaris, and they all decided that infidelity
for either couple was impossible to imagine and, if it had
been true, one of their kids would have gotten wind of it
by now. For their part, it didn't answer any questions, and
they had no desire to delve deeper.

The evening had been quiet after that. Tessa and
Lacey went off to plan their new endeavor. Vivien had
worked in the back office on some design ideas. Kate
disappeared upstairs to make travel arrangements and
pack.

Worst of all, Jonah came home glum, and holed up in
his room.

They didn't even have a final dinner as the ad hoc

family they'd become over these last few weeks, and that sent Eli to bed early and unhappy. Now, sipping his coffee, he studied the horizon, wondering when the rest of the house would be up.

"Dad!"

He turned at the sound of Jonah's voice as he barreled up the stairs from his first-floor bedroom. "On the deck, son. Join me for coff—"

Jonah shot out through the sliding glass doors, his face bright. "Meredith is a genius!"

He almost choked, not sure what surprised him more —the compliment for Jonah's sister or the expression of sheer joy on his son's face.

"What happened?"

"She found a program at Northwest Florida State, which is twenty minutes from here in some town called Niceville, if you can believe that."

Eli put his cup on the table, standing up. "I know exactly where that is. Very close and very, well, nice."

"I knew there was a school there, but when I checked their site, it said culinary *management* only, which isn't what I want. I want culinary arts, but Meredith—holy cow." He gave a laugh and shook his uncombed hair back. "My girl is unstoppable when she wants something, but this time I'm grateful."

His girl? My, how things changed. "Tell me what she found."

"That community college is starting a flagship culinary arts program in the hospitality department *this summer*."

"What's all this I hear?" Kate came out to join them, looking dressed and ready to travel, but Eli didn't let that dampen his excitement for what Jonah was saying. "You found a program?"

"Right over the Bay Bridge," he told her. "Apparently, it's going to be run by a local chef who wants to take very few students, so"—he made a face—"I'll need to interview and cook something. I'm thinking that Brazilian shrimp should do the trick."

"Anything you make will wow him," Kate said, reaching to give him a hug. "I'm so happy for you, Jonah."

"Well, no congrats yet, but it's a first step." He let out a sigh and looked at her, then Eli. "I'm really grateful to both of you."

"Us?" Kate asked with a quick laugh. "Your father's the one who's helping make this happen."

"But you..." He pointed to her and nodded, as if he didn't have to say anything, the connection between them palpable.

"You provided the inspiration and encouragement," Eli finished for him, taking a step closer and hoping his feelings for this woman weren't too obvious. "Thank you, Kate."

"And you provided the means," Jonah said to Eli. "I just hope I can get accepted to the program."

"You can live here," Eli said, not even giving the idea a second thought.

"What?"

"You went downstairs early last night," Eli said. "You missed the news that Vivien, Tessa, and Lacey are staying through November. We'll get you a proper bed and you can live and study here, and use our kitchen."

His jaw loosened as he processed this. "I was seriously going to live in my van, but...wow." He looked choked up as he reached for Eli to give him a hug. "Thank you, Dad."

Eli patted his back warmly, knowing that at that moment, he couldn't be happier.

Well, he *could* be happier, he thought when he opened his eyes and his gaze landed on Kate, who watched the exchange with pure joy on her face.

He could be holding her and convincing her to stay for the summer, too.

Guess he couldn't have everything.

"Well, I hate to break up the party," Kate said with a wistful sigh, "but my flight leaves at eleven, so—"

"Please say we have time for one more breakfast," Jonah interjected. "We have to...oh, hang on." He pulled out his phone and tapped the screen. "Email from the assistant to the hospitality and tourism department dean." He took a deep breath and glanced from one to the other. "I'm scared to open it."

"Did you apply already?" Eli asked, astounded at the possibility.

"Meredith the Relentless sent an note to the department asking what the requirements were and gave them my email." He held up the phone. "Let me go read this. I'll be back."

He disappeared into the house and Kate and Eli looked at each other, silent for a beat.

"You did this," he finally said. "You stepped in and saved my son."

"Not a chance I can take credit for that, but I'm delighted I could play any role at all in this new season of his life. And sad I won't be here to watch it unfold."

He looked at her for a long time, taking in every feature and trying to imagine what he could say. Only one word would do.

"Stay," he whispered.

She blinked, a little color draining from her face. "You know I can't do that."

"Doesn't stop me from asking," he said. "Don't you get the summer off? Aren't you on a school semester schedule in that lab?"

"Yes," she said. "But...my mother. My kids. My life. Even thinking about it doesn't make logical sense."

"Logic is overrated," he said, only half joking. He could tell she ached for her children, and certainly couldn't fault her for that.

She looked like she wanted to say something, but closed her eyes, tamping down whatever it was, so he just reached for her hand.

"Let me take you to the airport," he said. "Surely you agree that's...logical." Although when it came time to say goodbye and he wanted to kiss her? Then what?

Jonah came out, interrupting the conversation and looking far less excited than when he'd left.

"What did they say?" Kate asked.

He huffed out a breath. "I have everything school-wise, but they want restaurant experience."

"You have plenty of that," Eli said.

"Yeah, but they also want the one thing I doubt I can get from anyone. A letter of recommendation."

"Oh, son. I'll write—"

Jonah held up his hand to stop Eli. "Not from a family member. From someone I've worked with in the past year at a restaurant or in food service."

"Well, surely there's someone," Kate said.

Jonah winced. "Someone, somewhere over a bridge I burned. I'll have to give it some thought, but..." He shrugged, looking defeated.

"Don't let one roadblock stop you," Eli said. "I'm sure you'll think of a manager from one of your jobs."

He shook his head. "I don't know, but...I'm going to go downstairs and think about who I haven't ticked off and try calling them. Don't leave without saying goodbye, Kate."

She gave him a warm smile. "I won't. In fact, I have to go finish packing."

She stepped inside, and Jonah followed, leaving Eli right where he'd been a few minutes ago. Only now his coffee was cold, his hopes were dashed, and he really, really didn't want to say goodbye to Kate.

AFTER A HUG-FILLED goodbye to the rest of the household, Eli and Kate took off for the Destin-Fort Walton Beach Airport, which was tiny in comparison to most, but slammed with spring break travelers.

There was one parking lot, packed and overflowing.

"You can drop me off, you know," she said as he circled the lot a third time.

"I want to walk you in and say goodbye."

When she didn't say anything, he stole a look at her.

"What?" he asked, unable to read the expression behind her glasses that, for once, were on her nose where they belonged.

"I was thinking about how sometimes things don't add up properly and they still feel right," she said. "That's kind of a hard concept for my scientific mind to conceive."

"Things like what?" he asked.

"Like your faith and my...feelings."

He saw the lights of a car pulling out and drove closer to the spot, processing exactly what she could mean.

"Your faith doesn't make sense to me," she continued. "Normally, religious people kind of irritate me."

"I get that," he conceded. "I don't like to think of myself as 'religious,' per se."

"You go to church every Sunday. Alone, too."

He didn't realize she'd noticed that he quietly disappeared on Sunday mornings to attend a small nondenominational church he'd found in Destin. "I do, but I don't expect my faith to make sense to you. I haven't pushed it on you, have I?"

"Not at all," she assured him. "But my point was it is very right for you. I sense it."

He waited while an SUV pulled out and slid his truck into the open slot, eyeing the clock to see how much time they had to just sit here and talk. Whatever it was, it wasn't enough.

"And your feelings?" he prompted. "You mentioned those, too."

She shifted in her seat, unbuckling her seatbelt as he turned off the ignition so his brake lights didn't give someone hope that he was leaving.

"Feelings," she said on a sigh. "Not my favorite subject, as you can imagine. But, yes...I'm having them."

He smiled, taking off his seatbelt and turning to her. "Does that scare you, Kate?"

"Not exactly, but it does...present a problem that doesn't have a solution. The scientist in me hates that." She took her glasses off to look into his eyes. "The woman in me doesn't seem to mind."

For some reason, those words did stupid things to his insides. Things he couldn't remember feeling in a long, long time.

He put a hand on her cheek, loving the feel of her skin against his palm. "You want to tell me what kind of feelings they are?"

"No," she said with a quick laugh. "But I do want you to know they are real and keep me awake at night."

Very slowly, he grazed the pad of his thumb over her chin, searching her face. He was determined to memorize her cheekbones and the fine lines around her eyes, the shape of her lips, the hint of dimples, and the way her dark bangs fluttered around rich brown eyes that were as warm and grounding as freshly tilled earth.

"Same," he finally whispered. "And I have no idea what to do about that."

"Nothing," she said.

He gave a dry laugh. "Well, that doesn't make sense."

"Eli, my life is in Ithaca, New York. My family is there, my job is there, my cat is there." Her earth-toned eyes glimmered at that, and maybe with a few unshed tears. "But my heart, at the moment, will be in the same place it was at the end of every summer for seven years." She smiled. "In Destin, belonging to a sweet kid with blue eyes named Eli."

Oh, how had this happened? How could he feel so disappointed after these amazing weeks? Because he was not ready to say goodbye. This couldn't be over before it even started.

"Can I call you?" he asked.

"Of course."

"Can I visit?"

"Yes, but—"

He slid his finger over her lips. "No buts. We'll take it from here and see what happens."

"Nothing can happen," she said. "It's kind of hopeless, you and me."

He drew back, giving her a look. "I don't believe in hopeless, Kate." He was a little surprised at how vehemently that came out, but it was the foundation of who he was. It was important to underscore that. "I don't think there is such a word as hopeless. There's never not hope."

Her eyes shuttered, doubt etched on her features, but she smiled. "Okay. I'll hold on to that."

He leaned in closer. "And hold on to this." Before she opened her eyes, he kissed her, as lightly as possible.

She made a soft whimper in her throat, then wrapped her fingers around his neck, tunneling through his hair, pulling his head closer to deepen the contact.

Their first kiss lasted for less than three seconds, but it was pretty much the best three seconds of his life.

As they parted, her eyes were definitely filled with tears.

"Don't walk me in," she said gruffly, inching away. "Please. I...I just want to go by myself and remember that kiss."

He nodded, respecting the request, slowly drawing away. "I'll get your bag."

With that, they both climbed out, and he reached into the cab and pulled out her single roller suitcase and a small backpack with the Cornell logo on it.

She pulled up the carry handle, tugged her backpack on her shoulder.

"Well, I guess you're over Tessa, then," she teased as she smiled up at him.

He laughed. "Completely. But her sister? Whew." He looked skyward. "Another Wylie to wreck my heart."

Laughing at that, she took a few steps backwards, turning the suitcase. With her free hand, she blew him a kiss. "Bye, Eli!"

He just smiled at her, feeling the pressure on his

chest. He stayed very still, resisting the urge to do something dumb and dramatic like run after her.

Instead, he watched shoulder-length hair swing as she walked to the end of the parking lot, crossed the street, and disappeared into the small terminal.

The drive back to the Summer House was slow, sad, and quiet. It wasn't until he pulled into the driveway that he looked down at the console and saw her glasses resting in the cup holder.

"Oh." He picked them up, giving a quick laugh. She had more, he knew, but...now he had these. Maybe he'd deliver them in person.

As he was walking toward the house, Jonah came out of the garage, holding his phone up.

"Dad, you are not going to believe this." He waved the phone. "She wrote me a letter of recommendation."

He almost asked who "she" was, but he knew. It wasn't Meredith. He gave the glasses a slight squeeze.

"She emailed it to me to send to the admissions office —a top research scientist from Cornell University!"

Of course she did, Eli thought. Because Kate Wylie was made of goodness. "What did she say?"

"Oh, please. It's over the top." He glanced at the phone. "She said she cooked side by side with me for several weeks and found me to be..." He chuckled. "I can just hear her saying this: 'Creative, inspired, and talented in the kitchen as well as excellent with instructions, and eager to learn.' And get this—she said, 'Jonah Lawson would be an asset to any college or university and Northwest Florida State would be fortunate to have him as a student destined for greatness in the culinary world. We'd certainly be thrilled to have him at Cornell, but your flagship program is a tremendous draw for him.' Man, I love that woman!"

Eli smiled and knew that if he didn't already, he certainly could love her, too. So he clung to the hope she didn't believe in, grasped the glasses she couldn't keep track of, and hugged the young man she'd helped save.

"I'm so proud of you, son," he said, his voice thick.

"You will be, Dad. I promise."

As Jonah headed back inside, Eli stood for a long moment in the shadow of the house and looked up at the sky.

"I hope You have a plan," he whispered. "I'm counting on it."

Chapter Twenty-two

Tessa

The salty Gulf breeze teased loose strands of Tessa's hair as she walked with purpose up the driveway of Garrett Fischer's house.

Lacey's pep talk, delivered with animated fervor before she left to run some final errands and triple-check things at the catering kitchen, had buoyed Tessa this morning. Jonah's "get pumped" music had rocked the Summer House. Vivien had helped her pick the perfect outfit and Eli, bless his heart, had said a quiet prayer for her success.

If she had nothing else, she had these friends, and they had changed her life.

Today, if everything went well, it would change again —her business would be launched. She and Lacey had poured everything into planning this dinner party—their first big outing for Tessa Wylie Events.

And maybe, at the end of it when he wasn't her client anymore, there could be someone special in her life.

She'd be lying to herself—something Tessa Wylie never did—if she didn't admit she was pretty darn excited about seeing Garrett Fischer today. They'd texted a few times right after he left for Miami, but she hadn't heard from him in several days.

But that didn't worry her. He'd be here. What did her old boss at the Ritz always say? It isn't the ten things you plan to go wrong, it's the one you never dream of that will get you.

Not today, she thought as she reached the house. *Nothing will go wrong.*

Looking up, she took in the glorious beach house, loving the combination of gray shingles and pristine white trim set against the deep blue sky. Despite its grandeur, the place exuded a breezy elegance, its tall windows reflecting sunlight and seafoam. A house fit for a party meant to impress the guests—and the client.

Her kitten heels clicked confidently against the stone walkway as she approached the door, her mind racing through the final checklist. Chairs, flowers, music, catering—it was all on the way.

Garrett's confidence in her had been infectious; his praise and trust had reminded her of who she used to be before the setbacks and heartbreaks had chipped away at her self-assurance.

She adjusted her tailored linen blazer, the one Vivien had insisted made her look "both bossy and approachable," as she rang the doorbell but fished for the keys Garrett had given her in case he hadn't come back from Miami yet.

The chime echoed as the door swung open, and Tessa froze at the sight of a woman she'd never seen before.

She was in her early fifties, but strikingly made up with sharp cheekbones, perfectly highlighted hair, and an expression so icy it could have frosted glass. She wore a tailored silk blouse and gold earrings that screamed Old Money.

"Can I help you?" the woman asked, her tone clipped, her manicured hand resting on the doorframe as if she were guarding the house.

Tessa blinked, the first real wisp of worry curling through her. "I'm Tessa Wylie."

The woman's eyes narrowed as she scanned Tessa from head to toe, her lips twitching into a faint, disdainful smile. "Are you from Fiona's property management company or the housekeeping outfit? I can't keep track of who he brings through this place."

Tessa's stomach knotted, a cold dread beginning to seep in. "I'm the event planner for today's party. I'm here to set up, and the vendors will be arriving shortly," she said.

"Oh, right. The planner. He might have mentioned you in passing."

"I've been working with Mr. Fischer for several weeks to plan a dinner party," she said carefully. "And you are...?"

She flicked a brow of surprise, like a celebrity expecting to be recognized. "I'm Caroline Fischer, Garrett's wife."

The words hit like a slap. Somehow, Tessa managed not to catch her breath. She couldn't do anything about the blood that drained from her face, though, except pray that *Mrs. Fischer* didn't notice.

Never, not once, not one single syllable he'd spoken indicated he was married. No "we" was mentioned, no partner alluded to, no single breath about a wife. Just lingering glances, carefully crafted compliments, and a flirtation that had felt...real.

He was a snake. And she was a fool.

Tessa angled her head and refused to be defeated. "Lovely to meet you, Mrs. Fischer." She extended her hand and smiled. "I am certain you're going to be delighted with what we have planned."

"I'm not certain of that at all," the woman said. "I'm sure Garrett mentioned that I'm very particular when it comes to parties."

"Actually, he didn't," she said. "But he did give me carte blanche, so you don't have to do anything but enjoy your guests. May I come in?"

The woman looked past her as a large white truck with the Chair Affair logo pulled into the long driveway.

"Oh, the chairs are here," Tessa said.

"They don't come with the tables?" Caroline asked.

"Not the ones I wanted. Only one place in Florida has acrylic Chiavari chairs, which will be stunning on your—"

"Acrylic?" She practically spat the word. "This isn't a twenty-two-year-old's wedding, you know."

Tessa drew back at the tone and the comment. "They don't block the view."

"They're cheap," she volleyed back.

Tessa turned as a truck door slammed and a burly man came closer. "Ms. Wylie? I have fifty—"

"Take them back," Caroline called, just loud enough to stop the man in his tracks. "I hate them."

"Oh, no, you don't," Tessa said quickly. "Otherwise, we won't have chairs for the guests dining on your deck."

The other woman's green eyes narrowed. "Can't you find chairs I like? You're the event planner."

"No, but I might be able to scare up chair covers, which will be lovely and I'm sure will make you very happy, Mrs. Fischer." She turned to the delivery man. "Bring them around the side to the upper deck. Thank you."

Caroline still stood in the doorway, distaste etched on her features as she stared at Tessa.

Tessa took one step closer, her pulse pounding. "Now, if you'll let me in, your husband hired me to coordinate every detail of this party, which I intend to do without any trouble."

Caroline's laugh was chilly and fake as she gave Tessa a once-over. "Oh, yes, I'm sure Garrett hired you for your...*skillset*. But I'm his wife, and I'll decide what stays and what goes. Get covers for the chairs."

The insinuation stung, but Tessa won Round One because Caroline walked away and left the door open, presumably inviting entry to her home.

Tessa followed and caught sight of the woman rounding a massive flight of stairs, her voice echoing back as she called, "I changed the menu."

Excuse me? Surely Tessa hadn't heard that right.

"We're serving filet mignon tonight," Caroline declared. "It's Garrett's favorite."

Tessa followed, anger rising again. "We're serving lobster tails and scallops," she said tightly. "The menu was chosen weeks ago, and the caterer is already preparing it."

Caroline spun on her heel, trying to look innocent, but failing. "No, they aren't. They couldn't handle the filet order, so I canceled them."

Tessa froze. "You...*what?*"

"Honestly, I cringe at catering like that," she said. "I'm stunned Garrett didn't tell you to use a private chef. Maybe he assumed you wouldn't know any, but they're around. It's late, but if you throw enough money at people..." She gave a humorless smile. "And, isn't that what he hired you to do, Tessa?"

Tessa's vision blurred and suddenly the term "seeing red" made sense. The caterer was *canceled?* The chairs needed covers? She wanted filet? This was a disaster.

"I'll be upstairs," Caroline said, her foot on the first step before she turned. "Sorry about the kitchen. I had some friends over last night and we left a bit of a mess. You'll have to clean it."

She waltzed up the stairs, leaving Tessa fuming and... no, not broken. Could this witch break her that easily?

Yes, a small, hated voice inside her whispered.

It was the same voice that taunted her as a child when she couldn't read or as a college student when it took her ten times as long as anyone else to complete an assignment. It was the voice that told her she was "beautiful but stupid" and if she couldn't charm her way through a situation, she might as well give up.

Only one person could ever quiet that voice...and he was gone.

She walked into the kitchen and gasped at the mess, not quite able to take it in. Some friends? The place was littered with empty wine bottles, a half-eaten charcuterie board, dirty glasses, and an overflowing trash bin.

How would she ever—

The sound of screeching tires broke through her spiral, making her rush to the door in time to see Lacey leap out of her car.

"Did you cancel the caterer?" Lacey demanded.

"No," Tessa said, her voice cracking as she walked outside. She flicked her hand to get Lacey back in the car and climbed in the other side for privacy. "Caroline did," she said as she slipped into the passenger seat.

"Who is—"

"His wife."

Lacey's mouth formed a perfect 'o'. "His...*what*?"

"His spouse. His better half. His beloved Missus. You know, the one he *never mentioned* to me."

"Well, who cares? We have problems to solve, Tessa Wylie, and we are not going to let anyone ruin this party."

Tessa nodded, tears burning her eyes. "It might be too late."

"No!" Lacey's eyes narrowed with determination. "We're not giving up. This is our first big event, Tessa. We've worked too hard to let this ruin us. We can fix it."

"How?" Tessa asked. "We're out of time, out of resources, and completely screwed. Oh, and the kitchen looks like a frat house on a Sunday morning. And, Lacey, we need a private chef!"

"We have a private chef," she said. "His name is Jonah. And a staff—Eli and Vivien. And me and you and..." She grabbed Tessa's arm. "You can do this, you know. I don't know where you get the idea you're not capable and smart and fabulous. I want to be you when I grow up."

Tessa blinked. "Really?"

"But first I have to grow up and that means a good job, which I have as the second-in-command at Tessa Wylie Events. So get it together, boss! We will show Garrett and Caroline what we're made of, and they will fold in the face of our greatness!"

She sounded so much like Artie Wylie, Tessa could have cried. It was like he'd been reincarnated as a twenty-four-year-old angel with a big heart and bigger ideas. And he'd come back to do what Artie always did—encourage and delight her.

Tessa took Lacey's hand and squeezed it, so overcome with emotion, she couldn't talk.

"Am I right?"

"So right," Tessa agreed. "You go get the team. Tell Jonah it's his job to find filet mignon for fifty. Grab a ton of seafood, too, in case we need it, or he can make an appetizer. The theme is seaside—serving filet is just dumb. The tables are in the garage, so I'll get the chair crew to bring them up. If she hasn't canceled the florist, they should be here soon."

"That's what I'm talking about. Oh, look." She pointed to the rearview mirror. "Florist is here!"

Sighing with relief, Tessa reached for the door handle. "Go tell the crew we're doing a dinner and... and...and I love you, Lacey."

Lacey leaned over and planted a kiss on Tessa's cheek. "If I didn't have the world's most awesome mom, I'd want you to be mine."

She sucked in a soft breath, expecting the words to stab at an old wound. Instead, they were like a balm. All she could do was smile. And get to work.

TESSA STEPPED into the gourmet kitchen, her nerves barely contained under what she hoped was a polished exterior. The late afternoon sun bathed the space in a golden light, the Viking stove alive with sizzles and steam, promising perfection.

Outwardly, everything glimmered with effortless elegance, but inwardly, her thoughts churned—would Garrett even show up?

The Guptas and their three adorable daughters were here, the girls happily ensconced in the upstairs media room. Caroline took over the hostess duties with surprising ease, chatting with Sai and Priya as if they'd met before.

Where was the host? Would he miss his own

birthday party? Was that why Caroline showed up unannounced?

She couldn't worry about that now, not with her crack team of dear friends—an architect, a designer, an aspiring student chef, and, of course, her young protégée —working in choreographed syncopation, like seasoned party professionals.

The scent of Jonah's Brazilian shrimp appetizer sautéed in cast-iron skillets filled the air, mingling with the faint sweetness of freshly baked bread cooling on the counter, and the salt-infused breeze wafting in through open windows.

Vivien stood at the sprawling marble-topped island, a white apron covering the black T-shirt and pants they'd all agreed to wear, dicing herbs under Jonah's watchful eye.

Eli had turned a café-style eat-in area into a working bar, shaking a cocktail mixer with an assuredness that matched his easy smile. Lacey flitted around the room, arranging hors d'oeuvres on sleek silver trays with the precision of a jeweler setting gemstones.

Beyond the bustling kitchen, the Gulf provided the perfect backdrop to the outdoor party, a stunning azure today, dotted with frothy waves and the occasional gull swooping overhead.

Music floated in from outdoor speakers, the soft, jazzy playlist that Jonah and Lacey had put together setting the perfect tone for an elegant evening ahead.

"Keep the parsley rough," Jonah said to Vivien, who

nodded, her brow furrowed in concentration. "It's garnish, not confetti."

"Got it," Vivien replied, her tone tinged with determination.

"Tessa!" Eli called, holding up a frosted glass filled with a frothy sage-colored liquid. "Come taste the signature cocktail."

She crossed the kitchen, accepting the drink.

"You said wine only with one specialty drink," he said. "What do you think of this one?"

She inhaled a bright, fresh scent, definitely strong enough to carry a punch. She sipped and closed her eyes with a moan at the mix of flavors. "This is... fantastic," she said, taking another sip. "What's in it?"

"It's a twist on our favorite gin and tonic, with some muddled cucumber and a splash of elderflower liqueur," Eli said. "What should I call it?"

She closed her eyes and took another sip, ancient memories rising to the surface. "A Bonfire."

He chuckled. "Perfect."

"So are you," she said, beaming up at him. "Thank you, Eli, and thank you for...forgiving and forgetting. I feel your grace."

His jaw loosened at the words, and a bit of color left his face. "So you *do* remember."

"What I'd like to forget is the way I behaved." She added a tight smile. "You definitely deserve better. At least, a better Wylie girl."

He sighed. "I don't deserve..."

She put a hand on his arm. "She'll be back. You'll see. We just have to—"

"Tessa."

She spun around at the man's voice, spotting Garrett standing in the middle of the kitchen.

For a moment, she just looked at him, taking in the expression of...what? Regret? Guilt? Shame? Whatever it was, she wanted him to wallow in it.

"You made it," she said simply.

"And you made it...happen." He gestured toward the bustling kitchen. "Somehow, despite everything, you're making me look good."

"As I was hired to do."

He eyed her, clearly uncertain where to go next. "Can I talk to you privately?" he asked.

She opened her mouth to say she was too busy, but decided not to give him the satisfaction.

"Of course." With a quick glance at Eli, she walked toward Garrett, who led her to a small, water-facing balcony off the kitchen.

"Tessa," he said on a sigh. "I'm so—"

"Late," she interjected. "But no worries. Your wife was here."

He winced. "And I, uh, understand she made some last-minute changes. She fired the caterer? And changed the menu?"

She lifted a shoulder. "All in a day's work for me."

He cocked his head, searching her face—no doubt expecting some reaction. Fury? Jealousy? Disappointment? Honestly, he wasn't worth the effort for any of those—not when she had a party to coordinate.

"I should have told you," he finally said.

"You think?"

"I might have given you the impression that I was..."

"Single? In the market for more than a party planner? It's fine, Garrett," she said, already lighter just by letting him off the hook. He wasn't worth anything more. "I admit, I gave it a passing thought myself. Like, maybe, you were different. But turns out it's not even worth a passing thought."

She waited a beat to relish the look of true self-loathing she saw. But that was enough. She had work to do, a party to hold, and a business to build.

"Everything's fine," she added quickly. "We've recovered nicely, as you can see, and you will still have a memorable and flawless event."

"I owe you an apology."

"Nope, but my fee has tripled, so you'll owe me that. And now, why don't you meet your chef, and he can go over the new menu with you? But don't make any changes, please."

Without waiting for his response, she breezed back inside and he followed her to the cooktop.

"Chef Jonah Lawson, this is Garrett Fischer. Chef, tell him your revised menu."

Jonah nodded, wiped his palm on his apron, and shook Garrett's hand. "Hello, Mr. Fischer. We're starting with Brazilian shrimp," he said. "It's a signature dish of mine inspired by a woman named Ivette, who cleans...up on the cooking contest circuit."

Tessa bit her lip, knowing full well the recipe came from the lady who mopped Kate's lab.

"Excellent," Garrett said, looking impressed. "And the entrée?"

"Per Mrs. Fischer's request, we have Wagyu filet mignon with a red wine reduction, roasted fingerling potatoes, and grilled asparagus. For dessert, a citrus panna cotta with a raspberry coulis. Although your wife has asked for cupcakes and candles."

Tessa shrugged. "I know you don't want singing, so take it up with her."

He laughed. "I will. But, wow. This is so impressive."

"I also heard Mr. Gupta's daughters are dining upstairs," Jonah added, throwing a look at Tessa. "I took the liberty of whipping up some *Wicked*-themed green ketchup dip to go with kid-friendly chicken fingers and fries."

Garrett's face lit up. "That's... incredible. Thank you."

"We aim to please," Jonah said, turning back to his work.

Tessa introduced Garrett to the others, who were all perfectly professional and warm, earning her client's palpable amazement.

"I don't know how you pulled this off, Tessa."

"I believe the expression is 'a little help from my friends.'"

"I am so grateful," he said. "If I can do anything for you—"

"You can get out and have fun and impress Sai Gupta so he joins your board. That was the real point of this party, right? Oh, and happy birthday."

He looked hard at her, a little longing in his eyes. "I think I lost sight of the purpose of the party," he admitted.

"Maybe you lost sight of a lot of things," she said softly. "But I didn't, so..." She flicked him away. "Let me get to it."

He left the kitchen and, in a matter of seconds, Tessa actually forgot all about him. Which made him...like every other man she'd ever met.

A few hours later, dinner was served without a hitch. From the side of the deck, Tessa watched the guests gathered at large round tables—and *uncovered* acrylic chairs because she won that battle, too.

The partygoers all looked good in the soft light from glowing wall sconces. The air was alive with the hum of conversation, the clink of glasses, and the distant splash of the surf.

As her gaze moved over the tables, she paused at the one where Garrett and Caroline chatted with Sai and Priya Gupta, and three other couples. Immediately, she noticed the Guptas hadn't touched a bite of food.

Of *course* they didn't eat beef. She'd suspected that could be the case.

She whizzed into the kitchen. "Jonah! I need two seafood plates, stat!"

He leapt into high gear, pulling out gorgeous mahi that he'd had in reserve for just a moment like this, tossing them into a hot pan.

"Let me dress these up," he said, pulling out a glass bowl of his delicious mango salsa. "I'll add some heat to bring this alive." While the fish cooked, he chopped some additional jalapeño, folded it in, dressed the dishes, and handed her two plates that looked like art.

"Bless you," she whispered, scooping them up. "Follow me, Lacey, and gracefully sneak their plates away. I'll manage the excuses."

The two of them were barely noticed at the table when they switched out the entrées before the others had eaten much.

Priya looked up with a question in her eyes and Tessa met Caroline's sharp gaze from two seats away.

"Entirely my fault, Mrs. Gupta," Tessa said. "Your host and hostess did specifically ask that you get the mahi in mango salsa." She gave a warm smile to Caroline. "So thoughtful of you, Mrs. Fischer."

Sai's face lit up, and Priya's gratitude was clear.

"Thank you," Sai said to Caroline. "It's the little things that mean a lot."

"Like the movie and dinner for my girls," Priya chimed in. "I was worried they'd be bored to death at this event and last time I checked, they don't want to leave."

Caroline's brows lifted, her eyes silently expressing thanks to Tessa.

After that, it was smooth sailing—unless she counted the look of pained discomfort on Garrett's face when

Caroline insisted the entire party sing "Happy Birthday" and Garrett blew out a candle on a cupcake.

By the end of the evening, the guests were mingling with coffee or cocktails, the sound of laughter, music, and conversation filling the air.

As Tessa came down from checking on the sleeping girls upstairs, Garrett was waiting at the bottom of the steps.

"Tessa," he said, looking up at her. "I can't thank you enough. This was... beyond anything I could have hoped for. Sai Gupta's agreed to join the board. You saved the day."

"That's what you hired me for," she said with an easy smile.

His expression softened as she reached the last step. "Please, I just have to say...I know I should have told you about Caroline."

"Yes, you should have," she said, her tone light but pointed.

"Can I make it up to you?"

"Oh, yes, you most certainly can."

A glimmer of hope lit his eyes. Hope she was about to dash. "Name it," he said.

She crossed her arms and studied him, deciding just how far she'd take this. *Far.*

"A five-star review, quotes for my website, and at least five local references for more business. Big ones with fat budgets."

Garrett laughed, nodding. "Done."

"And a glowing letter of recommendation for Chef

Jonah," she said, knowing Kate's letter would probably get him into the program he wanted, but this certainly couldn't hurt.

"It will glow like the sun," he promised her. "Anything else?"

Oh, yes. There certainly was. "My friend, Vivien? She is an interior designer launching a new business in Destin."

"Yes?"

Just then, Caroline came around the corner. "There you are," she said to Tessa. "I was looking for you in the kitchen. And you're here, chatting it up with my husband."

"Not chatting," he assured her. "But lining up recommendations. Tessa was just mentioning that her friend Vivien is an interior designer opening her business here in town."

"Vivien who helped serve dinner?" Caroline asked.

"Vivien Lawson is a gifted designer," Tessa said. "She's staging the house where I'm staying and it's simply stunning. Do you know anyone who might—"

"Yes," Caroline interjected, her gaze direct and far kinder than when they'd met. "As a matter of fact, Fiona Buckman is here. She runs the property management firm that handles this house and many just like it. She just mentioned that she's got several high-end rentals that need complete remodels, as well as a house she just moved into in Indian Bayou. Why don't I introduce her to Vivien right now?"

Tessa beamed at her. "You won't be sorry, Mrs. Fischer."

"First of all, it's Caroline. And second, I admit I wasn't sure about you at first."

"That's fine," Tessa said, and meant it. This had gone too well to hold grudges.

"Honestly, after watching you tonight, I realize I had nothing to worry about," Caroline said. "You made it all look effortless, which I know it isn't."

Tessa accepted the compliment with a tip of her head. "Thank you."

"Let me go make that introduction. I hope Vivien has no issues with strong, opinionated women."

"She was raised by one," Tessa said. "She can handle anything."

"And would you leave some cards, Tessa? Several people have asked me who planned the event, and I'm happy to give you a referral." Caroline stepped away and Garrett turned to Tessa.

"You, Tessa Wylie," he said, "are a complete surprise."

"Surprise? You didn't expect party perfection?"

"I didn't expect you to be smart, classy, and full of poise," he said, his voice carrying a note of something she couldn't quite place—admiration, yes, but maybe a tinge of regret. "I certainly didn't expect all that from a beautiful woman I found lurking under my boardwalk."

She laughed at the memory. "Did you know I was there?"

"I saw you disappear," he told her. "I wanted to find you, so I walked down while I was on the phone. I had no idea you'd save my behind on a party, which you absolutely did."

"Happy I could help," she said. "And thank you for the kind words. They remind me of my father."

He made a face. "Your father? Not what I was going for."

"Trust me, it's a compliment. He was a great man."

"He raised a great daughter," he said, adding a warm smile.

For the first time in longer than she cared to admit, Tessa felt like she wasn't defined by her looks, her weaknesses, or her past missteps. She'd broken her pattern, found strength in herself, and couldn't help hoping she could finally create the kind of future her father always said she deserved.

"Oh, Garrett, I have one more request, actually." She felt a smile pull at her cheeks as she regarded the wealthy man standing in front of her.

"Anything."

Tessa arched a brow, straightening her back. "I want the boat."

Garrett laughed softly, drawing back with obvious surprise at her boldness. But perhaps more surprising than that was his response. "It's yours."

She gasped, not expecting that.

"I was thinking about selling it," he said. "And honestly? I owe you. What will you call it?"

She knew instantly what to name that boat. "*Good Time Girl.*"

Chapter Twenty-three
Vivien

Late that night, Vivien leaned back in her prized Frontgate recliner, her bare feet aching after all the hours of physical labor as she gazed at the moon hung low over the Gulf.

It had been a good, satisfying, and successful day. One that left the impromptu party crew on a high that they were still enjoying hours after they'd cleaned up and come back to the Summer House.

She couldn't help but marvel at how everything had come together for Tessa and Lacey, especially after the near disasters earlier in the day. They'd pulled it off, and now, as they sat together with Eli's signature cocktails in hand, the world seemed... right.

Almost right. Close to right. There was something tapping on her heart, and no matter how she tried, she couldn't ignore the thought that had taken hold that day.

She tried to pinpoint when the idea hit her, but couldn't. It was sometime between that morning when Lacey announced they were going to work together to pull off a massive dinner party—reminding her of the night they'd all made an anniversary dinner—and right now, as she lifted her plastic cup when Jonah asked for a toast.

"To Tessa and Lacey," Jonah said, raising his drink. "For pulling off what can only be described as a miracle."

Tessa grinned, the flush in her cheeks more from pride than the cocktail she'd barely touched. "Please. It was the definition of a group effort." She lifted her cup. "To the A-Team. Don't think I won't use you all again on our next project."

"Which could be soon," Lacey chimed in, her voice brimming with excitement. "Didn't someone tell you about a lady who owns a bridal salon and wants a grand opening event?"

"Yes!" Tessa said. "And weren't you talking to a couple who want to throw a Fourth of July beach bash that's going to be twice the size of tonight's party?"

"I was," Lacey confirmed.

Tessa leaned over to give Lacey a high-five, which somehow morphed into a hug. "You're a gem, sweet girl." Over Lacey's shoulder, she winked at Vivien. "She's mine now."

"Business only," Vivien laughed. "And speaking of, I think I got a new client tonight, too."

But Vivien wasn't focused on the woman who'd asked her to set up a time to look at a Victorian house that needed an overhaul. Instead, she just watched her daughter and Tessa, not the least bit jealous of the friendship that had formed between them. Both of them radiated pure joy.

Tessa had changed so much this past month, she mused, eyeing her friend.

The uncertainty and doubt that hung over her when she'd been discovered camping out in the downstairs spare bedroom seemed to have melted away, replaced with confidence and determination. Lacey, too, had found her groove, proving that her boundless energy could be channeled into something extraordinary.

They'd all changed over this past month, to be honest. Jonah had come back after years of estrangement, his life situation demanding he take a new direction. Eli had fallen into the first soft cloud of an unexpected romance, and it had softened him. Kate's influence could be felt on both of the Lawson men.

And Vivien...well, she liked being Vivien Lawson now. She'd well and truly let go of her old life and marriage, with just pings of sadness and regret lingering in her heart. Most of all...she never wanted to leave this place.

Oh, Viv. Never say never, right? Because she had to leave eventually.

Didn't she? The thought made her sigh and feel that knock on her heart again.

"And to Chef Jonah," Eli added to the toasting. "For not only saving the dinner but turning it into a masterpiece. Garrett couldn't stop raving about the food."

Jonah waved off the group cheer. "It was nothing. Just doing my job."

"It was not nothing," Tessa said firmly. "That mahi

you whipped up in record time? With the mango salsa? I've never seen gratitude like that on anyone's face. Sai Gupta might've signed on to Garrett's board tonight because of your cooking."

He managed a sheepish smile. "The host did ask for my email because he wanted to write a glowing recommendation of my cooking in case I needed it." He narrowed his eyes at Tessa. "Not sure who told him I might, but it's going right into my application to the program."

The conversation flowed easily, punctuated by bursts of laughter and teasing. But Vivien didn't say much, letting her gaze wander back to the moon. All the while, there was that idea dancing over her heart again.

Actually, not dancing. More like stomping in demand to be...considered.

"You're quiet," Eli said, nudging her arm. "Something on your mind?"

Vivien turned to him, looking into her brother's kind blue eyes. It was time to talk to Eli, but it had to be alone. "Any chance I could talk to you privately for a moment?"

He sat up. "Everything okay?"

She nodded. "I just...have an idea." And it was a doozie, she thought as she put her drink down. "Something I'd like to run by you."

"Sure. Talk inside?"

"Yeah. I'm going to run to the bathroom for a sec," she said. "Meet me upstairs in a minute."

As Eli's expression turned curious, Vivien's nerves

buzzed as she headed up to her room. In the ensuite, she rinsed her face, calming herself before she faced Eli. She was asking for a lot—but she had to ask. She had to.

"What's up?" Eli called as he tapped on her bedroom door.

"Come on in."

He walked in and glanced around, looking uncertain. She waved him to the open doors and out to the balcony, which seemed as good a place as any to present her idea. The voices and laughter floated up from the deck below.

What if Eli thought she was being foolish? Or, worse, selfish? But the thought of what was at stake gnawed at her heart and gave her courage.

"Listen," Vivien began, leaning against the railing. "I have an idea. Bear with me—it's crazy."

"As crazy as the time you wanted us to have a crab racing contest and three of them got lost and ended up in Uncle Artie's suitcase?" he joked.

She chuckled at the memory. "Maybe...worse."

"The sandcastle contest? Boys versus girls? That was the same year, I think, the summer we met the Wylies."

"Oh, yes!" she said, that memory particularly fresh from her diaries. "I happen to know the girls kicked butt in that contest."

He drew back with a scoffing laugh. "Are you kidding? Peter and I had a *bridge* over our moat. You just won because Crista cried."

She smiled, knowing he was right. "Got any more memories from when we were kids here?" she asked.

"About a million. Why?"

"Because that's my idea—making memories."

He studied her, a frown pulling. "What do you mean?"

"I mean..." She sighed. It was time to dive in and she knew the water wouldn't be warm, at least not at first. "What if we didn't sell this house, Eli? Not in November, not...ever."

He just stared at her.

"I wouldn't suggest it if you'd fronted this rebuild, but since it came out of the profits from over the years..." Her voice faded as he stayed silent. "I know, it's giving up a lot of money."

He snorted. "Millions. With an S at the end, Viv."

"You can't put a price on those memories, Eli, or on the value of owning a place like this," she said softly. When he didn't laugh in her face or run screaming from the balcony, she pressed on.

"We could have more memories like that," she said. "With our families, and then theirs. Crista could bring Nolie. And Meredith, if she ever takes a vacation, would love it here. I'm never going to get Lacey to leave, and Jonah might come back with...your grandchild."

His eyes flashed at the word. "My...yeah. I...I see where you're taking this, Viv. What really matters in life, huh?"

"Seriously," she pressed, leaning forward. "We know firsthand what summers in Destin meant to us and we could spend so much time here—summer vacations, holidays as a family, special occasions. We could gather as a family...or two."

"Two?"

"With the Wylies."

A million emotions sparked in his eyes as he processed that.

"Why couldn't Kate come here with her kids? And Tessa?"

"One reason—and I don't think I have to even say her name."

Of course. Maggie. "Maybe she'd get over it."

He shook his head. "You heard her that Sunday at Crista's house. She never wants to set foot here again."

"But we do!" Vivien insisted. "And she said we could do what we want—"

"With the *money*," he finished.

"With the *house*," she corrected. "What if we want to keep it?"

He was silent for a few seconds, his sharp brain processing, no doubt going through all the possibilities, the pros, the cons, the long list of people and things that would be affected by such a wild decision.

"I don't know, Viv."

Okay, okay. Hope climbed up her chest. That wasn't a *no*.

"This place is magic, Eli," Vivien continued, reaching for his arm to make her point. "It's not just a house. It's a family. It's memories and laughter and connection. Generations could grow up here, just like we did. Doesn't that sound better than a million bucks in the bank?"

He finally turned away, looking out to the moonlit beach, swallowing hard. When he closed his eyes for a second, she knew he was praying. She just hoped God thought this was a good idea, too.

"We'd have to get Crista on board," he finally said, and she almost jumped for joy.

"Of course!" Vivien said. "Maggie leaves tomorrow for a month-long trip. We could get Crista to come down for a few weeks, with Nolie. Maybe Anthony. We'll give them the main suite and they'll fall madly in love with the place and then we'll hit her with the plan."

He thought about that, but slowly shook his head. "I want to be straight with her," he replied. "No subterfuge. If you and I agree that we want to think about this, let's call her before she takes Maggie to the airport. If she loves the idea, she can maybe feel out Maggie in the car and get a first response."

Vivien tipped her head. He was probably right, but she liked her plan better. "Maggie will instantly say no, and Crista will do whatever Maggie says. You know that."

"Maybe. But maybe our mother will see the benefit and respect our decision."

Vivien almost laughed. "Are we both talking about Maggie Lawson?"

He smiled. "If anyone's going to get her on board, it will be Crista," he added. "She has some sway over Maggie—it was Crista's idea for her to take this gardening club trip to Europe."

"I didn't know that," Vivien said.

"I picked it up between the lines. I'm not sure living with her is as easy as Crista makes it look."

Vivien rolled her eyes. "I can only imagine. But you know what Crista might really like, then? A getaway at the beach."

He nodded, still quiet, not yet committed.

Vivien slid her arm around him and dropped her head on his always-strong shoulder. "Hey, do you remember what happened the next morning, after the sandcastle contest?"

He narrowed his eyes, squinting at the beach. "I don't, no."

"Come here." She tugged him toward the room. "I have to show you something."

He followed her in and waited while she went around the bed and pulled out the bright pink Caboodle.

"Ah, the Destin Diaries," he said on a laugh. "Did you write about the sandcastle contest?"

Smiling, she flipped to the last entry she'd read and brought it over to him. Side by side, they read together.

AUGUST 30, 1989

Yesterday might have been the best day of the whole summer! We had the big sandcastle contest on the beach, boys versus girls. And guess what? WE WON! (Okay, fine, maybe it was because Crista cried when her really terrible tower fell over, and the parents didn't want to deal with her meltdown. But a win is a win, right?) Tessa and I worked so hard on the little seashell walkway, and Kate's windows were so perfect they looked like something out of Cinderella.

The boys' castle was good, I'll admit. Peter added a spiral tower with driftwood sticking out, and Eli naturally went over the top and made a moat and it had a draw-bridge out of sea grape leaves. Best part? It was still standing this morning when we woke up—both castles! They weren't even wrecked by the tide.

Tessa went fishing with Uncle Artie super early (she's way braver than me because no way am I touching slimy bait), and our parents took Crista into town for pancakes because, of course, she "needed" them after crying her way to victory.

That left me, Kate, Eli, and Peter on the beach. And we had the BEST idea! Instead of letting the castles just sit there, we decided to add on to the castles and make one big compound.

Kate said there is something called a "castle keep" (why does she know everything?) that is the strongest part of a castle, so we built one! Eli designed it and then built this amazing bridge that connected everything. Peter made four turrets—one named for each of us. That's what holds the whole thing together, Kate said.

We called it "The Summer House Keep" which I loved. It was so pretty! Kate and I pretended to be princesses and the boys thought we were so dumb, but then they played along. I got saved by Sir Peter and Eli was a prince looking for the Holy Grail and he called Kate "Lady Katie." It was silly, but I'll never forget it or the Summer House Keep.

It's so weird to think that summer is almost over. Tomorrow we have to start packing, and I already feel sad about it. But the best part is that everyone keeps saying, "We'll be back next year!" I can't imagine not coming back here. This place feels like home, more than Atlanta ever could.

The Summer House Keep got wiped out by high tide today, but it doesn't matter. We'll just build it again.

Vivien

For a moment, Eli just stayed very still, staring at the page. When Vivien looked up at him, she saw the mist in his eyes.

"See what I mean?" she whispered.

He sighed, running a hand over the splash of pink and purple on the girlish cover.

"I remember those turrets so clearly now," he said softly. "Peter and I argued over how to build them. I wanted visual perfection, with balance and symmetry. He said it had to be secure so no one could storm the castle. As if it mattered."

She laughed. "The architect and the cop. Makes sense." Then she leaned into him. "It mattered then, and it matters now."

A faint smile tugged at his lips. "All right, Viv. Let's call Crista tomorrow."

Vivien nodded, though her heart fluttered with nerves. "I just hope Crista sees it the way we do. If she doesn't..." She trailed off, unwilling to voice the fear that she might still buckle under the weight of Maggie's opinion and demands.

She might have shaken off Ryan, but her mother was another story.

Eli gave her a reassuring squeeze on the shoulder. "If she doesn't, we'll figure it out. But we have to try, Viv. This place is worth fighting for."

Chapter Twenty-four

Eli

Eli actually loved the idea of keeping the house in the family, and hoped Maggie might see the real benefit of it. She wanted them to be happy —any mother would. And if having a luxurious beach house that they shared made them happier than extra money in the bank, then surely Maggie would agree they should keep it.

Frankly, whether they kept it or sold really should make no difference to her.

But her issues with the Wylies ran deep—deeper than the house or she would have sold the property years ago.

That's what kept Eli awake all night—whatever Maggie hated about Artie and Jo Ellen, would it affect his relationship with Kate? Because, if he was being completely honest, that relationship, whatever it was or could be, had become one of the most important things to him, if not *the* most important thing.

He thought about Kate day and night and wanted to talk to her constantly. If she felt the same way, there had to be a solution. There had to be a future. There had to be hope.

But he wanted to get the Maggie roadblock out of the way—or at least get to the bottom of it.

So he felt strongly that they had to tell Crista that the Wylie girls had been here, which he knew she would report to their mother. And then, he hoped, Maggie would at least tell Crista *why* she had an issue with a family she hadn't seen in thirty years.

If he knew why, he could solve the problem. He hoped.

"You ready?" Vivien asked, tucking her legs under her on the seat across from him, the morning light pouring over the patio deck.

"I'm ready." He picked up his phone and tapped Crista's name. While it connected, he quietly closed his eyes to pray for God's help on this.

She answered on the first ring, of course. Perfectionist Crista was always on top of every aspect of her life.

"I'm leaving in an hour," she told them after a quick greeting and some light small talk. "Mom's flight doesn't take off until three, but the gardening group is getting to the airport four hours ahead of time." She laughed, sounding a little lighter than usual. "I can't imagine their poor tour guide when they get to the Netherlands with four septuagenarians who want to see every tulip in Holland."

"And what are you going to do for a month without Maggie?" Vivien asked.

"A lot less," Crista said. "Not that she's difficult, of course, but just having one less person in the house makes my life easier. Nolie will miss her desperately, but

Mom has appointed her little namesake as the keeper of Aunt Pittypat, so I guess Nolie will be sleeping with a dog for a month."

"Well, maybe you could bring Nolie and Aunt Pittypat down here for a visit," he said. "I'd like you to see the house."

"Oh...I don't know about that. I'm not sure I could..."

Eli and Vivien shared a look, knowing the rest of that sentence. If Maggie didn't go, then Crista wouldn't, either.

"You need to come down," Vivien said.

"Oh, please don't tell me there's some weird government problem," Crista said. "Ever since Mom told us about this, I'm dreading that a federal agent is going to show up and take it away from us."

"I've worried about that myself," Eli said. "But it's not happening. It's ours and, uh, that's what Vivien and I want to talk to you about."

"Mmm?" She sounded surprised. "What do you mean?"

"Crista, we think we should keep this house and have it as a family gathering place," he said. "All of us would own it and have full access to it. You and Anthony could bring Nolie down every summer and she could have that same magical childhood we did."

That was met with dead silence, and Vivien dropped back on the sofa, closing her eyes.

"That's why you need to see the place," Eli said quickly. "And hear us out. Yes, it's a lot of cash, but this house is spectacular, and we could make so many memories here. Nolie would love the beach."

Again, long silence.

"Destin's changed, of course," he said. "But this beach has the same magic it always did."

"I'm not opposed."

Vivien gasped and covered her mouth with two hands.

"Really?" Eli asked, feeling a huge smile form.

"I'm not convinced, either," Crista said. "But I could see the appeal of having a beach house. It's worth talking about with Anthony, I suppose. And weighing what we'd be giving up financially."

"You'll love it here," Eli said. "We've really been enjoying it. The Wylies have, too."

"The *what*?" She barked the word. "What did you say? Have you been in touch with them?"

Eli's eyes shuttered. "Actually, Kate and Tessa have been here—"

"Are you out of your ever-lovin' minds?"

"Crista." Vivien shot forward. "How can we hate a family when we don't know what they did? You—and Mom—are hanging on to thirty-year-old grudges like we're the Hatfields and McCoys or something! Why should we hate them?"

"I don't know," she answered, lowering her voice. "But Mom does, and we need to respect that."

Eli didn't need to respect it. And Crista needed to see the house and meet Tessa. Kate, too, if he could get her down here, even for a weekend.

"Why don't you just visit?" he asked. "Let's plan a long weekend while Mom's away—all of you come and just see what this is all about. Then we'll make a decision."

She was quiet again, but it didn't sound like that furious silence. This was way better than he could have hoped—not the flat-out rejection he'd been dreading.

In the background, he heard a loud squeal.

"Nolie? Nolie, are you okay? Did something break? Magnolia Merritt!" On a noisy grunt, they heard movement on Crista's end. "I have to go. Let me..."

"Think about it?" Vivien asked.

"Yeah. I'll call you guys. I have to go."

With that, the call ended, leaving Eli and Vivien staring at each other before they both broke into wide grins.

"She doesn't hate the idea!" Vivien practically squealed.

He wasn't quite so optimistic, but he felt better than he had before he made the call. "I don't know. Maggie could snuff this out with one breath, and we may never know why."

Vivien sat back, thinking. "Maybe they did have affairs. Maybe they swapped."

"Stop it." He shot her a vile look.

"Well, what made things get that messy?"

He huffed out a breath. "Maybe it'll come to light now."

"How?"

"Crista will tell her in..." He looked at his watch. "Five, four, three..."

Vivien shook her head. "You really think Crista has the nerve to mention that the Wylies have been here?"

"Yes," he said. "And, if we're lucky, that will be enough for us to get some information about that big breakup."

She stood as someone knocked on the front door. "The carpenter is here to install the built-ins. What are you doing today?"

"First? Calling Kate." He smiled. "Then after that..."

"Nothing else matters," she joked as she walked to the door.

She wasn't wrong.

The minute she was gone, he called Kate, pathetically desperate to hear her voice.

"Well, hello, there," she answered, and he could instantly see her smile, and it lifted his heart.

"There's the sound I needed to hear," he said softly, not caring if they weren't there yet—he was crazy about her, and she needed to know it. "What are you doing, Lady Katie?"

She trilled a laugh. "Well, I'm under fluorescent lights on a snow-encrusted day testing the stability of the new capacitor design."

"You had me at fluorescent," he joked. "Because the sun is blinding here at the Summer House and the only thing missing is you."

"Stop, you're killing me." She sighed. "Maybe I'll get back this summer."

"Or sooner. And Christmas. And Easter. And...the year after that, and the year after that..."

"What are you talking about, Eli?" she asked.

"We—Vivien and I and maybe Crista—are thinking about keeping the house in our family. And, anytime you want to visit and stay, your family, too."

All he heard was the soft intake of her breath.

"How does that sound?"

"Incredible," she said on a light laugh. "But...I'll believe it when I see it."

"Have you talked to Jo Ellen about Maggie?" he asked. "Did you tell her what the Cavallaris told us—regardless of their discrepancies?"

"I haven't," she said. "She's struggling with her hurt ankle and seems as down as she's been since my dad died. I haven't had the heart to bring her lower. I told her about all of you, though, and how awesome you are. Especially you." She chuckled. "I'm guilty of talking about you a lot."

"I'm guilty of thinking about you a lot."

There was a stretch of silence on the line, adding to Eli's physical ache to just reach out and hold this woman.

"So will you come back...sometime?" he asked.

"I'm thinking this summer," she promised. "With my kids, although I don't know where we'll stay."

"Jonah and I will finish the apartment above the garage so it's done by the end of May. It's two bedrooms, so they can stay there. You can be in your old room."

"It's not my room," she said. "I happen to know that Lacey moved in there with Tessa's help yesterday."

"It will be yours in my mind, every time I pass it. I swear I can smell your perfume."

He heard her laugh. "Come here and you could get a whiff of eau de capacitor."

"I'd take it, Kate. Want me to visit Ithaca?"

She didn't answer right away, and he squeezed his eyes, hoping he hadn't pushed this too far, too fast.

"Kate?" he whispered after way too much time ticked by.

"Oh, how I wish you made sense," she finally said.

"Can I be clearer? I'd like to come and see you."

"Not that kind of sense," she said. "The logical kind. The math kind. The provable hypothesis based on facts that fit together."

"This is the illogical kind," he said. "The impossible dream of two people who fit together... perfectly."

She gave the sweetest little grunt that just made his heart ache more. "I don't know where we go from here, Eli, but..."

He waited for her to complete the thought.

"But I don't want to give up," she said. "I've got a crush on you that's thirty-some years old and it isn't going anywhere."

He punched his fist into the air, biting his lip to keep from letting out a hoot of victory.

"That's all I needed to know, Lady Katie."

She chuckled.

"Do you remember when you got that name?"

She sighed softly. "The Summer House Keep," she

said. "I remember the sandcastle. I remember... everything."

He closed his eyes and squeezed the phone, as gone as a man could be. "I'll call you soon," he said. "And I'll text. A lot."

"Good. I'll overthink every message."

Laughing, they said goodbye, leaving him far happier and more hopeful than he'd been since she left.

He got up to find Jonah—they had to start on that apartment. Kate would be coming back, with her kids. And he couldn't wait.

ELI AND JONAH started that same day by reviewing the blueprints for the apartment and the project tasks— drywall, hardwood, fixtures, electric, paint, flooring, and finishings. Jonah was invested enough to volunteer to go to Home Depot by himself with a list a mile long.

In the afternoon, Eli met with Don, his general contractor, and finalized the last financial draw, happy to be completely finished building this house. There was one final inspection, a rubber-stamp closing on the project, and the house was done.

And after dinner, he took a walk by himself and texted Kate three different pictures of the sunset.

When he walked into the house, he was greeted by the familiar sight of Lacey and Tessa, papers sprawled over the dining room table, chattering about some marketing plan they were cooking up.

Lacey always did the fine-print stuff, he noticed, and Tessa handled the big-picture ideas. The two of them were slowly becoming a well-oiled machine and he had high hopes for their little business.

Vivien was at the counter, talking to Jonah. Even after a full day of work on the apartment project and making them a delicious dinner, Jonah had decided to tackle a hollandaise sauce that he promised they could have on eggs Benedict tomorrow morning.

"I'm the official taster now," Vivien told Eli, taking a spoon Jonah offered. "I'm no Kate, but I'll have to do."

For now, Eli thought. Because Kate was coming back. He clung to that hope with two hands.

"Ooh, tasty." Vivien smacked her lips. "Perfect consistency, too, Jonah."

Watching the interaction, Eli closed his eyes and said a silent prayer of gratitude for the peace in this home. It permeated every corner, and he didn't want that to change. He felt the warmth, the goodness, and, yes, the magic of Destin.

"Where's my phone?" Tessa said, looking around and touching her watch. An electronic beep echoed from upstairs. "Oh, I left it in Kate's room while I was helping you move in there, Lacey. Yes, we shall forever call it Kate's room." She winked at Eli as she stood and jogged toward the stairs. "So, let's get her back!"

Eli chuckled at the echo of his own thoughts, his attention pulled by headlights that suddenly beamed through the front window.

"Who's here at this time of night?" Vivien asked,

leaning back from her seat at the bar to peer out the window.

"Maybe Kate came back," Lacey teased.

With a jolt of hope he knew was ridiculous, he went straight to the front door. As he got there, he heard a car door slam outside.

He touched the switch to pour light over the person coming up the stairs, squinting through the side panel.

What the heck?

For a moment, he just froze, unable to believe what he saw. She was here already?

"Crista?" he croaked the name as he flipped the latch on the door.

"What?" Vivien's barstool scraped the floor. "Did you say Crista?"

He opened the door before his youngest sister could even knock. "Yes!"

"I have to talk to you," she said, her ebony eyes flashing as she stepped right into the entry. "I have to talk to you and Vivien and it's really important."

"I'm right here." Vivien rushed into the entryway, arms out. "What a wonderful surprise! I can't believe it!"

But Crista didn't hug her sister. She just held up both hands, a little breathless. "What you are not going to believe is what Mama told me this morning."

She sailed past both of them, tossing a handbag on the entry table without even looking around. Then she came to a dead stop and gasped.

"*Jonah*? What are you doing here?"

"Hi, Aunt Crista," he said, coming around the island. "I'm living here now."

"Me, too." Lacey rushed closer. "It's great to have you here. Did you bring Nolie?"

She looked from one to the other, her expression slightly frantic. "*All* of you are here? The whole..." She shook her head. "Never mind. That shouldn't surprise me. What is it about this town that makes me the family pariah?"

"No!" Vivien exclaimed. "We're so happy—"

"You won't be," she interjected. "When I tell you what I drove five hours and fifteen minutes to say to your faces, you will *not* be happy. You might abandon the idea of keeping this house and you will, I assure you, never lay eyes on anyone with the last name of Wylie ever again."

Eli jerked back. "What?"

"Didn't you say you'd seen them? Wylies? That they'd been here? You have no idea what that family did to us, Eli."

"Crista, stop," he said, praying Tessa didn't hear that. "Whatever you are about to—"

"You need to know this!" she insisted. "You need to know that if it weren't for Arthur Wylie, our father would still be alive. He would never have gone to jail, only to die alone in his cell."

All of them just stared at her, shocked into silence.

"It's true," she said. "Some ethics professor, huh? Our dear 'Uncle Artie' totally stabbed his best friend in the back, and we would still have a father if it wasn't for that snake. Now do you want to talk to anyone named Wylie?"

"This can't be true," Eli said.

"Oh, it's true. Mama told me today. It's why she doesn't want to come here and why they never spoke again after that. But when I told her you said you saw those Wylie girls, she exploded. She called them the devil's daughters."

"Excuse me?"

Every single one of them turned to the landing where Tessa stood. Her face was bloodless, her lips quivering, her eyes fierce and golden like a lioness about to strike.

Crista gasped, her jaw dropping. "Are you...who I think you are?"

Tessa managed a shaky breath. "I'm the woman who's going to kill you if you speak one more word against my father."

"Tessa." Crista hissed the word, stepping back as if in fear. "I...I can't talk to you. I'm sorry, but I think you should leave. I don't...you shouldn't be here. You need to leave this minute."

Jonah took a step and closed his fingers firmly around Crista's arm. "And you need to chill the hell out, Aunt Crista."

She wrenched free. "I will not chill. I can't be in the same room as a Wylie."

Eli held up both hands. "Will you please be reasonable, Crista?"

She brushed him off, her dark eyes wild, "Reasonable? Her father basically *killed our father*!"

"He did not!" Tessa lunged forward but Jonah shot in front of her. "He did no such thing!"

Separated by Jonah and Eli, Crista crossed her arms and narrowed her eyes at Tessa. They stared each other down, the peace of the room shattered by the crackle of tension.

"I have the facts," Crista ground out. "And you probably know it's true! Why would you come here? How could anyone in your family have the nerve to even speak to a Lawson after what that...that...*traitor* did?"

Tessa closed her eyes, looking like she couldn't even breathe at that moment. And Eli knew exactly how that felt because every word his sister spoke was an unbearable weight on his chest.

"As far as I'm concerned," Crista continued, fighting for calm, "your whole family has blood on its hands. You are not welcome here."

Instantly, Lacey came to stand next to Tessa, a supportive arm around her friend. "She is so welcome here."

"Lacey!" Crista exclaimed. "Did you hear what I said?"

"The whole beach heard you," Lacey said. "But that doesn't make it true."

"It's not..." Tessa rasped. "It can't be. He'd never...my father didn't have a disloyal bone in his body."

"Really? Well, that's not what I heard this morning."

"He's not here to defend himself," Tessa said, putting her fingers to her temples as if she could not process what was happening. None of them could. "He's dead and you can't talk about him like this! He's dead!" Her voice cracked and she looked like she might buckle if Lacey hadn't been holding her.

"I'm sorry for you," Crista said. "Sadly, we know how hard it is to lose your father. But, under the circumstances, I think it's best if you leave our house."

"Crista!" Vivien glared at her. "You don't even know this woman. You're just doing what you always do—parroting Maggie."

"I don't want to," Crista insisted, glancing from one to the other. "I know you all think I'm Maggie two-point-oh, but it's not true. This is not a rumor or gossip or a memory. He was the reason Dad went to jail...*where he died.*"

Still pale, Tessa held up a trembling finger and pointed it directly at Crista. "You have no idea what you're talking about. My father was a paragon of virtue and integrity. No finer man ever lived. And yours?" She gave a mirthless laugh. "A common criminal convicted of fraud, embezzlement, and theft."

Eli felt the words smack him.

Tessa looked at him, her face crumpling in sorrow. "I'm sorry, Eli, I know that hurts you. But...but..." She held up both hands, taking a step backwards. "Never mind. I don't want to do this. I don't...I can't..." She took another step. "You win. The Lawsons win. I'll leave now."

She turned and strode to the back of the house.

"Tessa!" Lacey ran after her, leaving the rest of them in shocked silence.

Vivien stared at Crista. Jonah looked like he'd been kicked in the solar plexus.

And Eli... could barely breathe.

Shaking, he walked out of the room to the deck, sucking in salt air so he could think and pray and figure out how to fix this impossible knotted mess.

What if *betrayal* was at the root of the decades-old feud? What if —

"Eli." Vivien came out behind him, putting a hand on his shoulder. "Crista's always been a drama queen. Although, even for her? This was a lot."

He looked at his sister, knowing there were tears in his eyes. "This could...end everything."

Vivien shook her head. "No, no, it can't. We can't let history repeat itself, Eli."

"I think it just did." He looked past her into the living room where Jonah spoke softly with Crista.

"We'll change her mind," Vivien insisted. "We'll get to the bottom of this. We will not roll over and die over our mother's thirty-year-old allegations. We've never heard anything like this before. She could have just pulled it out of her imagination because she heard we talked to the Wylies."

He closed his eyes but all he could see was Kate. Her smile. Her eyes. Her damn missing glasses.

"I love her," he whispered, the revelation shocking him—sort of. He'd already known he loved her, he just hadn't acknowledged it. If he didn't love her completely, he knew he could. And he wanted to.

"But I love my mother, too," he said. "And I don't want to have to choose sides with my own family."

"Then don't," she said. "You're an architect. Bring the two sandcastles back together before the tides wash it all away."

"How?"

She looked hard at him, her eyes swimming in tears. "Build a bridge. You did it once before and you can do it again."

He closed his eyes on a grunt. She was right...but could he do that? Could they survive this? He had no idea, but he had to try.

Because he would not let life break their hearts or steal memories they hadn't even made yet. He would not let his father rise up from the grave and take his joy again.

He would not lose this house, this family, or the woman he loved.

Don't miss The Summer We Danced, the next book in The Destin Diaries series!

The Destin Diaries

Other family saga beach reads by Hope Holloway and Cecelia Scott

Hope Holloway

Coconut Key

Shellseeker Beach

Seven Sisters

Cecelia Scott

Sweeney House

Young at Heart

Collaborations by Hope and Cecilia

Carolina Christmas

The Destin Diaries

Visit www.hopeholloway.com and www.ceceliascott.com for details about all of their books!

About The Authors

Hope Holloway is the author of charming, heartwarming women's fiction featuring unforgettable families and friends, and the emotional challenges they conquer. After more than twenty years in marketing, she launched a new career as an author of beach reads and feel-good fiction. A mother of two adult children, Hope and her husband of thirty years live in Florida. When not writing, she can be found walking the beach with her two rescue dogs, who beg her to include animals in every book. Visit her site at www.hopeholloway.com.

Cecelia Scott is an author of light, bright women's fiction that explores family dynamics, heartfelt romance, and the emotional challenges that women face at all ages and stages of life. Her debut series, Sweeney House, is set on the shores of Cocoa Beach, where she lived for more than twenty years. Her books capture the salt, sand, and spectacular skies of the area and reflect her firm belief that life deserves a happy ending, with enough drama and surprises to keep it interesting. Cece currently resides in north Florida with her husband and beloved kitty. Visit her site at www.ceceliascott.com

www.ingramcontent.com/pod-product-compliance
Lightning Source LLC
LaVergne TN
LVHW091500230625
814460LV00010B/53